PSION GAMMA

ALSO BY JACOB GOWANS:

PSION BETA

PSION GAMMA

BY

JACOB GOWANS

Published by Jacob Gowans 2011

To my Fellow Bookworms who took a chance and bought Psion Beta, *for their enthusiasm for a sequel, and their continued support.*

ACKNOWLEDGMENTS

*

After such unexpected success with *Psion Beta*, I have many people to acknowledge for making that happen and for helping *Psion Gamma* reach its full potential.

My first thanks go to the members of Cougarboard, an online sports forum. With opened arms and minds, they read and encouraged others to read *Psion Beta*, helping word about it to spread. They also helped me with names of characters both foreign and domestic.

My second thanks go to those who participated in a fan-workshop of *Psion Gamma*. Their feedback and ideas and criticisms helped shape *Gamma* into a much better novel. These people are: Scott and Britta Peterson, Michael Sheldon, Anna Bean, Joel Mietus, John Wilson, Jana Jensen, Alyssa Penney, Dan Hill, and Kirk Anderson.

My third thanks go to family and friends who supported the projects and told others about *Psion Beta*. Special thanks to Rawl and Carol Crosby, my in-laws, who let me litter their table for two months with manuscripts while I lived with them after finishing dental school and prepared for licensing exams.

More special thanks go to Britta Peterson, for her work on the cover, and to Shannon Wilkinson and Caity Jones for editing the final manuscripts.

*

Psion Gamma

1 | Fallout

December 19, 2085

COMMANDER BYRON SAT IN HIS OFFICE surrounded by medals, pictures, and other personal effects. On his holo-tablet was a classified report from the New World Government Health Center Department of Psychology. He had already read the report twice, but wanted to peruse it once more before retiring. The day had been long, most of it spent at his desk on the sixth floor of Psion Beta headquarters. A long sigh escaped him, one of many that day. He stared at the wall facing his desk and watched a particularly large cloud slowly drift by, gently swirling as it did so.

He liked the cloud screensaver on his wall screen. It reminded him of flying, one of his favorite things. It also helped days like today become a bit more tolerable, when all he did was fill out paperwork and spend hours on conference calls and read reports on the upcoming launch of the first moon colony. He rubbed his eyes to make the bleariness go away.

Suddenly the clouds disappeared and his screen displayed a message from his son, Albert:

We need to talk. Can I come up?

Byron quickly answered his son in the affirmative and began separating his files into finished and unfinished stacks. He had just sorted the last of them when a soft buzz came at the door. Albert's face appeared on the wall screen. Byron touched a button at his desk to unlock the door.

He studied his son's face, trying to read his emotions. For the last few weeks his son had worn the same brooding, torn expression. Now it was different.

"Hey, buddy. How are you?"

"Fine," Albert said as he took the seat opposite the commander. Byron never allowed Betas into his office, but entertained plenty of Alphas and members of Psion Command.

"Did you watch the Hurricanes last night?"

"No, but—"

"No?" Byron drummed his fingers on the desktop. "Pushing for the division title now."

"Really, are they?" There wasn't a hint of interest in Albert's tone.

"Yep, they won seven of their last eight matches. They even beat the Furies four to one last week. Did you catch that?" Byron knew the answer to his question, but wanted to hear the words from his son.

"No, I guess I missed it."

"Ah, well, it was a great game." Byron smiled sympathetically.

The old Albert rarely missed watching his favorite football club, the Helsinki Hurricanes. And given that the Hurricanes were vying for a spot in the World Tournament . . .

Commander Byron closed his eyes. How many hours had they spent together cheering the Hurricanes either at home or at the field? Hundreds—maybe thousands. He wanted to push the issue, but his son was clearly all business.

"So, what did you want to talk about?" he asked.

"I'll show you." Albert held up a memory cube. There was a flash in his eyes, a little bit like the old Albert. He had inherited that spark of life from his late mother, Emily, but his mission last month to Rio de Janeiro had all but extinguished it. Byron hoped its disappearance would not last. The Alphas needed someone with his son's enthusiasm.

"Is it alright if I load this up, Dad?"

"Sure."

After tinkering for just a couple of moments with Byron's computer system, Albert directed Byron's attention to the wall screen. "Okay, it's starting."

A program Byron had never seen before appeared on his screen.

"So the Alphas assigned to work with me on this are Ho Chin and Djedaa El-Sayid. I, uh, I assume you know them . . ."

Byron nodded and glanced to the wall on his right where a picture of every Psion Beta who had passed under his command hung in very neat rows, including Ho and Djedaa.

Albert noticed the glance and rolled his eyes at himself. "Right . . . Well, they're helping me compile all the information from the mission and organize it into a format that can be analyzed chronologically. At the same time, they're designing hyper-software that will start doing this automatically for all missions."

"Sounds like a good idea."

"Yeah, well, Ho Chin is really good at that stuff. And Djedaa, she's just brilliant at problem solving. It's taken us a while because we can only do it in our spare time."

The screen changed into two line graphs, side by side, each with nine different colored lines. Each line had dots at varying intervals. Almost all the dots were blue, but two lines ended in black dots.

"So each colored line represents a different member of my team's heart and breathing rates. This line is mine." Albert spoke fast as he pointed at the gold line almost filled with blue dots. The excitement lacing his voice was unmistakable. "All of the blue dots represent voice communications received and sent. These black dots mean heart rate or breathing rate stopped. Basically . . . estimated moments of death." Albert drew his finger along a purple line. "That line is Martin's." Then he moved to the light blue line. "That line is Sammy."

"Okay," Byron said.

Albert licked his lips and continued. His hands were shaking just slightly. "The only part of the graph we need to be interested in right now is toward the end. Where the three explosions occurred. The first bomb exploded here."

He pointed to an area on the graph where all the heart rates except two picked up speed. He tapped the screen urgently, and Byron wondered if he wasn't understanding something Al wanted him to see.

"That was when I ordered the cruiser to detonate the proximity mines the Thirteens had set up to block our entrance. A few minutes later, here, was the second explosion—that one was caused by a Thirteen. The third was here, and after we ran out of the building."

Byron finally understood. "You mean—"

"Yes!" Albert said, his face beaming now. "Sammy's vitals ended before we even blew into the building, before the first explosion! I saw him alive before the second explosion went off—the one that tore up that end of the hallway. From what Kobe could piece together from his broken memory, he was laying against the brick wall that fell down after the second explosion."

"You mean, he—"

"Do you see it, Dad?" Albert tapped the walls screen repeatedly, sending ripples away from his fingertip. "There is no way Kobe could have survived the weight of the brick wall falling on him."

Commander Byron didn't answer his son, but listened intently.

"So Kobe must have had help. Sammy survived through the second explosion, at least long enough to save Kobe."

"But you just said the weight alone could have killed him." Byron rubbed his eyes again. "And if you did not see him when you were leaving, he had to be under that wall. Even if he was alive at the time, the third explosion . . ."

"I don't know what happened in between the wall falling and the Thirteens running away. The hallway was full of smoke."

"I remember Gregor reporting that the third bomb was a class C explosive, is that correct?" Byron asked.

Albert's expression changed at this question. The spark left his eyes and he looked on his dad with wariness. "Yes," he admitted.

"And the explosive was at the top of the pile, correct?"

"I know it's not likely, but there's a chance," Albert said. The strain in his face aged him almost ten years. "It's possible!"

"Al—" Byron started to say.

"Don't patronize me, Dad. All I'm saying is it's possible. He could have made it."

"I know—"

"Well, then we should go back! Who cares about the danger? I owe it to him." Albert stabbed repeatedly into his own chest with his finger as he said these last words. His face was flushed and his body trembled.

Byron spoke gently. "Please let me finish before you raise your voice. I agree with you. Okay? You are right. I will take all this to the Command. I will tell them that they must act if there is any chance he survived. Samuel was resourceful . . . and very smart."

"So—" Albert started to say, but his father cut him off by speaking over him.

"However," he waited until he had his son's attention again, "you need to be patient. It takes time to organize a run into enemy territory. This is not going to be directed as a rescue mission. It will be to recover Samuel's body. Wrobel and two others on Command both think the factory might be under surveillance in case we try to do just that. You understand that risk, right?"

Albert was about to protest again, but stopped himself. Byron appreciated his display of self-control.

"I am proud of you for doing this, Albert." He fixed his gaze on his son. "But do you really believe Samuel is alive?"

The whites of his son's eyes had taken on a pinkish hue. "I'm just trying to make things right." A tremor shook Albert's voice.

"I know." Commander Byron's voice had turned very soft. "Sit down for a second, okay? Otherwise I might start thinking you—"

"I've heard you say that a thousand times," Albert said as he sat, but he wasn't wearing his teasing smile.

Commander Byron looked at his son expectantly. "So?"

Albert just shrugged. "How are Kobe and Cala?"

"Cala is starting to look like her old self again," Byron explained. "Should be back soon. She is one of the lucky few to survive an attack like that from Thirteens. Survivors are rare."

"And Kobe?" Al pressed.

Byron picked up the holo-tablet with the psych report from NWGHS Medical Center. It detailed the latest information about the rehabilitation of Kobe Reynolds. He frowned as he scanned the words. "I am not allowed to read you most of it, but . . . 'More evidence of psychological trauma continues to be found . . . Patient continues to blame himself for the death of Samuel Berhane . . . Undetermined if patient is a danger to himself, although at this stage he appears to be depressive, not suicidal. Date of release currently unknown.'"

Al stared at the pictures of the Betas on the wall. "It's weird how Cala was the one who was hurt the worst—"

"And Kobe is the one who has the most trouble coping with it," Byron finished. More than that, Kobe had flown off the handle not long after returning from hospital after the Rio mission. Byron first noticed signs of night terrors haunting Kobe's sleep. Then his performance in instructions and simulations dropped to abysmal levels. He lost his temper at anyone who mentioned Samuel's name, and assaulted Ludwig Petrov in the Arena. Almost two weeks ago, Byron made the decision to send him in for help. It hadn't been easy. He and Kaden had to help the medics restrain Kobe just to get him out of the building.

The commander watched his son, realizing that he wasn't looking at Kobe's picture, but Martin Trector's. "I spoke with Martin's parents again a couple days ago. They are still struggling to come to terms with his death."

Albert stared down at his feet. "Martin was hilarious. Not the best at anything in particular, but he was a loyal friend. I wanted him in Rio with me for that reason." Albert flicked something out of the corner of his eye. "I miss him, Dad. His parents shouldn't have been told that weapons malfunction baloney. They should know he died a hero."

"We call it the Silent War for that reason," Byron answered solemnly, but he knew his explanation wouldn't help his son. "Even people like Martin's parents cannot know about it."

"And why not?" his son asked suddenly. "Because we're afraid people will lose faith in the NWG?"

"It is not my decision, Albert. The Scourge was not that long ago. Billions of people died. Billions. How popular do you think a war would be? A war of any size?"

"He was too young, Dad." Albert's words came out like a croak and his eyes were red. "Sammy was too young. I should've picked someone else."

Byron turned and looked at the rows of pictures with his son. They were all too young. Each picture had a unique story to tell. Some stories were particularly painful to recall. They made him wonder if he merely spent his days cutting short children's adolescences. For a long time he'd resented his own teenage years. His youth had been robbed from him.

It was the curse of being a Psion. He tried not to dwell on thoughts like that. They made him feel pessimistic, something he couldn't afford. Besides, he enjoyed working with the Betas. He loved watching them shoulder new responsibilities with a courage most adults have forgotten. He believed all youth had a well of untapped strength. Sometimes he thought of himself as a gardener, tending seeds, protecting them from the elements, helping them grow strong and self-reliant. All of the pictures represented, in some fashion, his children. His life's work.

But now I do the same thing to others that was done to me. Does that make me a hypocrite?

Questions like this were often on his mind lately, cropping up at inopportune times. As always, he reminded himself that it was a time of war.

In his experience, war made hypocrites out of everyone. It turned black and white into gray; right and wrong into neutral, perhaps war could even mix water and oil. He considered himself to be a man with clear principles and allegiance, and yet, some days, when he thought too much about the people he fought against, he questioned—even doubted—himself.

He still believed he was a good man doing the right things, but when he looked over all the pieces of metal sitting on the shelves to his left (awards, they called them) all he saw were decisions he'd made: battles he'd fought: people who had died from his choices. Had he done right in those moments? Did the benefits outweigh the cost?

Commander Byron cleared his throat. Albert blinked twice and looked at him. "Have you spent much time with Marie lately?" he asked his son.

Albert shrugged. "A little."

"Is she upset that we canceled the mission for her Psion Panel?"

"I don't know."

"After what happened, I doubt there will ever be a Panel mission again." Byron searched for more words to say, but couldn't come up with much. He was thinking about the night of Albert's mission. How eight hours had turned into ten. Then twelve. He had gotten so worried that he'd thrown up, something he hadn't done in years.

And now Albert seemed intent on cutting himself off from everyone around him. He should have graduated to Psion Alpha two weeks ago, but had requested that his commencement be delayed to work on his project of reconstructing the Rio mission. On the surveillance cameras stationed in the sim rooms, Byron watched his son work like a man obsessed. Albert pushed himself eight to ten hours a day, rarely taking breaks to eat or exercise. Nothing would stop him until he figured out what exactly had gone wrong and knew for certain that Samuel was dead.

"Just remember that no matter what happens, you did your best." All the care and worry he held for his son came to a crest, and he felt it in his throat and heart. For Albert's sake, he maintained his calm. "Let go of all this guilt. You did your very best. You have been more diligent than we— than I could have asked."

Byron glanced wistfully at the holo-records of his late wife Emily and his son. He saw the jewelry box displaying her wedding band and engagement ring. Behind the box was a leather-bound, glass-covered frame with two halves: in one half was their marriage certificate, and in the other was a picture of their wedding in a large white castle in Bern, Territory of

Switzerland. He missed his wife badly right now. *What would you say to him, Emily?* he asked her.

"Your mom is proud of you. I hope you know that."

Albert nodded silently and stood to leave. As he reached the door, Byron called out to him.

"I love you, Al."

"I love you, too, Dad."

2 | Glasses

December 19, 2085

MIRTH RANG THROUGH THE CAFETERIA at Brickert's joke. Sitting next to him, Jeffie giggled hardest, clutching her sides as if they hurt from all the laughing. Her golden blonde hair, tied into a ponytail, bounced on her back. The light in her bright green eyes lit up as her smile grew, stretching her face until the corners of her nose flared out.

I love it when her eyes do that.

In celebration of Al's graduation from Psion Beta, food and decorations filled the cafeteria. Finally, after living six years at headquarters, he'd be moving on and joining an Alpha Squadron. Marie solemnly watched the party from a distance as Alphas spoke enthusiastically about Al's future.

Kobe and Kaden stacked their plates obscenely high with cake, pie, and pastries. They walked delicately, trying to balance the towers of food threatening to topple. Miguel and Martin chanted at them, cheering them on.

Across the room, platters of chicken, ham, roast beef, and turkey let off pillars of steam each time someone cut off a small slice of meat. Cooked vegetables, boiling gravies, and sparkling salads were nearby, waiting to adorn the entrées. Another table bore circular arrangements of fruits surrounding fountains of fondue.

Just give me a handful of that food. One plate. That's all.

Kawai, Natalia, Brickert, and Jeffie chatted on about their sims and instructions, comparing who was further and giving each other tips. Brickert made another funny comment, and everyone laughed again. His eyes shone with delight, basking in the attention—especially the looks Kawai discreetly shot him when no one else could see.

Brickert's sisters were right. It's easy to tell when someone likes your friend, so much easier than telling if someone likes you.

As the laughter died down, Brickert, still smiling at himself, got up from the table with his empty bowl and crossed the room to the ice cream dispenser. As he reached for the handle, a small red ball formed on the lip of the nozzle and glistened in the light. The drop grew unnoticed until it was too heavy to cling to the plastic and splashed on the spill guard below.

That's not right! Brickert shouldn't get ice cream from there!

Sammy desperately tried to cross the cafeteria and stop his friend, but his legs were now made of mud and he could barely move. He yelled and screamed but, despite his protests, Brickert's hand reached up and pulled down on the handle. Instead of ice cream, thick red blood gushed into his bowl spilling up the sides and over the edge. At first, Brickert didn't notice. He was too busy looking back at his friends and laughing with them. But when he turned back and saw the blood covering his arm, dripping down onto his shoes, and pooling around his feet, he screamed. It was high pitched, toe-curling—a wail that echoed around the room.

Like the Aegis I blasted into that hot field . . .

Then everything in the room sped up to a hyper-fast pace. Every head jerked around to see what would cause someone to scream out like that. The lights in the room went dark. Sammy continued to run across the cafeteria, but he hadn't sped up like the rest of the world. Panicked voices yelled out in the dark, but were silenced by animal-like shrieks that filled the cafeteria. Red eyes shone in the blackness, approaching from impossible directions: the ceiling, the floor, the walls. They grew brighter and more menacing as they drew closer.

Red eyes! I have to warn them!

"THIRTEENS!" Sammy shouted as he jerked awake.

Gasping for air, he sat up shakily. Drops of sweat matted the edges of his shaggy, curly brown hair and trickled down his face. "It was a nightmare. Get over it! Only a nightmare." He put his hand on his chest and clutched the skin over his heart. "Just calm down . . ." Gradually, his breathing slowed.

"It was so real," he told himself.

That described most of his dreams lately. He lay back down and stared up at the ceiling of the bunker. Then he closed his eyes.

In his head he could still hear perfectly the voice of the women over the intercom at Psion Beta headquarters saying, "Good morning, Psions.

Good morning, Psions." He muttered the same words several times using a falsetto voice in a well-practiced imitation.

"Get up. It's a big day."

His bed was made of torn cushions, laminated maps, and polyester stuffing. He never bothered making it. He wouldn't know where to start.

The morning routine was always the same. He'd become so dependent on routines and schedules after nine months in headquarters that he lived one now to keep himself grounded. First, he splashed water on his face. Then he coaxed crusty toothpaste onto his finger from an old, worn tube and rubbed his teeth until he heard squeaking. When he finished, he pulled on the same torn, smoky-gray jumpsuit he'd worn for the last four weeks and started his exercises.

Four weeks.

Four weeks without any human contact. Four weeks stranded in the secret compound of a resistance group underneath a factory in Rio de Janeiro. Four busy weeks.

No.

Four frantic weeks. Four nerve-frying weeks. Four panicked weeks.

The first week he'd spent just figuring out a way to leave the bunker underneath the factory. When he finally managed it, he explored the factory and security records only to learn that Al's Rio mission had gone wrong because a Psion—not just a Psion, a member of Psion Command—Commander Wrobel—had betrayed them and organized an ambush. The image of a Psion and a Thirteen working together was like a nail in his brain. He dreamed about Wrobel or Thirteens or both almost every night. During the day, he bent his willpower on one thing: finding a way to get back home and warn Commander Byron about the traitor.

- 15 -

The task was daunting. How could he travel halfway across the world to Capitol Island? How would he move safely through CAG-controlled territory? Travel and communication between CAG and NWG territories was highly regulated and closely monitored. He couldn't just take a jaunt from Rio de Janeiro to New York City to London and tell everyone he was traveling for pleasure. Nor could he simply pick up someone's com and call Byron. The CAG operatives would be on him in minutes. Besides, everyone back home probably thought he was dead.

He had no money, no identity, no contacts; nowhere to start and nowhere to go.

During the second week in the bunker, people had come and dragged away bodies. He'd heard the muffled sounds as their feet crunched the rubble above and muttered a few words here and there. That day was one of the most terrifying of his life. He'd shut off the generator and crawled into a corner where he huddled for hours trying not to go mad.

Since then, he'd either heard or imagined hearing random sounds: small things like distant shouts, always in very short, staccato-like bursts. They sounded eerily similar to the Thirteens' bizarre form of communication. Occasionally rubble tumbled down through the ceiling hole. Those times were always followed by long, sleepless nights.

He knew that eventually people would come back to the factory. It was just a matter of when. Many nights he lay on his makeshift bed, wishing he had somewhere to go and thinking about all the things that might go wrong when he tried to leave.

The only thing he had to wear was the torn, gray flight suit that every Psion wore. What if someone was watching the facility and recognized his clothes? He'd have to swipe something immediately after he left, even if it came from a dumpster. And another thing: his voice. He didn't have a local accent. He wasn't sure how similar English here was to his South African vernacular. What if he gave himself away as a foreigner the first time he spoke?

He'd spent days scouring the few rooms in the bunker for anything useful. There were many broken gadgets on the shelves and scattered across the compound floors. Possessing a limited knowledge of mechanics gleaned from his instructions at Beta headquarters, he set out to fix whatever he could, hoping something might be worthwhile. After many frustrating hours of tweaking and tinkering with unnamable devices in various states of disrepair, he managed to put a couple things back into working order.

The first was a flashlight. He even found a battery for it, and it lasted roughly five seconds before dying out. Another discovered device was a small black pair of thick glasses that Sammy originally thought was old-fashioned, pocket-sized binoculars. The strangely tinted glass lenses were not broken, but the frame had been damaged in several places. He messed around with some honey from the food stores and balls of cotton for hours before getting the frame to hold together long enough to look through.

He was so disappointed that the stupid gadget wasn't binoculars that he almost chucked the glasses across the room. One thing stopped him. In the corner of the room, on one of the maps he'd been sleeping under, were blue and red markings he hadn't noticed.

He walked across the room, pressing the gadget against his face, and looked again at the maps.

"I'm sure they weren't there . . ." He looked at the map without the glasses. No markings. Again with the glasses. Markings.

Some letters and numbers had been scrawled across the page, but most of the markings were thin arrows radiating outward and inward to and from little blue houses drawn like a box with a triangle on top. At first glance, Sammy thought of missile strikes.

"What is this all about?" he asked himself, then immediately answered. "Some kind of special ink that only these lenses pick up."

He looked a few more times with and without the lenses at different maps.

"Yeah . . . Must be."

He'd thought the maps were peculiar from the start. They'd been hidden in a room full of bird cages (and a few dead birds), and he had dragged them out to help make his bed. After discovering the markings, he'd gone over all of them again with the special glasses. Once he sorted out the marked and unmarked ones, he examined just the marked maps.

Some were of North America, South America, or both. Others were of only one territory. They all had one thing in common: CAG territory. After staring at the writing and symbols for two days, he'd gone to sleep with maps on the brain. That night he dreamed about catching a chicken and eating it. In the dream, he'd done all the work himself; feeding, killing, plucking, dressing, and roasting. Just when the time came to eat, the chicken jumped off the platter and flew away. When Sammy woke up, he could *see* the answer.

"Carrier pigeons. The dead birds were carrier pigeons."

He jumped out of bed, found the glasses, and went over the maps again.

"The blue houses represent the other resistance compounds."

He traced his fingers all over the maps. "These lines were pigeon routes. All of them centering around . . . this one." Sammy jabbed his finger into the map of Mid-American Territory. There, in blue ink, was a mysterious inscription that appeared to have been scrawled out in haste: *Sedgwick C. Plainpal.* And it was right over the city of Wichita.

"That has to be the main compound of the resistance. But what does 'plainpal' mean? And who is Sedgwick C?" He searched through his memory. Thanks to his Anomaly Eleven, his brain was like a powerful computer in many ways, but nothing he could think of matched such an odd description. "But if these people were fighting the CAG . . . maybe they'd help me."

The new revelations from the maps had been enough to light a fire in Sammy. He spent more time poring over the maps, interpreting data, plotting possible destinations, and the safest routes to travel.

This new hope helped push away his fears of the unknown. His information was likely very outdated, but still useful. Most of the blue routes and stations radiated outward from that area. If there were any resistance left, wouldn't it be there?

With no better alternatives, he resolved to make for Wichita. As for Sedgwick C. and "plainpal," he hoped to find out the meaning of that either when he got there, or sometime along the way. To prepare for his departure he made himself a serviceable traveling bag out of a cushion cover and some wire, then stocked it with food, water, and some maps.

When he'd given the Psions a month to come back and look for him, he knew it was time. Staying any longer might cost him his sanity. He'd debated for days whether he should leave a message in case Alphas came looking for him. In the end, he decided against it. The CAG was more likely to come snooping around. If Alphas hadn't come by now, they weren't coming.

The horrible dream with Brickert and the bloody ice cream stayed with him all morning as he got everything ready to go. His preparations took about an hour. Then he set about making the chamber look as if it had never been touched. Any evidence of his stay was removed; he wiped down every surface he could think of. When he finished that, he slung his pack over his shoulder with a satisfied sigh. He paused with his thumb on the generator kill switch, watching the machine chug away. The exhaust pipe made a faint rattling sound where it passed through the wall, though he'd grown so used to it, he rarely notice the noise.

"Lucky me this place was here," he told himself. Brickert would have agreed, but Al would have said it was something more than luck.

So many emotions gripped him, but he swallowed hard and pushed the button. He went to wipe it with his sleeve, but decided to leave it.

Who knows, he said to himself. Without another glance, he traced the familiar path to the hidden door, and left the bunker.

He emerged in the noon-day sun from the trapdoor in the middle of the lawn of a large chemical engineering plant. Before anyone could notice something out of the ordinary, he hopped out and erased all traces of the door by smoothing out the grass. He intended to walk to the air rail hub in downtown Rio de Janeiro. According to the maps, the landmark closest to the hub was Estádio de Maracanã. Once he found that, he would easily find the air rail station.

Heading westward, Sammy hoped daylight traveling would be safer because he could appear less conspicuous in crowds. With a seven or eight kilometer walk to make, he tried to keep a good pace. He stayed on the lookout for clothes: shirts, shoes, a pair of pants—anything to get out of the clothes that told a Thirteen or Aegis what he was.

For the first hour or more, he passed mostly industrial buildings, shops, and truck yards. On multiple occasions, trucks flew by him on the road, paying him little mind. He spotted several dumpsters, but nothing inside he could use. When the landscape changed into homes, Sammy grew nervous again. When he was unable to take it anymore, he scampered down a bank, landed in a creek running alongside the road, and smeared mud over the holes and blood stains in his jumpsuit.

About halfway to his destination he found a tattered rag of a shirt strung out over a bush. It had two long tears down the back, several frayed edges, and yellow food stains, but smelled fit to wear. It covered the top half of his jumpsuit, which let him breathe easier.

It was a hot day and stiff breezes whipped regularly through the street. On the back of these winds, he caught a whiff of something that stunk like the bottom of a garbage can. He turned into an area where the sidewalks were busy with pedestrians and mangy, stray dogs. It took considerable restraint on his part to not rush over and speak to someone. He hadn't had human contact in a month. Most of the kids played football in the streets, dispersing only when a car rumbled through the game. Then they'd converge back into the road as though nothing had happened. Dogs chased and nipped at each other. Flies or fleas swarmed most of them. One dog took quite a liking to Sammy, sniffing and barking happily at the food in his pack. Sammy ignored it for two blocks, and the dog left him alone.

Rows of townhomes lined each side of the street with dusty windows and crumbling eves, each missing several bricks from the siding. They had all been turned into shops or churches. A police car roared down the cobblestone street with sirens blaring. Kids scattered like roaches and heads popped out of windows to investigate. Sammy hadn't seen or heard a siren since he'd run from the Shocks back in Johannesburg almost a year ago. Instinctively, he ducked into a small shop selling heat-blown glass. He peeked out the window, ignoring the sales clerk's attempts to coerce him into buying a glass flower. It took about five full minutes before he felt safe to continue traveling.

Not long after leaving the shop, he came to it:

Estádio de Maracanã. The largest football stadium in the world.

Sammy had heard about it, of course. Anyone who knew football had heard of Maracanã. Still, the sight of it mesmerized him. It stood like a bright white temple calling out to its people. This stadium held over a quarter of a million spectators. Four towering statues of stone honored the Great Ones: O Fenômeno, Copa, Pélé, and O Rei. The grounds around the stadium bustled with activity.

The air rail hub was a block away. The surrounding streets were busy, too. According to flyers pasted on every flat surface he could see, two local football clubs were inside battling for a regional title. From inside the stadium's bowels, a soft buzz of noise echoed out of the semi-open dome. As he passed by the magnificent structure, the buzzing grew louder until it turned into a dim roar of cheers, horns, whistles, and shouts. It built in crescendo until one tumultuous eruption of sound like thunder filled Sammy's ears, startling him. Half of the stadium bellowed out its approval while the other half whistled in anger.

As he drew closer to the hub, he heard a voice over the intercom announcing the arrivals and departures. He passed a large pink sign with a suspicious looking man in a black hat and coat. Underneath the image, in bold letters, he read: *KEEP THE PEACE! CALL IT IN!* After over three hours of walking, he finally reached the hub. The main building was a long, low oddly-designed structure with strange angles to the roof and windows. Next to it stood a large parking garage of similar architecture. Buses and taxis lined the roads coming and going. Sammy passed them all, picking up his pace in anticipation.

As he crossed over the threshold of the front doors, a wave of noise greeted him. The busyness of couples saying good-byes and hellos, parents directing their children around, and shops and restaurants providing their services warmed his soul in a way that made him feel silly and juvenile. It also made him miss his friends quite badly.

So many people . . .

Instantly, he felt out of place. It was one thing to be dressed the way he was on the streets of Rio, and another to be dressed that way in an air rail hub. The state of his clothes received several stares and a few pointed fingers from people walking past. Most of them spoke in English, but he caught snatches of conversations in other languages, most he believed to be Portuguese. Parents steered their children away from him. He tried to ward off these worries by returning these looks with a simple smile, but their suspicions resurrected his old fears. He sought out an electronic ticket vendor and brought it to life with a touch of the screen.

Number of Passengers:
One
Round trip or one way:
One way
Destination:
Wichita
Wichita, Mid-American Territory. Correct?
Yes

```
Closest Hub: Topeka---Distance: 8800 kilometers.
Fare: $130.00.
Accept?
```

His heart sank. Where was he going to get one hundred and thirty dollars? Even if he could somehow miraculously find a job and work for wages, hard currency was a thing of the past. He had no account to put his funds into. Sammy's dad had told him about how he used to carry money around for many years, but Sammy had only seen it in history museums. In the NWG, no one carried money. If the CAG was the same way, someone would have to buy a ticket for him.

He sat down to consider his choices, mildly aware that just a few meters away, hanging on the wall, was another one of those pink signs: *KEEP THE PEACE! CALL IT IN!* Thoughts streamed through his head presenting him with dozens of variations on three main possibilities: he could go back to the compound and try his luck there, he could look for work, or he could steal. With enough patience, he could finger enough things to pawn and pay someone to set up an account for him.

The idea of stealing turned his stomach. He'd done all that before and he'd hated it. *Maybe, in my case, stealing is justified. I have to get back and warn the commander.* These rationalizations didn't make him feel any better. And if he were caught, the consequences could be catastrophic. He resolved to spend the rest of the day trying to barter a deal with someone to pay his fare to Topeka in exchange for work.

He went through the entire hub, talking to all the restaurant and shop managers, explaining that he was a runaway and needed help getting back to family up north. As he expected, no one needed help from someone who dressed or sounded like him nor were they willing to bother with his dilemma. One burly man with big bushy arms jabbed a meaty finger into the pink sign hanging just outside the front of his restaurant and said, "Beat it kid, or I'll call YOU in."

Sammy left in a hurry, pleading his case with the few remaining shops. When he knew he'd gone to them all, he left the hub and hit the streets.

The football match had ended. Fans, wearing combinations of black and blue or green and yellow, flooded the sidewalks around the stadium. Sammy pushed his way through crowds and tried to spot places shabby enough that he could find some type of work. He headed back for the rows of stores and shops he'd seen earlier.

For the rest of the day, he went door to door giving each owner or manager the same story he'd told in the hub. He was from the north, hence the accent, and was trying to get back after running away. The pink signs weren't seen as frequently around these parts, but he still found no success. As the sky turned from blue to a reddish-orange and the summer heat faded, Sammy strongly considered going back to the compound for the night. He turned onto another road just as the streetlights blinked on above him.

This row of shops was just like the dozens of others he'd knocked on. Five or six doors down, under the illumination of a dim bulb hanging above the front door, he saw a small man wearing an apron over his clothes with a package tucked under his arm. The man turned over the sign so it read: CLOSED and locked up the shop door.

Sammy picked up his pace. "Sir! Excuse me, sir!"

The man looked up at Sammy running toward him and took a step backwards toward the door. His apron was red with blood. When Sammy saw the blood, he stopped quickly. Then he relaxed. Above the man's head hung a large green and yellow sign:

Butcher/Açougeria.

"Yes?" the man asked in a soft voice. "I just closed up. What do you want?"

He was a short man with badly receding dark hair. His face was round and full, but lined. His eyes weren't hardened like most Sammy had seen today. This was a man waiting to pass judgment.

"My name is Albert," Sammy said in his most friendly tone. "What's yours?"

"Floyd." He extended his hand to Sammy. "Hernandes."

Sammy took it and shook firmly. "Hi. I need a job, sir. Just temporarily. I'm trying to get up north, and I have no money."

"Well, I can see that." Floyd glanced twice at Sammy's clothes. Sammy couldn't tell if Floyd's expression was of disgust or concern. "Forgive me for prying, but where are your parents?"

Sammy used the same story he'd used all day. "I grew up north until my parents moved here. But I ran away from my home. I have an uncle in Topeka. I'm trying to get to him, but I have no money."

"Your uncle can't help?" he asked.

Sammy shook his head.

Floyd stared at Sammy, debating with himself.

"I'm not trying to play a trick—"

"You're a climber?" Floyd pointed a finger at the spikes sticking out of Sammy's shoes.

"Sort of. It's been about a month since I've done any. These are my only shoes."

"They can't be too comfortable."

"They mash my toes, actually." Sammy gave them a wiggle along with a sad smile. *Please, please, please say yes.*

Apparently satisfied that Sammy was desperate enough, Floyd answered, "How much money do you need?"

"A hundred and thirty dollars. I can take care of myself once I get my ticket."

Floyd pursed his lips. "Your accent, where is it from?"

"Northern Lakes Territory. I grew up there."

Floyd nodded. "Can I trust you?"

Sammy was surprised by the directness of the question. "Yes sir. I'm not looking for a handout. I just want to earn some money and make my own way."

The man nodded. "I respect that. You know something about butchering?"

"Nothing at all," Sammy answered with a note of pleading in his voice. "But I'll do anything you ask."

Floyd's lips pinched tighter, and he scratched his chin. Then he looked up at the setting sun and asked, "And you have a place to stay the night?"

"I can make do."

That seemed to clinch it. "No—no, I won't hear of that. It's almost Christmas. You come with me. I don't live very far," Floyd said. He put a hand on Sammy's shoulder and immediately pulled it away with dirt sticking to his fingers. "Maybe you need a shower, too, huh?"

Sammy chuckled out of embarrassment. "I'd forgotten all about Christmas."

"Really?"

Sammy nodded. It was more than he could have hoped for. "Thank you. Thanks so much, sir."

"Please call me Floyd. You can stay with my family through the holidays, help me out in my shop since we'll be busier than usual, and I'll have you on a rail a week after that. Sound good?"

"Yes, it does. Thank you so much, Floyd!"

"Not a problem. You go by Al or Albert?"

"Al's just fine."

3 | Denial

December 19, 2085

INSIDE SIM ROOM SIX, Jeffie screamed and swore until her lungs hurt. She didn't curse often. Her father didn't really care, but her mother hated it, so when she did swear, she made it count. With her temper being so close to the surface the last few weeks, it was a good thing her mother wasn't around. It was partly Sammy's fault. He'd tried to watch his language around her, but when he got angry he could string together a very interesting combination of words.

In her left hand she held a Fletcher, a nasty device that spat out barbed, armor-piercing rounds; a tiny gun with massive recoil. She hated the . . . *darn* . . . thing. Ever since breaking her ankle in that dunking contest a few months back, Jeffie had developed excellent aim with her blasts. When she started Weapons Training three weeks ago, she'd hoped that talent would carry over. Instead, she'd dropped four spots in accuracy rankings and one spot overall. That really pissed her off.

She stared at the target hanging ten meters away. The sim unit wanted her to make three consecutive shots into a twelve centimeter circle in under three seconds.

"When am I going to get this right?" she yelled to no one. "It's not even that difficult!" With her earplugs in, she barely heard her own voice.

The unit restarted. She prepared herself and then fired the Fletcher. Her first shot landed half a centimeter outside the target area. The hole in the target blinked red three times, then disappeared. She swore again. It was obviously going to be another bad day.

Bad days were the norm lately. A month ago, Jeffie had the worst day of her life. Worse than the day she broke her leg in a spelunking accident. Worse than the day her basketball team lost the regional championship. Even worse than the day her favorite grandmother passed away. It was the day Sammy didn't come back.

☺

She got up early that morning to give Sammy his birthday present. Everyone else in headquarters had given him clothes just as she and Brickert had planned. She'd been eyeing this amazing blue hoodie at the mall, but decided against it, no matter how well it would bring out the color in Sammy's eyes. Instead, she opted to give him a kiss.

She'd never initiated a first kiss, but after waiting several weeks with no signs from Sammy, she'd gone to Kawai for help. Kawai went to Natalia and asked her to find out from Brickert when Sammy planned to step up the relationship. Kawai reported back that when Natalia had asked the question, Brickert had just laughed. He'd laughed for almost a minute straight.

"Sammy's never kissed a girl," Kawai and Natalia explained to her. "And he has no clue what 'taking it to the next level means.'" Jeffie figured it served her right for crushing on a guy who'd spent time in an all-boys juvenile center and had no sisters.

When Sammy's name had been called out by Commander Wrobel to go on Al's mission to Rio, Jeffie got nervous. And no matter how hard she tried, she couldn't shake the feeling. Somehow, she got it into her brain that if she gave Sammy a kiss on the cheek first, and promised him the real thing when he got back, he'd have to make it back safely. Logically, it made no sense, but emotionally, it was the perfect plan.

Sammy's mission was supposed to be no more than eight hours. At fifteen minutes after the eighth hour she started glancing worriedly at the clock hanging above her bed. At half an hour past, she sent a text to Byron asking if the team had reported in yet. Byron never answered her. After one hour she knew something had definitely gone wrong. Another hour went by, and she panicked. Rosa Covas, whose sister was also on the mission, joined Jeffie in the dorm, and they tried to console one another.

When she couldn't stand it any longer, she went to the fifth floor and waited. Finally, Al walked through the door, but he was a bloody mess. He wouldn't speak to her, but his face told her everything she needed to know.

Brooding isn't going to help you, Jeffie. Get your head back in the sims. The voice in her head sounded an awful lot like her father's. Obediently, she walked to the panel on the wall and punched the command to restart.

With the Fletcher in her hand, she continued shooting. But her problem didn't go away. Each time the holo-targets appeared, her mind superimposed on it the image of a grotesque Thirteen with the red-melted-into-black uniform and haunting red eyes surrounding the pupils. Then, inevitably, she would shake ever so slightly. The trembling hands threw off her aim.

Glaring at the target, she pulled her hair into a tighter ponytail to cool her neck and face. She rehearsed in her mind the mantra of steps Commander Byron had taught her, but it didn't help the shaking. She gritted her teeth and let the urge to swear pass.

"Focus!" she hissed at herself.

Jeffie restarted the trial again. The trembling in her hands had subsided a bit. She fired the first shot. Hit. The shaking in her hands got worse, but she worked through it and fired off the second shot. Hit. Now her hands were doing a lively jig. Her face contorted as she tried to concentrate on staying still. She fired the third shot. Miss.

More swearing ensued. Then another memory of Sammy filled her thoughts.

⑤

"Does it ever scare you?" she heard herself asking him. They were sitting in the cafeteria, late on a Saturday night, the Game having ended only a couple hours ago. Sammy's team had won, of course, and most of the Betas had gone to bed, exhausted. A few were gaming in the rec room. Jeffie had forced Sammy to stay up with her and talk.

He picked a peanut butter chunk out of his ice cream bowl and ate it, looking at her with a puzzled face. "Does what scare me?"

"Oh, come on, you know . . . one day we're going to be soldiers—agents—whatever you want to call us. We'll really be fighting for our lives."

"Yeah, sure. Sometimes. But that's not going to be for a while, right? I mean, we still have years of training. I think by then I'll be ready. Don't you?"

Jeffie nodded. Her chair had a squeaky leg, and she subconsciously rocked on it, enjoying the noise. "Some days I think it's exciting. I get this rush during hand-to-hand combat in the sims. I never felt anything like it during a basketball game—not even the close games."

"Really?" Sammy wore an expression of genuine surprise.

"Yeah. Is that bad?" she asked, mortified that Sammy might think she was a freak.

"No—no, not at all. Just interesting."

"And why is it . . . interesting?" Jeffie intentionally employed the tone of voice her mother had taught her to use when she wanted to make it obvious she was flirting. As usual, it had no effect on Sammy. He was the smartest boy in the world and oblivious to everything going on around him.

Sammy fumbled with his words as he scratched his head. "I—I don't know. I think I do, too, sometimes. I mean, I get excited when I pass a trial."

"But I'm saying I enjoy beating the crap out of people."

In that way she loved, Sammy's eyebrows furrowed together as he thought about her response. She could sit for hours and just watch him think.

He made a gesture with his hands to show her he'd given up trying to figure her out. "It's probably got something to do with psychology. Your older brothers; fighting, wrestling, all that stuff."

"Maybe . . . but they were never much of a challenge."

Sammy snickered, and she took the opportunity to steal from his bowl. "Combat totally changes once you get into the advanced level. It's scary sometimes."

"Really?"

"Yeah. The first time I fought a Thirteen . . . I was so scared I could hardly move."

"Have you ever had a time when you're just absolutely terrified, and you feel like all that emotion is going to blow up inside you? I used to get that right before a big game."

"I hate that feeling."

"What do you do for it?" she asked quietly.

"I breathe. Deep breaths. And I tell myself I have ice in my veins."

"Seriously?" Jeffie laughed. "Ice?"

"My dad used to say it. Anyone who's really good in clutch moments, he'd say, 'That man has ice in his veins.' So I tell myself I have ice in my veins."

Jeffie didn't say anything except "Hmm."

"Yeah. Panic is probably the worst thing that can happen, don't you think? When—when I found my parents—you know, dead and all that blood, I went crazy. I didn't know what to do, where to go. It was almost like being blind even though I could see. So, if I'm in a situation or a fight where I think I might lose, I tell myself that, and I force myself to think

- 34 -

logically about my best chances, and usually go with the first thing that comes to me."

✿

Jeffie recited Sammy's words as she prepared to fire the Fletcher. *Breathe, Jeffie. You have ice in your veins.* She already knew the steps to fire an accurate shot. Thinking of the conversation with Sammy helped calm her. Instead of embracing her fiery hate, she reminded herself that if she allowed her body to tremble, she'd never pass the trial and never advance to the sims she wanted to be in more than anything: Advanced Combat.

Holding the image of Sammy in her mind, she aimed steady and true. In one fluid motion, she pulled the trigger. The Fletcher jerked her wrist upward. A small mark appeared on the target over the left side of the breast where the heart would be. Then she quickly reset her position and fired again. And again. Three hits.

That's three less Thirteens, she thought with a satisfactory nod.

She left the sim room two hours later. Brickert was just coming through the stair door. He'd been letting his brown hair grow a little long recently, almost shaggy. It brought out the blue in his eyes and made him look older, although he was still shorter than everyone else.

He called out to her.

"Hey, Brickert. What's up?"

"Staying late again?" he asked. His eyes told her he knew exactly what she was doing.

"Yeah, just trying to do some more weapons training . . . I'm finally done with the stupid Fletchers. What about you?"

"I left my com in the sim room. Took it off during one of my trials. I think I need a new one. This one digs into my ear."

"Oh."

"Are you all right? You don't look so good."

Jeffie rolled her eyes. "Nice, Brick. Very smooth. Didn't your mom ever teach you how to talk to a girl?"

Brickert's cheeks grew red spots. "Uh . . . no—sorry. Have you seen Al?"

"No. Why?"

Brickert shrugged. "Marie's looking for him."

"Why doesn't she just com him?"

"She tried. I think Al's locked himself in the sim room hunting for more mission data."

Jeffie saw how nervously Brickert was watching her, which wasn't like him. In fact, they'd grown a lot more comfortable around each other over the last month. They'd needed to in order to stay sane, she believed. Now she wondered what he was going to say next.

"Al—he's borderline obsessed about the mission, I'll tell you."

"Wouldn't you be?" Her tone came across more forceful than she meant it to be.

"I don't—I guess so." Brickert's cheeks were now bright red, and he looked like he wanted to turn around and leave. "I'm not saying Al shouldn't try. But there's a point when you have to acknowledge that—that you've done everything you can do, and let other people handle it from there."

"It's what he should be doing, Brick! Not waiting around for—for whatever . . ."

The words flew out of her mouth before she even had time to think about what she was saying. Heat rose to her head and flushed her face. For the last month, she and Brickert had carefully stayed away from this subject

- 36 -

based on some unspoken agreement. She hadn't discussed Sammy with the other Beta girls, she'd declined an invitation from Commander Byron to talk about him, and she'd told the woman from crisis therapy that she wasn't interested in sitting down with her, either. As the weeks had passed, she'd assumed Brickert shared her feelings about not discussing the topic of Sammy.

"He was my friend, too. The best friend I've ever had, I'll tell you!" Jeffie couldn't ignore the look of pain in Brickert's face. It was as if he were finally saying things he'd wanted to, but hadn't let himself. "I miss him. Sometimes I think of a funny thing to say and I turn to say it to him, but he's not there. I got so used to having him around. I—I lost a brother, Jeffie. I lost a brother!"

"I know, Brick." Jeffie took a step closer to Brickert. She thought about hugging him, but couldn't see herself doing it.

"And now Al's tearing himself up about this! Marie's beside herself because he's so withdrawn from her. They've got plans to get—you know—plans for the future. Now every time she brings it up, he just runs to the sim room. At some point, people have to let go. Right?"

All the sympathy Jeffie had felt for Brickert vanished with that question. She stepped away as if he was contaminated. "No! Al can't stop looking! It's too soon!" She didn't know why she was yelling at Brickert. None of this had anything to do with him.

"Why not?" Brickert asked quietly with his gaze fixed on the floor. "Because it means Sammy is dead?"

Brickert's words punched her in the stomach. Even after a month, she still expected to see Sammy in the cafeteria eating his bowl of creamed oatmeal. She looked forward to fighting with him about whose breakfast was healthier, which movies were better, who Brickert really had a crush on. She missed those stupid arguments. She missed everything.

"He could be alive. I don't see why everyone has a problem believing that!"

"I know," Brickert pleaded with her. "I know. But I've talked to Gregor and Kaden and others who were there—"

"—even Kobe?"

"Except him. But I did try . . . when he was here. He didn't want to talk to me. Everyone's said the same thing. They didn't see a way Sammy could still be alive."

Jeffie folded her arms and looked away now. "I've heard all that . . ."

"I want him to be alive, too, I'll tell you! But as much as I wish it were, it's—"

Jeffie fixed him with a murderous stare, daring him to say what she thought was coming next.

"—it's not likely. You heard the commander's speech at Martin's funeral. You know what happened, Jeffie. It kills me, too, but I don't want to live the rest of my life waiting for my best friend to come walking through the door. I—" He dropped his voice again. "I don't want to be like Al." His chin quivered as he spoke and his eyes moistened, but he held strong.

Brickert's emotion got to Jeffie, but she refused to cry, too. She was so sick of crying. The first week after Sammy had (*don't say it!*) not come home, she'd cried herself to sleep so much that she didn't want to cry ever again.

Brickert's cheeks grew red spots. "I'm sorry. I didn't mean to hurt your feelings." His eyes flickered over to sim room six. "I just—I don't know what to say."

"I know," she whispered.

"I want to believe it. I do."

Jeffie nodded, holding her stomach tightly. If she let go, she'd throw up. "I just wish I knew one way or the other. My mind tells me he's gone and—and Kawai and Natalia and Brillianté are bent on helping me accept that. But when I dream, Brickert, he is always alive."

4 | **Butcher**

December 24, 2085

FLOYD HERNANDES owned a comfortable two-level home located in a sprawling, middle-class neighborhood, or *bairro*, as Floyd called it. Sammy wondered why Floyd didn't just call it a neighborhood, but he quickly learned that the butcher slipped in and out of using Portuguese without thought.

The Hernandes family consisted of Floyd's wife, Karéna, and their four children: Rianna, Adam, Rebecca, and Rosalina. The girls, whose ages ranged from twelve to eighteen, were enthralled by "Albert" and flirted shamelessly. Rebecca, the girl closest to Sammy in age (and extremely pretty), was particularly keen on him. They all looked like Karéna: tall and slender with long dark hair and big brown eyes.

Adam, on the other hand, was short and round like his dad. Sammy didn't think Adam liked him very much. He guessed it was because Floyd was so hard on his son, but treated Sammy like an honored guest. The family set up a cot for him in Adam's room on the far wall from Adam's bed. Late into the night, Adam peppered Sammy with questions about his parents, his life, and plans for the future. The interrogation aside, it was Adam's tone Sammy found most annoying. He seemed bothered by Sammy's "northern" accent and frequently told his sisters off for spending so much time around a complete stranger. Sammy tried not to let any of it worry him. He had more important things to think about.

Christmas at the Hernandes' began early on Christmas Eve and was unlike any holiday celebration Sammy had ever seen. Festivities were big, noisy, and continued into the night. He had never been to such a party. Hordes of family and friends descended upon the Hernandes house: first cousins, second cousins, third cousins . . . it made no difference. All were like siblings in this family. They ate, sang, played, and danced. Then the cycle repeated itself. Sammy had no choice but to have a good time.

Rebecca, the middle of the three daughters, spent a good portion of the day trying to coerce Sammy into going on a walk around the block with her. At first, he saw no harm in this and nearly said yes, but then he saw another young couple in the family returning from a "walk around the block" and they both appeared fairly disheveled. Not wanting to incur any more suspicion from Adam, he politely declined Rebecca's offers.

Finally, at midnight, the whole crowd went outside and lit fireworks with the rest of the neighborhood. Rather than waiting until morning, as Sammy was used to, the Hernandes celebrated Christmas Day as soon as it was Christmas. No sooner had the last firework exploded, then they went inside and opened presents.

Sammy expected to receive nothing. What more could he want than food, shelter, and a job? The Hernandes family thought differently. From his newfound friends he received a change of clothes and a leather necklace from which hung a miniature replica of the Cristo Redentor carved from wood.

"Now you'll have something to wear besides Adam's old things," Karéna told him.

"And you can remember your time here after you go home," Rebecca added.

Sammy thanked them so many times they had to tell him to stop.

The day after Christmas, Floyd woke Sammy and Adam early in the morning to drive to the family shop and prepare it for opening. They got up, bleary eyed and yawning from the previous days' festivities, and headed to the car.

Floyd had already taught Sammy how to wrap meats. "That's all you'll do is wrap them up," he'd explained on Sammy's first day in the shop. "Cutting meats is too difficult. You can never learn enough in one week. Even I haven't perfected my craft, not after many, many years."

So Sammy stayed in the back of the store with Adam and Fernando. Fernando was an apprentice and cousin of the Hernandes family. Judging by the tattoos up and down Fernando's arms, he had a thing for the Catholic saints. When Sammy asked him about them, Fernando just chuckled.

"You gotta have someone watching your back, right, man?"

Sammy also quickly learned that Fernando's favorite thing to say was *man*. "You got that order, man? You need some help, man? I met this girl the other day . . . so hot, man! She melted my teeth, man!" It wore on Sammy's nerves.

When Floyd was in front with customers, Fernando took over the responsibility of cutting meats. Sammy discovered he actually enjoyed butchering once he got past the goriness of it. Floyd's shop had an amazing collection of knives and tools. Fernando said that they prepared over three dozen kinds of meat and fish. Occasionally they special ordered them for the wealthy customers. Before Sammy wrapped them, Fernando and Adam diced, sliced, peppered, or tenderized the cuts until they met Floyd's demanding specifications.

From morning until evening, whether it was salami, turkey, beef, mutton, or whatever, Sammy prepared and packaged the cut meats alongside Adam and Fernando. Even though the two boys helped him and showed him how to do things, Sammy felt like an outcast. Part of this feeling came from the fact that Adam still did not like Sammy, and his distrust slowly carried over to Fernando. He often caught Adam watching him from the corner of his eye, and had to endure Fernando double checking most of his tasks. He was fairly sure they were trying to catch him stealing, which he found humorous, given his past criminal behavior.

In fact, he'd been very careful not to do anything unusual around the family, particularly Adam. He also kept a close guard on what he said about himself, always making sure he kept his story straight. He did not want to arouse any doubt surrounding his circumstances. As far as Floyd and his wife knew, he was Albert, a fifteen-year-old boy who ran away from his abusive parents, and was now traveling to Topeka where his uncle and aunt lived, although his family had originated in the far northern territories.

It was a different kind of busy than he was used to, but he gained a new understanding of the meaning of a hard day's work when the shop was clean and closed. Blood and bits of meat decorated his apron like a morbid Rorschach pattern when he hung it up. They all climbed back into Floyd's truck and drove home. Most of the conversation centered around football matches, the day's orders, and dinner. Sammy stared outside, watching the city go by as they drove. He let his mind wander, subconsciously counting the funny pink signs posted every couple kilometers reminding people to KEEP THE PEACE! At dinner, Floyd mentioned how impressed he was with Sammy's hard work.

"If you weren't headed north I'd keep you on as a third apprentice," he added. "Your work ethic might rub off on the other two."

Floyd's daughters thought this was the best idea they'd ever heard and begged Sammy to change his mind about leaving. Adam, however, was visibly chafed by the comment and made Sammy pay for it the next day.

"Really, Albert?" he asked as he held Sammy's most recently wrapped log of chuck beef in his hand like a club. "A retard could wrap this meat better. Quit being such a hobo."

"Hobo," Fernando chuckled in the corner, not looking at Sammy. "That's funny, man."

Adam threw the meat back into Sammy's chest and ordered, "Redo it."

Sammy bit his tongue and did as he was told, but this only empowered the two boys.

As the days passed, Sammy knew his work was getting better but their taunts became worse. Adam always made sure he gave Sammy a bump each

- 44 -

time they passed. Soon, the bumps turned into trips or shoves. Fernando wasn't as bad. He just liked finding ways to get Sammy to do things for him. Sammy had seen it all before. Bullies at school and the Grinder all used similar tactics.

A voice in the back of his head reminded him that doing anything to retaliate could undo his whole plan. With only two days left, he could deal with it. The closest he came to losing his cool was when Adam intentionally body checked Sammy, then punished Sammy more with a full strength shove.

"Watch it!" he hissed at Sammy.

"You watch it," Sammy replied.

Adam faced Sammy, trying to stare him down, but Sammy didn't budge. He had a few centimeters' height advantage over Floyd's son, not to mention months of training. Before the moment between them had passed, Sammy took a deep breath. *If I gave him just the tiniest glimmer of how lethal I can be . . .* But he knew he couldn't. He gazed at Adam calmly and raised a finger slowly until it was right in between Adam's eyes. Adam seemed mesmerized by the finger. *Just blast him with one finger, right in the forehead.*

Don't do it, Sammy. Bad bad bad idea. You're going to Wichita!

Adam looked past the finger, into Sammy's eyes, and swallowed hard. *There's fear there. He knows I'm serious.* Then, as if he'd snapped out of a trance, Adam snarled and pushed Sammy away.

After that, both boys did their best to avoid each other. Perhaps Adam didn't want to know what would happen if he pushed Sammy hard enough, or maybe he finally realized Sammy had no intention of sticking around.

The morning of Sammy's last day at the butcher shop, Floyd put an arm around him and gave him a smile.

"Got the ticket for you. Rio to Topeka. It's under the front counter, and I'll give it to you as soon as we close up. It's good for any time. So you can leave tonight or in the morning. Either way, you'll have enough time to shower and change. I'll get you a lift to the hub if you want."

"That'd be great, Floyd." Sammy said with much sincerity. "Thanks so much again for everything."

"It's been my pleasure, Albert. My pleasure. Sure wish you'd stay, though. Live with us, be like one of our own . . . marry Rebecca." Floyd chuckled at his own comment and rubbed Sammy's back with his open palm.

"I wish I could. Really."

Floyd clapped Sammy on the back and returned to the front of the store. "No need to worry. I've got until the end of the day to convince you otherwise!"

Sammy went back to his duties wearing a huge grin, even the sight of Fernando and Adam looking over their shoulders at him and chuckling couldn't bring him down. *I can't believe it worked!*

Floyd gave him a particularly large order of thin-sliced beef that needed spicing, tenderizing, and wrapping, then announced he was going across the street to take his lunch break. The other boys cut it and left Sammy to do the rest of the work. When he finished, Fernando told him to wrap up the rest of the meat and put it back in the cooler. He noticed a strange tone in Fernando's voice, but ignored it.

The cooler was big and old, one of its casters had fallen off long ago. A block of wood had been jammed in its place to stabilize the base. Sammy had to walk into it to place the meat in its spot. His breath billowed around his head and his arm hairs stood on end. Just as he started to hang up the

- 46 -

meat, he saw the door start to close behind him. Dropping the meat to the floor, he rushed over and threw his shoulder against the cold metal.

"He caught me!" Adam said with a cold laugh. "Get over here and help!"

Sammy had no desire to be locked in until Floyd got back from lunch, so he shoved again. He shoved it hard enough that it rocked the standing cooler on its base. Through the space in the door, Sammy heard Fernando hurrying over to help. Sammy slammed his shoulder into the door three more times, rocking the cooler more each time.

Adam shouted out a curse and let go of the door, leaving Sammy to pop out of the cooler like a pressurized cork.

"Watch out, man!" Fernando warned Sammy, but it was too late.

A big box full of Floyd's old, worn knives had been shoved on top of the cooler. Sammy, in all his pushing, had tipped the cooler off the block of wood, and the box slid off and tipped its contents right onto him.

He didn't think. He just reacted.

With both hands, he fired blasts repeatedly at the oncoming blades, jetting half the knives across the room, and pushing the rest harmlessly out of the way. Part of his blast must have connected with Adam, because during the commotion he hit the ground hard.

"Albert! Are you all right, man? It was Adam's idea! It was supposed to be a joke, man. You know, to scare you!"

"I'm fine. No thanks to your stupid joke, *man.*" Sammy took several breaths to calm himself. The last time he'd been this mad, Byron had pulled him off Kobe in the cafeteria.

"It's a miracle! The knives! They—they flew! Did you see that? The holy saints are watching over you, man!" Fernando crossed himself multiple times with great fervor.

Adam lay on his butt, staring at Sammy with a pale face and frightened expression. Finally, he managed an apology and began cleaning up the mess he'd caused. But the damage was done. The mood in the back of the store turned quiet and awkward. Adam said nothing else and went out of his way to avoid looking at or being near Sammy. When Floyd returned, his son immediately took his lunch break.

Another big order came in right after Adam left. Since Fernando needed help, and Floyd didn't want Sammy carving the meats, Floyd sent him up front to man the cash register until Adam got back.

Sammy had only been up front for about thirty minutes when a large white van pulled to a stop across the street about thirty meters up the block. On the rear side door was painted a pink square with a suspicious looking man in black. And in big bold letters above him: *KEEP THE PEACE!* And below him: *CALL IT IN!*

A group of kids who'd been playing football in the street scattered and didn't come back. Sammy swore under his breath as the air in his lungs grabbed hold to the walls of his chest. The doors to the van opened and six men in strange clothing clambered out. He didn't need a second look to know what was going to happen next.

Adam . . . what have you done?

The six men were Aegis, the soldiers of Thirteens. Sammy was sure of it. They weren't wearing their usual mottled green and brown uniforms. Instead, they'd chosen to go with black suits and ties, white shirts, dark fedoras, and large sunglasses covering their faces. One man had a white stripe on his hat and another running down his tie. He motioned with his head and the group broke in half.

Sammy's mind began calculating a way for escape, but there was no way he could get away without a fight. And if he chose that path, he'd draw all kinds of bad attention to the Hernandes family.

Three of the Aegis, including the striped man, sauntered toward the front of the store and three disappeared around to the back, cutting off his escape. While he could see them, they couldn't see him. He looked around the store quickly. He grabbed the ticket under the register, slipped it into a small plastic bag, and stuffed it into the darkest corner of the nearest cabinet, beneath a can full of old receipts. No sooner had he finished, the bell over the door jingled.

Sammy wiped down the counter by the register as if nothing was wrong. An observant inspector would have noticed his slightly shaking hands and his breath coming a little quicker, but these men didn't seem to be anticipating any problems.

Floyd came out from the back just as the man with the stripe crossed the threshold. Sammy didn't know if Floyd recognized these men, but judging by the way his boss' eyes moved back and forth between the three men and the van parked across the street, Floyd sensed something terribly amiss.

"Can I help you gentlemen?" Floyd asked. His voice was cool but controlled.

"Actually, you can, Mister . . .?" The striped man stepped forward with a hand outstretched.

"Hernandes. The owner. You guys are government?"

At that moment, the other three men in suits emerged from the back of the store with Adam and Fernando in tow. Hernandes let out a strangled cry and started toward his son. Two of the men stepped in and blocked his path.

"Calm down," the man with the white stripe said. His deep voice had a uniquely nasal tone that struck Sammy as odd. He also had a small scar above his upper lip that twisted up to his left nostril. "We're here because of a call placed about thirty minutes ago. Someone reported an unusual incident here."

"What do you mean?" Floyd demanded. "Who called you? I don't know what you're talking about."

The striped man lifted his sunglasses so Floyd could see his eyes. They were light gray and colder than the meat locker. Whatever doubt Sammy had that this man was an Aegis was now gone. Fear flooded his very soul. "We ensure the safety of our citizens. That's all you need to know. Now, who placed the call?"

"No one here placed any—" Floyd protested as he turned his head back and forth between the Aegis and his employees. He stopped when he saw Adam step forward with a trembling hand raised into the air.

"I did."

"Adam?" Floyd faced his son and put a finger to his chest. "What on earth were you calling about?"

"Albert's a freak, Dad!" Adam said.

"No, it was a miracle, man," Fernando insisted. "You should have seen it, Uncle! It was a miracle."

Floyd turned now to the man Sammy thought of as Stripe. "I have no idea what's going on here. My son made a mistake. Please leave."

"Is this the boy you called about?" Stripe questioned Adam, but looked at Fernando.

Adam shook his head. "Him," he said, pointing an accusing finger at Sammy.

"Let's go."

Three pairs of hands seized Sammy at the same time. He'd been expecting this, but Floyd and Fernando had not. They both started forward to protest Sammy's removal, but as soon as they moved the other three Aegis pulled out weapons.

"Don't do anything foolish. We're just taking this boy in for questioning. Public safety."

"Questioning?" Floyd shouted. "Do I look stupid? Why the guns if he's only going in for questioning?"

"To ensure your safety. This boy could be dangerous. Thank you for your cooperation."

"I'll be fine, Floyd." Sammy gave his friend a look that begged him to drop the matter. "Thank you so much for your help." He didn't want harm to come to the family, even if Adam was a dirty little rat.

Fernando and Floyd gave only empty protests as Sammy left the store in the hands of six Aegis. As he crossed the street he heard the fading sound of Floyd screaming at his son.

"You should have talked to me before you called someone! We took him in! He was practically family!"

One of the Aegis slipped thick magnetic cuffs around Sammy's wrists and activated them. They clamped firmly, locking his arms together, robbing his wrists of any movement, and forcing his palms to face each other. Sammy wondered if he could break them with a strong enough blast, but knew that attempting it would expose him immediately as a trained Psion. At this point, as far as he could tell, the Aegis had no idea who he was. He saw no need to tip them off. They opened the rear doors of the van and tossed him inside. He landed hard on his shoulder. The thick door shut tightly behind him. A wall of solid black material sealed him off from the rest of the vehicle, extinguishing all light to his section of the van.

From the vibrations in the floor, he felt the van's electric motor whir to life. As he was carried away, his mind surged with frustration. What more did he have to do to get back home? He'd only been hours away from the air rail.

Lying on the thin rug with his arms bound tightly behind him, he tried to formulate a plan to escape without using his blasts. It was impossible. He decided that his best chance would be surprise. *One good blast should do it . . . As soon as they open the doors, I'll pounce.*

Within the pitch black compartment of the van, he lost all sense of direction. He felt the van lurch down a short, steep drive, then level off. After coming to a quick halt, he heard the muffled sounds of doors opening and slamming shut. He tensed his muscles, ready to try to break the magnet cuff seal with a strong blast. Then he heard the sound of hissing gas and knew he was in trouble.

5 | Recruits

January 7, 2086

"IT SOUNDS LIKE you got yourself some good kids, Walter." Commander Wrobel's voice came through the cruiser's speakers loud and clear.

Commander Byron and Dr. Maad Rosmir sat in the pilot chairs of Byron's personal atmo-cruiser. Behind them, in the passenger seats, three nervous recruits stared out their windows as the cruiser cut through the snowy fog over Western Europe. The last time Byron and Dr. Rosmir had taken this trip together was almost a year ago. Samuel had been in the back of the cruiser, strapped down with several Elite guarding him.

"No bad ones yet. Am I right, Maad?" Byron smiled at the doctor.

"I don't know," Dr. Rosmir replied. "That Albert kid is a bad apple if I ever saw one. Not very bright, either."

Wrobel's laughter was loud enough to make the sound break up in the speakers. Byron chuckled, too.

He and Dr. Rosmir had just finished picking up the last of the recruits from a city in the Territory of Mediterranea called Ancona, right on the Adriatic Sea.

"A new record breaker, is that what you told me?" Wrobel asked.

"Correct," Byron answered. "Youngest Psion ever—sitting right behind me." The recruits couldn't hear his conversation due to the soundproof partition Byron had activated. It sealed off the cockpit, but he could still watch them on screen.

Commander Wrobel snorted. "You and your statistics."

"More important to us," Dr. Rosmir added, "is they're all healthy. Makes my job much easier. I don't think Psion Command appreciates how difficult my work can be."

Commander Byron gave Dr. Rosmir a quick nod. "Victor, I will check in with Command when we get back to headquarters. Until then, you take care." He pushed a button and ended the call. A moment of silence passed between the commander and the doctor. Then Byron tapped the digital clock on the control panel. "Two hours from Rome to the Island . . . What do you want to talk about?"

Dr. Rosmir laughed and let another long silence pass before he spoke. Byron didn't mind the quiet, it was Rosmir who rarely left time unfilled with conversation. Two things the commander had learned about Rosmir very quickly: he liked to talk and he wanted everything neat. The second attribute made him a very fine surgeon.

"How's Al doing?" Dr. Rosmir finally asked.

Byron recognized the walking-on-eggshells tone in his friend's voice. He'd heard it several times in the last month and a half from many different people. "Hard to say. Sometimes I think he might be snapping out of it, other times . . ." He checked his altitude and speed, and then turned on autopilot, something he didn't normally do. "His graduation is in two weeks. I really hope getting out of Beta and being surrounded by Alphas helps him."

"I'm sure it'll do him some good," Maad offered. His focus shifted to scouting out any bit of dirt under his fingernails.

Byron nodded, even though he didn't necessarily agree with the assessment. "I have a couple people who will keep an eye on him. Not that I want to do that. I want him to have his autonomy, but if this obsession with his mission keeps going like it is, it could ruin his life."

"And Kobe? Any news lately?"

"He is getting better. Though I have some other news you might be interested to hear."

Dr. Rosmir stopped working under his nails for a moment to glance at Byron.

"Psion Command voted today to risk going to Rio and recovering Samuel's body."

"That's good news, right?" Dr. Rosmir asked. "I mean, last time we discussed it, you didn't think you'd get enough votes."

"Wrobel and Iakoka still vetoed it, but I persuaded Commander Havelbert to change her mind. Four votes to two . . . we go to Rio."

Dr. Rosmir flicked away whatever he'd unearthed under the nails on his left hand. "As intimately acquainted as I am with Psion politics, I still never understand you guys. You have an equal vote to the other five members of Command—"

"Only on matters relating to Betas," Byron cut in to remind him.

Dr. Rosmir raised a finger. "Exactly, and Sammy was a Beta."

"But Alphas are being sent to recover him, not Betas." Commander Byron cleared his throat. "You also should know that I will be honcho on the mission since Samuel was my pupil, and that I have asked that you come along to provide your expert forensic abilities."

Dr. Rosmir's mood changed quickly. His expression was surly and tension crept into his voice. "No, I hadn't heard that."

The words hovered in the air. On the window behind the doctor, flakes of ice and water streaked the cockpit glass as it seeped out of the thick clouds around the cruiser. Byron didn't need to ask his friend how he felt about the decision. He'd known for a very long time.

Maad Rosmir was among the earliest recruits after the Psion Corps split into Psion Alpha and Psion Beta. At the age of seventeen, he'd finally gotten up the courage to learn to drive his family's car. As his father sat in the passenger seat teaching Maad how to operate the vehicle, a large truck that had lost its brakes slammed into the side, T-boning them. Maad's father died instantly. The only thing that had saved Maad was his undiscovered Psion abilities.

Byron investigated (just as he did almost all such accident survivors) and flew to the Territory of India. He met with Mrs. Rosmir and Maad, explaining who he was and what he had to offer. When he told Mrs. Rosmir her son had a genetic anomaly, she burst into tears, thinking her only boy was going to die. An hour later, after she'd finally calmed down, she encouraged Maad to go to Capitol Island. Maad refused, stating his duty now was to take care of his mother.

Fortunately, Mrs. Rosmir proved more stubborn than her son. India was no place for him. It still had not fully recovered from the Scourge, even after thirty-five years. India's tightly packed urban population had been ravaged by the disease, and had lost over seventy-five percent of its population. Maad left his mother and went with Byron to headquarters, eventually becoming one of the most valuable Psions that Byron had trained.

As he watched his former pupil squirming in the copilot's chair, the commander felt sorry for him. "Maad," he said softly, "you make me nervous just looking at you. Relax. We are not due to leave for weeks. Besides, General Wu will assign a full squadron to come with us."

Dr. Rosmir played with his pocket-watch as he nodded his head. With such wide eyes and a fearful expression, he looked very much like the young recruit Byron had flown in from Bombay several years ago. In another setting, Maad's reaction might be funny, but the commander was not amused. The idea of combat or any kind of danger had never sat well with the doctor.

"Will you protest my request to have you come with me?" Byron asked him.

Still playing with the pocket-watch, Dr. Rosmir answered, "I have to get over it sometime. Even if it's not combat."

"You never know . . ."

Dr. Rosmir smacked his hand on the armrest. "Don't tell me that. That's the last thing I need to hear." Commander Byron offered a sincere apology, which Dr. Rosmir waved off. "I know you're just looking out for me, Commander. Don't say sorry for that."

Byron checked on the kids in the back by glancing at the screen. The two boys were talking to each other now. Byron didn't bother turning on the microphone to hear them. Judging by her eyes, the girl was listening even though her focus was still on the window where she rested her forehead. He turned back to the doctor. "You mind if I ask you something personal?"

"Sure, go ahead," Dr. Rosmir said heavily.

"Were you ever angry that I stopped you from taking the Psion Panel?"

Rosmir didn't answer right away, but Byron expected that. After all, he was asking about something that had happened well over a decade ago. Maad spat out a one-word answer that Byron couldn't hear.

"I missed that."

"Bitter," Dr. Rosmir repeated. "Not angry. I understood. I understood better than I let on. But honestly, how could I stay that way? You gave me exactly what I wanted. I felt trapped in that place—no offense. When you told me they were letting me go to medical school . . . it was like getting a get-out-of-jail-free card. I knew I wasn't any good at combat." Rosmir looked over at Byron and saw something in his face. "What?"

Byron stared back puzzled. "What do you mean, what?"

"You have that look. Okay, fine, so I was terrible at combat."

"I said nothing!" Byron protested. But he probably had made a face, even if he hadn't meant to. The truth was, no pupil of Byron's had performed as abysmally in the sims as Maad had. Despite all the extra help the commander had devoted to tutoring him, Byron knew he wouldn't pass the Panel. Psions were not created equal. It came as no shock to him. Not after Elite training. And in his tenure as the head of Psion Beta, he'd seen a wide range of abilities come through.

You have your natural fighters like Kaden and Albert, and the ones who struggle— the Gregors and the Maads. And all kinds in between. That is how life goes.

"How long did it take to get approval for me to go to school?" Rosmir asked.

"Oh . . . about six months." Byron checked the figures in his head and confirmed it.

"All the way up to General Wu, huh?"

Byron nodded and drummed his fingers on his knees. "We lock down the Betas. Most of them never seem to miss normal life. It surprises them. Limited contact with family, friends. Cooped up in that building for years in most cases. We ask a lot of these kids. But the structure and the schedule is something they come to rely on. Most of them, at least. I thought Samuel was going to fight it a lot harder than he did. A few incidents, but . . ."

Byron brushed his thoughts away. "Yes, it went all the way up to Wu. Even his thick skull could see we needed a Psion with a medical degree. I think your case helped open everyone's eyes. It helped people see that not every Psion is meant to be a soldier, even if they can shoot energy out of their hands."

"I can't complain. You put me through King's med school and the top surgical programs."

"And we gave you a very nice infirmary."

Dr. Rosmir rubbed his hands together gleefully. "When I show other doctors where I work—and that's not very often, believe me—they drool all over themselves. Every one of them."

Byron laughed and Dr. Rosmir let out the over-the-top cackle that he was famous for.

"And look at you now," Commander Byron said. "Every recruited Beta goes through you. Every sick or injured Alpha goes through you. You see firsthand the horrors of this war—probably more than anyone else. You know what we call you in our meetings when you are not around?"

"What's that?" the doctor asked.

"The sixth commander. Think about it. You are at almost every Psion Command meeting. You know more than most of them what is going on around us. You work with my counterpart at the Anomaly Fifteens—"

"And I work with Elevens now, too."

"See what I mean? Anyway, we got way off the subject. I guess what I want to say is, after all you have seen and done as a Psion, it surprises me that flying into Rio puts you on edge."

"Flying into Rio doesn't put me on edge. What might be waiting for me in Rio—that puts me on edge."

Byron couldn't stop another chuckle. He checked on the kids in the back once more. They all seemed fine. The girl had joined in the conversation, talking animatedly with both boys, who gave her their full attention. "She's going to be trouble, that one."

Rosmir looked at the screen. "The Plack girl? What makes you say that?"

"Years of experience. She's outgoing. Pretty. Young. The young ones get awfully bored with headquarters by the time they graduate. Remember, she turned twelve just a few months ago. I think she should room with Gefjon. They have a lot in common." Byron kept his eyes on the screen as he answered. He always found it fascinating the way kids could just start up a conversation about anything. So much more relaxed than adults. "How many of the Placks tested positive for the Fourteen?"

"Just the oldest girl," Dr. Rosmir answered. "But she turns thirty in a year. We'll just send her the pill to take every month. She was very cooperative about it. He watched the screen, too. Byron recognized the look in his friend's eyes as nostalgia. "How long does it take you to get a feel for a new recruit?"

Byron shrugged. "It depends. With some of them I can tell right away. Others, it takes a month or longer. But all of them surprise me sooner or later. People are simply unpredictable. Just when you think you know someone . . ."

"They throw you a curveball."

Commander Byron answered with a thumbs up. The remainder of the trip passed in more comfortable conversation. The weather was much milder over Capitol Island as the atmo-cruiser touched down on the rooftop of Beta headquarters.

"Just landing now, Major Tawhiri," Byron spoke into his com. "You are relieved of duty."

It was standard procedure for an Alpha or higher to be at the Beta building at all times to supervise the Betas. The Alphas referred to this assignment as "babysitting." And the man who normally got that job was Major Tawhiri.

"Anything unusual I need to know about?" Byron asked as the major came up to the roof toward the cruiser.

"Nope. Everything's hunky-dory," Major Tawhiri answered. They shook hands briefly. "You've got the best job in the world, Walter."

"Yep. Maad will take you home. Thanks for the help."

Byron opened the door for his newest recruits. The first to step out was the girl, Strawberry Plack. She had long dark hair, darker than her brother, Brickert's, but the same blue eyes and red spots on her cheeks. Behind her came Antonio Otravelli, an older recruit. Almost sixteen. He was the boy they'd picked up from Mediterranea. He'd been in the middle of a karate tournament championship when he'd accidentally blasted a kid trying to drop kick him. Byron spent almost a week and a half fixing that nasty problem.

Bringing up the tail came Hefani Ndumi. Commander Byron couldn't say enough good things about Hefani. He was just an all-around great kid from a tiny village in Southwest African Territory. Byron had heard about him almost eight months after he'd manifested signs of Anomaly Fourteen.

He stuck to the same routine, ushering the recruits downstairs with the sim room all set up for his presentation. Three holo-chairs were waiting for them, each with a com box on it bearing their engraved names. Six eyes stared up, watching him expectantly, nervously, but all with some measure of trust in their eyes.

Trust. They trust me.

He had told their parents he would be training them to become government operatives. He had made them all sign non-disclosure agreements that included severe penalties if breached. He had promised them to do all he could to ensure their safety and education.

But he hadn't told them about Aegis and Thirteens. About the Silent War. About Martin or Samuel. Nor had he mentioned other deaths of Psions like his wife, Emily, or Blake Weymouth (one of the most valiant men Byron had ever met), or Takeo Soto, or James McEmery, or Liam Scoresby, or . . . The list went on and on. And it grew longer too often.

What if the next casualty is Hefani or Antonio?

The commander cleared his throat and began kept speaking about the history of the Psions. He knew the drill, but had a much harder time getting through what he wanted to say.

He thought of the words he'd said at Martin's funeral in Australia and how inadequate they had felt. He remembered similar words at the memorial service held for him at headquarters. Tears falling from the eyes of so many Betas, but he had not let himself shed any. He wondered how long it would be before he shed more.

He promised the recruits he would do all he could to ensure their preparation and training. After administering the New World Government oath, he gave them the tour of headquarters then sent them all downstairs to unpack and settle in. Upstairs, in his office, he sat in his chair and turned on the screens displaying dorm hallways, the cafeteria, the rec room, and each room on the upper levels.

New roommate orders had been issued the day before, and several girls were still moving their belongings around the halls. Brillianté and Asaki were now sharing a dormitory, allowing Kawai and Natalia to room together as they'd requested. On his screen, he saw Strawberry entering her new dorm with Gefjon.

He stared blankly, lost in the circular mazes formed by his thoughts. Suddenly, a small blue box blinked at him on the wall. "Commander Wrobel," Emily's voice announced to him.

"Accept the call," he stated while sitting up and composing himself.

"Did you get the kids tucked in, Walter?" Wrobel asked.

Victor Wrobel sat in the same office that had once been Byron's long ago, but Wrobel had certainly personalized it over the years. Wrobel's taste in furniture was fancier than Byron's. Three tall bookcases stood side by side behind him. They held no books. Instead, the shelves were filled with trophies, plaques, honors, and so forth. In the very center, just above Wrobel's head, sat a framed picture of the beautiful Claire Hardy. Near Byron, on the wall of all his Psions, hung a different picture of the same woman.

Commander Byron glanced one last time at the screen showing his pupils. "Snug as bugs. But I can tell you have something else on your mind."

Wrobel chuckled. "You think you know me so well . . ."

Byron raised an eyebrow. "I did train you."

"I didn't get a chance to talk about plans for Al's ceremony next week," Wrobel continued as if he hadn't heard Byron's comment. "We need to go over some details."

"Which ones?"

Commander Wrobel snatched a sheet of paper off his desk and squinted at it. He held it awkwardly at arm's length from himself. The last time Byron had seen someone do that was when his father had needed glasses, but hadn't been willing to admit it. "First of all, the parents of the graduate occupy a seat of honor at the ceremony. The only people who know you're his dad are the rest of us in Command."

"And Marie, his fiancée."

"Right."

"And Dr. Rosmir."

"Fine—fine," Wrobel said, looking almost annoyed with Byron's correction. "My point is do you want everyone to know? This was considered classified information when he enrolled."

"It was classified because the general likes to classify things. I just wanted Albert to have a normal experience in Beta."

"Still . . . you or the general has to declassify it."

"Consider it done."

"That's fine by me." Commander Wrobel went back to his list. Byron almost laughed at how much Wrobel had to squint. "Has Al agreed to speak at the ceremony? Does he understand that it's the highlight of the ceremony for the graduate to give a speech?"

"Come on, Victor, how many ceremonies has he been to? He knows how they go. Put it in the program. Who is in charge of the highlight tape?"

"I don't remember. I'm sure it'll be fine." Wrobel put his paper down and looked into the camera. "How's your kid holding up, Walter? He must be thrilled about going back to Rio."

"I have not told him about it yet."

Wrobel sat up in his chair. "Are you serious? You really should get on that. Unless, of course, you're willing to listen to some sense and not go back. It's too dangerous."

"Sorry, my mind is made up. If there is even a slim chance we find his body—"

Commander Wrobel swore under his breath, shaking his head. "And make the kids go through all that trauma again?"

"I know your feelings on the matter. No need to rehash them."

"We should have gone back sooner . . ." Wrobel lamented.

"You vetoed my motion then," Byron reminded him.

Wrobel pointed a finger at Byron. "Don't blame me. It's all this . . . red tape. It's General Wu dragging his feet. Special op units can't do anything without approval. When is the team going in?"

"Not long after Albert's graduation. Everything is almost arranged. He wants to be there in person."

"For Pete's sake, he ran that mission. He should be there! But let me ask you something, Walter, do you think that kid could be alive?"

"No. Albert needs some closure on this, though. Bringing Samuel back, even dead, will help."

Commander Wrobel shook his head. "I don't know. Those demons wouldn't leave a body behind. Who knows what they've done?" His gaze was fixed on a spot near Byron's Psion pictures, as though he was lost in thought. "You know that as well as I." Wrobel's sullen tone and distant expression put a damper on Byron's spirits. The last few weeks had been hard on everyone. Wrobel, normally enthusiastic almost to a fault, rarely fell into moods like this. It made Byron wish he and Victor had stayed as close of friends as they'd once been, long ago.

"Anywhichway," Wrobel said with a snap, "I'll buzz you again to finalize the program. I have to go."

Before Byron could even say goodbye, Victor was gone. From the rec room cameras, he saw Brickert going ballistic, hugging his sister in a death squeeze. Byron smiled. Protocol had prevented Brickert from knowing about his sister's Anomaly Fourteen, and Strawberry had been too young to bring to headquarters with him a year ago. On the other side of the room, Antonio Otravelli went around the room introducing himself to all the girls. Hefani seemed comfortable hanging back and watching others.

Byron sighed and switched off the cameras. "And life goes on . . ."

All the Betas attended Al's graduation along with a handful of the youngest Alphas at Albert's invitation. His new squadron leader and every member of Command took prominent seats.

"Albert is more than just an outstanding young man. He's more than a talented Psion," Wrobel said in his opening address to the crowd of about sixty people. "He is a great follower, a loyal friend, and an excellent leader. Psion Command has no doubts he will have a significant impact on our efforts. But as I just said, Albert is more than what many of you may realize. He is the first second-generation Psion ever born. He is the son of Walter Byron and the late Emily Hayman."

Byron heard a few gasps and mutters at Wrobel's words. Natalia turned to Kawai and mouthed, "I told you so!"

"This was kept hidden only to allow him the privilege of being trained as your equal and to prevent any thoughts of unfair treatment. All of you know Al has proven himself to be a capable and worthy member of the Alpha ranks. And now it gives me great pleasure to allow him the time to address you."

A standing ovation came from the audience. As Byron watched his boy stand and walk to the pulpit wearing an expression of anxiety and reluctance, a warm tightness filled his chest and he said a prayer of gratitude for such a wonderful son.

Albert cleared his throat and grinned nervously at Marie and Gregor. He had a note card tucked up his sleeve, and he inched it out just barely. "First of all, I have to thank three people in my life who have helped make me into what I am: my mother, my father, and my future wife, Marie. My mother gave her life in the war we are still fighting."

An image of Emily, aged but beautiful, sitting in the chair next to Byron was suddenly very strong in the commander's mind. In that instant, he missed her more than he'd done in years. Across the stage, Commander Wrobel's head dropped and his eyes closed.

"Her example has taught me to give all my energy and heart in training and to carry on the fight she died for." Byron had to close his eyes to continue listening to his son. "Marie and I met on her first day here. Despite her . . . reserved personality, I saw an inner strength that compelled me. I spent months trying to get her to open up to me, and I've found it was worth every second. She is a friend and support I will always treasure. I love you, Marie."

The commander glanced into the audience and saw Marie's eyes shimmering as she smiled back at Albert, her face as red as the stripes on her uniform. Her sister, Rosa, held her hand and smiled at her.

"Finally, I want to talk about my father," Albert continued. "He is—he is the greatest man I have ever known." A heavy weight settled in Byron's chest. "My father, despite having to disguise our relationship for the last five and a half years, has always been there for me. After my mother died in battle it would've been easy for him to throw himself into his work and stop raising a child. Instead, he has made time for me regardless of the demands of his job. Even lately, as I've struggled to—to get through the recent events—my mission and such—he has been there for me, constantly checking up on me. I hope I grow up to be just like him. I love you, Dad."

A large smile broke out on Byron's face. He opened his eyes to see his son looking back at him. He'd never felt so proud of anyone in his entire life. It was one of those rare occurrences when he knew he'd done a decent job raising his son.

6 | Disorientation

January 8, 2086

SAMMY HAD NO IDEA what kind of gas the Aegis injected into his compartment, but it stunk like burned toast and paralyzed his muscles. Wearing gas masks, the Aegis dragged him out of the van, patted down every inch of him, and then propped him up on a dolly. One of them buckled straps around his waist and shoulders before wheeling him behind the others.

Through drooping eyelids, Sammy saw that he was in a well-lit, underground parking lot. They passed two security cameras, which meant there were probably more, but he had a feeling whoever was watching those cameras didn't care about some kid being wheeled into the building on a moving dolly. Every pillar they passed had a large purple 'N' with a golden circle wrapping around it. Some of the walls bore this symbol, too.

They brought him to an elevator. Each Aegis except Stripe and the one pushing Sammy had a gun trained on him. When the doors slid closed behind them, Stripe pressed his thumb to a scanner above the columns of floor buttons. The panel of buttons swung open to reveal a second panel set into the elevator wall. Only three buttons were on this new panel: black, red, and white. Stripe pushed the black one.

The steel box descended for a long time. As it dropped, the effects of the paralyzing gas began to wear off. After coming to a smooth stop, the doors opened. Sammy expected to see a filthy, dark, dripping hallway straight out of every slasher film he'd ever watched late at night when his parents thought he was asleep. Such was not the case. They came to a pristine, almost gleaming, corridor. The walls were covered in a cream and gold wallpaper with a deep purple trim. The carpeting was a light tan with rich embroidery. The long hallway stretched on before them. Somehow this scared Sammy even more.

They went halfway down then took a right into another hallway, this one shorter and narrower. It was lined with four skinny doors on each side, each with a small circular window about two-thirds of the way up.

A thin, breaking voice screamed out from behind one of the doors. "Let me go! Let me out of here! I want to go home!"

Through the second window on his right, Sammy saw the source of the shouts: a thin girl with short black hair. She was on her hands and knees in the corner of a white room with a metal ring around her neck that chained her to the wall. Sammy thought she couldn't be any older than Jeffie. She looked up at them as they passed and screamed even louder. The Aegis made no sign that they heard her. At the end of the hall stood a tall black door. Stripe scanned his thumb again. There was a click, and the black door swung open.

The room beyond the door was scantily furnished. There were two chairs, one with heavy-duty arm restraints built into the rests, and one without any restraints at all. The second one looked more like an office chair. A table stood against the nearest wall with a white sheet concealing the identity of the oddly-shaped lumps atop it. Hanging from the ceiling was a helmet similar to the one Sammy used when he played virtual reality games at Psion Beta headquarters. The room was immaculate, probably even sterile, but despite the lack of smell, Sammy sensed death in this room. An awful chill ran up his spine and ended at the base of his skull.

While two Aegis removed the magnetic cuffs from Sammy's arms, three guns stayed trained on him. They shackled him firmly into the restraints on the armrests of the chair and his feet were placed in ankle-cuffs. When everyone seemed satisfied he was secured, all but Stripe left the room.

Stripe walked behind Sammy, who craned his neck to see what Stripe was doing. With great care, Stripe took off his hat, coat, and tie and hung them on a small, thin stand. Then he removed his glasses and placed them in the front pocket of his coat.

"Not the most comfortable clothes for traveling, you see. Especially in the middle of the summer." He began unbuttoning the cuffs of his white shirt, then rolling them up his arms in careful fashion. "But the rules are the rules. And I obey the rules."

"Why am I here?" Sammy asked. He checked the sturdiness of the restraints as subtly as he could.

Stripe did not answer immediately. When he came back around in front, Sammy got a better look at him. He had neatly trimmed and combed hair ending above his ears. His gray eyes, confident and intelligent, were not kind.

"You won't get out of those without help." Stripe gestured with his head to the restraints. "I saw you pulling at them. They're built to withstand six hundred kilos of pressure. So unless you have supernatural strength . . ." He let his words hang in the air as he measured Sammy up with a stare. "Why do you think we are here?"

Sammy lied as best he could. "I don't know. Did I do something wrong?"

Stripe frowned as if he found Sammy's words to be troublesome. "Wrong is a very awkward word, don't you think? Very arbitrary. You see, you may not have broken any laws, but you did do something that needs correcting."

"What do you mean?" Sammy asked trying to sound scared, like the girl he had passed in the hall. "What needs correcting?"

"No details. I just want to speak very clearly to you. I want you to understand every single word that I say. Are you listening to me?"

Sammy nodded, his eyes wide. The closer Stripe got to him, the more he could sense his own fear crawling across his skin like an army of spiders marching up his arms and shoulders toward his brain. Stripe's sharply cinnamon-scented breath hung in the air around Sammy's nostrils.

"Good. You seem like a smart boy. You're not screaming like most of the crap we get. We ran a DNA search for you on the way here. Nothing was found. It's happened before. Your family is one of the unregistered pieces of gutter trash, probably from the slums judging by the stench on you. I don't really care. The point is, one way or another, you will tell me who you are and where you are from. It's such a simple thing. If you tell me now, I can go have a talk with your family, and everyone will be happy. Including you. If you don't tell me, I have to make you unhappy."

Pieces fell together inside Sammy's head. *They kill Anomaly Fourteens . . . and probably their families, too.*

"Do you believe in God?"

Sammy hadn't decided one way or the other, but since he was pretending to be Al, he answered in the affirmative.

"Good for you. Do you pray?"

Again he nodded.

"If you don't answer every question I ask, you will come to realize through significant pain that there is no God. Have I made myself clear?"

"Yes."

"Did you understand every word that I said?"

"Yes."

"Then tell me your name and where you live."

Sammy said nothing, but his mind raced furiously. If he lied, they'd figure it out. What would be the point? Cold hard calculations flashed before his mind's eye and he resolved that the only way of getting out of the situation would be to wait for a chance to escape. That moment was not now, not in this chair.

Dread rose in him, filling his chest and settling over his heart. He would be tortured. He knew it. He wanted to cry. More fear hit him in a way he had not felt in over a month. *This is real. This is really going to happen.* He steeled himself as best he could against whatever was coming.

The Aegis smiled. His perfect teeth, end to end, side by side, framed by bright red lips was all Sammy could see. And for the third time in his life, Sammy prayed. *God . . . Please God, if you're there, please save me. He's going to hurt me.*

"So you've made your choice. Good. A little courage never hurt anyone." Stripe smiled as though he'd made a private joke to which only he knew the punch line.

Stripe stood up and flipped a switch on the wall. The helmet hanging ominously above descended until it was level with Sammy's chest. He put it on Sammy's head, snuffing out all the light. There was a loud sound, like metal scraping tile, followed by something heavy dropping into Sammy's lap.

"Lean forward and throw up in this. I don't like cleaning up messes."

The blackness inside the helmet was replaced by a kaleidoscope of images and movements. It reminded Sammy of going to a holo-laser show in a dome theater and thinking he was flying even when he wasn't moving at all. He picked up speed, traveling through a dimension of spirals and wormholes. He tried to close his eyes, but when he did a painful shock nipped his ear. His whole body convulsed as his eyes reopened. The Aegis snorted softly nearby, unseen.

As minutes passed, the movements became faster and faster until his eyes could just barely keep up with the swift changes in direction, jerking him around until his brain spun inside his skull. His mind, plunged into such disorientation, could no longer tell if he was sitting in a chair, hanging upside down, or twirling madly in space.

When his vertigo reached a critical point, he lurched forward and vomited into whatever sat in front of him. His eyes involuntarily closed, shocking him even more than the first time. He retched again and again until he heaved nothing but air and sound. The swirling and turning continued. Every so often Sammy believed he could withstand the pain of the shock just to keep himself sane. But each time he tried to close his eyes the voltage increased, and it hurt too badly to resist.

When Sammy finally lost all concept of spatial and time orientation, the helmet turned off and retracted back to the ceiling. He closed his eyes and heaved several more times, still feeling as though he were zipping every direction at once.

"That was fun!" Stripe said. His voice was like glass in Sammy's ears, thundering through and trying to shatter him. "Now I'm going to give you a tiny taste of what you can expect tomorrow if you decide to continue this silly farce. Your homework will be to think about this next experience every time you consider withholding information from me."

Sammy cracked his eyes open to see what the man could possibly be preparing to do. The world was spinning and in the middle of it Stripe stood using a small knife to break the seal on what looked like a tube of toothpaste. With protective gloves covering his hands, Stripe squeezed a small dollop of white cream onto his fingertip, and held the glistening droplet up for Sammy to see.

Sammy could only see a spinning ball of light.

"Do you want to tell me what your name is now?"

"No." He didn't remember screaming while the helmet had been over him, but the sound that came from his throat was a hoarse whisper.

"Could you at least tell me whether or not it's Muhammad, John, or Michael? Because I could eliminate an appreciable chunk of the male population . . ."

Sammy said nothing, keeping his focus on not retching.

"Did you know that there are only three connections between your skin and the sensory area of your brain? So when I do this—" he touched the glistening finger to the back of Sammy's left hand, "—you feel the change in pressure, temperature, and a slight wetness almost immediately."

The spot the man touched felt wet and cold on Sammy's skin.

Stripe continued very calmly, speaking as though he were sharing a great secret with his captive. It dawned on Sammy that this was a man who his father, Samuel Sr., would have described as being in love with his own voice.

"I've made the sensation of pain a special study for myself. It's so wonderful. It helps us feel alive. You probably don't know much about pain. But you're here, so I'll teach you."

As the wet dot on Sammy's skin began to warm, Stripe lectured about the different nerve endings in Sammy's hand and how they communicated with his brain. All Sammy heard were bits of words like pacinian, spinothalamic, and cortex. Normally his hyper-intelligent brain would have picked up everything instantly, but the tiny dot on his skin had grown uncomfortably warm, as if it were too close to a candle.

"Let me ask you a theoretical question. What if some brilliant researcher isolated a molecule that could duplicate the effect of temperature change on nerve receptors? The possibilities are endless!" Stripe exclaimed these last words in a rapturous voice. Then he got unnaturally close to Sammy's face again. His cinnamon breath permeated Sammy's entire being. The twisted scar on his lip filled Sammy's vision. "And, you see, here's one amazing discovery: a person can feel it without any damage to the skin. No death from dehydration . . . even when you experience such intense heat that your skin should be burning off your bones."

Intense pain blazed through the spot on Sammy's hand. He gasped sharply, groaning through gritted teeth.

"It's okay to scream. I know how badly this is going to hurt—curiosity got the best of me. Do you see this red tube?" he asked, holding it up for his prisoner to see.

Sammy opened his eyes and nodded quickly.

"Fire. It's what you're going through now. Do you see this one?" He held up an identical blue tube. "Ice. It makes it all go away, you see. You know how to get the ice, don't you?"

Sammy closed his eyes tight so he would not answer Stripe's question. He tried to push the pain out of his mind. He wanted to grab hold of anything that would take his mind off the blistering heat on his hand, but everything he thought of slipped away, leaving only pain. Blinding pain. He wanted to yell and scream and thrash unabashedly. But he wouldn't allow himself to, even if he couldn't stop tears from leaking out of his eyes.

Wait for your opportunity to escape. DO NOT SHOW WEAKNESS! he ordered himself in a voice that sounded much like Byron's.

Immeasurable time passed and eventually the pain subsided. Sammy could open his eyes now. Stripe had stopped spinning and was now watching him with his immaculate teeth bared and an unreadable look in his gray eyes.

"Impressive," he said. Sammy wasn't sure if Stripe was grinning or grimacing. "Not a peep. But remember two things when you go to your room tonight. Number one, that was a very very very tiny little drop on your hand. What if I rubbed it all up your arm? On your ears? On your lips?

And number two, you've only met fire. I have other tubes. Enough to keep us busy for a long time."

Stripe dragged out the word *long* as his eyes bored into Sammy's, waiting to see if he would break.

"No one ever holds out. In the end, I always win. ALWAYS. Maybe that's why I like the game so much." He gave Sammy a slight touch on the shoulder. "Have a nice rest."

After Stripe left, two different Aegis with guns took Sammy into the same room he'd glanced into minutes or hours (or maybe days?) earlier. They left him no opportunity to venture an attack. The young girl with dark hair in the corner was asleep. The men secured his neck to the wall with a chain and checked his arm and leg restraints. After they left, he either passed out or fell asleep.

His rest was fitful. It didn't seem long before he woke to the sound of the girl being taken from the room in the same fashion that Sammy had been brought in. He watched them go, the girl crying as she was led away, probably to the same room with the black door. His mind raked over his situation for a long time, more than he could keep track of. But then he fell asleep once more. When he woke for the second time, the girl was crying again.

"Are you okay?" Sammy asked her.

Either the girl didn't hear him or didn't understand him.

"Hey," Sammy called out a second time. "Are you all right?" he peered across the room at her. Her short hair didn't hide her face well. Tears streamed down her cheeks. She clutched her left arm as if it were badly hurt, but he saw nothing wrong with it. Copious amounts of drool fell down her lips and onto her soiled shirt.

"Do you have a name?" he asked. "Can you help me or can I help you?"

When she failed to respond a third time, he stopped asking questions. He huddled against the wall, angling his head so he could watch her across the way. Somehow, he fell asleep in that position.

The next day, the cell door opened and a bowl of soupy oatmeal slid across the floor to him. Some of it sloshed over the sides as it came to rest near Sammy. Another bowl slid to the girl. He'd thought she was sleeping, but the moment the bowl came to rest, she picked it up, drained its contents, and sucked up whatever had spilled near her. Sammy picked up his own bowl and sampled the contents.

It tasted like worn socks blended into small bits. However, he was famished, so he finished it. The girl eyed the little puddle of sludge near his knees, but he wasn't about to eat off the floor. Moments later, in walked Stripe.

"Good morning," he said. "Did you sleep well?"

Sammy didn't answer.

"Was it better than the gutter you came from?"

More Aegis came in. This time they were wearing their regular uniforms—the green and brown clothes with the pattern muddied in such a way that it hurt Sammy's eyes to look at it too long.

"Are you ready to play?"

Sammy was led into the room with the black door. He felt the same fear he'd felt the day before. The guards secured him to the chair and left.

The scent of cinnamon was present again when Stripe got close to him. "Did you do your homework?" was the question.

When Sammy wouldn't answer, the helmet came down. His breakfast came up within five minutes of swirling lights and flashes. When Sammy was good and dizzy again, Stripe spoke up.

"Are you ready to tell me your name so you can leave?"

When Sammy didn't answer, the creams came out. This time, Stripe introduced Sammy to pressure. He smeared it across the back of Sammy's hand and waited. Slowly the cream went to work, inducing the most bizarre sensation that someone was sitting on him. As the pressure built, Sammy's hand began to ache, then worse. At its peak, his hand felt like it was being crushed under an immense weight. All the while, Stripe spoke to him in a calm voice about the history of his pain research and how humans had evolved an especially keen perception of pain.

"We are meant to perceive pain more than other animals. Pain defines us; molds us from infancy. Nothing makes a more indelible impression on our minds than pain."

About ten minutes into the pressure cream, Sammy started to cry. He stared at his hand, knowing nothing was wrong with it, but unable to stop imagining a giant boulder squashing it. He tried to imagine all the different things that could cause such agony: anvils in cartoons, furniture falling over, an elephant stepping on him—anything to keep his mind off the pain.

A voice in his head begged him to tell Stripe his name, but the voice wasn't strong enough and Sammy pushed it away. Somewhere far from his consciousness, time ticked away until Stripe called it a day.

As the Aegis led Sammy out of the room, Stripe spoke to him. "It doesn't have to be like this. Remember that. It can all go away. Remembering that will be your homework today."

In his cell, as Sammy cradled his hand, which still throbbed horribly, he thought about what Stripe had done to him. His gut told him that Stripe hadn't expected him to break. *Maybe he's just testing me.* The idea that Stripe had even worse tools on hand that he hadn't used yet kept Sammy up late that night.

He waited with dread for Stripe to come back for him the next morning, but Stripe never came. The girl across the room slept most of the time, but Sammy didn't think he would get her to talk to him, anyway. He passed the time in silence, thinking about how he was going to escape. He thought back to the Grinder and how he'd managed to break out of it.

Anyone on the receiving end of the Juvenile Delinquent Education Facility in Johannesburg called it the Grinder. The education given there was two-fold: learn your books and learn to never come back. Six hours a day spent in class. Six hours a day of manual labor.

As the son of a territorial prosecutor, Sammy knew the theory behind facilities like the Grinder: make prisons miserable, show the prisoners a better way while they serve time, and allow them a chance to reform. According to his dad, the system worked.

Sammy never thought he'd actually experience the Grinder for himself. When he ran away from his foster home, stealing food inevitably followed. He knew it was only a matter of time before he was caught, but he didn't care. After seeing his first foster father, Calven, die of a stroke, he wouldn't be transferred to another foster family. He couldn't do it.

Within several days' time, security at a grocery store caught him trying to leave with a cart of over a hundred and fifty dollars' worth of food. The police arrested him and put him in a cell. Appearing before Judge Hill, a good friend of his father, had been the most embarrassing moment of his life. However, the judge was sympathetic to Sammy's unique situation and gave Sammy the territory's minimum sentence for theft: nine months.

Bitter, frustrated, and lonely, Sammy arrived at the Grinder and immediately sought out others who shared his hatred of just about everything in life. It didn't take long to find them. Seven boys, all between the ages of twelve and fifteen, formed strong bonds of friendship. They hated the building, they hated the guards, they hated the work, they hated the crappy food, the phony counselors, the uncomfortable cots, and they hated most of the other kids there, too.

After serving five months of his sentence, Sammy's uncanny ability to think deeply showed itself. It happened late one night while he lay on his cot listening to the night sounds of the forest that bordered the Grinder. The idea to break out settled over his mind. He could not and did not resist the idea. Lying there, he saw the way out. He just needed time to work out the details and get everyone on board.

The Grinder was a single building, large and rectangular, with only one floor. The front third of the building served as the administrative area. It held the main reception area, offices for the directors, the warden, security, and several counselors.

The middle area of the Grinder was the factory and the gathering room. In the gathering room they ate meals, attended group sharing sessions, and played indoor games on Friday nights. They also had several smaller classrooms. Whenever he got bored during classes, Sammy looked out the barred windows and watched other boys work the farm to grow their food. Beyond the farm's high fence stood a beautiful green forest.

The last area of the Grinder, closest to the forest, was the quarters, or "cells" as Sammy referred to them. All of the cells had tungsten-plated bars on the windows and opened only from the outside.

Security was tight. Cameras left no room for privacy. When a fight broke out, security was on it in seconds. If one of the rougher kids threatened a counselor, security was on it in seconds. Even someone loitering around the halls got pestered by security. All security wore the same stupid uniform: a blue shirt with a sewn-on yellow badge and khaki pants. The kids in the Grinder called the members of security "Blues."

Crop and livestock from the farm provided their food. The factory and kitchen turned raw food products into edible meals. With one hundred and nine boys in the Grinder, the manpower to make it work was in place. The boys did all the cleaning as well. Two teams of eight were assigned each night to mop, sweep, scrub, collect garbage and dirty linens, or any other oddities that needed doing. Assignments for night shifts came about once a week.

From the very start of planning his escape, Sammy knew it would happen while on cleaning duty. Since Sammy and his friends were all on cleaning duty together, they could meet in the gathering room, go through the factory, and exit out the factory's emergency doors in the back. From there, they'd have to sprint across the grounds, climb the fence, and disappear into the forest.

He saw two obstacles in this plan. First, the door between the factory and the gathering area was locked. Sammy's friend Watch, their best thief, was given the task of jimmying it. He learned to pick it while Chuckles and Honk kept lookout.

The second problem was more difficult to solve. They needed more time to get through the factory. Sammy reckoned that the moment they picked the lock, the Blues would know. He and his friends would have to make a beeline for the emergency door. But security had their own door into the factory, and it was much closer to the emergency exit, making it very likely the Blues would cut off their escape.

Breakfast held the answer.

"Brains, eat," Chuckles ordered as he folded a large slice of French toast into his mouth. "You need food or you're going to waste away and die. And if you die, then we're stuck in here, forced to become rehabilitated citizens. You know, boring people. And I don't want to be boring."

Sammy ran the calculations through his head again and cursed out loud. "I can't stop thinking about it! How are we going to find more time?"

"Maybe you're thinking about this all wrong, Brains," Gunner suggested. "Try it from a new angle."

"No . . . I'm not." He rubbed his temples as if he could somehow massage his brain into giving him the answer. "We pick the lock and open the door. Five seconds for all of us to go through it. We sprint across the factory. Twenty seconds for most of us. Twenty-five for Chuckles' fat butt."

Fro-yo and Honk laughed at this. Chuckles flipped them off.

"The Blues realize what we're doing in five seconds. They reach the factory door in . . ." He looked at Watch to finish the sentence.

"Six seconds tops," Watch reported.

Sammy flipped his fork up in the air and caught it by the handle. "By the time we're halfway through the factory, the Blues have cut us off because they're that much closer to the exit."

- 84 -

"Only if they catch on right away," Feet pointed out.

"I'm assuming the worst," Sammy said. "Less surprises that way."

"If Brains says so, it must be true," Fro-yo said while examining his hair in the reflection on the back of his spoon. "If you're going to do nothing but think, can I eat your toast?"

"Why do you care what you look like?" Sammy asked as he pushed his plate over. "I see no girls here."

Fro-yo grinned and winked at Sammy, then puckered up and kissed the air. "Be a pal and pass the butter, will you, Feet? Brains didn't even have the decency to butter his own food."

"It's not butter," Feet said. "It's margarine."

"So what? They taste the same."

"No, they don't," Chuckles responded. "They're totally different. Butter is made from milk. It's sweeter and healthier. Margarine is oil based and tastes like—"

"Butter isn't healthier than margarine," Feet answered back.

While his friends argued, an idea clicked in Sammy's head. He went over it repeatedly during his morning classes. During his work time in the factory, he double-checked the whole plan once more, making sure he hadn't missed something.

At dinner time, he announced quietly that he had the solution. They would escape in three days, on their next cleaning night.

The night of the escape, Sammy stayed in the gathering room and mopped so he could keep a watchful eye on everything else in operation. Watch was entrusted with the sacred task of picking the lock while the others pretended to be cleaning. What they were really doing was packing food and supplies to keep them alive as they wandered through the forest.

It went like clockwork. When the packing was finished, Feet gave Sammy a thumbs up. Sammy mopped his way over to the factory door and gave the waiting Watch the go-ahead. About a minute later, all hell broke loose.

The seven of them hustled into the factory just as the security door burst open. There were fewer Blues heading them off than Sammy had expected. But the Blues didn't get very far.

Earlier that day, just before the factory had closed down for dinner, Honk had accidentally spilled a large can of mustard on the factory floor while preparing sandwiches for next day's lunch. When he reported this to the supervisor, he was ordered to clean it up immediately. This he did, except, instead of using cleaner, he used a large tub of melted margarine as his cleaning agent, coating a very large portion of the floor near the security guards' door.

When the Blues came out of the door, they slipped and could not get back up.

Sammy and his gang howled with laughter as they raced down their own clear path, burst through the emergency exit, and emerged in the blustery night air. He noticed Gunner, Honk, and Fro-yo had grabbed makeshift weapons along the way, others had not. He'd told them they wouldn't need them.

He was wrong.

Three more Blues blocked their path into the forest, wielding the only weapons the Blue were allowed to use: pepper spray and clubs. Sammy realized security must have had access to some other exit he didn't know about, giving them a quicker route to the grounds.

"Remember your promise!" Sammy bellowed as he ran straight for the nearest guard.

"Never come back here again!" Feet yelled.

The pepper spray was unleashed as the Blue raised his club. Sammy threw his shoulder into him and ran on, ignoring the stinging in his eyes.

The two other Blues gave just as much fight before bowing to the overwhelming numbers coming at them. Honk and Gunner swore in anger as the pepper did its work.

"Keep going to the fence!" Sammy shouted.

Chuckles hit the ground screaming, clutching his face when they were only a few meters from the fence. The rest of the Blues emerged from the factory exit. Sammy ran back to help Chuckles as his friends scaled the fence. When the boys had all crossed, they ran for the woods, shouting taunts and obscenities at the Blues who didn't even bother to give chase.

⑤

Ten more days went by and Sammy relied more and more on his memories to get him through his time with Stripe. He saw no chance for escape. Guards escorted him through the halls at gunpoint, and his arms stayed shackled whenever they moved him.

On his fifth trip to the room with the black door, he was caught off guard. After the escorts secured him to the chair and left, Stripe sat down in his chair. He was wearing the same suit Sammy had first seen him in: the one with the striped tie and white shirt. Stripe flattened his tie against his chest and stomach with a sigh.

"I can't do this anymore," he said in his unusually deep, nasal tone, looking at the floor. "I can't stand hurting you. Or other people, for that matter."

Sammy stared at Stripe with his mouth half-open. He didn't believe he'd heard Stripe correctly, but then Stripe looked up. In his cold gray eyes Sammy detected no sign of humor or deceit.

"They expect me to play this role for them. To be this sick man." He looked at his hands as if they were giant mutant fish fins or something similarly awful. "I hate this. I hate this. GAH!" He slammed a fist down on the table and made both Sammy and the cream tubes jump.

"I don't understand, Stripe," Sammy said hoarsely.

"What was that?" Stripe asked. "What did you call me?"

"Stripe." Sammy realized then that he'd never called the man anything out loud before. "It's just . . . I don't know."

Stripe looked down at his tie, then over to the hook where his hat hung serenely in the corner. He smiled a little. "No, that's okay. You can call me that."

"I don't understand what you mean when you say that you hate this."

"They make me do these things to you. They make me do them because they have to have information to keep people safe. We have to know who the families are to test them and see if there are others. It's all about ensuring the safety of our people. So they try to get us to scare it out of you. And if that doesn't work, we have to hurt you. They watch me to see if I'm doing my job right."

Stripe's comments didn't make sense. It seemed to him that there were several holes in the logic he was hearing, but for the first time in a while, he couldn't put a finger on what they were. And he desperately wanted to believe that Stripe was telling the truth.

"Can you imagine what my wife would think of me if she saw what I do every day? Or my children?"

Sammy heard real dread in Stripe's tone. "But you aren't being watched now, are you?"

Stripe shook his head. "Sometimes they are. Sometimes they aren't. I can tell when, but they don't know that I know. Does that make sense?"

Sammy nodded and licked his lips. Perhaps Stripe could help him after all. Maybe Stripe even wanted to.

"If I can manage it, I'll sneak you out of here and take you back to your family. How does that sound?" Stripe stared into Sammy's eyes. Excitement and kindness blazed in the Aegis' eyes, and Sammy couldn't look away. "I'll help you if I can. But you need to help me, too."

Sammy's heart was thunderous in his chest, and his arms trembled from the wonder of the moment. But he couldn't say yes. Not immediately. Something told him to wait, even if just for a little while.

"Can I think about it, Stripe?"

Stripe nodded. Sammy relaxed even more. "I'll go easy on you today, okay?" Stripe said gently. "They'll know if I don't do anything, but I'll cause as little pain as I can."

When Sammy returned to his cell, the girl was gone. He wasn't sure if she'd been taken to another room, but he didn't miss her. All she did was cry and drool and not talk. Still, the room felt a little emptier without her.

He couldn't sleep. His mind turned over his conversation with Stripe. As the hours passed, and the girl didn't come back, he knew she wasn't returning. He didn't know how he knew that, but, deep in his soul, he knew it and he didn't question it.

She talked. She told them who she was. They finally broke her and she talked.

The next thought in his mind was: *But not Stripe. Stripe wasn't there. He was with me.*

Either Stripe is toying with me or he's the one being played by someone even higher up. Perhaps Stripe believed he could help Sammy, but the moment Sammy told Stripe his identity, he'd end up like the girl that never returned. It didn't matter which reality was true. Sammy knew he couldn't tell anyone.

The next day, Stripe came into his cell just after Sammy had licked the last bit of soupy oatmeal from his bowl.

"Good morning," Stripe said. "Did you sleep well?"

Sammy sort of shrugged. It was the same thing every time Stripe arrived.

"Was it better than the gutter you came from?"

The old Stripe was back when the black door shut, leaving them alone.

"I want to introduce you to a friend of mine," Stripe said. "Mr. Wake-up." He then waved a wire in front of Sammy's face. "This will make sure I don't give you more pain than your body can tolerate. I don't want you passing out on me."

He gave Sammy a wink. "Anything you want to tell me before we begin?"

Sammy shook his head. Stripe looked disappointed. Then he put Sammy through the ringer. Fire on Sammy's lips and nose, so it felt like his face was melting off, and sharp on the soles of his feet, as if he'd stepped all over glass. It was just as bad the next time. And the next. Sammy yearned for the nicer Stripe to come back—for a day when "they" weren't watching. He didn't know how much longer he could hold out as the pain Stripe inflicted on him grew worse.

As the torture went on, Sammy coped by forcing himself to build on the lies he'd told Floyd Hernandes. He was Albert, a boy who'd run away from abusive parents. He loved swimming and building model train sets.

His favorite color was fire engine red. His father was a pilot, his mother a nurse. He liked enchiladas more than anything. And when the moment came that Sammy's courage ran out and he could take Stripe's methods no more, with tears streaming down his dirty face, he screamed out, *"My name is Albert!"*

Stripe sat next to Sammy and put his hand on Sammy's trembling hand. The hand was warm and soothing. In a soft, nasally voice, he asked. "Albert what?"

"ALBERT CHOOCHOO!"

7 | Hooks

January 19, 2086

"GOOD MORNING, PSIONS. Good morning, Psions. Good morning, Psions."

Jeffie lay in bed with her eyes open, staring at the ceiling. The woman's words didn't even register anymore. She was thinking about the dream she'd just had—the one the alarm had interrupted. The image of Sammy kissing her, wrapping his fingers in her hair, faded away with a slow sigh of longing.

Two months . . . It's been two months.

Beneath her, Strawberry Plack stirred. "Unh . . . what time is it?" Her pillow muffled her voice and made it deeper.

Jeffie glanced across the room at the clock blinking dim red numbers. "Almost seven."

"Feels like . . . earlier. Is it time for the Game?"

"Yeah."

"So stupid." Strawberry's feet hit the floor and she wobbled wearily.

Jeffie smiled as her roommate left the dorm. Each morning, with fanatical consistency, Strawberry did the same thing: roll out of bed, change into her jumpsuit (today it would be the noblack color for the Arena), then head for the bathroom to shower and do her make-up. That was Strawberry, the girl who thought it a sin not to look perfect. Jeffie considered her to be a nice change from Brillianté, her old roommate, not that there'd been any bad blood between them.

Still, it amazed her how different she was from Brickert's sister. Jeffie was tall and blonde, Strawberry a short brunette. Jeffie played sports, Strawberry liked to dance and couldn't dribble a basketball. Jeffie wore make-up, but Strawberry would not, could not, leave the girls' floor without it. Jeffie loved competition, while Strawberry could not care less about winning. They rarely saw eye to eye, yet they had quickly become friends.

When Strawberry came back in the room fifteen minutes later, she noticed Jeffie hadn't moved.

"Is something bothering you?" she asked in her cheery, naturally high-pitched voice.

Jeffie shook her head slowly.

"Come on. Tell me what's up."

"Nothing—really, nothing. I've got to get ready."

Jeffie recognized the extra buzz in the cafeteria when she sat down, but it didn't interest her. It usually meant someone new had been picked for honcho or Byron had thrown an insane scenario at them. She was sitting between Brickert and Strawberry, letting her oatmeal fall off her spoon and into her bowl like snow sliding off a hot roof. Natalia and Kawai were across from her, talking with Brickert and Strawberry. The panel on the wall had only lit up minutes ago, but several bodies were congregated in front of it, blocking the wall from view.

"What do you think is up?" Brickert asked.

Kawai and Natalia just shrugged. Jeffie didn't even answer.

"Okay, well, don't everyone jump up all at once." Brickert let his fork clatter to the table. "I'll check it." He had to stand on his tiptoes to see over Rosa's shoulder. When he sat back down, he turned to Jeffie with a huge grin and said, "You're up."

"Huh? Me?"

"Yeah, you're honcho. So is Miguel."

"Miguel?" Jeffie repeated in astonishment. "They're putting me up against Miguel on my first run? Yes! That's way better than going up against . . . I don't know—Kaden or Marie."

"Hey, Jeffie!" Miguel called out a table away. "Good luck!" He gave her a wink and then went back into conversation with Ludwig and Kaden.

Kawai came back from examining the panel. "Kaden's on the other team, but I think you can do it. Miguel's nowhere near as good as his big sis."

"He hasn't lost his last three times at honcho, though," Natalia said. "Or is it four? Shoot. I can't remember."

"No, it's his last two," Asaki told her from the next table over. "Sammy beat him, remember?"

"Either way," Brickert said, "he's really good!"

"You've got the better team," Kawai reminded her.

Jeffie attempted to clear her thoughts of Sammy beating Miguel, but couldn't. She forced herself to smile back at Kawai. "I'll beat the pants off him."

"The Game's not about winning, Jeffie," Brickert replied in a mock bossy tone, "it's about—"

"I know what it's about, *Commander.*" She flipped her hair over her shoulder and swallowed some oatmeal. It didn't go down easily; her throat was too dry. She loved what she was experiencing now. The pressure. The need to win. The drive to be the best. It was in her blood—in her DNA. *Tvedts are winners. Tvedts thrive under pressure. Oh gosh, I sound like my dad.* Then her father's voice came back to her as clear as if he were in the cafeteria with her.

🌀

"This is not just a bunch of games, girls. It's the Under-16 Olympics!" Coach Tvedt yelled at twelve girls sprinting up and down the basketball court at the end of their final practice before their first game. Jeffie was a full line ahead of her teammates. She mopped her forehead with her blue and white jersey and pushed on as her father gave them his standard motivational speech.

"I know each of you want the championship just as badly as I do . . ."

Jeffie knew her father well, but she doubted he wanted the trophy as badly as she did. She'd lost count of how many times she had dreamed of standing on the pedestal with a gold medal around her neck.

"So you're going to have to be perfect!" he roared at them. "You can't make bad passes. You can't take bad shots. If you play your game the way you should, none of the territories will beat you. Some of them won't even be able to give you a lick of trouble." He blew the whistle once and the girls, conditioned after months of practice with him, doubled their efforts. Then he blew the whistle twice, shrill and commanding, and they stopped. Jeffie bent over to catch her breath. "First game is tomorrow. Shower up! Be in bed by 2100 because rise and shine is at 0600."

"Go Norway!" all the girls yelled as a team. Then they ran to the locker room.

⑨

Shaking herself out of the memory, Jeffie looked at the panel to see exactly who was on her team.

Team 1: 5th Floor	Team 2: 5th floor
Alanazi, Cala	Ndumi, Hefani
Covas, Marie	Covas, Miguel (*)
Enova, Levu	Covas, Rosa
Etoille, Brillianté	Otravelli, Antonio
Ivanovich, Natalia	Petrov, Ludwig
Nujola, Kawai	Plack, Strawberry
Plack, Brickert	Reynolds, Kaden
Tvedt, Gefjon (*)	von Pratt, Gregor
von Pratt, Parley	Zheng, Li Cheng
Yoshiharu, Asaki	

Victory: 2 Games of 3
Maximum Game Length: 90 minutes
Start Time: 07:00
See special rules

Kawai was absolutely right. Jeffie did have the better team. But that didn't make the pressure go away. It would still be a close match. Her chances of winning were good, but not absolute. Not only did she have the extra player on her team, but Miguel was honcho of all three nukes. *New recruits*, she corrected herself. *Remember how you hated that name?* She finished her meal and left to put on her suit. Fifteen minutes later she marched her team into the Arena.

Almost a year ago to the day, Jeffie had arrived at Psion headquarters. In that period of time, she had played something close to fifty Games, one every Saturday. Only rarely did the Game setups repeat themselves. And she had never played one like this. Even the oldest Betas hadn't heard of a setup like this.

"This is going to rip my arms to shreds," Cala said when she saw the Arena.

"You can say that again," Asaki muttered.

The ceiling of the Arena was decorated with blunted hooks big enough to grab comfortably. The special rules on the panel informed Jeffie that a small chair would be suspended on each side of the playing area. While the entire Game would be played hanging from the hooks, players could use the chair to take a two-minute rest. However, after the two minutes ended, the chair would dump out whoever was sitting in it. The first team to eliminate the other team's players would win the Game.

"Communicate with me when you need a rest," Jeffie told her team as they arranged themselves in the attacking formation she had chosen. "And you don't have to rest the full two minutes."

She divided them into two groups of four and one group of two. She put herself into one of the foursomes. Hook after hook, they made their way into the middle of the field. The two foursomes were assigned to corner individuals on Miguel's team. The group of two, which Jeffie called her rovers, was made up of one weak and one strong player. Their job was to stay moving and assist either unit. They had to always be ready to pinch off from either group.

She felt confident in this strategy. And for good reason.

Miguel came out with his team divided into thirds. The first group of three clashed directly into Jeffie's four and were beaten back by her group's superior skill and larger numbers. It did not take long for Jeffie to notice that one of Miguel's groups of three was comprised solely of the three newest recruits.

Why would he do that? In her mind, the better strategy was to scatter the worst players throughout the groups. She ordered her second team of four to go straight at the newbies.

While en route, all the hooks moved randomly about the ceiling, and then came to a stop. The new configuration gave Miguel's team the advantage. Four of Jeffie's team wound up pinched between the three newbies and Miguel's three best players. Jeffie ordered her two rovers to help them. Parley was the first to go down. He lost his grip on a bad swing. Jeffie panicked watching him fall. Even though she knew the floor would be softened for the Game, falling four floors was still falling four floors.

Brickert, who was also a part of Parley's group, got caught sandwiched between Miguel and Gregor. Before the two rovers on her team could help, Brickert had been eliminated as well. Jeffie's one player advantage had now turned into a one player disadvantage.

Asaki and Natalia, the last two in that group, called for help. Had it not been for the inexperience of the newbies, they would have gone down next. The arrival of the two rovers behind Miguel's three rescued them. Jeffie's four against Miguel's six was enough to win that small battle. All three newbies went down, plus Gregor. The hooks scattered again. Jeffie ordered the rovers to stay with Asaki and Natalia. Miguel only had five players left against Jeffie's eight. Her two groups of four relentlessly chased down Miguel's remaining players. The match only lasted twenty-five minutes.

⟡

"Ladies and gentlemen, with tonight's win, Team Norway advances to the semifinals to play Australia in two days," the booming voice of the announcer called out to the exiting crowd, "Judges from the media have voted All-Territorial guard Jeffie Tvedt as the game MVP. Tvedt and Vernika Salvensen combined for forty-eight of Norway's points. Tipoff for the semifinal matchup is 1900."

Toting her second MVP placard and her game bag, Jeffie followed her dad to the rail to take them back to the hotel. The rest of the team had met up with their own parents to celebrate the win. Coach Tvedt, as usual, wanted his daughter in bed and resting.

"Not bad, girl," her dad said. "You had two . . . maybe two and a half solid quarters. But you stopped attacking in the fourth. You had Mediterranea's forward on her heels whenever you wanted."

"That whole team was a walkover," Jeffie responded with a flippant expression. "I'm surprised they got as far as they did. Their ball handling was crap. I figured it'd be better to not push it too hard in the fourth after we were up by fifteen."

"Yeah, but I told you to push it, didn't I?" her dad reminded her. "You can't go easy on any teams in the tournament. Remember what I told you?"

"Put your foot on the throat and crush it," Jeffie muttered as they stepped onto the rail. Her ears popped as the door sealed shut. The rail sped along through the clear tube, moving from the south of Paris to the north.

The lights of the city passed them on both sides. As always, Jeffie made it a point to watch as they went by the Arc de Triomphe. It was her favorite landmark in the whole city. Victory. The only thing that mattered. She was a winner, born into a family of winners. She allowed herself a sigh of happiness. Life was perfect right now.

"Nervous about Australia?" her father asked.

"I don't think so," was her answer. "Should I be . . . Coach?" She put an extra emphasis on his title.

Her dad held his trusty notebook that he always carried with him. Inside, he kept detailed thoughts about each team they played. Right now he was leafing through his notes about Australia. "You're going to be in a tough spot on defense. I'm sure they'll put their forward on you. She's got a six centimeter height advantage on you. Long arms. She's three years older, too. You've got to play tough if you want to get her into foul trouble early."

"Dad, come on, we're unstoppable. Even if she has a good game we've got five great players, they've got one."

"They're not a bad team, just streaky. Give them some credit."

"Look who's worried now! You said they'd only be a lick of trouble!"

"Yeah, well, I've been watching them closely since the tournament started—"

"Don't worry, Dad. We're going to get the gold."

"I'll show you some stuff at tomorrow's practice before the other girls get there," he said, grabbing his briefcase as the rail came to a stop at the north Paris station. "In the meantime, get a good sleep . . . and don't stay up all night talking about the boy teams."

Jeffie saw her dad's sly grin. "Jerk."

The strategy used for the first Game had worked so well in the Arena that Jeffie only made a few small adjustments before sending her team back out on the hooks. She felt focused, poised, and ready to hand Miguel his second loss so she could call it a day.

Not surprisingly, Miguel had made some big changes. As Jeffie watched his team swing out to meet hers, she noted their approach in a phalanx formation, the tip of the angle pointing toward her team. As Miguel's bunch made their way toward her groups, Jeffie countered, telling her groups to get in position to surround his.

Is Miguel really this stupid?

Before her best fighters could finish carrying out her orders, Miguel surprised her. His weakest players attacked Jeffie's best, but not with feet or hand blasts.

Antonio, Strawberry, and Hefani all let go of their hooks and grabbed onto Marie, Parley, Cala, and Levu. Antonio was the one who attached himself to two people. It was a brilliant idea, and better yet, it was unforeseen. Jeffie didn't know what to do to counter it. She watched as the additional weight of the clingers did the damage intended. Two of her team went down immediately. Marie and Parley both managed to blast Antonio's helmet, but now, with his suit securely locked around their bodies, they couldn't shake him. They, too, had to let go of the hooks.

This left the teams even number-wise, but talent-wise, it wasn't close. Jeffie's best players were gone. Brillianté and Asaki were separated from the rest of Jeffie's team, and surrounded by four of Miguel's. Both girls managed to take one of Miguel's players before going down. That left Jeffie, Kawai, Natalia, and Brickert against Miguel, Gregor, Kaden, and Li.

As much as she loved Brickert, Kawai, and Natalia, Jeffie would not have picked them to be the ones left in the Game against Miguel and his oldest, most experienced players. Natalia went first, then Kawai. She and Brickert managed to take out Kaden, but Li got her from behind. She screamed in frustration as she fell . . . and it was a long way down.

◉

"Listen to me, girls," Coach Tvedt said over the booming music and cheers of the crowd. There was a stern edge in his voice. "We're down by ten! Losing is not going to happen, do you hear me?" The team sat around him on stools wiping sweat off their faces and sipping energy drinks. He jabbed his finger into the air at the scoreboard hanging above the basketball arena. "When this game ends, we will be up by ten. At least. We've got twelve more minutes of play time. Vernika, get up in number ten's face every time she shoots!" Coach put his hands in Vernika's face as if she did not know how to follow instructions. "You're giving her way too much space! She won't go around you, she's not fast enough. Maia, watch those picks. Jeffie, do you remember what we talked about yesterday in practice?"

"Yes, Coach," she said through gasping breaths.

"Do it."

"But—"

"Do it," he repeated more forcefully. "We're all counting on you. Now get it done girls!"

"TEAM!" the girls shouted.

As Jeffie and the other four starters walked back to the court, her teammates on the bench cheered them on. Jeffie eyed her defender: Laura Ruth Grimes, from Melbourne, and eight (not six) centimeters taller than her, and at least fifteen kilos heavier. And a weak right ankle.

Cheers for Norway clamored loudly in her ears as she passed the ball to Vernika, the point guard. At the top of the key, Vernika slung the ball to Maia, the small forward, who bounce-passed it back to Vernika as her defender pressed down on her. Jeffie jostled with Grimes for position to get the ball, and Vernika threw it to her. Using her long arms, Grimes reached around Jeffie and batted the ball away to another Australian player who dribbled down court.

The Australian coach signaled for them to slow the tempo to run more time off the clock. The Australian guard called the play, and glanced quickly at Grimes. Jeffie knew where the ball was going. Her conscience pleaded with her to not do what she'd been instructed. Jeffie tried to box out the larger girl, but she was too big—too powerful to defend. The guard drifted the ball to Grimes, who stepped around Jeffie to meet the ball for an easy lay-up. Without even thinking, Jeffie deftly moved herself into position. As Grimes went for the lay-up, Jeffie stepped on her right foot, pinning it to the ground. Grimes' body elevated, her foot stayed down.

Grimes cried out in pain and curled to the floor.

Doctors and coaches rushed onto the court to treat their star player, while the Australian head coach screamed at the referee to penalize Jeffie. As she walked back to her team huddle, she felt sick and refused offers to drink anything. The referees came over to Jeffie's dad, and said, "I didn't see anything; we're not calling a foul. Keep the game clean, Coach."

While the team doctors worked to help Grimes off the court, Jeffie and the other girls talked more strategy. Meanwhile, the feeling in her stomach grew worse. She had seen that kind of injury before. Grimes might not play again for a long time.

"Don't worry about that, girls," her dad said to the team. "She'll be just fine."

Without even a glance at Jeffie, or an acknowledgement of what she'd just done, her father told them that they had to take advantage of this opportunity. When the referee blew his whistle to resume the game, Jeffie's sick feeling melted away, and she was all business once more.

Grimes' replacement could not stop Jeffie from getting to the basketball hoop. In the last ten minutes of the game, Jeffie scored seventeen points and led her team to a twelve-point victory, winning a third MVP award and earning a spot in the finals. The Australian players glared at her as they walked through the line shaking hands. The coach stopped her as he shook her hand.

"Do you feel good about yourself?" he asked quietly, wearing a fake smile on his face. "I hope you sleep well tonight, cheater."

Jeffie stammered to say that she hadn't meant to hurt Laura, but that was a lie.

"Save it," the coach said, and moved on.

Later that night, as they passed through downtown Paris, the rush of victory faded and the sickness returned. Her dad sensed what she was thinking about and tried to cheer her up.

"Come on, kiddo. You didn't hurt her on purpose. She's going to be fine." Her dad had the same look he always wore when he felt the topic of discussion at hand was not worth his time.

"But—"

"Look, sweetie," Now he sounded slightly annoyed. "It's part of the game. People get hurt, if you're not tough enough, or your body can't handle injuries, athletics is not the place for you. She needs to learn that—and the sooner the better."

Jeffie did not know what to say. Maybe her dad was right. What did she know?

"I am proud of the way you stepped up today," he continued. His face beamed at her. "Very proud. I've got a surprise waiting for you when you win gold on Saturday."

"Really? What?"

"Take a look." He handed her a small white envelope.

"Should I open it now or wait till Saturday?" she asked, hoping he let her open it right away.

"Go ahead. Look."

With anxious fingers she pried up the top, and pulled out five shining tickets.

"Oh my gosh! Is this what I think—Oh my gosh, Dad! Tickets to the New World Cup! We're going to all of Norway's games! This is so great! Thank you, Dad. You're so awesome!"

"You're welcome, kiddo. You deserve those."

Byron gave them a long, welcomed rest in between the second and third matches of the Game. Everyone's arms ached. Jeffie needed time to think of a new strategy to prevent Miguel from pulling down her best players again. She considered telling her team to each pull down one person, and since her team had the extra player, they would be guaranteed a win, but she suspected Miguel might anticipate such a strategy. In the end, she decided to split her team into two groups of three and two groups of two. By keeping themselves in smaller groups, they could avoid the problems from the last match.

Her plan was working. Miguel's team could not gain any upper hand on her four groups. The only problem was that her team was very tired and moved slowly. Every time she saw her chance to take advantage of a situation, her players were scattered throughout the Arena as the hooks rotated.

The resting chairs became important in this match. Jeffie tried to get her weaker players rested at the same time as Miguel's stronger ones, but it was too difficult to coordinate this strategy effectively, especially with the moving hooks pushing people who needed a rest farther away from the chair.

After a half hour of futile battling, Jeffie felt as though her arms had grown three centimeters longer. Her shoulders and hands were half numb. But the fatigue gave her a new idea: block the opponents' chair. She gave instructions, ordering Parley and Levu to this assignment first. Meanwhile, the two players who would relieve them were sent to rest up until the hooks moved again. Miguel countered this by trying to surround the two players, but Jeffie kept her team close enough to prevent a focused attack. When the hooks rotated, carrying Levu and Parley away to opposite sides of the Arena, it was Marie and Kawai's turn.

⑤

"At the end of the first half of the Under-16 Olympic Basketball Championship," the announcer declared, "Spain leads Norway by one basket."

Coach Tvedt walked his team briskly to the familiar locker room. He did not wait for them to sit down before beginning his pep-talk.

"Why are they getting so many rebounds?" he half-asked, half-shouted. "Jeffie? Jnomu? Maia? You are my rebounders. Any answers? Your job is to get the boards. Spain pulled down fifteen offensive rebounds in the half!

- 106 -

FIFTEEN!" He kicked a chair and sent it spinning across the room. "Twenty-one second-chance points! We should be killing them out there!"

"Coach, they're playing so physical, and they're not getting called for it," Jnomu, the starting center, explained. "When we do the same thing, we get called on it almost every time."

"I don't care! Box them out. Hook their shorts if you have to. You've got to shut them down! This is it girls. This is the game. You will not get another chance!"

Brillianté and Asaki moved in to cover Miguel's team's chair after Marie and Kawai. So far, both teams had only lost one player apiece: Strawberry for Miguel's team, and Natalia for Jeffie's. That was fine by Jeffie, she could afford to lose one player for each of Miguel's. Her strategy was starting to show some promise. Miguel's team had been cut off from their chair for over twenty minutes, and the fatigue was becoming quite apparent. While Jeffie's team followed her instructions, Miguel ordered everyone on his team to meet in the middle of the Arena, surrounding Jeffie's team.

Seeing the trap, Jeffie ordered all her players to meet Miguel's in the middle. So far that day, most of the action had played out in carefully controlled skirmishes between small groups, but now, in the middle of the Arena, everything exploded into an all-out brawl.

"Don't let his little leeches grab onto you again!" Jeffie shouted into her com.

I am not going to lose this. No chance. Tvedts are winners.

Back and forth like a ping-pong match, the lead exchanged between Spain and Norway. With only two minutes left, Norway held onto a one-point lead, and retained possession of the ball.

"Slow it down, Vernika," Coach Tvedt screamed from the sidelines.

Like a well-oiled machine, the five Norwegian starters moved the ball around the court. Jeffie tried to lose her defender, Raquelle, but the girl was like a rubber band. The further Jeffie got from her, the faster Raquelle snapped right back. Jnomu set a low screen for Jeffie, freeing her up to take a pass. With two quick steps she put up an easy lay-up. The crowd roared its approval.

"Three point lead for Norway!" shouted the announcer.

Jeffie felt the fervor of the crowd and knew her moment had come. The championship was hers . . .

After two quick passes, the ball was in the hands of Raquelle, Jeffie's Spanish opposite. Raquelle backed up on Jeffie, leaning her weight into her to scoot closer to the basket. Then she shifted her weight back and forth in attempt to shake off Jeffie. When that did not work, Raquelle threw an elbow into Jeffie's stomach. Jeffie took the blow and hit the wood, waiting for the whistle. Raquelle, meanwhile, turned to the hoop for an easy bucket.

More cheers from the crowd. Jeffie's dad yelled from the bench. "You don't call that a foul? How can you not call that?"

With sixty-five seconds left, Norway had the ball and a one-point lead.

"Freeze it! Freeze it!" her dad yelled.

In an arc around the circle, four of the girls passed the ball around, running time off the clock, always careful to keep it out of range of Team Spain. Vernika tossed the ball to Jeffie, but gave it too much air. With forty seconds left, Raquelle darted out from the key and smacked the ball down court, racing after it before it went out of bounds. She recovered the ball just inside the sideline, ran ahead of the stunned Norwegians, and laid the ball gently off the backboard, into the hoop.

The Spanish fans went crazy.

"Time out!" Jeffie called. "Time out!"

⟳

Marie, Cala, and Jeffie were the only survivors of the dogfight left on her team. Still tangling with them were Miguel, Li, and Kaden from the other. Each were paired off: Kaden against Cala, Jeffie kicking and blasting at Li, and brother Covas trying to knock off sister Covas. She had no further instructions to give her team. All her attention was focused on Li. The numbness in her hands and shoulders had spread through her arms except for the occasional sensation that a thousand pins were poking through her flesh.

She flung her legs up in the air in another attempt to blast Li's helmet or hands. Anticipating her move, he swung his own legs up, and wrapped them around her waist, catching her in the horizontal position and trapping her legs against his chest.

That was stupid, Li.

As he yanked down, trying to pull her off the hooks, she lifted her body higher, hooking her ankles over his shoulders. Realizing how close she was to deactivating him with a foot blast, Li stopped tugging and released his legs and one hand, to put distance between them. Before he could get his second hand back on a hook, Jeffie wrapped her leg around his shoulder, and wrenched as hard as her muscles would allow.

"Bye bye, Li!" she called out in her most friendly voice, though she doubted he could hear her.

Her next closest target was Miguel. He was still fighting it out with Marie not far from where Jeffie hung. Rather than using their legs, the siblings were going at it with one hand apiece trying to wrest the other's hand from the hook or get a palm on the other's helmet. It reminded Jeffie of when she played chicken on the monkey bars with her brother as a young girl. Marie wrapped her arm around Miguel's waist, and her leg around his leg. Miguel craned his head around to see Kaden finishing off Cala, and with a pleasant voice, shouted to Jeffie, "Good luck!"

In one swift movement, he reached his free leg around Marie, who had just gotten the leverage she needed to pull him down. He released his grip on the hook, and clutched Marie over the shoulder. Marie tried to hang on and shake her brother off as Jeffie raced over to help, but Miguel reached up, seized Marie's helmet, and gently blasted. Marie's muscles tensed, and she free-fell to the ground with Miguel still gripping her tightly.

He shouted in gleeful triumph. As he fell, the sound of his voice shrunk until Jeffie could barely hear him. Focusing her attention onto Kaden, she swung out to meet him.

Crunch time, Jeffie.

⑨

"Crunch time, Jeffie," her dad told her during the timeout. "The refs are letting you play physical, so you give it right back to that girl. They won't call a foul on the last play unless it's a blatant charge. Hold the ball out, bring your elbow down, move right around her."

With thirty-five seconds on the clock, Jeffie in-bounded the ball to Vernika and sprinted down the court to receive the pass. Vernika rocketed the ball across to Maia. Like a beehive in synchronized motion, the defense shifted toward the ball.

Fifteen seconds.

Maia took two dribbles and bounced it back to Vernika, who immediately tossed the ball to Lise, the other forward. The defense collapsed around her, and she dumped the ball off Maia, who gave it back to Vernika.

Seven seconds left.

Vernika passed the ball around her defender and over to Jeffie, who caught it and backed up against Raquelle. From only a few meters away she looked into her dad's eyes—her coach's eyes—and saw him give her the nod.

Three seconds.

For an instant, she saw the gold medals around her teams' necks, and made her choice.

Twisting her body around, she jammed out her elbow and jumped for the hoop. She did it so perfectly it looked like Raquelle had simply gotten in her way.

Two seconds.

Her elbow caught Raquelle in the stomach as she turned her body with her pivot foot. A whoosh of air left her defender, and she doubled over.

One second.

Jeffie released the ball and watched it go. The ball circled around and around the hole, and then dropped through.

The buzzer rang.

The Norwegian team leapt into the air, screaming and crying. Norwegian fans leapt to their feet in the stands. Jeffie's teammates attacked her with hugs and screams.

"You did it!" Vernika yelled. Jeffie could see her dad running toward her, clipboard thrown aside.

"That's my girl!" her father yelled as she was lifted into the air.

Atop her team's shoulders, she felt like the whole world was beneath her. She looked back and saw Raquelle still on the floor and gasping for breath. Her teammates and coach were helping her to her feet. Jeffie realized she'd caught the girl right in the plexus and knocked all the air out of her.

"That's my girl!" her father yelled again, even louder.

The medal ceremony took place right after the game. Australia, without its star player, had lost in the bronze match to the Territory of Oceania. Jeffie stood in the center of her team on the tallest platform covered in red carpet, with the Spanish team on the right, and Oceanians on the left. The judges came and placed the gold medal around her neck. She'd waited for this moment—dreamt about this moment—since she was six.

As the NWG anthem played, most of the Norwegian team cried. Not Jeffie. Her father would never have let her hear the end of it. All three teams stood in the sign of respect with the left hand tucked behind the back, and the right hand over the heart.

Raquelle stood on the very end of her team's platform. About halfway through the ceremony, she bent over and threw up, clutching her stomach and crying. Jeffie looked down at the gold medal swaying softly against her red and blue jersey. It was not as shiny nor as pretty as she'd imagined.

Of all the players to be stuck fighting, why did it have to be Kaden?

With her aching limbs ready give out any minute, Jeffie had to make this quick. Kaden was stronger than her; his arms were much bigger. He moved in close, oozing confidence in his ability to end the Game in his team's favor.

"You're not taking my victory away from me," she grunted through her teeth.

Then she lashed out with a swift kick to his solar plexus. Rather than taking it, Kaden swung his body backward in a tremendous display of his strength. Using his momentum to carry him forward, he gripped his legs around her like a vice, and pulled. Jeffie resisted with everything she had left, squirming her hips and torso to give him less grip on her, making him work just as much.

Kaden let go with one hand and shot a blast at her helmet. In such close range, Jeffie had no choice but to use her own hand to shield. She felt their two opposing energy forces pushing against each other like two magnets repelling them. If she didn't get her other hand back on a hook in a few seconds . . .

Apparently Kaden was in the same boat. He jerked his hand back up to grab a hook, and Jeffie did the same. She also managed to pull herself up and wrap her feet onto Kaden's chest until they were both almost completely horizontal. Before she could send a foot blast at his helmet, Kaden released his grip on her with his legs. As he pulled away, Jeffie kicked him savagely in the side, then blasted his chest with her feet. The noblack suit absorbed most of the blow, but Kaden was rocked back, his hands fumbling to keep his grip.

Jeffie knew she could win it right here with a well-placed kick to the groin. The suits could take a lot of impact to protect the Betas from hard falls, but they could only do so much for some areas of the body. Technically there were no rules, but still . . . she knew it was totally wrong.

Kick him in the groin! Coach Tvedt told her. *You want to win, don't you?*

She saw herself applauded by her peers for winning her first Game as honcho. She tasted victory in all of its sweetness.

Tvedts are born winners. It's in our DNA.

She saw herself with a gold medal around her neck.

But instead she reached out to blast his helmet.

Seeing the danger, Kaden rolled his body up between his arms in a neat flip. His head was now completely out of reach for her shot. He let go of the hooks and jumped on her. Still off balance with only one hand supporting the weight, her grip slipped off the hook and she tumbled. In the air, they fumbled around until their hands locked so neither could blast the other's helmet. As the suit sensed her rapidly increasing velocity, her helmet clamped over her face, muting out the stream of swear words she shouted all the way down.

"A draw!" she stormed in the cafeteria during dinner. "A stupid . . . freaking . . . draw!"

"Let it go, will you, Jeffie?" Kawai requested matter-of-factly. "At least you didn't lose."

"Besides," Natalia added, "No one wins their first turn at honcho."

Jeffie refused to be consoled even though the day was almost over. In her family's case, being a winner also meant being a terrible loser. It did not bother her in the least that her friends were exasperated with her mood.

"It's true," Asaki said, overhearing them from her table with Brillianté and Rosa. "I didn't win my first—in fact, I don't think anyone has. Even Al. It just takes time. But you were really good."

"That's right," Kawai agreed.

"How can—?" Jeffie tried to finish her sentence, but the words caught in her throat. Hot tears welled up in her eyes. "I can't believe this!"

Almost everyone looked up to see what she was shouting about.

"What?" Natalia's eyes were wide with bewilderment as she spoke. "What's the matter?"

"Sammy! Sammy is the matter! He did it. He won his first time as honcho. How can you guys have already forgotten that?"

No one said anything, everyone just looked at each other.

"I haven't forgotten, Jeffie," Brickert said solemnly. He swallowed hard as he spoke up, but his characteristic red spots weren't there. "He was honcho against Marie and Kobe. You were on his team. So was Natalia."

"Did you hear what you just said?" Her voice rose in accusation at everyone but Brickert. "Do you guys even listen to yourselves?"

"I'm sorry," Kawai said. "I didn't mean to downplay what he did."

"What he *can do*, you mean to say, right?" Jeffie said even louder. "You all act like he's dead! 'Was my best friend.' 'Downplay what he did.' You even act like what he did wasn't special."

"We all loved Sammy," Natalia quickly offered. "He was great. No one said he's dead."

"You guys all act like he was some sort of god," Antonio declared from across the room. He was a tall kid, about as tall as Sammy. His jet-black hair was trimmed close on the sides with a long wavy style perfectly in place on top. He had a confidence in his hazel eyes perhaps only Kobe or Al could match. He put up his hands when she looked at him. "I don't mean to disrespect him. I'm sure he was good, but I'm good, too. Hey, I might even be better. Who knows, right? No reason other people can't do just as well as he did here. Right?"

Everyone in the room turned to watch Jeffie. On their faces she saw expressions of fear and caution. Kawai and Brillianté looked ready to pounce if things turned ugly. She ignored them all. Slowly, she placed her hands flat on the table and stood up. Cold fury flooded her veins as she faced Antonio with no desire to hide her emotions. He did not look nearly as confident under her glare.

"He. Is. Sammy. You have no clue what you're talking about. There will never be another Sammy."

She turned and left, heading for her bedroom. Once around the corner, she heard Brickert. There was no kindness in his voice, either.

"I'll tell you, Antonio, you'd better run it by one of us before you try to speak to her again.

8 | Dilemma

February 17, 2086

ALPHA HEADQUARTERS shared little resemblance with its Beta counterpart. While Psion Beta was just a single building, Alpha was a sprawling campus built to house and support thousands of Alpha operatives. That included the Elite, Psion Alphas, Ultra Alphas, and Tensai Alphas: Anomalies Fourteen, Fifteen, and Eleven.

Exercise and training facilities claimed their own spaces, and other small structures housed things like the food courts, recreation areas, and shopping centers. Each Alpha had his or her own comfortable but efficient personal living quarters. Some lived alone, some Alphas preferred having roommates, and others were married with families. Housing occupied almost a fourth of the total area. The rest of the property was dedicated to work: mission planning centers, hangars, weaponry stations, simulators, intelligence stations, and a transportation hub.

Before landing on the airstrip, Commander Byron called for a small ground car to meet him. He'd never actually lived at Alpha, but he had no problem finding his way around. After all, years ago he had designed most of the layout, and more recently he had helped Albert move into his new quarters.

The scenery was a frosty one. The roadways were clear, but the trees still bore heavy snow and most of the grounds were pure white. The air carried a clean and fresh scent which Byron let drift in through the half-opened window of his one-man vehicle. The quiet droning of the car's electric motor allowed his thoughts to stray ahead to what he wanted to say to his son.

He drove along at a slow pace. Several Psions going about their business waved at Byron, but he hardly noticed them. After a five minute drive, he pulled up to number seventy-two and rang the bell.

"Come in," his son's voice shouted from behind the door.

"Hello," Byron called out as he entered.

"I'm back here in the kitchen. Just grab a seat."

Byron looked around at Albert's living room. Each Alpha received the same basic furnishings for their quarters, but Albert's place looked drastically different. Over the walls hung blueprints and floor plans from the Rio factory, designs of various explosive devices, and mission timelines. Across the coffee table lay open books, each with a title describing something to do with Albert's mission.

Byron sighed as he sat down on the couch. On the mantle over the fireplace, he saw what he had been looking for: a small holo-pic of Albert and Marie, almost unnoticeable amongst all the paraphernalia surrounding it.

Albert entered from the kitchen with a plate of sandwiches. A steady dripping came from the kitchen sink, each drop making a small *plop*! The noise grated on Byron's nerves, bringing back horrible memories of being down in the sewers. Even his heart rate picked up noticeably.

"Hungry?" Albert asked his father, shaking the commander out of his reverie of bad thoughts.

"No," Byron said. "Thank you, but I ate lunch before I came."

Albert took a large bite of one and sat down.

"Is—is there a dripping coming from your kitchen? Do you hear that?"

Albert cocked his head to listen. With his mouth still full, he said, "Yeah. The sink. If I don't turn it really tight, it does that. But I always forget."

"Can you please make that stop?"

"You're so weird, Dad." He stood up and returned to the kitchen. When he disappeared from view Byron wrung his hands together, willing himself to calm down.

His son returned momentarily. "What's up?"

The commander fixed Albert with a look. He didn't want to come down hard on his son. Albert was nineteen, after all, and that made it harder to offer counsel. "Look around your home. You tell me 'what's up?'"

Albert's blank expression told the commander all he needed to know.

"Look around your home," he repeated. Albert's eyes roamed the room for about half a second. "What are you doing to yourself? Anyone who walks in here is going to think you are obsessed with your mission."

"Maybe I am obsessed." Byron hadn't seen the dullness, the lack of enthusiasm about life, in Albert's eyes for weeks but he saw it now. His son took a second bite of his food, chewing it without any savoring. "So what?"

"We are going to Rio to recover Samuel's body. In two weeks. All of the arrangements have been made."

"Excellent!" His son stood up with the sandwich clenched in his hand. "Has my squadron leader approved for me to go?"

"Of course she has. She is probably too afraid to tell you no."

"Then I'm in. With your backing, Command might even let me lead the mission."

Byron motioned for Albert to sit back down. "Please. There is something else you need to consider."

"What—?"

Commander Byron raised a hand and Albert obeyed, taking his seat again. The sandwich in his hand was now forgotten as he waited. Byron chose his words carefully. He'd had enough estrangement in his family to last a lifetime.

"We only have a small window of opportunity to arrange this excursion. Unfortunately, it coincides with Marie's graduation ceremony."

"Is there any way—?"

"No. It has to be then, or we wait weeks longer."

Albert put the sandwich down on his plate and grabbed his head with both hands. Byron watched him, hoping he'd done the right thing by intentionally creating this scheduling conflict.

"Can't you reschedule Marie's ceremony? I've got to be able to do both!" Byron was pleased to hear the frustration mounting in his son's voice.

"No. People, like Marie's entire family, have already made their plans to attend. Then we begin Ludwig's Panel, and after that is Cala's. Then—"

"I get the point, thanks." His son stood up and combed his fingers through his brown hair he'd always kept neatly groomed. As he stood, several books slid off the coffee table in a cascade. Byron watched everything passively, missing the days when his son's problems were much simpler.

"Make a choice, Albert," he said bluntly.

"What?" Albert's expression told Byron he didn't believe what he'd just heard.

"Make a choice. Make a choice and stick with it. I know you blame yourself for what happened, but you did not make a mistake."

"What do you know about mistakes, Dad?" Albert said in a controlled, but raised voice. "You've lived a perfect life! Everyone around here looks up to you and admires you. Every Psion here would lay down their life for you. My mistake killed people!"

"You were roundly commended for your decisions. Remember that? Do you think we withheld criticism from you just because of the deaths?"

Albert didn't answer.

"What do you think you should have done different?" Byron pressed. "Tell me, please, so we can discuss it."

Albert sat back down, ruffling his hair even more. It was plain to see these things had weighed heavily on his mind for a long time.

"I should have confirmed our exit points. The brick wall . . ."

"The intel you used to plan the mission was recent."

"Not recent enough!" Albert paused for several seconds, as though debating whether to speak what was on his mind. "Dad, I think someone tipped off the Thirteens. Someone on our side."

"We investigated that option already. Command was very thorough. No records of communication with CAG from anyone who knew about the mission. We looked over the ship—"

"Ho Chin and I went over the ship again. Whoever examined it wasn't thorough enough. We found very small scratch marks on the modulator where it had become dislodged. That's why we couldn't send any type of signal to you that we were under attack."

"Scratch marks? How long have you known about this?"

Albert nodded. "Since last night. Ho Chin wouldn't tell me over the com. He told me to wait to tell you in person, too."

The sink in the kitchen began to drip again, but Byron hardly noticed the noise this time. He couldn't believe what he was hearing.

"Does anyone else know about this?"

"No. We both figured you were the only person we trust enough to tell. All the equipment was tested two days before the mission. Then the cruiser was put on lockdown."

"Only Psion Command, Dr. Rosmir, and squadron leaders have access to a cruiser in lockdown," Byron added. "If it was tampered with . . ." He shook his head. It was something he never thought he'd hear himself say.

"I still could have prevented it, Dad," Albert continued. "If I'd checked the exits . . . we could have radioed back immediately for clearance to continue. Instead, I just sent in our updates, not even checking to see if they were being received."

Silence reigned in the room save for the occasional drip from the faucet. Byron felt like he finally understood his son's issues. He indeed had made a mistake, albeit a small one that almost any other honcho would have made, including himself. Albert sat on his couch with his face in his hands.

"I have made mistakes, too, Albert."

Albert made a rude sound and shook his head.

"I have. Some of them I have never been able to forget. I work with Victor Wrobel nearly every day, and seeing him reminds me about the greatest mistake of my life. I doubt he even realizes it."

"Dad . . ."

"He and I used to be best friends. We were both in the sewers when your mother died. So was Claire and Blake Weymouth and—"

"I know all about that. You've told me plenty of times."

"Our relationship has never been the same since. We are still friends, but it changed. We lost four good soldiers in that one battle." He looked at his son, hoping Albert would look back. "And I was the honcho."

"You think he blames you for what happened?" Albert asked. "After all this time?"

Byron didn't answer. The truth was, he didn't know. "For a long time, I blamed myself for what happened. It took me years to talk to him about it. We were traveling to Sri Lanka to investigate a terrorist cell. He said he had forgiven me. I should have reached out to Victor sooner. I might have saved a special friendship. If you keep this obsession up, you are going to lose Marie. Now, I need to know, are you going to Rio or to Beta headquarters?"

Albert looked stunned, staring straight into his father's eyes. "I . . . I, uh, need to think about it. I'll let you know."

"If I had said something like that, your mother never would have married me." Emotion laced Byron's voice, and he fought it back so he could speak clearly. "Do you know why she loved me so much, Al? Do you want to know the secret?"

Albert did not respond, instead he shooed a bug away from his food.

"Because I put her first. Always. But Marie has been riding in the backseat of your life for three months now. Bless her heart for being so patient with you, thinking you are going to move past this. What happens when we find Samuel's body? Burned and decayed. Then what? What are you going to do with this shrine?" He gestured to the fireplace, the table, the posters—all of it. "What are you going to tell Marie when you come home after missing one of the most important ceremonies of her life?"

"Dad, I—"

"No, please hear me out," Byron said with a raised hand. "She will know she comes second in your mind. Not behind you or Samuel, but behind this war. Behind this suit you wear now. And she will still marry you, but neither of you will be as happy as you could be. Do you want that?"

"Of course not. But I've got a responsibility to—"

"You do not!" Byron's voice rose despite his attempt at self-control. Instantly he regretted his actions and took a moment to calm himself. "Forgive me, but this responsibility is not yours. Your accountability for Samuel ended the moment you finished your briefing two months ago. You have a duty to two people. Your squadron leader second, and Marie first." Byron dropped his voice, pleading in a whisper. "Do not miss this! Let other people take care of this now. Look around your room. Remember what I always taught you? You worship what you put on your walls. If you want your life to center around work then, by all means, come with us to Rio. If you want to live the good life, as your mother and I did, stay here and be with Marie."

"My mind doesn't simplify things that easily. I—I should be able to do both."

"Trust me. It is impossible."

Albert took another bite of his sandwich, but it was much smaller and he barely chewed it. Byron wanted to press further, but after nineteen years of raising this boy, he knew when to talk and when to shut up. He busied himself by taking a long drink of water from the glass his son had set in front of him. It cooled his throat and calmed his nerves.

"I didn't want this to happen." Albert's voice was heavy and he put a hand over his face. "I haven't meant to neglect her."

"I know. But you still need to fix things."

"How?"

"If she were Emily, I would know what to say, but only you know Marie well enough to make that judgment."

Albert nodded. He looked at his plate of food and pushed it away. It was Byron's cue to leave. He stood up, hugged his son, and said goodbye.

9 | Escape

February 19, 2086

ALBERT CHOOCHOO RESTED IN THE CORNER of the white room with his neck secured by a collar that kept him chained no more than a couple meters from the wall. He laid his head on the floor, unsure if he was awake or asleep. Things like consciousness, time, and location weren't terribly meaningful to him. All he really knew was Stripe, pain, and the black door that came with both of them.

Life had gotten worse after telling Stripe his name. Visits into the room with the black door became more frequent, the pain more severe, but Stripe hadn't lost his patience. Every so often, he'd plead with Albert to reveal his real name so he could help him. But Albert didn't understand. He had already told Stripe his name. Why didn't Stripe believe him?

Everything was so confusing now. Was it days—weeks—months—years he had already endured in the chamber with the black door? He had no clue. There were no Mondays, Tuesdays, or Wednesdays. There was only fire, ice, pressure, sharp, and others. Sensation after agonizing sensation until his mind fragmented inside his skull.

He spent so many hours alone in his cell that he began looking forward to time with Stripe. At least with Stripe, there was still the hope that he was on Albert's side.

He had grown used to the devices Stripe used on him. Some days were worse than others. He no longer threw up after wearing the helmet, but he still felt woozy and disoriented. The pain levels he endured depended solely on Stripe's mood.

His cell door opened and a bowl of sludge slid across the floor. Albert devoured it in four seconds. His hands trembled uncontrollably as he held the bowl to his mouth. This moment was what he looked forward to each day. He opened his eyes to see if Stripe was coming.

"Good morning, Albert," Stripe said.

There's his voice . . . If Stripe was nearby, then everything was okay.

"Did you sleep well?" His voice was a salve, a balm of great relief. Seeing him was like seeing the face of an angel of mercy. "Was it better than the gutter you came from?"

Albert nodded.

"Are you ready to play?"

"Yes," he whispered hoarsely, "I'm ready."

Albert allowed himself to be led from his cell. He didn't even notice if guns were trained on him or not anymore. His existence was contained between these two rooms.

Stripe performed his work. Each time—sometimes sooner, sometimes later—Albert broke down and cried like a baby. Today was no different.

Right on cue, Stripe said the same thing he always said, "Just tell me what I need to know, Albert, and the pain goes away."

The black door opened before Stripe had finished, a rare occurrence.

"A word with you," said a man wearing the same green-brown uniform as Stripe.

Stripe stepped out, but didn't close the door completely.

"Orders came down today," the new man said. "They think you're wasting time."

"No. I've never failed to finish an assignment. I'm not giving up." Albert heard the care in Stripe's voice and was touched. He didn't care so much about the words, but the tones.

"It's not my call."

"You have sway. Use it. I've learned more from him than I have with the last ten they've brought me. Give me more time. I have to break him"

Stripe came back in and slammed the door shut. Albert noticed Stripe was angry. He braced himself because when Stripe was angry, the pain was worse.

As more time passed, Albert noticed a sense of urgency from Stripe. The pain was worse than ever. He had long ago learned why the girl had drooled on herself the way she had: after spending so much time screaming, his jaw was too tired to close, so the spittle just rolled off his lips.

One morning, maybe even the next day, another boy appeared in his cell. *How long has he been here?* He screamed and cried and begged the way Albert and the girl had before they realized how useless it was. The boy was talking to Albert, but Albert didn't really care to pay attention because he knew the boy didn't matter. In fact, it angered Albert that someone else would be brought into his little room and invade his privacy. He wanted to hurt the other boy.

After finishing his sludge, Stripe came and went through the usual questions and statements. He motioned to two heavily armed friends, who entered the room and grabbed Albert. Floating down the hall, Albert saw the black door open, heard it close behind him, and felt the hard wood of the chair beneath him. With guns trained at his head and heart, he allowed the chair restraints to be tightened into place. Stripe knelt in front of him to check the security of the bonds at his feet, too.

"Did you do your homework like I asked?" Stripe asked.

Instantly, tears flowed down Albert's cheeks. He had tried so hard to finish his homework, but he had not been able to do it.

"I couldn't. I'm sorry, Stripe. I couldn't. I'm sorry."

"I've given you harder assignments than that since we've known each other. Why was this one so difficult?"

"I don't know," Albert wailed. The shame of not being able to do his homework was so embarrassing . . . but he had tried so hard.

"Then you know I have to hurt you more today, don't you?"

Weakly, Albert nodded. He understood.

"I know I've said it before, Albert, but you are so lucky. You know why, don't you?"

Albert nodded again, albeit reluctantly. "Most people have to learn pain through cruelty and anger. But you care about me."

"Yes. I do," Stripe said, his eyes searching Albert's. Albert wanted to scream out the truth for Stripe. He wanted to give Stripe whatever was wanted. But Stripe spoke again. "Let's try one more time. Maybe you can do it after all. Which would you prefer today? Sharp or pressure?"

At that question, Albert lost his senses completely. All the rage he'd felt toward the other boy in his cell was gone, replaced with helplessness, weakness—surely he was not responsible enough to make such an important decision. Certainly Stripe could choose. He always made the right choices. Albert managed to voice this to Stripe.

"If you can't pick one," Stripe said paternally, "I'll have to do both."

It was no use. Albert could not pick between them. "Okay," he mumbled through tears and uncontrollable gasps for air.

"Others have told me that the combination of these two sensations is like an alligator biting them. Perhaps you'll experience similar results. Let me know."

Albert nodded as Stripe turned to his bench to grab the appropriate tools and tubes. He carefully selected the right ointments to administer, wearing a grim smile the entire time. As Stripe rolled up a leg of Albert's pants, Albert experienced a mixed rush of terror and excitement at what was about to happen.

It's going to hurt! HURT! No more pain!

But Stripe needs to do this to me. He needs to know where I'm from, he reminded himself. *I should tell him. He's kept me alive. They wanted to kill me, but he wouldn't let them.*

You can't tell him, Albert, repeated the small voice in the very back of his head—the voice getting quieter every day. *Remember the girl!*

Goosebumps formed on his leg as the creams were applied to his skin. Stripe artistically placed both types in such a way that the pressure would be more widespread, and the sharp would be in rows, like a mouth of jagged teeth.

"I was quite liberal, this may be worse than anything you have yet experienced."

Beads of sweat formed like a crown on Albert's temples and forehead. Slowly the pain began to set in. His mind went elsewhere . . .

"Things aren't always what they seem, Sammy," his father said as they walked side by side through the African wilderness. Dry grassland and muddy slopes stretched out for miles around. In the eastern sky, the red sun was rising, already warm so early in the day and casting its light far out onto the landscape. Not a trace of wind was to be found.

Sammy bounced his binoculars on his hand as they walked. They were a cheap pair, picked up last minute at a gift shop near the preserve check-in. "I know, Dad, but sometimes it's hard to tell what's real and what isn't."

"There's a trick," his mom added from the other side of Samuel Sr. "You watch closely, for a long time, and eventually the truth is revealed."

"Do you want to see an example, Sammy?" Brickert asked. "Look over here at this waterhole. Seems normal right?"

They stood at the top of a long, deep slope of mud and sparse grass. Down at the bottom was a puddle of water not much larger round than a child's pool and probably less deep. Due to the nature of Brickert's question, Sammy assumed there must be something wrong with it. He watched closely for several moments but saw nothing.

"Right," Sammy answered, "totally normal."

Feet and Chuckles tugged his sleeve and pulled him down behind a dried shrub. Feet lifted his binoculars, silently telling him to use them now.

"Wait here patiently and watch the water." The excitement in Feet's voice was contagious.

Together, Sammy, his parents, Feet, Chuckles, and Brickert squatted down and spied on the waterhole from only thirty or forty meters away. The waterhole was as still as death on their side. Across the way, up the opposite slope, a herd of gazelle approached, the leaders eyeing the waterhole for several minutes. Sammy wondered what they were looking for. He saw no ripples of water, nothing. But his heart beat faster as he sensed something going on, something perhaps he had no way of detecting.

As the sun climbed higher in the east and the temperature rose, the adventurers continued to watch and wait, almost perfectly motionless. The gazelle continued to inspect the hole, darting in and out in quick movements. One gazelle in particular seemed determined now to make its way to the hole. Sammy squinted at the animal. It had Jeffie's face.

As it drew closer to the water, its behavior became more curious. Every few steps, the gazelle with Jeffie's face got spooked and ran back a meter, maybe two, but it always made up the distance and then some, drawing closer and closer to the water's edge. Sammy licked his own lips in thirst, knowing what a powerful temptation drew that Jeffie-gazelle. And sure enough, it conquered the nervousness of the beast. Twitching in apprehension, the gazelle lowered its head to the water.

The tension surrounding Sammy was palpable. *Something's going to happen, but what? What does everyone else see that Jeffie and I can't?*

Small ripples, emanating from the gazelle's lapping mouth, traveled across the small waterhole. Its ears twitched often and its muscles jerked every few seconds as though it wanted to run but needed the water too badly. *What is it so afraid of?*

From deep within the muddy water, a huge crocodile raised its body up, with its jaws wide open, and crunched its teeth down around the neck of the Jeffie-gazelle. The gazelle's body jumped back, finishing the commands of the now disconnected brain.

"Remember, Sammy," the five people around him repeated in unison. "You must watch and wait."

Pain jerked Albert—*no, Sammy!*—out of his reverie and he screamed in utter agony. His cries were so guttural—so visceral—he did not even recognize them as his own. In his ears, a grown man was in the room with him, dying.

"It hurts, Stripe! *Please!* It's eating my gazelle!"

Stripe had not lied. This was the worst pain he'd ever felt. He looked down at his leg and saw the monstrous crocodile biting, gnawing, tearing at the skin and bone of his leg. At any moment the entire appendage would be ripped away.

"Stripe, please! It's going to kill me."

Tears poured from his eyes, blinding him of everything but Stripe's face, which leaned slowly to his.

"I can make it stop, Albert. But only I have the power to do that. There is absolutely nothing anyone can do for you. Do you understand me?"

"Y—y—Yes! I understand! Please make it stop! Please! I'll do whatever you say!"

"Anything, Albert? Will you tell me where you are from?" Stripe asked softly. "Will you tell me your real name?"

"I—I—" Once more he gave into that visceral scream in order to quiet the voice in his head begging him to not give Stripe what he wanted. "It's going to eat me! Stripe! Please help me! Please stop it from killing me!" He struggled against his bonds, horrified at what was happening to his leg. But the bonds held him fast, and he could not escape the massive reptile eating him. The pain expanded, filling him, and then it leaked out of his pores like a noxious gas, surrounding him, suffocating him.

"You have to tell me where you are from. It is the only way I can call this alligator off."

"I—I CAN'T! It's a crocodile! It's a CROCODILE! Please stop it!"

This continued for hours or years. Albert-Sammy begged and begged, but his pleas became quieter and quieter. Finally, Stripe put the helmet on him. As the pain became dull and bearable, a sound like thunder filled Albert-Sammy's ears as the black chamber door burst open.

"Why didn't it work?" someone shouted.

Albert-Sammy couldn't see who it was with the helmet forcing him through endless swirls and cascades of color. Exhaustion had consumed his body and mind. Even the slightest breath required effort.

"Did you see how close he was?" Stripe asked, then immediately answered himself. "On the brink. He stands on the very brink, and tomorrow I can push him over it." There was a healthy measure of both confidence and fright in his voice.

"I will be here tomorrow, watching you perform your task. If you can't break him . . . then so be it. We've wasted enough time on this trash."

"Don't worry, sir. I will grind him more than he has ever imagined."

The black door shut. Stripe commenced tidying up the room. Meanwhile, Albert-Sammy sat reeling and twitching spastically in his chair. Something had snapped inside of him. One memory he had not lost lay deep inside his splintered mind. A word had triggered it.

Grind.

As shattered and as broken as he was—a shell of what he'd been when he first entered this nightmarish place—the word still brought back emotions of incalculable hate. This powerfully intense fury swept through him, leaving him consumed and exhausted.

Grind.

He mumbled the word to himself over and over again as Stripe dragged him back to his room and fixed his neck to the wall via the metal ring.

Grind.

It was coming back. Like a bathtub slowly filling itself, a memory surfaced.

Grind.

As he sat in the corner of the room, aching in never-ending pain, he heard a familiar voice talking but ignored it as usual. He focused whatever brain capacity was left in him on one single thing.

Grind.

A puddle formed in the bottom of the tub that was his mind.

Grinding.

The water kept coming, soon the bath was half full.

Grinder.

With nothing to stop it, the water reached the brim of the porcelain.

The Grinder.

It spilled over the sides, onto the floor, bringing with it every last detail of the memory he had almost completely forgotten. He remembered the Grinder. He remembered the abandoned grocery store. He remembered Psion Beta headquarters.

I'm not Albert Choochoo. I'm Sammy.

The memory of the Grinder set him buzzing. He kept thinking back to it, remembering how exhilarated he and his friends had been as they'd hit the trees and knew they'd escaped. Nothing could touch them. They were kings of their own destiny.

I've escaped once, said the small voice in the back of Sammy's head. *I can escape again. Watch and wait. Watch and wait. Watch and wait.*

But Stripe needs me here, replied the other voice.

Stripe hurts me. I hate him. I've got to get OUT of here!

No. There's nothing but Stripe. I am nothing without Stripe.

Sammy let out a sob and grabbed his stomach, wishing it were time to eat.

"Who are you?"

The sound came from the far end of the room, startling Sammy. He jerked up, crouching like an animal. The room was dark, but not so much that he couldn't make out the shape of another person peering back at him. It struck Sammy that he had heard this voice before, perhaps more than once. This time, however, the words spoken had registered with him.

"Who is that? Who are you?" Sammy asked back, shocked. For days or weeks now, he'd thought he was alone in this room.

"I'm over here." Then the unseen person sniffed loudly. "And I asked who you were first."

Sammy peered into the darkness, but could not see more than a vague shape. *It's a trap!*

"I said, who are you?" the voice repeated.

Sammy shook his head at the sound. "I'm not answering you."

There was another sniff. "Why not?" The voice was so young—young and pushy.

"Because you're here to kill me. Did Stripe send you?"

"Who is—?"

"Don't lie to me!" Sammy bellowed, struggling against his restraints.

"Take it easy! Okay? My name is Sapo. I—I want out of here."

"What kind of name is Sapo? A fake name?"

"It means Toad."

"Your name is Toad?"

"No. It's what everyone calls me. I'm really Rulé. Rulé Prado. Can you help me get out of here?"

The desperation in Toad's voice touched Sammy, but not enough. "I can't help you. I don't know what I'm going to do tomorrow. I might have to talk."

"Huh?"

"Never mind," Sammy said testily. "What happened to the girl?"

"What girl?"

"There was a girl the first day I came here. She was like . . . I don't know . . . young. She wanted something . . ." He tried so hard to remember what it was, but nothing came to mind when he thought about it. In fact, his brain was so muddled that he quickly forgot what he'd been thinking about.

"What girl?" Toad repeated with a sniff.

"Forget it."

"There's no girl here now. But I am, and you've got to help me get out of here. I don't think they're going to let me go. They told me they'll bring my family, but I've been here for almost a week."

Another sniff.

"Why did they take you from your family?" Sammy asked, his curiosity aroused.

"I don't know. I was at a camp party. We were having races . . ."

He was still talking, but Sammy heard nothing after "at a party." He thought of being at a party with the Hernandes family.

His body tensed suddenly, wracked with immeasurable pain as he remembered countless sessions in the black chamber with Stripe.

Fire. Ice. Stretch. Pressure. Sharp. Ache.

Oh, Stripe. Why did you do these things to me? How long have I been here? A scream in his mind went on and on and on . . . *He needs me! He NEEDS me!*

"Hey!" Toad yelled. "HEY!"

The boy's shouts snapped Sammy out of his reverie of insanity. His skin was damp from sweat.

"What?" he screamed back, infuriated at everything in the world. "What do you want?"

"How are you going to help me?" A small sniff.

"I don't know. I'm sorry, but I don't know what to do anymore." Riding the roller coaster of emotion, Sammy went from the heights of anger to the depths of despair in under three seconds.

Toad kept talking, but Sammy stopped listening again. It all seemed like mumbo jumbo to him, anyway. He was uncertain of the future and fell into an uneasy sleep filled with nightmares and monsters and most of all . . . grinding.

"Good morning, Albert. Did you sleep well?" Stripe asked indifferently. "Was it better than the gutter you came from?"

Toad muttered faintly in the corner of his room. Sammy looked over at him, forgetting to answer.

"Are you ready to play?"

"Yes," Sammy answered, "I am ready."

"Today will be different," Stripe explained as the Aegis moved Sammy with extra care to the black door chamber. "Someone will be with us, observing."

"Is that good, Stripe?"

"Yes and no. He may kill you if you do not give us the information we have been asking for."

"I don't want to die, Stripe," Sammy said in a weak voice.

"Then you should cooperate, and I will do what I can." There was an edge in Stripe's voice that didn't register with Sammy. He was still trying to sort out what Stripe was saying about dying.

Inside the room, his escorts seemed on edge. With unnecessary roughness, they shoved him so hard he lost his footing, and fell into the table. He hit the edge of the tray of Stripe's tubes, spilling them.

"Careful!" Stripe yelled.

Sammy hit the ground and rolled. A pain stung his thumb. He'd rolled onto the small knife Stripe used to open the seal on his cream tubes. Without thinking, Sammy grabbed the knife and carefully closed his fingers around it. The Aegis hurried to pick him up and dragged him over to the chair.

"Leave the magnet cuffs on him today. I need his arms behind his back to keep his chest taut."

"Protocol says we use the chair restraints," an Aegis said. "They're safer."

Stripe's tone told Sammy he was in no mood to be questioned. "If we don't get what we need today, the protocol will mean nothing."

Sammy kept his fist tightly closed around the blade. The Aegis still put the ankle restraints on, and gave Stripe a nod. As they left, Stripe got his tools ready.

"What's wrong, Stripe?" Sammy asked in a weak voice. "Are you mad at me?"

Then the door reopened. In walked a tall man of Asian descent with short hair, half a nose, and two long scars running down the left side of his face. The red sclera surrounding his brown eyes were fixed on Stripe.

At the sight of the red-melting-to-black tunic and pants, a dragon's rage flared inside Sammy so hot and wild that it made his lungs burn when he breathed.

"What is he doing here?" Sammy shouted the words, his voice already hoarse from yelling at Toad. Spit flew from his mouth as his legs kicked against his restraints. Tears from the betrayal he felt fell from his eyes. "What are you doing with him, Stripe?"

Both men looked at Sammy with bewilderment.

"Do you know this man, Albert?" Stripe questioned.

"A Thirteen?" he said. "Of course I know him!" His mind was too far gone to realize the fatal mistake he had just made.

While Stripe looked back and forth from Sammy to his superior, the Thirteen stared curiously at Sammy. He approached the chair with an obvious menace until their faces were only centimeters apart. The red sclera of his eyes shined dangerously against the deep brown of his irises.

"Who are you, boy?" the Thirteen asked. His eyes remained perfectly fixed on Sammy's face. Stripe stood behind him with a similar expression of wonder.

With his arms cuffed behind his back, Sammy realized the purpose of the blade in his fingers. He scowled back at the Thirteen as he oriented the knife how he wanted it.

Thinking about the endless torture and hell underneath a building in Rio de Janeiro filled his body with an energy he hadn't felt since the first time the helmet had been put on him.

No guns in the room pointing at me now.

Clutching the small handle of the knife between his right thumb and index, he blasted from both palms with maximum effort. In one fluid motion, he broke the powerful magnetic bond of the cuffs, swung his arms around in front of him, and sliced the Thirteen's throat, spraying himself in blood.

Stripe sprang across the room for a weapon. Reacting quickly, Sammy reached out, threw his weight forward, and dug the blade into the back of Stripe's left knee. As Stripe's leg collapsed, he screamed in agony and hit the floor, clutching it.

Sammy removed the ankle restraints and magnet cuffs from his wrists as Stripe crawled across the floor. Seeing this, Sammy grunted in anger and kicked Stripe away from the table.

"You said you'd help me," Sammy reminded Stripe with another kick.

He looked down on the man he'd seen as both savior and tormentor and felt more empowered than he'd ever felt in his life. He leaned over Stripe, just as the tormentor had done so many times to him.

"Are you ready to play?" he asked him quietly.

Stripe gazed at him for a long time before answering in a whisper, "Make it fast."

Sammy crouched down and stared until he made up his mind. Then he stood back up. He turned to the table of tubes and chose two: fire and sharp. In three flicks of his blade, Sammy removed much of the suit that was covering Stripe. He ignored the whimpering and pleading from the fully-grown man below him. Raising the tubes high over his head, he squeezed . . . and squeezed . . . until the contents of both were completely gone.

After removing and pocketing Stripe's finger, he left the chamber. Two Aegis were standing just outside the door. Sammy blast-jumped into one, killing him the same way as the Thirteen. He grabbed a fallen gun and checked it, shielding with his other hand. *No identifiers on the grip.* He raised it and sent half a dozen bullets into the last Aegis. Then he calmly continued down the hall with Stripe's gut-wrenching, cream-choked screams following him through the chamber door.

To Sammy, it sounded more like music. He let himself into his cell and released Toad.

"Let's go."

As they made their way out of the building, Sammy happily killed anyone who crossed their path.

10 | Tango

March 3, 2086

IN A STEALTH ATMO-CRUISER above the Atlantic, Byron piloted a crew consisting of himself, Dr. Maad Rosmir, and the Alpha squadron named Tango. Dr. Rosmir sat next to him in the cockpit, catching up on journals on his holo-tablet. The passenger area was a ruckus. The Beatles pumped through the speakers on a portable player. Sung Ju tried to sing along, but she didn't quite have the vocal range to match. Two other Tangos were going head-to-head on a portable holo-game, and on top of all that, five more were playing a very competitive match of Texas Hold 'em.

Commander Byron paid little attention to any of it. His mind had gone back to the same questions that had plagued him for the last two weeks. Had someone sabotaged the cruiser going to Rio? Had someone tipped off the CAG that a Psion team was coming? Who would do that? Why?

The day after Albert told him about the modulator, Byron had gone down to the hangars and inspected everything himself. The damage to the equipment was minimal, almost non-existent. No wonder it had been missed during the initial checks. With such little evidence, conclusions couldn't be drawn.

Treason is an unthinkable act. Maybe I am naïve, but there is not one person I know who would do such a thing.

There was always the chance that some bizarre event had caused damage to the modulator, and that the Thirteens had coincidentally put up the brick wall that blocked Samuel and Kobe's exit, and that they'd been monitoring activity at the Rio factory . . . but who was he kidding? The more he analyzed Albert's debriefing statements, the more he saw the obvious truth staring back at him: the Thirteens had been too prepared for the Betas' arrival.

He couldn't bring the information to Command. The mole could be any of them. It could be more than one. The ramifications if it was one of them would be enormous. For now, the only people he trusted were Albert, Ho Chin, and Djedaa El-Sayid.

He steered his focus back to the mission as they approached CAG territory. Sometimes Byron found it hard to believe he had grown up on this hemisphere, back when the world was still united under the New World Government. Each time he flew into enemy territory, he thought of the same conversation, the one that ended with his own father throwing him out of the house. He tried not to think about that now. The man who'd said those words, if he was even still alive, was thousands of kilometers away from Rio.

Byron glanced over at Dr. Rosmir who was poring over another article on his tablet. His face was pale, even with his dark skin. His eyes shifted rapidly back and forth across the screen. Byron pitied his friend, but he needed him along, just in case . . .

"Are you holding everything down okay there, Maad?" he asked.

Dr. Rosmir bounced in his seat, as if he'd been startled. "Oh—yeah—fine. Just getting through all this information. Sometimes I think there's no bottom to the well."

Byron watched him for a moment longer, hating that he had to suspect his friend as a possible traitor simply because he was one of the few people with access to the hangars. Such was war.

During Tango's briefing, Byron had given each member of the squadron specific orders for the investigation. In teams of two, every centimeter of the factory was to be searched, every Alpha armed with heavy-spread hand cannons and bomb tracers. The principal target was Samuel's body, but they were to report anything suspicious.

Byron, with Dr. Rosmir and one other soldier, would go directly to the hallway where the two bombs had detonated. A reasonable estimation was that the team would only be there for two or three hours, four or five if there was a lot of heavy work to do.

They landed in the loading square, exactly where Albert's team had landed three and a half months ago. Byron rubbed his face.

"I hate days when I feel my age," he told Dr. Rosmir. The doctor gave a sympathetic chuckle back as a response.

"What odds would you put down that we even find a body?" he heard one Tango ask another as they geared up.

"Ten to one," came the answer.

"More like a hundred to one," Shamila said. Shamila Bessette was the squadron leader and acted all the part. "Find it anyways."

The fraternizing stopped as they went to work. Byron noted the squadron's discipline with a touch of pride. As the overseer of Beta headquarters, he knew each Psion personally, including their strengths and weaknesses. He'd chosen Tango Squadron because it was the only squadron made up entirely of Psions. All others included some combination of Psions, Ultras, and Tensais.

Teams paired off with efficient execution, entering the building through different routes. Most of the warehouse looked like a warzone. All the loading doors had been blown away, the dock itself cracked in four places, and two areas sagged under their own weight. Byron, Dr. Rosmir, and Shamila went around the building. Blood stains soiled the cement walkway as they approached the stairs that led down to the basement.

"Should I collect samples, Commander?" Dr. Rosmir asked.

"Not yet. The pilot said he fired on the enemy in this area. How about we take a peek around first?"

Getting inside wasn't as easy as he'd thought. Two bombs had gone off near the entrance. The bottom steps were badly damaged. A huge pile of wreckage comprised mostly of brick, cracked plaster, and drywall filled the doorway, which had miraculously held strong.

Commander Byron sent Shamila in as the point, Rosmir in second, and he covered the three-person team from the rear. They took caution, trying to be as silent as possible. Inside was the epicenter of the storm. Black soot and ash covered what was left of the walls. Several places had blown clean through into the adjacent offices and hall. Above them, Byron saw a gaping hole where the ceiling had collapsed.

"We're gonna have to move this piece by piece, aren't we?" Shamila asked.

"Should I call in for help, Commander?" Dr. Rosmir asked.

"No, I want to do the work myself. Shamila, please stand guard outside while Maad and I get to it."

"Yes, sir."

"Thank you."

Dr. Rosmir gave Byron a puzzled look. The commander ignored it and put on his working gloves, handing a pair to the doctor when he was finished. "This is something I want to do in private; just you and me. They never knew Samuel."

Together, the two men heaved and hauled both massive and small chunks of the pile further down the hall. The amount of rubble and debris, combined with the awkwardness of the lifting and moving, made the work slow. Byron held his breath with each piece they cleared away, wondering if it was the one that would uncover his pupil. After almost an hour of work, Byron knew Dr. Rosmir had to take a rest. The doctor hadn't complained, though sweat poured down his pale face. They went outside and Shamila reported on her squadron's progress.

Commander Byron kept the respite brief. He wanted to find the body and get back to safety as soon as possible. After another ten minutes, Dr. Rosmir came up with something. "I found a body!"

They quickly dug to uncover it, but after only a glance Byron knew it wasn't Samuel. It was a Thirteen. He was so badly burned that the only recognizable feature was a tuft of blond hair. They grabbed him by his uniform and heaved him out of the way.

Dr. Rosmir bent down to inspect the spot where the Thirteen had been. "Check this out. It's Sammy's Beta transmitter . . ."

"Still in decent shape," Byron muttered as he turned it over in his hand. "But not what I came here for."

He handed it back to the doctor, who slipped the metal into his pocket. Just as they returned to work, crunching noises echoed from down the hall and around the bend. Byron stopped in a half-squat and looked at Dr. Rosmir. The doctor reached for his weapon, hands trembling. Commander Byron stood back to full height. The crunching stopped for a few seconds, but Dr. Rosmir didn't relax. Then the noise started again.

Dr. Rosmir cursed under his breath several times as he drew out his weapon.

Byron allowed himself to wonder if it could possibly be Samuel. It was a stupid thought. More likely, knowing what he knew now about the possibility of a traitor, more Thirteens had arrived to welcome them. Neither he nor Dr. Rosmir moved. The sound drew closer. Rosmir's gun pointed steadily at the end of the hall. Byron drew his own weapon. He fingered the switch to the light beam, trying to decide if he should turn it on.

Finally his patience ran out. He flipped the switch, and in a soft voice called out, "Samuel?"

The crunching noises stopped.

"Samuel?" he repeated just a hair louder.

The crunching began again but at a slower pace. Whoever it was stood just around the corner.

Two eyes appeared at the end of the hall, much lower to the ground than Byron had expected. They reflected back two ghostly dots, but Byron couldn't tell who or what it was. The eyes watched them but did not move. Dr. Rosmir turned on his laser sights and trained it between the eyes.

"Samuel?" Byron asked one last time, louder than before. Two high-pitched, ear-splitting sounds rang out in the hallway. It was a dog. A chocolate Labrador, Byron noted, as it came fully into view. Dr. Rosmir sighed, his hands trembling as he lowered his gun, then holstered it. The dog approached them for a pat and rub. When he smelled Shamila, he pushed past them toward her.

"That was a nice surprise," Dr. Rosmir commented.

"You look like you just lost two years off your life," Byron told his friend.

Dr. Rosmir shook his head and got into position to lift the next piece of debris off the pile. "You going to help or make jokes?"

After all they had done, the once daunting task now seemed quite manageable. With only a few more heavy loads remaining, the bottom of the pile wasn't far away. Byron felt some concern. What would he do if they reached the end of all this mess and Samuel was not there? What then?

He put off those questions and focused on finishing the task. They came to a particularly large chunk of the brick wall. Byron, feeling his age a little more than he'd care to admit, had to call Shamila in to help lift it off the pile.

"Prepare yourself," he told Dr. Rosmir and Shamila. "He's probably under this."

Together the three of them lifted at one end, standing the giant slab against the wall.

"Holy heavens," Dr. Rosmir said. "Am I really seeing this?"

Byron turned back to see what Dr. Rosmir saw: a hole in the floor the size of a square of sidewalk grinning back at them. "I see it, too."

Shamila peered into the black square, running her hands along the smooth sides. "How does something like that happen?"

"Flare please," Byron ordered.

Shamila handed him a flare. The commander jammed it against the wall, and it ignited, fizzling and popping merrily. They all watched as it dropped meter after meter after meter until—

CLUNK!

It landed on the ground and rolled out of sight.

Byron looked at Shamila. "Maad and I are going down there." Now he spoke into his com. "I need two sets of repelling equipment and one of those boomlights brought to me."

"Right away, sir," the voice of Robert Greene answered in his ear.

In under five minutes, with the rappelling gear secured and a light in hand, Byron jumped down into the hole and blast landed safely at the bottom. Immediately he dropped into a defensive stance and shined his light around the room in all directions.

"It's safe," he said to his com. Dr. Rosmir lowered a forensics kit down the rappel line and followed suit with his own land blasts. With two boomlights, the room was nice and bright. The walls were of strong sturdy brick. Shelves lined over half of the room and a giant generator took up a large portion of one corner.

"Geez . . ." Dr. Rosmir said. "What do you make of all this?"

"Looks to me like a bomb shelter. Who knows how old it is, but I see no sign of Samuel."

Trying not to let his hopes get too high, Byron circled the room looking for any definite sign of habitation. If Samuel had been here, he did an excellent job of hiding his tracks. Byron felt a touch of pride at that.

Dr. Rosmir, meanwhile, got busy with his kit. Byron had seen him use things like this before and knew better than to offer help. The kits were expensive, complicated, and extremely handy in investigations such as these.

Rosmir took out a long skinny can and sprinkled powder on the floor all around where the two Alphas landed. Then he sprayed the powder with an aerosol can, and waited. Byron marked areas around the room with a special pen that could only be seen with wavelength altering contacts. Both he and Dr. Rosmir had one to wear when they needed it.

"Come see this, Walter," Dr. Rosmir said.

The commander noticed that his friend had used his first name, something he only did on rare occasions.

"What is it?"

"Can't you tell? Look . . ." he said pointing to small color variations on the floor.

"You seem to be forgetting that I did not attend medical school, and never bothered to memorize the color code for chemical traces."

"No—no, I haven't forgotten," Dr. Rosmir said with a bemused smile. "I'm trying to prolong your suspense." He pointed out several spots to Byron. "This faint orange is caused by a reaction with hydrochloric acid. See it?"

"Not really, no."

"It takes lots of practice. Hydrochloric acid is found in the stomach. It comes up with vomit. But since it's such a common acid, even in cleaners, there's only one way evidence of vomit can be used in a court of law."

"How's that?"

"Pepsin and pepsinogen—enzymes also secreted by the stomach, but never found in your household cleaners. All I have to do is spray this over it, and if it turns blue—"

With a quick spray over the orange spots, even Byron could see traces of blue.

"Voila!" Dr. Rosmir exclaimed.

Byron smiled and clapped him on the back. "Well done. So we know someone threw up here."

"And not too long ago," Dr. Rosmir added. "Within the last six— maybe seven months."

"Any signs of blood?"

"Yep. But nothing like what we'd have seen if the boy had fallen down the shaft to his death . . ."

"Can you get a DNA—?"

Dr. Rosmir shook his head. "Not from vomit. I can run the blood when we get back, but it still won't tell me if he survived or not."

Byron frowned. No trace of Samuel here. None upstairs. What if he hadn't fallen down the hole? What if his body had been taken away with all the others?

"I marked some areas for fingerprints," he said, pointing around at the pen marks he had made. "Take that side of the room."

None of the places Byron circled yielded results.

"I must be missing something," Byron said with a frown as he turned around on the same spot, letting his gaze fall everywhere. "A little blood and vomit. No note, no fingerprints. No fingerprints anywhere."

Dr. Rosmir held his hands in the air like he was about to play an invisible piano. His eyes were closed. "The kid wakes up here. He's alone. He finds food and water. What does he do?"

"Stays, hoping someone will come and get him."

The doctor nodded. "I go along with that. But how long does he wait? A week? Two? A month? More?"

Byron shook his head and kept looking around the room for clues. "So he lives in here for some time. After a while, assumes no one is looking for him. Then what? Where does he go? What does he do?"

"That's what I'm figuring. He has to know he can't stay here forever, but just in case someone comes looking, what does he do? He leaves . . . something. Maybe a note? A sign? Nothing at all?"

"Samuel is smart; too smart to leave a note. Maybe . . . something."

"So what? Where? Where would he leave it?"

They spent a half hour searching for and talking about possible messages or symbols Samuel might have left to tell where he might go. They found nothing.

Byron scratched his head in frustration. "All we have is a spot of vomit and old blood. Come on, Samuel. Where would you leave a message?"

Dr. Rosmir snapped his fingers. "What is the last place he touched? A door? A light switch? Maybe turning off the generator?"

A smile spread across the commander's face. "You want to do the honors?"

Dr. Rosmir sprayed a small aerosol over the generator kill switch. Sure enough, a nice fat fingerprint appeared in green. Byron used his scanner to make a copy of the print, but hardly needed to see the results of the analysis. And yet, he hadn't needed to see anything so badly in a long time.

It was Samuel's print.

Byron's knees almost gave. He caught himself as they bent. It was too much to believe.

"Walter, are you all right?" Dr. Rosmir asked. "Wasn't it his?"

The commander dropped the scanner at the doctor's feet. Rosmir picked up the scanner and belted out a laugh.

"He's alive . . . what a lucky kid!"

The two combed every centimeter of the underground shelter, making sure that nothing was overlooked. When Byron believed they could glean no more information from the bunker, he told Tango squadron to prepare for takeoff. Dr. Rosmir was just about to climb back out when Byron put his hand on his shoulder.

"I need to talk to you privately," he said.

"Okay."

"Only we know Samuel is alive. I want it to stay that way . . . for now."

"But why?" Dr. Rosmir asked. "How can we organize a search if—"

"Tomorrow, I am going to bring Tango Squadron right back here to start a search, and I am going to forbid them having any contact with Command other than myself." Before Dr. Rosmir could protest, Byron stopped him. "I have my reasons, and I'm leaving it at that."

"What are you telling Tango? And Psion Command?"

"I will tell Tango what they need to know . . . tomorrow. Command will think we found no sign of his body or of survival."

"Walter—"

"I need your trust on this. I will keep you up to date with everything Tango finds, but I need you to have some faith in me."

Rosmir responded with a sound of exasperation, but Byron knew he had his confidence. He patted the doctor on the back and climbed out of the hole. The rest of Tango waited in the cruiser. Byron told them he and Dr. Rosmir found nothing in the bunker.

Once in the cruiser, Byron pointed them back to Capitol Island. Not long into the journey, he sent a text to his son:

A critical matter requires your urgent attention back at A. headquarters. Can you return to base immediately following the ceremony? Bring Chin and Djedaa. Samuel is alive.

All speed, Dad.

He and Dr. Rosmir spent a good length of the trip discussing in private how he was going to explain the disappearance of Tango squadron. He'd need to come up with a very good excuse. Eventually things were going to come out, and Psion Command would be furious with him. Technically, he had the authority to give such orders, but he knew he'd be in hot water with General Wu. Before they landed, another thought struck him, and he sent a second text to his son.

And do not say anything to anyone. Even Gefjon or Marie.

He had much more work to do than he'd anticipated. And he was thrilled about it.

11 | Graduation

March 3, 2086

JEFFIE AND BRICKERT moved down the aisle between the two large sections of chairs in sim room one looking for a good place to sit.

"Over there," Brickert suggested, pointing to her right.

Jeffie counted the number of available adjacent chairs. "Not enough for everyone."

"You mean, not enough for Strawberry and Antonio," Brickert said, "which is more than fine by me."

Jeffie reprimanded him with a look and continued meandering up the aisle, waiting for the crowd of Alphas, Command, and Betas in front to clear out.

"Do we really want to sit that close?" Brickert asked. "I'll get sick during the highlight video."

"Oh, quit whining!" She punched him on the arm playfully.

Brickert smiled back, and all she could do was shake her head. She looked back to see if their friends were following behind when someone tugged on her sleeve urgently. It was Al trying to squeeze between three members of Marie's family. He wore a very strange expression.

"Hey, Al! What's up?" She hadn't seen him since his own graduation.

"I need to speak with you in private." He kept his voice quiet, and she barely heard him over the din. "You know . . . after this is over."

"About what?" she asked.

Brickert turned an ear to catch a piece of their conversation.

Al opened his mouth to speak, but Marie's father cut him off. "Al, let's hurry now. It's about to start."

He shot her a look of hopeful reluctance and mouthed: "After." Then the tide of the crowd pulled him away from her and to the front of the audience where family received special seating for the ceremony. Jeffie's mind froze on Al's expression and she forgot all about trying to find a seat.

"Jeffie?" Brickert snapped his fingers in her face. "Earth to Jeffie?"

"What?" she finally answered.

"What did Al want?"

"He wants to talk to me after this is over."

"Did he say what about?"

"No, he didn't." But she had a pretty good idea. *It's about Sammy. What else could it possibly be?*

Brickert ended up choosing their seats, as Jeffie was too lost in her own thoughts to really care anymore. Twice, he had to steer her by the jumpsuit

- 157 -

so she wouldn't walk into someone. Natalia and Kawai arrived shortly and sat with them. Just before the ceremonies began, Strawberry ducked in with Antonio, taking the seats to Jeffie's right.

"Where's Hefani?" Antonio asked.

Jeffie pointed two rows up where the other new kid was sitting. She hated having Hefani around. He was nice, polite, and extraordinarily humble, but he shared too many similarities with Sammy. Often, Jeffie would see him and immediately think of her best friend. It wasn't that they looked exactly alike. Sammy was taller, bigger, and much better looking with his strong chin and cute, stubby nose. Hefani kept his hair long and hardly ever spoke unless Antonio was around. But his dark skin and hair often made her do a double-take.

She didn't remember much of Marie's ceremony. It seemed as though a box of fireworks had been crammed inside her head and lit, causing her imagination to explode with daydreams of both wonderful and devastating tidings. What news could Al possibly have? Had they heard from Sammy? Were they going back to look for him? So many thoughts and ideas battled for the spotlight that she began to hate Al for making her wait for their conversation.

"I am not telling you how many boys I've kissed," Strawberry whispered in mock offense.

"Come on. Don't be such a prude," Antonio answered under his breath. "I'm sure someone as cute as you has had a little experience!"

"Oh, right. Nice try, but—"

"Can you two act mature for two hours?" Brickert hissed, leaning across Jeffie to talk to his sister. "I'll tell you . . ." he added under his breath to Jeffie, who answered with an indulgent smile.

"Sorry," Strawberry replied, beet red.

Antonio hitched a cheesy grin on his face, and they both turned to watch the proceedings.

"Thank you," Jeffie breathed to Brickert. "I didn't want to have to say something." No matter how great of a roommate Strawberry was, she seriously lacked social etiquette whenever Antonio was around.

Most of the Betas were getting bored with the graduation ceremonies. This was their third in about two months, after attending Al's and Gregor's. They were all fairly similar except for the highlight reel; an impressive collection of recordings of the graduate in the Arena and simulation fights. That was everyone's favorite part. Each time Jeffie tried to pay attention, her thoughts strayed back to Al. *What could he possibly need to talk to me about?* Whatever it was, it seemed urgent.

Brickert leaned over and again interrupted her train of thought. "Would you mind if I sat in on your conversation with Al?"

"It's fine with me if it's fine with him."

"Great. Thanks." He beamed at her.

"Can you two act mature for two hours?" Antonio hissed at them, grinning as he did so. Jeffie glared back, and he shut up.

Finally the highlight reel began. Jeffie watched it with mild interest. When it ended to thunderous applause, Marie got up to speak. Sensing the end of the meeting, Jeffie sent several glances at Al as if her eyes could hold him in place until she reached him. He was sitting between Marie's parents and her littlest brother, Domingo. Jeffie wondered vaguely if he, like Strawberry, had already tested positive for Anomaly Fourteen, but was too young to be recruited. Every few seconds, Marie's mother or father would lean over and whisper to either Al or each other about something in Marie's speech. Seeing Marie's parents in the same room with their daughter reminded Jeffie of a late night with Sammy not long after he had beaten four Thirteens in one sim.

◎

As he told her about beating the sim, he practiced levitating his ice cream spoon in one hand while using his other hand to spin it. Jeffie knew he'd picked the idea up from watching Kobe, but she didn't mention it.

"I'm kinda jealous of the relationship you had with your parents," she told him.

"Come on . . ." he responded, getting a really good spin on the spoon before it tipped over off his blast, "you make it sound like yours are terrible."

He sat in his favorite gel chair, propping his legs up on a second one, the way he always did during their late night talks. He wore his old jeans and a T-shirt Al had given him a couple months ago with the Helsinki Hurricanes' logo on it. Jeffie hated the Hurricanes, they were a big rival of the Oslo Otters. So, naturally, Sammy wore it more often.

"I didn't mean it to sound that way." She watched him spin the spoon, wishing he'd put it away and look at her. "They're not terrible. I—I just wish they had been more down-to-earth."

He dropped the spoon again, and didn't bother to pick it up. Instead, he looked at her with that blank expression he wore when he was just listening to what she had to say. He probably did not know it, but it was the perfect way to get her to keep talking.

"My dad was my basketball coach ever since . . . oh gosh . . . ever since I was old enough to be in recreation clubs, I guess. Did I ever tell you he fudged my age on the application to get me in?"

"No" Sammy smirked at her. "But I'm not surprised. In fact, I could see you doing the same thing."

Jeffie threw a gel chair at him. He blasted it away without much effort. "Thanks for the workout."

"You're welcome. Anyway—where was I?"

"Fudging your age," he told her.

"Oh yeah, so I was six months shy of the cut-off date, and he marked my half birthday on my sign-up form. He told me the bigger sin would be to not let me play."

"Do you think he was right?"

"Playing with older girls definitely pushed me harder. But I was six! I mean, who cares about that stuff when you're six? They don't even care if you double-dribble until the eight and nine-year-old league. But if I double-dribbled or traveled or fouled out—it was like a cardinal sin!" Jeffie clutched her face in mock terror. "My dad would make me run lines after practice."

"Really?"

"Oh yeah! The same with my brothers. That's why they're playing professional sports all over the continent—two play for football clubs and one plays basketball. At least, that's the reason my father told everyone."

"He's probably right."

"You know, the only time my parents ever got into arguments was when my mom wanted to take us to her film shoots. She wanted us to be well-rounded; he didn't want us to miss practice. So, finally, she decided to direct a documentary on the Norwegian territorial football squad, and my dad had to let us go. I was nine then. We liked being on her film sets so much he had to let us go more often."

"You got to do some pretty cool stuff," Sammy remarked. "What are you complaining about?"

"But they weren't my best friends!" she shot back. "Aren't they supposed to be? I don't know. Your parents sound so great."

Sammy shrugged in his chair, causing the gel to squish inside. "They were."

Jeffie mocked his nonchalant shrug several times until he smiled. "My dad was more concerned with winning and getting us sports scholarships to whatever school we wanted to attend. My mom was determined to culture us in the arts, but she rarely went to my games. She missed all my Olympic games because she was filming the first basketball holo-film. Ironic?"

"You were in the Olympics?" Sammy asked.

Jeffie's expression told Sammy that the answer should be obvious. "Of course I was. But do you see my point?"

"Yeah, sure I do," Sammy said as he got up to get more ice cream. "Do you want more?" he called back.

Jeffie grumbled a bit to herself about whether she should and then reluctantly answered, "Yes."

Sammy came back, grabbed her bowl, and filled hers up as well. When he handed it to her, he said, "Don't take this the wrong way, but I want to spend my life with someone like my mom. She was my best friend. I could trust her with anything."

The words burned themselves into her memory. At that moment, she realized she wanted to be the person Sammy was talking about.

"What is that face for?" Sammy asked.

Jeffie mentally slapped herself. "Nothing . . . I just think you're really lucky. And I wish my mom and dad had taken more time to be my friend."

"You should remember that when you have kids someday."

"Okay, can we talk about something a little less serious?"

Sammy just laughed.

⑤

Jeffie's patience ran out about twenty seconds into Marie's speech. She could hardly sit still, glancing every few seconds at Al, who seemed to have no problem listening to his girlfriend's discourse about how grateful she was that her mother and father had taken a leap of faith and accepted Byron's offer.

"Calm down," Brickert hissed at her. "Everything's going to be fine."

Jeffie ignored this, glancing again at Al. This time he was reading a text on his com. When his holo-screen disappeared, Al sat up straighter and looked to his left and right as if he were making sure no one else read the message.

More questions jumped to Jeffie's mind and she tried to keep track of them. As Marie wound down, Jeffie tapped her feet to a fast beat in her head and ignored the annoyed looks from Levu and Cala. A half-second after the ceremony finished, she sprang from her seat like a jack-in-the-box and made her way toward Al.

But Al, it seemed, had forgotten about their conversation. She watched him worm his way over to Marie, hug her, and then whisper something in her ear. Marie nodded and hugged him again.

That can't be good . . . Jeffie increased her speed. Unfortunately, the entire Covas family had congregated in the aisle, blocking Jeffie's access to both Marie and Al. She tried politely to shove through the crowd but by the time she got through, Al was gone. Unwilling to give up, she raced through the hall yelling his name, and barely caught him on the stairs to the rooftop.

"Hey! Where are you going?" she asked him a bit breathlessly.

"Oh . . . Jeffie. Hi." Al glanced back up the stairs and then looked at Jeffie. He still wore the same strange expression, only now he looked guilty, too.

"You said you wanted to talk to me, then you ran off. What's up?"

"Nothing," he said. He looked uncomfortable. "I just wanted to see how you are. I mean, how are you?"

"I'm fine. That can't be what you wanted to talk to me about. Is it?"

"Well . . ." Al stared at her blankly, then examined his watch. "I mean, yeah. I wanted to talk to you a bit more, just to see how you are. But I remembered I have an urgent meeting. It wasn't anything . . . Sorry if you thought it was something important."

Jeffie didn't know what to say. As she stood there in silence, Al ducked through the door with little more than a goodbye.

She ran forward to stop him, but too late. The roof door closed, and she didn't have the authority to open it. Frustrated and confused, she kicked the door. Her toe throbbed with pain. She ordered her com to call Al.

"Permission denied. Unauthorized number."

She cursed at herself for forgetting she couldn't call Al anymore. *Second option: find Marie.* She ran back down the hall and into the sim room. She had to wait until Marie's family finished hugging her before she could get near.

"Congratulations," she said with a semi-forced smile and hug.

"Thanks, Jeffie," Marie said. "How are you doing? We haven't talked much lately. My fault."

"No—no, I'm fine. I was wondering where Al went off to in such a hurry. He said he wanted to talk to me about something. It seemed important."

"Oh, I don't know. He didn't say anything about that. Right after it ended, he said he had to leave. Apparently that was urgent, too. Sorry . . ." She said this with a sad, knowing smile that made Jeffie feel uncomfortable. The idea that Marie thought she understood what was going on in Jeffie's life stirred upsetting feelings.

She has no idea what I feel.

With no more desire for company, she went to her dorm and sprawled out on her bed. She wanted to stop caring about what she'd thought Al would say. She even felt a little ashamed at some of the daydreams she'd invented. *Sometimes you can be such a silly little girl.* Stupid. Childish. If it had been anything of significance, Al would have made sure to tell her.

The feeling of loneliness hit her harder than it had since the first days when Sammy didn't come back. Sure, she had Brickert, Strawberry, the other girls, but they were not Sammy. She could not have the talks with them that she had been able to have with him. Sleepless and solitary, she let memories of Sammy pass slowly in front of her inner eye. Tears wanted to come, but Jeffie refused them.

Her door opened suddenly and she sat up, startled. It was Strawberry. She was crying. Jeffie's sisterly instincts took over, sweeping away the self-pity in which she had been wallowing.

Plenty of time for that later.

"What's the matter, Berry?" she asked.

Strawberry, in a move that was so typical of her, hid her face. Jeffie knew how much her roommate hated crying—or anything else that caused her make-up to run. But she was actually kind of glad Strawberry was upset, because it made her forget her own feelings.

Strawberry shook her head and went to her closet as if she was looking for something.

"Hey," Jeffie persisted, "talk to me."

"It's . . . nothing," Strawberry said through small sobs.

"If it's nothing, then I'm sure you won't mind if I mention it to Brickert."

Strawberry laughed a little and sniffled. "You wouldn't tell him! You'd be breaking my sacred trust."

Jeffie smirked at her friend. Strawberry could be funny, even when she felt totally miserable. "Will you talk you me now?"

"Oh . . ." she shrugged. "It's Antonio."

"I knew it! I'm going to pummel that boy." Jeffie said it with more sincerity than Strawberry probably believed. Otravelli had already gotten off on the wrong foot with her by way of his cocky nature and his tactless remarks about Sammy. "So what happened?"

"It's so stupid! During the ceremony we had talked about playing some games together, but when I went into the rec room to find him, he was already hanging out with Natalia."

"Okay . . . why didn't you talk to him?"

"I did. But he blew me off like I was a little kid."

"I wouldn't lose any sleep over *Antonio Otravelli!*" She pronounced his name like she'd heard in mafia movies. "Especially if he's making nice on Natalia. He won't get far."

Strawberry laughed at Jeffie's impersonation, but beneath Jeffie's words hid an even greater pearl of truth. Since Natalia had arrived at headquarters, she'd suffered from a major crush on Brickert. Unfortunately for her, Brickert had eyes for the older girls, and Natalia's thirteen month gain on Brickert did not seem to qualify her for his affections.

"I try not to . . ." Strawberry answered distantly.

For a long moment, the two roommates sat in silence. That was another thing Jeffie enjoyed about rooming with Brickert's sister: she was fun, but she did not always have to be talking. On the other hand, Brillianté, Jeffie's last roommate, always had something to say—be it gossip, overly personal information, or opinions. Brillianté fit more into the Natalia and Asaki mold than Jeffie did.

Strawberry broke the silence by clearing her throat.

"Yes?" Jeffie asked, reading her friend's noise.

Strawberry hung her head down over the bunk's edge so she could look at Jeffie, and asked, "Will you be upset if I ask you about Sammy?"

"No . . ." Her answer came before she'd even thought about it. But she found that she really did not mind. "Besides, I know you've wanted to for ages."

"It's just that everyone talks about it—about you two—like you were Romeo and Juliet or something. Was it really like that?"

Jeffie lay back on her bed and stared up at Strawberry's bunk, pressing her feet up on the supports of Strawberry's mattress. "We never even kissed, Berry! Romeo and Juliet made it to first base, didn't they? I read it for school, but Tvedts aren't known for being readers." She pushed hard against the wood, feeling it flex slightly under the strain. Every time she did so she wanted to push until it broke. "But sometimes I thought about being with him forever."

"What was it about him? Why was he so different?"

"Has anyone ever told you about what we were like when we first met?"

Strawberry, still hanging over the side of the bed to look at Jeffie, shook her head, a curious expression on her face.

"We didn't get along at all. I mean, I couldn't stand him!"

"Really? Why?"

"Because I was such a brat."

From the look on her face, Strawberry was not buying it.

"No, I mean it," Jeffie said, laughing again despite herself. "I'd come from this family where winning was everything, but Sammy was the golden boy. He won everything he did—every Star Racer match, every Arena Game, anything he tried. It drove me nuts!" Her temperature rose, even now, at the memories of losing to Sammy.

"Sammy the Great. That's what Kaden called him the other day."

"Pretty much . . ."

"So? What happened next?"

"He did something crazy, Berry," Jeffie said, now getting into her story. The memories brought a smile to her face. "Absolutely crazy!"

"What? Tell me!"

"He let me win. He gave me something no one else had. I mean, obviously he knew how competitive I am—was—"

"Am," Strawberry decided for her.

Jeffie rolled her eyes. "Well, believe me, this kid liked—*likes*—to win, too. But he knew it was more important to me." She frowned at herself for the faux-pas she had made.

Strawberry looked at her with a clueless expression. "He let you win?"

"Yeah. Get it?" she said, laughing again. "Since the day I met him, I resented him for being so good at everything. But to him, my friendship was more important than winning."

"Huh . . . And he never kissed you?"

"I'm sure it wasn't that way in his head. He was just trying to make me happy so I'd stop being such a—well, a nasty person to him."

"And then?"

"I fell . . . hard!" she said.

Strawberry burst out in laughter. Her laugh sounded almost exactly like Brickert's, not that Jeffie would ever tell her.

"Yeah . . . it was pretty bad."

"And? What happened? What did he do?"

"Nothing."

"Nothing? I don't get it."

"Neither did he!" Jeffie exclaimed. Both girls giggled in fits. "He's so clueless. It's really, really sad. But, honestly, that was another thing that ended up making it even worse for me. He wasn't ever obsessed with kissing or whatever. He was my best friend. We talked and laughed, and he liked me. I knew it, but I waited one day too long to take the first step."

Suddenly her ache was back and worse than ever. All the reminiscing had done was make the hole inside her bigger and fresher and harder to fill.

Strawberry noticed the change in the atmosphere and asked, "Are you okay?"

"I don't know. I just wish—not that I'd gotten to kiss him, per se. I mean, I wanted to kiss him so bad, but it's not that."

Unable to hold it in any longer, Jeffie covered her face with her pillow and muffled a scream. She kicked the wooden paneling, wishing she could just snap it in two. Somehow it would make her feel better. Instead, she pounded the bed with her fists.

"I'm sorry for bringing it up," Strawberry said. "But I'm really glad you talked to me about it."

"It's not that, Berry. It's just . . . I feel like there's this huge gap inside that needs to be filled." She lowered her voice as she continued. "And what if he really is gone—gone for good?" Saying those words hurt like an elbow to the stomach. Though, strangely, she was glad she said them. "And what if no one will ever be able to fill it up again? I mean, what if no one can ever take his place?"

Strawberry was quiet for a moment, then spoke. "I don't know. Sorry. I wish I'd known him, though. Did Juliet ever find someone else after Romeo died?"

Jeffie rolled her eyes. "Sometimes it's easy to remember you're barely thirteen."

12 | Ride

March 3, 2086

WITH ALL THE RECKLESSNESS of a runaway train, Sammy and Toad sprinted out of the parking garage, up a cement slope, and out onto the sidewalk. This escape felt different than the Grinder. It was experiencing real freedom for the first time. The afternoon sun shined too bright, the smoggy city air smelled sweet, and no downtown, inner city block ever looked so beautiful as the one he looked down now.

It was like waking from a horrible dream that had lasted days and days and days.

He didn't have a clue where they were. And for a little while, he didn't care. His head was pounding in the center of his forehead, and he wanted to put as much distance between the building and himself as possible.

Side by side, they sprinted down the street for several blocks. There were no sirens, no shouts, no sounds of anyone following them. He spotted a cramped alleyway splitting two tall buildings. A large dumpster blocked off most of the entrance. Without a word to Toad, Sammy turned into the alley and leaned on the wall to catch his breath. Toad's steps continued to patter down the sidewalk, then stopped and came back.

He leaned next to Sammy, and for a couple minutes, they did nothing but breathe the air of freedom. Still panting, Sammy talked out loud to himself.

"So that's it? We just walk away? What happened to the part where they chase us?"

Toad's eyes roamed from Sammy's hands to his neck to his face. "You killed everyone who's supposed to chase us."

Sammy stared back at Toad, who backed away as if Sammy might be combustible.

"You did. You killed like six or seven people."

"Eight. They were going to kill us."

"Okay, now what are you going to do?"

Sammy put his hands to his throbbing forehead and slid down the wall until he was crouching. He hadn't thought past getting out of the building. That seemed to be a gigantic feat in and of itself. *What am I going to do now? How do I get rid of this kid?* Part of him wanted to just sit down and have a good long cry. Part of him wanted to keep killing, maybe even Toad. Part of him wanted to go back and put a knife to his own throat, but he shook all this away. He was on an adrenaline high, and he had to ride it out before exhaustion set in.

The word *ride* stayed in his brain and reminded him of his air rail ticket. He looked out into the city skyline, saw Maracanã in the distance, and ran in that direction.

"Wait for me!" Toad called after him.

It was about thirty minutes of jogging before they reached the stadium. From there, Sammy knew where to find Floyd's butcher shop.

When they came to the street, he hung back to check for signs of anything suspicious. After watching for several minutes, he went to the spot where Floyd hid a spare key and unlocked the back door. Not daring to turn on any lights, he crept into the front section of the store and opened the cabinet where he'd hidden his ticket.

It was still there.

Toad pulled a face of disgust. "You smell really bad. And you have blood all over you. Are you hurt?"

Fumbling it in his excitement, Sammy opened the bag and removed the ticket. It looked as good as new, perhaps just a tad frayed at the edges.

No reason it shouldn't work.

"What's that?" Toad asked, plugging his nose and leaning over on his tiptoes, probably to see what piece of paper would be so important to come all this way for.

"It's my ticket out of here," Sammy told him.

"Where are you going?" Anxiety laced the younger boy's voice and he sniffed several times in a row.

"North," Sammy said and held the ticket possessively. "So, you're welcome for saving your life. Make it a good one." He looked through the windows to double check that they hadn't been followed. It looked safe, but could he really be sure?

"You're not just leaving, right?" Toad asked. "I need your help."

"No you don't. You know your way around here better than I do. Go back to your family and tell them to move away."

"Please come with me. You—you know how to fight. You killed all those people in the building." Toad's face paled as he said this.

"No, you'll be fine. Just go." He waved the boy away and spat a piece of dirt or grime out of his mouth. Toad backed up hesitantly. Sammy glanced at him, then looked away. Did he really believe Toad was going to be fine?

I don't want to take care of him. I don't need that right now.

But he knew he was wrong. Sending Toad back to his parents was ushering him to a violent death. Sammy knew he had done terrible things in the last hour, but those men were his enemies. Toad was not.

"Actually—wait. You can't go back to your parents."

"Why not?"

He didn't have time for Toad's ignorance, nor did he want to explain how he knew things. "I—I don't know! I have a bad feeling about it. The people who took you may have already gotten to them."

Toad rounded his small frame onto Sammy, as menacing as a small figure could be. He was probably a year older than Brickert and maybe, *maybe*, a centimeter or two taller. "What do you mean?" he asked with a whirlpool of emotion in his voice.

Sammy closed his eyes and said it. "I'm saying they're dead."

Wham!

Toad's small fist slammed straight into Sammy's jaw.

Sammy swore loudly, grabbing Toad by the neck and throwing him bodily into the closest wall. "What was that for, you little—?"

"Take it back!" Toad screamed in his face, but tears pooled in his eyes.

Sammy glanced out the windows again to make sure no one had heard Toad's yell.

Wham!

Toad's next punch caught Sammy in the back of the head. Sammy's foot shot out and swept into the boy's ankles, catching him off balance and sending him to the ground. Toad landed flat on his butt.

Sammy lowered his face down to Toad's as he grimaced up from the dirt. Sammy's eyes narrowed, his lip curled up, and he felt positively murderous. "Don't punch me again," he hissed. "And *shut up!*"

From the look on Toad's face, he wouldn't need to be told twice. But instead of retaliating as Sammy expected, he began to cry. Large tears spilled over his big hazel eyes as he quaked violently.

"Please . . . say they're not dead . . ." he moaned. "Please . . ."

Sammy watched him. His first instinct was to distance himself from the scene. His mind was still waking up from the fog of being in that building, and that spot in his forehead was knocking a little harder. He had important things to do. He needed to get out of this shop. He needed to get up to Wichita.

WICHITA! Sedgwick C. Plainpal.

This kid was slowing him down. But something in those tears touched the scraps of humanity inside Sammy that Stripe hadn't managed to snuff out. He couldn't leave Toad to fend for himself. *Especially if his parents are dead—murdered by some freak in their own home. Toad will walk home and find the door open. Then he'll follow the trail of blood and find their bodies.*

The hypocrisy was too great.

Resigned to his fate, he sat down on the floor next to Toad and awkwardly put his arm around Toad's shoulder. For the first time, he noticed how dirty the floor was. It wasn't like Floyd to leave the floor unmopped at the end of a work day. They sat there for a while, Sammy letting him empty out his tears. He felt no emotion for the kid, more like a mental connection. In his own emotions, a small dam had been placed inside of him, and as long as that was in place, Sammy wouldn't need to cry for himself, Toad, or anyone else.

"Can we go back and check?" Toad asked when he finally stopped crying. "Just to be sure? I have to know."

"No. We can't. It's probably best to never know."

"That's stupid!" Toad said through a husky voice and a big sniff. "Like you would know anything about it!"

"I do."

"Oh yeah? How?" Toad replied quietly and folded his arms across his knees.

"Both my parents died."

Toad looked at him for a long time but did not say anything. He just sat there, centimeters away from Sammy, occasionally sniffing.

"Ready to go?" Sammy asked him.

"No."

"Well, I'm going now. You can either come with me or go to your house and wait for them to find you."

"Can't I go live with my grandparents?"

"No." Sammy rubbed the pulsing point on his head to try and stay calm. "If you go any place where someone knows you, you'll die. You're coming with me."

Toad sniffed once more, and Sammy thought he was going to start crying all over again. Instead, Toad seemed to pull it together. He might be done crying for now, but the tears would come again later.

Sammy got up and brushed the dirt off his pants. As he stood, the ache in his head made white lights burst in his vision. He steadied himself against the wall and grabbed his head. Toad watched him with wonder and a little bit of worry. *We are a pathetic sight*, Sammy realized. He hadn't changed clothes in days . . . maybe even weeks. Nor had he eaten a proper meal in the same amount of time.

He smelled himself and instantly pulled away from his armpit. "I really do stink, don't I?" Sammy said.

Toad nodded, almost smiling, but not quite getting there.

They took five minutes to clean themselves up at the sinks in the back of the store. Sammy was still pretty wet when he put his clothes back on, but he smelled a lot better. A long drink of water helped take the edge off his headache.

"All right," he said to Toad. "Let's go to Maracanã."

They had no need to speak during the walk, which turned out to be much quicker than Sammy expected. Between his growing exhaustion and murmuring stomach, it was a miserable hour and a half. Despite his own discomfort, his mind kept going back to Toad, wondering what the kid was going through.

He could almost sense the thoughts trickling slowly through Toad's mind: trying to imagine what his parents might be doing. Or, if they were dead, what they looked like, and how it happened. Were they riddled with bullet holes and covered in blood? Perhaps poison gas had been pumped quietly into the home, and the entire family had just never woken up. If

Sammy had to guess, he would have picked the former. At least, that had been his experience with the enemy thus far.

Thirteens picked the most violent, hands-on ways to kill. And Sammy had no doubt Toad's family was dead, be it now or in the near future. It made him hate the Thirteens even more. Hate like a blackness filled him, leaked out of him. He wanted to kill someone. He wanted to watch the lights go out in their eyes.

It made him feel good for a moment. And when the moment passed, he felt completely sapped again.

Something unnatural dwelt inside him. Something powerful. That thought of violence and death had given him a fleeting moment of pleasure, but when it passed, it left him feeling ashamed, tainted.

No noise came from Maracanã that evening, but the hub was plenty busy. No one in the crowd seemed to care that Sammy was messy, damp, and still somewhat smelly.

They passed several of the *KEEP THE PEACE! CALL IT IN!* signs as they walked through the main concourse. Sammy clutched his ticket and tried to calm himself.

His lip and hands trembled. He had to get out of the crowd right now. Seeing his chance, he grabbed Toad by the sleeve and pulled him into the nearest men's room.

"What's the matter?" Toad asked.

"We need a plan," Sammy explained, trying to hide the panic growing inside him.

He sat on a sink as he thought. Time passed in relative quiet. A few men and boys wandered through to do their business. Some spared a glance at Sammy and Toad, others didn't care why two boys were hanging out in a bathroom. Toad said nothing, but sniffed every so often.

Yet nothing came to mind for Sammy.

Finally, Toad looked at him expectantly. "So?"

"Do you have money to buy a ticket? Like a link to your parents' account or something?"

Toad shook his head.

What is the plan? Sammy wondered. He slammed his fist against his forehead, trying to force something to come loose in his brain. The jarring did nothing but make his headache pulse more angrily at him. He shifted in the sink as his butt started to go numb.

Toad sighed deeply.

Sammy scowled at the kid. "I have a thing for coming up with plans. Just give it a second. Okay?"

"Okay. Take your time."

A few more minutes passed.

"I have an idea."

The words rang in Sammy's ears. They weren't his own, but Toad's. Sammy, swallowing a lot more than his saliva, asked, "What's your idea?"

"We'll need to do some dumpster-diving."

After explaining his plan to Sammy, Toad led them back outside where they looked through the dumpsters on the far west end of the hub near the maintenance equipment and service ways. Sammy counted about eight dumpsters in all. They only had to climb into three. The first two emanated such foul smells that Sammy had trouble joining Toad to look through them. It took about a half hour, but they finally found what Toad wanted: a large red suitcase, no larger than a kitchen cupboard, and in good enough shape to travel. The rubber on one of the wheels had only a few more rotations left to give, and the broken handle twisted when they pulled it. Otherwise, it was all they needed.

Soon enough they were back in the bathroom, washing themselves as best they could to get rid of their stenches. Then they locked themselves into the larger handicap stall at the end of the line. Sammy didn't think Toad's plan was going to work, and had no trouble letting him know it.

"Trust me," Toad insisted. "I know I'm right."

He unzipped the suitcase and climbed inside, then ordered Sammy to zip him up.

"You're sure you want to do this?" Sammy asked. "It's going to be awful."

Toad nodded, shaking the whole bag. "Just don't bump me around too much. And bring me back in here if there are any problems."

Like I needed to be told that, Sammy thought. *He thinks I'm a moron.* But it bothered Sammy that he hadn't been able to come up with a good plan. He picked up the case by the handle and wheeled it back into the concourse.

Toad only squirmed and jostled a couple of times during the walk to the information desk. Behind the desk sat a woman who wore heavy makeup, a skewed maroon vest, disheveled curly hair, and a taut face. When she turned her attention to Sammy, he saw her invisible well of impatience brimming over. He'd seen the look before in his mother's eyes, usually after a particularly long day.

He forced a smile and said, "Hi."

The woman eyed him as if he were an exceptionally nasty piece of manure. Sammy gulped but kept the smile.

"Long day?" he asked.

"You're only making it longer."

Sammy dropped the grin. The woman—he saw that her name tag said *Danielle*—was about to open her mouth and say something else, but he cut her off.

"I'm sorry, Danielle. I didn't mean to be insensitive, but I need your help . . ."

She watched him again, then a small smile raised her lips. "How can I help you?"

"It's my ticket. Someone purchased it for me, and I wasn't able to use it until now—a family emergency—but I desperately need to get up north."

"Let me see it."

Sammy pulled the ticket out of his pocket and handed it over to her. Under Danielle's severe scrutiny, he felt a twinge of embarrassment at its condition, and gave her a genuinely embarrassed smile.

"Forgot you'd bought it?" she asked him knowingly.

"Yeah," he weakly laughed. "Sorry, but it's—it's all I've got."

He did not bother to hide the tone of desperation in his voice. If she did not let him through, he was screwed. For the first time, it seemed, she noticed Sammy's clothes, his hair, his state, and probably his smell. Her eyes traveled up and down, and back to the ticket.

"Normally you'd have to buy a new one. This one's two months old. Our policy for ticket use ends at forty-five days. Why are you headed north?"

Sammy couldn't believe what he'd just heard. Sixty days. Eight weeks. Two months. He'd been kept in that room by Stripe for two months. Flashes of cream tubes and kaleidoscopic swirls of color filled his vision.

"Hey, are you still with me? Why are you headed up north?"

Sammy blinked several times and wiped the corner of his right eye. "Um, my family—my dad's parents are up there."

"Just the one bag?"

"Yeah."

"Carry on?"

"Yes."

Danielle typed for a few seconds and then handed Sammy a new ticket. Sammy took it with the same reverence he'd shown the old one.

"You know you get a free meal here at the hub with your ticket, right?"

Sammy's whole face brightened. "Really?"

"Yep." With one of her long fake fingernails, she showed him a small M on his ticket. He was almost certain there hadn't been one on his old ticket. She gave him a small wink. "Head on over to security to have your bag inspected."

"Thank you, Danielle," he told her very sincerely.

"Safe traveling," she said, her face now cheerful.

He smiled again and pulled the bag toward security where three lines formed. Sammy chose the middle. Each person had to walk past a team of dogs ready to sniff clothes and bags for traces of bombs or drugs. The dogs were all shepherds—some German, some Belgian. He wondered if any of the chemicals Stripe had used on him would be detected by the dogs. Fortunately, he didn't have to stew for long. The line moved quickly and though the dogs spent extra time sniffing at his bag, they let him pass.

The Rio de Janeiro Air Rail Hub had nine rails extending out from the city like the sun's rays in all different directions except directly south. Sammy wanted rail number three going straight to Panama City. Once he checked in with the rail attendant, he found another bathroom, locked himself in a stall, and unzipped the bag. Toad rolled out of it.

"Oh, that sucks," he muttered, and immediately set about stretching his legs.

"The stupid dogs kept sniffing the bag."

Toad's neck and ears turned red. "Yeah, well, all that running gave me bad gas."

"You need anything?" Sammy asked.

"Do you have any money?"

"No. But we get a free meal."

"Cool! Just let me walk around for a bit."

"Boarding is in less than thirty minutes. It takes us all the way to Panama City. No stops in between."

"After that?"

Sammy read off the itinerary on his ticket. "To Guatemala City. Then to Mexico City. From there we stay on the same rail, stopping in San Antonio, Dallas, Oklahoma City, then Topeka. You're sure you want to do this?"

Toad rubbed his legs with a frown, avoiding Sammy's eyes. He didn't seem sure at all. He'd be leaving his home city, probably forever. "Why to Topeka?"

Sammy didn't bother answering. His mind was on the free meal they were about to eat. They boarded after chowing down a slice of pizza each and sharing a soda. Sammy heaved his luggage up into the overhead storage compartment and took a seat by himself, hoping no one would sit next to him.

The rails in Rio were smaller than the ones Sammy had ridden with his parents in Africa and Europe, but the windows were bigger. Sammy's dad had once called the rail car an oversized medicine pill, and Sammy still thought the description was accurate. These cars held about forty people, with one engineer sitting up front in a small booth. Most everyone around him was reading or working on their holo-tablets. Two boys, who reminded Sammy bit of Kobe and Kaden, were playing video games. In front of him, a man with a tall spike of hair wearing a skeleton-band t-shirt rocked out to some music.

Once everyone was situated, the engineer disappeared behind a small thin hatch up front, and the air rail came to life with all the fanfare of a gentle hum. Sammy noticed for the first time that his headache had subsided almost completely. To amuse himself, he tried to contemplate the massive amounts of energy it would take to move the rails at such speeds, but his mind became unusually clouded, and he let the thought go.

An ominous click sounded when the docking door closed. It was a peculiar click, very similar to the black door's click when Stripe closed it behind Sammy to begin their sessions. Sammy gripped the arms of his chair tightly as a flood of bad memories washed over him. Stripe had brought him through the black door almost every other day. He couldn't remember many details, but he saw enough in his mind's eye to make his whole body quake as if he stood naked in a snowstorm. Naked was how he felt. Stripe had done something to him.

As the rail car was released from its locks and began to levitate on its magnetic rails, an intense feeling of panic and hostility flooded his body, causing him physical pain. His body tensed up and he gritted his teeth. He must have made some kind of an audible noise because, when he opened his eyes, a few people were watching him, shaking their heads or muttering to those next to them.

The car began to move. The sensation of acceleration was brief. A minute or two later, they reached a constant speed. Sammy stood and went to the restroom in the back, ignoring the glances from a handful of passengers. He shut the door softly behind him and gripped the sink.

He had been too preoccupied to look closely at his reflection in the hub, but he did so now. His face was very thin, his skin an unhealthy pale color. His hair was long and matted. His eyes had a haunted look, which freaked him out the most.

Thoughts of eating mush and drinking bad water came back to him. What had been in the mush? He had no idea, but thinking about it made him nauseous. He remembered being sprayed down with a hose once or twice while the Aegis complained about his smell. He gripped the sides of the sink tighter, fighting back the urge to cry. His head felt like the mush had been shoved inside of it, pushing out his brains and poisoning him. Splashing his face with water helped calm him.

He sat on the toilet to relieve himself, but found that nothing would come from either end. *What is wrong with me?* He wondered. When someone knocked on the door, he hurried to get up and take a couple more drinks from the sink.

Back in his seat, he tried to think of other things, like Jeffie or Brickert, but they always had Stripe's face. Instead, he stared out the window and picked nervously at a thread hanging off his dirty shirt, waiting silently until the rail came to a stop in Panama City. He was the first to his feet, grabbing Toad from the shelf and beating the queue off the rail car.

Once in the hub, he went to the bathroom and let Toad out in one of the stalls.

"Oh man . . ." Toad moaned, "This really, really sucks."

"Do you want to switch?" Sammy asked testily. "Just ignore my legs hanging out of the bag. Maybe tell the other passengers you couldn't afford a coffin."

The layover was only fifteen minutes and the change in passengers was relatively small. The ride to Guatemala was short. Toad spent as much time as possible stretching his body out on the floor before they headed to Mexico City. Sammy badly wanted to sleep on this leg of the journey, but couldn't relax enough to doze off. The only thing keeping his mind off Stripe was focusing on Wichita.

If I can find the resistance, I can get home.

Toad complained a lot in Mexico City about his legs cramping. Sammy had little patience for it. He almost had to force Toad back in the suitcase so they wouldn't be late for the departure.

One stop in San Antonio. One stop in Dallas. Then Oklahoma City. Then we're there. He told himself this over and over as the rail car filled up to capacity and then moved off. Looking forward to Topeka, he started trying to think of ways to get from Topeka to Wichita without having to walk the whole distance. By the time they left Dallas, he still didn't have a clue. The problem was that he couldn't seem to hold a steady thought in his head for very long unless it involved Stripe or memories of horrific pain.

They hadn't been moving for more than two minutes out of Dallas when the engineer's voice came over the speaker system.

"Ladies and gentlemen, North-to-South Air Rails regrets to inform you of an unscheduled delay in the Oklahoma City hub due to small maintenance troubles. All passengers will be required to exit the rail car and allow our escorts to take you to a designated waiting area until the problem is resolved. A qualified technician will be at the hub on arrival. We expect only a twenty to thirty minute delay."

Maintenance troubles, my eye, he thought, sitting stiffly in his chair. *They've found me.*

Amidst the grumbles and empty complaints of the other passengers, he stood up, grabbed the suitcase out of the compartment, and set it on the floor. When he opened the luggage, Toad looked aghast at being exposed in his hiding place.

"Get out," Sammy told him. "Did you hear it?"

Several people in the rail car stared at them, some in shock or interest, others in amusement, as Toad emerged from the suitcase.

"Hear what?"

Sammy told him about the announcement. "We can't leave this to chance."

Toad nodded his little head with a sniff. "Okay—okay—okay—I think I know what to do."

"How do you know that?"

"From my dad. Um . . . can you do one of those special jumps like you did earlier? You know, back in that building?"

"Yeah."

"Okay—okay. I think we can get out."

Sammy followed Toad to the back of the car. Everyone aboard was watching now. On the ceiling was an emergency hatch about the size of a sewer cover. Toad pulled a red lever and several warning lights began blinking in the car. At least a dozen people cried out in anger.

A soft alarm beeped and the engineer came out from the front to investigate. He was a fat little man with thinning hair. When he saw them at the hatch, he started running to them.

"Get in your seats! You have no business being back here!"

They ignored him.

"You two are breaking the law, and I am ordering you to sit down!"

Sammy helped Toad climb out the hatch.

"You stay right there or I'll shoot you, kid!" the man said.

Sammy saw that he was holding a small concealable handgun. It was laughable.

"You're not going to fire that in a car full of people," he told the man.

The engineer cocked his gun, but Sammy blast-jumped, grabbed onto the ledge of the exit, and pulled himself up and out. Beneath him, he heard the angry yells of the engineer and the murmurs of astonishment from the passengers.

Toad closed the hatch under them, sealing them off in the tube on top the rail car. Air howled around them, whipping their hair and clothes with dangerous force. From his crouched position, Sammy looked and saw that every couple kilometers was a bright colored circle. Toad pointed at them.

"These holes let the air out of the tube. We have to jump through one of them!"

Sammy shook his head. "No way! It's too fast. I can't time it right!"

"I can. Trust me!"

"I don't trust you!"

A banging sound came from below them as the engineer knocked on the hatch. Sammy looked at Toad, who seemed scared but also surprisingly confident.

"Fine. But you better not kill us!"

Sammy watched the circles fly by at regular intervals. Toad ticked off each beat with a finger perfectly. They had only a few centimeters clearance above their heads, even crouching as they were. It was terribly cold, and Sammy's eyes were now watering from the constant wind.

Toad gave a thumbs-up, then began ticking down each circle.

Five . . . Four . . . Three . . . Two . . . ONE!

Sammy launched himself and Toad from the top of the rail car and they sailed up through the top of the tube. Some type of thin metal screen covered the hole, but they broke through it cleanly. Sammy scrambled to grab onto the ledge of the giant tube and almost lost his grip, but Toad let go and snagged on with perfect timing. With two hands free, Sammy used his other arm to secure his grip and pull himself up.

It was colder here than Rio, and the sun was setting over the tops of the trees of a wooded area that stretched as far as Sammy could see from the top of the tube. From what his jumbled brain could remember about geography and the maps he had studied, he guessed they were in the northern part of the Territory of Texas. Not too far from the Dallas hub.

Yee-haw.

He used his blasts to help them get safely onto solid ground.

"Okay, now what do we do?" Toad was already shivering and stamping his feet.

Sammy didn't answer right away. The only thing he knew for sure at the moment was that they had to go north. "We run and hide."

14 | Sewers

March 5, 2086

COMMANDER WROBEL SAT BEHIND HIS DESK filling out the ridiculous forms that never stopped coming. He paused from his work to crack his knuckles and rub his temples.

Despite being a member of Psion Command since its inception over ten years ago, Wrobel had the worst job of any Psion. He was the Beta-Alpha liaison. Commander Wrobel had something to do with anything that connected Betas or Alphas to each other or the outside world. When Psion Betas were deemed ready to graduate, he organized the Panel, the mission, and the ceremony. He selected which Alpha squadron a Beta should go into. If the Beta had excellent tactical skills, he sent them where a tactician was needed. If the Beta was good at weapons and demolitions, he found a place for that one, too. When Alphas needed new arms or ammunition, Wrobel signed off on the orders. When the food shipments came to Beta or Alpha headquarters, he signed those forms.

Forms. Forms. Forms.

He glanced at the art piece hanging on his wall—an oil painting of Sisyphus rolling his giant stone up a hill. He'd had that commissioned over six years ago during a particularly dark season of his life, and he'd paid handsomely for it. Claire had been a fan of Greek and Roman mythology. In fact, she'd learned Greek and Latin in her spare time. He doubted Walter remembered that little fact.

He dragged a finger angrily over his screen and enlarged several more files to review so he wouldn't have to squint to see them. The next order of business for the day was reading over contract offers for explosive providers for the next fiscal year.

Riveting.

A little red box popped up in the corner of his screen. Wrobel swore and hurried to save his work. Then his computer instantly turned off, and he bent under his desk to disconnect a wire from his hyper-drive, reconnecting it to a small black box no bigger than a domino. The small box was well-concealed in a corner underneath his desk. His computer came back online with a flashing red text on an otherwise blue screen:

Transmission incoming.

Beneath the message was a countdown from nine. When the countdown reached zero, the transmission went live. On his screen, Commander Wrobel saw the ugliest face he'd ever seen in his life. Severe burns had left the head completely bald and pitted. The face was mutilated with thick deep scars that would never lose their red tinge. One particularly nasty scar ran from the right side of the chin, across the lips, leaving them split and twisted, up into the nose where the left nostril was completely missing, and into a hollow pit where his right eye should have been.

"Diego, you handsome devil," Wrobel said. "To what do I owe this pleasure?"

Diego's voice was high and raspy and the lower lip twitched badly when he spoke, probably from all the screwed up nerve endings. Worse than that, however, was the empty eye socket twitching each time he blinked. It made Wrobel queasy.

"I just spoke with the fox."

Wrobel maintained his composure, but a wave of fear washed over him. Diego held a special place in the Thirteen hierarchy. He was supposedly one of few people who knew the location of all the Thirteen cells, as he acted as a sort of switchboard operator between them all. If a cell needed to get in contact with another, they went through Diego. He also was the only person Wrobel knew of who had regular direct contact with the fox.

Commander Wrobel had a pretty good grasp of the Thirteen organization after his dealings with them over the last few years. But the fox was still like the boogey man. People rarely dropped his name, but when they did, Wrobel knew there was some serious crap flying around. The fact that Wrobel had gotten a call from Diego immediately after Diego spoke to the fox . . . that was bad news.

"Samuel Berhane is alive."

Wrobel's stomach dropped, and he let out a very pretty curse. "That's—" He was going to say *that's impossible*, but he knew better. Diego. The fox. These people don't tell jokes. He swore again. "Whose fault is that? Mine?"

"The fox isn't assigning blame to you at the moment. But I assure you, there's plenty to go around."

"I told you in November that I couldn't confirm his death. I recommended that you send in a full team to sweep the factory!" Wrobel's breathing quickened as his temper flared up. "You didn't listen to me!"

Diego snarled as a nasty chuckle gargled from his throat. "That shouldn't surprise you. We lost a whole cell in Rio. Around here we call that a debacle. You're telling me I should have trusted your word after one of your teams wiped out a whole cell?"

"I warned you in my report that the kid was dangerous!" Wrobel was yelling and he didn't know why. He pulled his collar away from his neck which suddenly felt very warm. His large index finger pointed back at Diego. "You check it. I wrote that!"

"Shut it, Fourteen," Diego drawled. "Just shut it. Here's the straight point. Your kid is out. Fell into a hole in the floor that went straight down into the basement."

"Your cleanup crew got lazy."

"I sent in three Aegis to do the job a week after the battle. They didn't find a body, so they got out fast. They thought you were setting them up for another ambush."

Wrobel laughed an off-kilter chuckle. "Ironic. Psion Command thought the same thing about you."

"You don't understand, yet. It gets worse. We created a new cell and moved them down to Rio in December. The next month, Aegis picked up a kid downtown on a questionable complaint. They held him in an interrogation room for two months with no idea who he was. The kid insisted his name was Albert Choochoo. We had one of our best interrogators down there. The kid got loose and turned on the interrogator. Poured torture creams all over him and down his throat. Then he killed eight more on his way out the door. Got a picture of him on a surveillance camera leaving the building."

Diego held a picture up so Wrobel could see it, but the commander had to really squint to make out what was going on. It was Samuel—Samuel and someone else the commander didn't recognize.

"Holy—"

"Now you see why I'm coming to you."

Wrobel shook his head to himself. *Byron. Byron knows about this and hasn't told anyone.* He thought of Claire again. He thought of Sisyphus. *Later, Victor. Later.* This was worse than filling out forms. He cracked his knuckles again and shook the stiffness out. "So what am I supposed to do about it? You want me to fly to Rio and find the kid?"

"The kid isn't in Rio," Diego snarled. The angrier he grew the more his eye socket twitched. "We tracked him to an air rail hub, and he bailed out in Texas, north of Dallas."

Wrobel didn't know much about Texas. And he wanted to keep it that way. "Excuse me for a second." He stood and went to the small water fountain on the back wall near the door to his private restroom. It was a small chrome bowl polished to a high shine. The jet of water was nice and strong, the way he preferred it. He swallowed a large mouthful and felt three drops splash onto his shoe.

Drip. Drip. Drip. It was Claire's voice he heard in his head, not his own. *Sounds like this whole place has a bad plumbing problem.*

He rejoined Diego at the computer screen with a friendly smile.

"Where were we?"

Despite the difficulty in reading Diego's face, Wrobel could see that the Thirteen's expression was one of pure anger. "This problem is yours, you realize that?"

Wrobel disagreed with a simple gesture of his hand and a long blink.

"Your job was to fix the mission."

"I put everything on the line for that, too, didn't I?" Wrobel's patience snapped like a brittle bone. "I flew out there myself and gave you information as a gesture of good faith. The fox told me he wanted Samuel, so I handed you his head on a plate. Your men screwed this up—*your* people. If you can't handle less than a dozen kids, then that's your problem. I'm not cleaning up this mess."

"The fox says you will."

Wrobel's fury died like a candle being snuffed out in a hurricane. He swore silently. The fox says this. The fox says that. He couldn't do anything but say yes. "Fine. But I want that number this time."

Diego laughed. It wasn't a pretty sound, an awful mix of a grunt and water being sucked down a pipe.

Sounds like this whole place has a bad plumbing problem, Claire's voice said again.

Wrobel buried his anger. Long ago, his psychologist had told him he shouldn't do that, but he'd done it anyway. For years he'd buried his feelings one grave at a time, until he'd become a mental cemetery.

"Listen to me, Diego. I said I'd take the job. I asked for her to be in on this clear back in November. You said no. Now look where we are. Same situation; different place. If you want this done, you give me that number I asked for last time."

"You wiped out a whole cell in Rio," Diego growled. The deep scars grew redder as he got madder. "Now you're demanding the Queen's number?"

"That cell was wiped out because you didn't listen to me!" Wrobel let his voice rise, now undaunted by Diego's status with the fox. Enough was enough. "You know what happened there. Give me the number and I'll be out of your . . . hair."

An animal-like shriek came from Diego's mouth as he whipped a knife out of his belt and took a long lick of the blade. Wrobel watched with disgust and fascination. Diego punched numbers into an unseen console.

"There!" he screamed with frothy red spit flying from his mouth and more blood pooling on his lips. His voice was almost all rasp now. "If I ever see you in person, this knife will be in your back. I don't trust your loyalties, no matter what the fox says. You have now sent two dozen of our men to their deaths, Newgie filth."

"Thanks. But if you're so mad, why insist on always winking at me?"

As another terrible, murderous screech rang out, Wrobel pushed two buttons, and the screen went blank again. Grinning to himself, he rubbed his lips in thought. Was he doing the right thing, bringing the Queen into this? Rumor was that no one bested her in tracking. She was impeccable, her ruthlessness unmatched. He'd also heard some call her a wild card. But she was in the fox's inner circle.

His fingers hovered over the keyboard.

What are you doing, Victor? Bringing in these animals to kill a kid? Who are you?

Victor's hands shook, and he had to get up for another drink. His mouth felt like he'd been sucking on a sponge.

Drip. Drip. Drip.

Suddenly Wrobel was back in the sewers. Water was dripping around him like a thousand leaking faucets.

⑤

"Drip," Claire said as she and Wrobel crept through sewer pipes large enough they barely needed to bend over. "Drip. Drip. Drip. Sounds like this whole place has a bad plumbing problem."

"Tell me about it," Wrobel responded. "My waterproof boots are already water logged."

Walter's voice came over the radio. "Check-in please."

In succession, the Psion team checked in over their mikes. Blake Weymouth was one. Emily Byron was two. Victor Wrobel, three. Claire Greenwall, four. Muhammad Zahn, five. Annalise Havelbert, six. Jason Ling, seven.

"I have everyone's position on GPS," Byron said. "Claire and Victor, you are closest to the refugees. Move in."

"Moving in," Claire replied. She looked to Wrobel and winked. "Beat you to it."

Wrobel held an automatic rifle in one hand and a handkerchief in the other to cover his nose. The water he trudged through was murky and thick. Each step seemed to stir up new scents that assaulted his nose, even through the fabric stuffed up his nostrils. The moon above sent only the most fragile rays of illumination down through the storm drains. Lights adorned both Wrobel's and Claire's automatic rifles.

"You're such a silver spooner," Claire told him. "Probably the only soldier on earth who walks into a potentially deadly situation with a handkerchief over his nose."

"That's what you like about me," he retorted. "My quirks."

He flashed her a grin and she laughed at him. They pressed deeper into the sewer for another hundred yards until they heard some small sounds, like paper being rubbed against the wall. Claire put her hand on his chest to stop him. When he looked at her, she tapped her ear and pointed ahead. Wrobel nodded.

"This is a rescue party for a group of refugees seeking political asylum with the NWG!" Wrobel announced. "We are carrying deadly force. Please reveal yourselves!"

He exchanged a glance with Claire, knowing his face looked as worried as hers. Neither Psion had been in battle before, and neither knew exactly what to expect.

Byron buzzed in over the radio. "Move in on three and four's position for reinforcement."

A pair of hands appeared around a corner that Wrobel could now just make out with his light. In the distance, maybe thirty yards away, was a small alcove. Wrobel and Claire started forward.

"We're coming to you!"

As they drew closer, Wrobel saw a small crowd of people, almost thirty in total, hunkered down together, squeezed into a space no larger than a modest bedroom. They were a dirty, haggard, miserable looking bunch. The hands belonged to a man of about twenty-five with fair blond hair. With his unsteady hands, he grasped Wrobel's shoulders.

"Thank you," he said. "God bless you. We've been down here almost a week. Our food is about gone. The women have gotten most of it. My wife—she's pregnant. Help us. Can you help us?"

"We're going to do everything we can," Claire told him. "We can get all of you out of here today."

A woman and man in the back started to cry along with exclamations of gratitude from the rest of the bunch. From behind, more of the team came sloshing through the water. Byron and Emily were the first to reach them.

Walter spoke into his radio. "Have you got a fix on our position? Good. What is the closest you can get? Copy that." Byron shook hands with the same man who'd spoken to Wrobel. "Are you Robert Reynolds?"

The man nodded. "We weren't sure anyone was coming. I sent that message over a month ago to the embassy."

"We have got to get moving," Byron told the team. "Transport cruiser will land one block east behind that closed school. One through four stay here and keep watch. Five, six, and seven escort them up the nearest ladder to the cruiser."

⑥

The voices disappeared as Commander Wrobel relived the rest of that day in the sewer. He punched in the number and waited.

"Hello?" a female voice answered before he'd had a chance to mentally prepare himself for the conversation.

No image appeared on the screen, which meant the Queen chose to block it. His own image wasn't visible either. Her voice was soft, ageless in quality. She might be twenty, might be fifty, he couldn't tell. It carried a sweet, sultry undertone that he instantly found attractive.

"Hello, this is—"

"I already know. I hoped you'd call."

He found himself able to relax. Listening to her voice was like watching his mother knit in her rocking chair in front of the fireplace.

"And you know why I'm calling?"

"I do." He heard a touch of humor in her voice. "There's been a lot of talk . . . not about you—not all about you. You are connected to Rio, though, right?"

Wrobel rubbed his lip while his free hand scratched an itch on his thigh. "The Rio incident is complicated. Talk is talk, right?"

"Maybe," she answered, still with that humor in her voice. "It depends who's talking."

"Apparently the fox has put me in charge of this. I need help."

Not her, a voice told him. *She's not the answer to this problem. Why are you doing this, Victor?*

He closed his eyes and pictured Claire. Her Psion uniform torn to shreds. Bullet holes in her back. Streams of blood curling and uncurling in swirls of filthy water under the light of his gun. It gave him all the resolve he needed.

"Give me details. I've been bored."

15 | Kobe

March 5, 2086

SWEATY AND TIRED, Jeffie emerged from her sims with a lukewarm shower and dinner on her mind. Anything to get her thoughts off Advanced Combat. As usual, she'd spent an extra half hour in the room before calling it quits. When she turned the corner of the hall, she saw a figure about ten meters away walking with his back to her. He was wearing stylish jeans and a fitted shirt. Jeffie didn't recognize him, which made her suspicious. No one around here wore street clothes on a Tuesday.

"Hey!" she half-yelled down the hall. "Who are you?"

The young man turned to face her and smiled sheepishly. "Are you kidding? You don't know me?"

When she heard his voice, the rest fell into place. "Kobe!" She ran forward and hugged him.

"How are you?" she asked. Already she could see that he looked better than those first weeks back from Rio, particularly in the eyes. That barely-contained rage was gone. The last time she'd seen him, he'd been mentally unglued. It bothered her a little that her chief reason for expressing concern about his well-being was to see if she should ask him about Sammy or not.

His hands stayed in his pockets. "I'm fine. Excited to meet the nukes."

She stared at him expectantly.

"Really," he insisted wearily. "I'm fine. Don't I look fine? How are you?"

"I'm okay." In reality she was very frustrated. Seeing Kobe helped defuse her emotions a little, but she had just spent several miserable hours having her butt kicked around by Thirteens in the sims. Her growing wrath at her inability to defeat two of them had begun to wear down her optimism. She reached up and wiped a trickle of sweat from her hairline.

"Been working hard?" Kobe asked, watching her hand move.

Jeffie didn't answer right away. She was wondering why Kobe looked so different. They'd known each other for a year, even dated briefly, but now she saw a whole new side of him she'd never seen before.

"Sims," she told him.

"Yeah, I kind of figured since you came out of the sim room all sweaty-like."

She laughed. It was nice to see a bit of his old sarcasm again. "Couldn't pull one over you. Not that I was trying or anything." Her hand jerked for a second, rather awkwardly. She almost playfully punched him but realized that would have been border-line flirting. With Kobe, that always came so naturally.

"No, don't take the credit. I'm just quick." He gave her a small smile, smaller than the old Kobe's. "What unit are you working on?"

"In sims?" she asked.

He nodded.

"Two Thirteens."

"Yikes. How long?"

"Just a week," she answered with a phony, toothy smile.

"Not going well?"

She shook her head slowly, looking him in the eyes. "It would best be described as a thorough butt-kicking."

The small glow that had come over him the last two minutes faded away. His eyes became distant and haunted. She decided it would be tactless to push him for information about Sammy right now.

"You okay, Kobe?"

"You already asked me that," he said. "I'm fine . . . not lying, either," he added the last part because of the doubtful look on her face. "My head is screwed on just the way it's supposed to be." With a small sigh, he added, "But I better get used to answering that question because everyone's going to be asking me for the next month. Maybe I can get a recorder. Every time someone asks me, I can just push play: 'I'm fine. I'm fine. Really, I'm fine.'"

A small laugh came from Jeffie before she'd even realized it. She had not expected Kobe to talk about it. Perhaps he wasn't as embarrassed as she thought. "Um . . . have you seen Kaden yet?" she asked.

"No. I'm on my way down now, but he knows I'm getting back today. It's not like it'll be a huge surprise or anything."

"Well, it's a surprise to me, at least. A good one." She closed her eyes with an inward grimace. *What a stupid thing to say.*

"Thanks."

They looked at each other for a moment, and then he spoke up again, this time in a lower voice. "You know . . ." From his tone, Jeffie thought he was going to talk about Sammy. "The doctor I worked with at the hospital, he says I don't share my feelings enough. I don't confront awkwardness head on. It got me thinking. I never apologized for what I did back when— you know." He shrugged his shoulders as if that somehow indicated exactly what he meant.

"What are you talking about?"

"When we were dating."

"Oh." The tape of them kissing. She hadn't thought about that in a while. "Right. You never did."

"Sorry, Jeffer."

The word *Jeffer* caught her attention. While they'd dated, Kobe liked to play with her name. He called her all kinds of variations: Jeffanie, Jeffer, and Jeffing were just a few.

"No worries," she told him with a dismissive hand.

Kobe took her by the arm and pulled her close so he could speak right into her ear. "Look, tell everyone not to treat me all weird or anything just because I went wacko. I'm fine now. I feel good. And I want to live normally again. Can you do that for me?"

"Sure." It reminded her of when she'd broken her leg and everyone had showered their sympathies on her for the short time she wore a cast. She'd hated it.

He let go of her arm and smiled as they pulled apart. "Are you going down to the cafeteria for dinner?"

"Shower first. Then dinner."

They walked down the stairs and Kobe stopped just before they reached the cafeteria. "I know you want to talk about Sammy."

Twice during the first weeks after Rio, she'd tried to talk to him. Both times he would not have it. He changed the subject very abruptly and, after the second time, began avoiding her. She wanted so badly to hear from him what had happened. After all, Kobe had been with Sammy until the end.

Jeffie opened her mouth to protest that she hadn't thought about it, but Kobe pushed on.

"And I will tell you about what happened. I just need time. You know?"

"Yeah, sure. No worries." She didn't know what else to say.

"Meanwhile, if you want to do some gaming like we used to, let me know."

Jeffie froze at his request, knowing he was casually dropping an invitation to formally hang out. Without thinking, she blurted another "sure" and hurried to the showers.

After cleaning up, she went to the cafeteria and ordered a Mexican salad from the Robochef. The large room was quiet, which was nice. Most of the Betas were hanging out in the rec room, probably talking to Kobe. He'd been missed. Kaden, Ludwig, and Miguel had spent the better part of the last several weeks moping around. Hefani sat in the far corner of the room with Antonio eating a pizza. Jeffie tried not to look at Hefani, he still reminded her too much of Sammy.

When she'd almost finished her salad, Brickert came in and sat next to her.

"Hey," he said breathlessly and wiped his forehead with his sleeve. "Almost. Not kidding. I almost beat that stupid sim today. Once. Then every time after that, I sucked it up. I'll tell you, if I'd been a mop, the sim room would be spotless."

Jeffie smiled at the way Brickert could just joke it off, even though she knew his frustration rivaled hers. After talking to several of the older girls, Jeffie had come to the conclusion that everyone got to this point around their one year mark. Advanced combat training. Some arrived a little before, others a little after. Kawai was about as far as Jeffie and Brickert. Natalia, however, had slipped behind their group, and was still struggling with Weapons and Demolition.

"What about you?" Brickert asked. "Anything new happen today?"

Jeffie shook her head as she scraped up her leftover dressing onto some lettuce. "Oh wait, duh, Kobe's back."

Brickert didn't seem to care one way or another. "Did you see him, or did someone tell you?"

"I saw him less than an hour ago. I'm pretty sure the commander brought him."

Brickert reached past her and stole her glass of water. After taking a long drink, he set it back. "Thanks."

Jeffie crinkled her nose. "Gross. Keep it."

"Double thanks." After another drink, he wiped his lips. "I want to talk to Byron."

"About what?"

"Sammy's recordings."

She put down her fork and folded her arms. It was something her mother would do, but she didn't let that stop her. Brickert noticed the gesture and put his hands up in defense.

"You don't have to come with me. I've made up my mind."

The firm tone in Brickert's voice took Jeffie by surprise. It also made her angry. She wasn't used to Brickert standing up to her.

"I know I don't have to come with you," she replied, "and I have a reason for it if you'll just listen to me."

Red spots appeared on her friend's cheeks and his attention was on the glass of water sitting in front of him. "No, you don't," he blurted.

"Excuse me?"

He still couldn't look her in the eye. "You don't have a reason, Jeffie. Not a good one, I'll tell you. I mean, think about it. What are you going to say? That Sammy wouldn't want us to learn from his recordings? I know he would. I know him better than anyone."

"That's crap, Brickert."

He glanced up at her and then back to the table. "It's not! We've already talked about this. You said what you wanted to say. It's not crap."

"It is!" Jeffie said loud enough that Hefani and Antonio looked over from across the room to see where the commotion was coming from.

"Why do you think Sammy volunteered his time to teach Al in the sims? Why do you think he spent so much time going over his own recordings? He didn't just want to be the best, he wanted to show everyone what was possible. He told me exactly that!"

Jeffie stood up and looked down at Brickert. "Don't act like you know what he'd want just because you roomed with him."

"If he were here now, he'd be going into the sims to help us, I'll tell you. At first, it was about the competition to him. Being number one in everything. Later on, it was all about the war. He was so excited when he beat the four Thirteen sim because it meant that other people would start believing they stood a better chance against the Thirteens than before. If he could do it, anyone could. But if you're too afraid to go in there and—"

"Don't tell me I'm afraid!" Her warning was low and menacing.

Brickert stood up, too. His expression was both fearful and defiant. "You are. Okay? You're afraid. I can tell."

Jeffie tried to interrupt him again, but all that came out was an incoherent sound of disbelief.

"I don't know what your problem is, Jeffie. I thought you'd be in on this with me. You and I promised each other we wouldn't give up until we beat the four Thirteen sim. Remember? To do that, I need his help."

Without another word, he took his exit, leaving Jeffie wondering who had just flipped the universe on its head. She pushed her salad away and put her head in her hands. It was then that she noticed the room had gone silent, and when she looked up she saw Antonio and Hefani watching her from across the room. They instantly went back to talking when she saw them, but all this did was infuriate her more, so she got up and left.

Halfway down the stairs, she realized that, more than anything, she wanted to talk to her mom. Unfortunately, Jeffie had made it a habit to use her monthly call home on the first day of every month. That way, her parents always knew when she was calling and would be ready for her. That was five days ago. She still had twenty-six days to go.

The next day, Brickert acted as though nothing had changed between them. Jeffie didn't mention their conversation either, but it stayed on her mind most of the day. What did she have against viewing Sammy's recordings? As far as she could tell, she had no adverse feelings toward seeing Sammy. Quite the opposite, if she really thought about it. And there was no question that studying him would teach her more than anyone else here could.

So then what's my deal? She asked herself more than once.

The answer didn't come to her. Not that day. Nor did it come the next. After three days of not being able to come up with a good excuse, Jeffie figured maybe there just wasn't a good reason at all. Now the only problem she had was going back to Brickert and telling him he was right.

"Could you repeat that again for me?" Brickert asked when she apologized over breakfast. "I'm being serious. I don't know if I heard you quite right." Then he had to duck before her English muffin hit him in the face.

After a short discussion, they decided to contact Commander Byron and ask for a meeting. Neither of them had ever done such a thing, though Brickert had worked with the commander twice in the sims. Still, asking for a private meeting was another matter entirely, and they had no idea how he might react to their request.

"Should we just . . . call him?" Brickert asked.

Jeffie saw the hesitancy in Brickert's eyes, the spots threatening to form on his cheeks, and activated her own com. "You mean, should *I* just call him?" She rolled her eyes and told her com to call Byron.

Fifteen minutes later, they were in sim room one sitting down on plush blue holo-chairs. Commander Byron had his arms resting across his chest, probably wondering what on earth two Betas wanted to talk about on a Friday evening while everyone else was downstairs in the rec room playing the sweetest fighting simulator Jeffie had ever seen.

"So tell me what this is about," he said with congenial interest.

Jeffie looked to Brickert whose face again told her she had the responsibility to make the request. She replied with a scathing glare.

"Well," she started hesitantly, "we were—we wondered if you would release the holo-recordings of Sammy's sims for us to study."

The commander's face showed no surprise. Jeffie wondered if he'd been waiting for one of the Betas to make this very request.

He read something off his com screen and then put it away. "Neither of you has even reached three Thirteens yet," he stated. "Might this request be a bit premature?"

Jeffie thought for only a moment before giving her answer. She'd already spent the last three days mulling over the very same question. "No, sir, we don't. I think the sooner we learn how to win these battles the better. What good is there in waiting?"

Commander Byron observed her for a moment, then his attention shifted to Brickert. Brickert looked everywhere but back at Byron's eyes.

Byron answered in his unique, measured tone, carefully placing each word as she knew him to do. "Technically, I am not able to do that. The records of a Beta are considered his or her private property and they are also considered classified documents. Only Samuel or General Wu can clear them for you."

Brickert and Jeffie exchanged a private glance.

"All right," Brickert added quickly, "but we thought in light of everything that's happened . . ."

"Plus he's—well, he's our—" Jeffie started to say.

"I know," the commander said with an uncharacteristic interruption. Jeffie thought she'd upset him. If she did, he showed no sign of it. Instead of saying any more on the subject, Commander Byron simply fell silent and looked at them. Perhaps he was waiting to be convinced.

Finally, she spoke up again. "Sir, we realize the ramifications of this, but we also know the importance of what Sammy was—what Sammy *is*." For a moment she couldn't believe what she'd just said. "I don't think anyone, even Al, could teach us to fight like Sammy can."

"No offense or anything," Brickert said hastily.

The commander smiled briefly and said, "I agree with both of you. But laws are laws and nothing can be changed. I will have to see if I can have Samuel's records declassified, maybe on a limited basis. Is that fair?"

"That'd be great," Brickert assured him.

"Good," the commander said, standing up. "In the meantime, keep working hard." In two strides, he had left the room, leaving Brickert and Jeffie looking at each other.

"That was weird," Jeffie commented. "Wasn't that weird?"

Brickert didn't seem to know what to think. The holo-chair he'd been sitting on disappeared and he hit the floor. Jeffie started to laugh and helped him up.

As Brickert rubbed his bottom, he asked, "What do you think he'll come up with? Anything?"

"I don't know. Hopefully something useful."

16 | Texoma

March 5, 2086

SAMMY HATED TEXAS. At least, he hated Texas in early March. Harsh winds relentlessly blew down from the north, chilling them. It was their second day of walking, having spent yesterday's remaining sunlight walking twenty or so kilometers east from the spot where they'd jumped from the air rail. When exhaustion finally caught up to them, sometime in the middle of the night, they still couldn't stop to sleep because of the biting cold. Moving was the only thing keeping them warm.

By the light of the moon, they searched for shelter. After hours of wandering, Toad spotted a boarded up shack that did little more than shield them from the wind. They huddled together inside, too tired to keep watch. Sleep came in spurts of five or ten minutes before a loud sound or frigid gust of wind woke them. The moment light appeared through the spaces between the boards, they set off northward.

Most of the terrain was unused plots of farmland, which provided little cover. He knew they should be traveling at night to help conceal their movements, but at such temperatures, how could they? They crossed plenty of country roads, most in disrepair. Sammy focused only on putting one foot in front of the other. He had no thoughts, no ideas. Deep down, he knew this was a bad omen. The realization that something in his brain had changed, and changed drastically at that, had begun to dawn on him back when they were in the bathroom of the air rail hub in Rio.

But Sammy didn't want to admit it. He didn't want to acknowledge that his once stellar, keen mind was about as good as a scrambled egg dumped in his skull. Truth was, Sammy could no longer *see*, and after relying on that wonderful Anomaly Eleven for the last couple years, the possibility that it was gone was like losing a friend.

Other than helping him learn faster than most people and allowing him to *see* solutions to problems, he wasn't sure what Anomaly Eleven meant to him. What else would it affect?

What if I'm naturally a dumb person? he wondered as he fell asleep.

The second day was milder, and the winds eased up. They had no clue if they were headed in the right direction other than north, but moving seemed a much better idea than standing still. It also helped them to forget about their growing hunger. About midday they came upon water and drank until their bellies were so full they sloshed at each step. Every few kilometers, they saw a house or large barn, but didn't dare go near. No cars ever passed them on the roads, and eventually, even the roads became scarcer.

After night fell, they pressed on, making poor progress with very little energy and rougher terrain. Between exhaustion, hunger, and the cold, the boys were absolutely miserable. As they walked farther north, they came across more and more trees until they were in a forest. When they finally had to rest, they could do nothing more than put their backs up to a tree and try to sleep.

Sammy didn't know how, but he got more rest that night than the one before. He woke to the sound of Toad crying for his parents. His sobs were wet and pitiful, laced with a deep moaning that ached for comfort. Sammy watched Toad with a detached passivity that he'd never before experienced. For one who had gone through something so horrifically similar, Sammy had no desire to provide empathy. Only a sense of duty finally motivated him to speak to the younger boy. He reassured Toad that he, too, had once lived through the same trauma, and in time the pain inside would lessen.

Toad's crying only got worse. Sammy tried to have patience, but he had so little of it since leaving Rio. His emotions always flew from one extreme to the next.

"Can't you calm down so we can get going?" he finally asked Toad.

"No . . ." Toad moaned. "I don't even know where I'm going!"

Sammy reasoned that it was time to tell Toad at least some things. If Toad proved to be untrustworthy (though Sammy had no idea how Toad would tell anyone), Sammy would just kill him.

"Start walking with me, and I'll tell you where we're going," Sammy said. "Sound fair?"

Toad grudgingly agreed. Sammy kept his word and told Toad about his intent to walk to Wichita, not Topeka, and find a place called *Plain Pal* or a person named *Sedgwick C.* Naturally, this only brought up more questions from Toad, questions which Sammy flatly refused to answer. Most of them centered around why they were going to Wichita and how Sammy was able to do the things he did in the N building.

"Okay, what about food?" Toad asked.

"I don't know," Sammy answered. "We know they're onto us. Maybe they know where we were headed, maybe not. But if we steal or do anything to attract attention to ourselves, we're just helping them find us."

"I can't believe you didn't bring maps," Toad said as his feet crunched the hard dirt. "That wasn't very smart."

"I had maps." Sammy's teeth clenched as he spoke. The morning sun was low and its rays shone on them through a canopy of leaves. Sammy hoped for a warmer day than the last. "I wasn't planning to travel without them."

"What did they get you for?" Toad asked. "Those guys in the suits."

Sammy made a sound of annoyance. A switch had flipped in his brain, and all of a sudden he didn't feel like talking. Every step made him hungrier. He knew he couldn't keep the pace up all day, maybe not even half the day.

If something doesn't happen soon . . . he let the thought hang over him. *I shouldn't have shared that pizza with Toad.*

He enjoyed the silence; nothing but birds singing and air blowing around them. The serenity helped bring things into focus. They walked through patches of forest, then patches of clearing. Sammy preferred the forests because he felt safer under cover, even though traveling was slower.

Toad, on the other hand, didn't like the quiet. He tolerated it for several minutes at a time, but then came right back to pestering Sammy with more questions or talking about any subject under the sun. The only subject Toad avoided was family. "How did you get your superpowers?" "Where did you learn to use them?" "I can run really fast." "Do I have powers, too?" It reminded Sammy of his conversation with Feet in Johannesburg while they'd been trying to elude the Shocks.

"You aren't answering any of my questions," Toad reminded him.

"I know," Sammy said dully.

"How did you—?"

Toad stopped walking, but better yet, he stopped talking. It wasn't because they had just come to the edge of the woods or because the sun had finally found their faces again, it was because the end of the woods marked a large community, a town stretching on for . . . Sammy couldn't tell exactly how long.

He watched Toad's face as it turned from hopeful to confused.

"Do you feel that?" asked Toad. His breath condensed in the air, dying centimeters from his lips.

Sammy didn't notice anything at first except the pains in his stomach and shins. When he took a moment to really pay attention, he understood what Toad meant. The panorama before him was so static it could have hung on a wall. It was obviously an older town; the materials of the homes were quite outdated. The lawns were overgrown, the tall trees breached the borders of the houses, growing over roofs and into windows, and yet Sammy could still have believed the town was inhabited had it not been for the perfect stillness captured like a picture.

Toad stood next to him and gave a loud sniff. "Ghost town. They're all over, I think."

Sammy had seen them before in Europe when he'd gone with his family. According to Sammy's history instruction, the worldwide average of fatality was over fifty percent during the Scourge. In South Africa, the casualties had stayed close to twenty-five percent. But in places as densely populated as China, India, and the United States, much higher percentages were seen, even reaching ninety in heavily urbanized areas. After things began to settle, mass mobilization resulted, with people moving back into the more urban areas. In the end, the small and mid-size towns took the greatest hit.

The effect was eerie. No artificial light streaming from windows or street lamps. No cars humming down the street or even standing parked in driveways. No joggers on the sidewalks or dogs barking behind fenced yards. Perfect quietness prevailed.

"This is great," Sammy said, intruding on the pervading quiet. "Let's see what we can find."

They went to the nearest house. The front door was unlocked, so they let themselves in. Sammy couldn't help his nervousness when they went inside. After all, they were entering a house uninvited.

The rooms were bare of furniture, the walls of any decorations. Drab curtains still covered a few of the back windows. A thick layer of dust coated the carpet and any other horizontal surface. Sammy's mind instantly went to food, and it seemed that Toad's did as well, because they both tore into the kitchen in a frenzy. With bangs and crashes, they systematically opened each kitchen cabinet, the fridge, freezer, and searched frantically for a pantry. It didn't matter. There was no food to eat.

"Are you kidding me?" Toad shouted as he slammed the pantry door shut.

Sammy swallowed his own disappointment. "Look for blankets and clothes."

They combed every room and closet in the house and found nothing.

"I'm taking those," Toad said, pointing at the curtains. He ripped them off the windows and wrapped them around himself as blankets, then they moved onto the next house. And then the next house, and then the next house . . .

As the sun set that night, Sammy and Toad walked down County Road clutching the thickest curtains they'd found around their shoulders. Toad pulled a badly rusted red wagon behind him. The wagon contained all their treasures: a sealed bag of rolled oats, three cans of corn, one can of chicken, and a few odds and ends they'd picked up. They passed a sign dangling upside down, hanging on by one nail. The next bad windstorm would tear it completely off the post.

"Welcome to Cedar Mills. Great Fishing. Great People," Sammy read aloud while craning his neck. "I hope the sign's right about the fish."

"I'm depressed," Toad mumbled.

"What'd you expect?" Sammy asked, "A banquet?"

"No." Toad sniffed a couple times and rubbed his nose. "But I didn't think they'd be totally cleaned out. He kicked a rock and watched it roll end over end down the road. "Now what?"

"I wish I could cook," Sammy grumbled.

"Can we just eat?"

Sammy shook his head. They caught up to the rock Toad had kicked, and Sammy gave it another good boot. It rolled out of sight. "Let's pick a house to sleep in. We'll eat there. Maybe tomorrow we can find some more food. If not, we'll keep going north."

Toad picked the closest house, an older looking two-level on the corner. It felt good to rest. Sammy noticed how tired his legs had grown from all the walking.

They started a fire in a metal pail with some matches Toad had found earlier in a jar under a broken bedspring. Looking at their food, they had to decide which to eat. Corn was the obvious choice, as they had three cans. Sammy picked the meat to go with it. He used his knife to open the cans.

"Okay, what about water?" Toad asked suddenly.

"What about it?"

"I need some. I haven't had any in hours."

Sammy licked his own dry lips, almost annoyed that he was now noticing how thirsty he was, too. "Neither have I. We'll split what's in the corn can and get some more tomorrow."

They ate slowly, savoring each morsel. Sammy stared blankly into the flames as he ate. A dark mood passed over him as the tongues of fire danced, forming shapes that mostly resembled Stripe's face. He became so lost in his own thoughts, it took a minute to notice that, across the room, Toad was crying. It started with that annoying sniff, then more sniffles, and finally Toad shook as he covered his eyes and bawled.

"What are you crying about?" Sammy demanded. "I've had the same amount of food and water as you, and I'm not crying!"

Toad responded by curling his small body into a ball beside the fire. Sammy shook his head, disgusted with Toad but also with himself. It was like two different people lived inside his own head, the old Sammy, and the new one: a twisted creature who'd risen out of the broken, beaten, nearly-destroyed person, thanks to the care of Stripe. The new Sammy had neither time nor patience for crying and whining. This new fellow wouldn't mind leaving Toad behind to fend for himself or die. He might not even mind putting Toad out of his misery if things got bad enough. Fortunately, old Sammy was stronger now and held the new one at bay.

"I'm sorry," he said finally.

"I miss my parents so much, Sammy." Toad's voice was muffled by wet hands covering half of his face. "I don't mean to be a baby."

"I know." He felt inadequate to the task of comforting Toad, so he said no more.

Toad looked up at Sammy. Tears had paved little paths down his dirty face. Something was in his eyes that both scared and thrilled Sammy.

"Will you teach me?" Toad asked.

"Teach you what?" Sammy asked even though he already knew the answer.

"To fight. To kill them like you did."

Sammy did not answer for some time. He stared back at Stripe in the flames, hating him and in some odd way missing him, too. His silence seemed to help calm Toad. "I don't know, Toad. We'll see."

He wanted to say something else, something profound or sensitive, but nothing came. A blank slate. That happened too often lately. It drove home again the possibility that maybe his Anomaly Eleven was just . . . gone. Perhaps he should do something else, a kind gesture, like put an arm around Toad or give him a compliment. He opened his mouth to let out whatever would come from it, but Toad had fallen asleep.

Day two of searching the little town of Cedar Mills yielded a couple things Sammy hadn't expected. In one house they searched, they found an old Texas/United States map in a kitchen drawer. Sammy could barely contain his excitement. Upon perusal of the map, Sammy discovered the second thing he hadn't expected. They had to cross Lake Texoma in order to get to Wichita.

At first, Sammy couldn't believe it. He led Toad outside and they walked northeast about a kilometer. Sure enough, before them stretched a giant reservoir as far as they could see. Seagulls flew lazily along the coast, congregating cordially on the docks that stood empty in rows stretching out into the water. Several weather-beaten signs pointed in the directions of the Cedar Mills Marina Resort.

Sammy stared at the reservoir for a long time, enjoying the sound of the water and birds, feeling something in his soul he hadn't felt for months: peace. A part of him felt cleansed, whole. He wouldn't mind staying here longer, in solitude, right on the lakeside.

"When I get old, I'm going to live on the water," he told Toad.

Then his mind snapped back to reality and he swore out loud. Toad looked at him, puzzled.

"We have to find a boat," Sammy explained. "We're gonna have to row across the lake. Two or three kilometers up north."

Toad unfolded the map and traced his finger along a white line running north. "There's a bridge we could cross right here. Highway 377! We don't need a boat."

Sammy snatched the map from Toad and folded it carefully. "Think about it. We can't take the bridge. We'll be out in the open with nowhere to go if they find us."

"Give me a break! We won't even be on the bridge for a half hour."

Sammy's face grew hot and he struggled to maintain his calm. "You're right. We won't be on it at all. Can you take any of them on in a fight? If so, then you can help make decisions. Until then, shut up and do as you're told."

Toad took a swing at Sammy, but Sammy pulled back, letting Toad's fist hit air. A gentle blast put Toad on his butt in the sand.

"I told you not to hit me anymore!" Sammy growled.

"Then quit being a jerk! Okay? I asked you to teach me to fight, and you said you would."

"I said 'we'll see.' That doesn't mean yes. Now get up and help me find a boat and more food."

For most of the day they went through houses, one by one, street by street, until they'd gone through the whole little town except the northern-most street: Oxford. Several houses on this block were larger and older, two of them even boarded up and condemned. Inside the first condemned home, the wooden floors creaked under their steps. Some of the windows had been left open, exposing the walls and floors to water damage and debris. Sammy sent Toad upstairs to search while he went through the main level. He heard Toad stomp up the steps and the ceiling groaned under his weight.

The kitchen was designed in a rustic log cabin sort of way: stove and counter tops made of brick with wooden bordering. Sammy ran his fingers along the brick as he went from cabinet to cabinet, finding all of them empty. He went into the pantry, a small room filled with shelves. The floor was covered with a faded, dusty rug of red, white, and blue. In the back was a small cardboard box. Sammy crossed the small room to check it out. The floor under his feet gave an extra loud creak, startling him.

The box was full of empty glass jars and lids. Sammy kicked the box half-heartedly. As he crossed back to the door, he felt a pop under his feet.

At first he thought the floor was about to give way under him. He grabbed the rug and pulled it aside to inspect. Instead what he found was a square trap door, big enough for one person to enter.

He pulled opened the trap door and looked down into a small cellar not big enough to stand in. It was about twelve feet wide and went back under the house about thirty feet. The smell reminded Sammy of the walkway above the abandoned grocery store in Johannesburg, as if no one had been down there for a long, long time.

And it was filled with food.

Toad came running when Sammy called him. They went down together, and hauled up more food than they could hope to carry. Powdered milk, dried fruit, bottled water, guns, ammo, canned fruits and meats and vegetables, even dehydrated meals. Toad found toothbrushes and toothpaste. On the back wall hung two flags. Sammy recognized one as the Texas flag. It matched the symbol on the map they'd found. The second flag had a large snake and read: "Don't Tread On Me."

Their lunch of crackers with canned ham and apple chips was heavenly. They loaded two large packs full of supplies, then filled the wagon to the brim. Toad looked nervous when Sammy said he wanted to take a gun, but Sammy paid him no mind. In fact, he felt a lot better having it.

"We'll spend the rest of the day looking for a boat, then come back here for the night. First thing tomorrow morning, we'll row across the lake and start hiking to Wichita."

They did just that. Toad spotted a canoe resting on sawhorses in a backyard near the corner of Oxford and Old Castle. Sammy inspected it and found only small cracks in the red paint. The oars were in bad shape, too. Finding nothing better, they portaged the canoe over to the lake's edge before it got too dark to see where they were going.

After a large dinner and another night's rest in the old house, they woke up with the sun and headed out with the packs and wagon. The weather was lousy, but they had ponchos now, so Sammy didn't mind as much when the gray clouds unleashed a steady drizzle on them as they loaded the canoe.

"Do you know anything about rowing?" he asked Toad.

"Sure, I've seen it before," was Toad's answer.

"Where?"

"In a movie."

They got the canoe into the water and Sammy told Toad where to paddle. The weather made the water choppy and steering more difficult. The lake was only about two kilometers wide where they decided to cross out. They were well out of view of anyone who might be driving across the bridge, but the going was slow. Toad dropped his paddle twice and Sammy had to fetch it before the canoe passed right by it.

About a third of the way across, Sammy noticed the canoe was taking on water.

"Is that from the rain?" Toad asked, pointing at the small puddle in the bottom of the canoe.

"Just keep paddling," Sammy told him. "We're fine."

But as he examined the canoe more closely, he realized that what he'd thought were chips in the paint were actually cracks in the canoe.

He began paddling faster. Toad wasn't able to keep the pace, which threw Sammy off. Most of the canoeing he'd done had been with his father on the lakes near Johannesburg. He knew his father's routine well.

Canoeing with Toad was much more difficult. He tried giving orders to help Toad, but it only made the process more confusing. About halfway across Lake Texoma, the canoe started to creak and squeak like a giant rat. Sammy saw that part of the wood was now leaking water steadily, and the puddle had grown much larger.

He moved the packs to a safer place and paddled with more vigor.

Come on, Sammy! You can do this.

Toad heard the noises of the packs being moved and turned to see what was happening. His eyes got big when he saw the water, and he started sniffing again.

"Are we sinking?" he asked.

"Just paddle," Sammy ordered. "Don't worry about it."

But they needed to worry. The canoe was moving slower than ever. The muscles in Sammy's arms burned. His body was out of shape, having wasted away from no exercise and little food for two months.

The northern shoreline was still about a kilometer away. Sammy encouraged Toad to paddle faster, but this only made Toad nervous, causing him to drop the oar again.

"Come on, Toad!" Sammy shouted. "I need you to do better than this."

He reached for the oar as it came within his range, but the wood was now quite wet. When his fingers touched the oar, they slipped off. He swore loudly as he watched the paddle float away. He considered braking and circling back, but they simply didn't have time to do that. The water was coming in too fast.

"Can you swim?" he asked Toad.

"Yeah, can you?" Toad sniffed several times in rapid succession.

"We aren't going to get anywhere in this piece of junk. Grab your pack and swim to shore. Take off your poncho first."

They took off their ponchos and left them in the canoe, which now held about ten centimeters of water with more flowing in. Sammy jumped first.

About ten seconds later, Toad joined him. Sammy treaded water as he watched for Toad to resurface. The canoe began to sink. Sammy shook his head as he thought of the wagon still inside with everything they'd stacked on it. Then the canoe went down.

It's not fair. What's the point in letting us find all that food?

Toad made his way over to him doing a bad impression of the side stroke. "I can't swim with this pack," he gasped, spraying water from his lips. His dark hair clung to his skin, covering his eyes. "It's so heavy."

Sammy turned and began to swim to the north shore. "You're not eating any food out of my pack if you let yours go."

The swim was exhausting. His arms and legs ached with fatigue. Toad was far behind him now, barely keeping his head above water. They hadn't made much progress, maybe another quarter of a kilometer. As much as Sammy didn't want to admit it, the pack was killing him, like trying to swim with a rock strapped to his back.

He turned back to meet Toad halfway. Toad's breaths came in desperate gasps. Sammy helped him get the pack off. For about two seconds he considered swimming with both packs, but as soon as the weight hit him, he realized what had to be done. He let Toad's pack go, allowing it to sink to the bottom of the lake. The rest of the swim passed slowly. Every stroke sapped the last bits of his strength. Toad swam behind him doing a lazy breaststroke. The pack on Sammy's back grew heavier until he felt like Atlas with the whole world on his shoulders.

Just a little farther, he kept telling himself. *Just a little farther.*

Then, forty meters from shore, Sammy's body gave out, and he dropped like a rock. The only thing that saved him was his height.

His feet touched the bottom while his nose stayed above water. A sigh of relief escaped his entire body. The rush of adrenaline that flooded his body in the wake of having been moments away from drowning allowed him to push on to the shore. There, he fell down to the beach and closed his eyes. The sounds of a wet and tired Toad dragging his feet through the sand came from behind.

"I can't go on anymore today," Sammy said.

He didn't care that it wasn't even noon yet; he needed rest. When he finally felt able, he sat up and pulled the pack off his shoulders. The fatigue in his arms and hands made them quake as he tried to pull open the zipper. Everything inside was wet. He dumped the contents onto the ground. Three large cans of peaches—still edible. Two cans of mandarin oranges—also good. An almost full bag of apple chips—all mush. A large sealed bag of rolled oats—saved. Matches—all but ruined. Toilet paper—now pulp. Toothbrushes. Toothpaste. Floss. Hand sanitizer. A flashlight—probably ruined. No gun. No ammo.

Somehow, he'd switched packs with Toad. In doing so, he had left the gun and most of the food in the lake.

Sammy dropped the bag and covered his face. If he hadn't, he might've killed Toad right then. Instead of food or something useful, Toad had filled half his pack full of worthless crap. With hundreds of kilometers still to go, all they had in their possession was five cans of fruit, oats, a wet map, and oral hygiene products.

The next morning, Toad and Sammy started the long walk north to Wichita. The map dried out pretty well over the night, and was mostly legible. If his measurements were accurate, they were roughly five hundred kilometers from their destination. If they kept a good pace, they might make it in nine or ten days. However, he didn't know what the terrain would be like, and he didn't know how far they'd be able to walk on such little food.

The first few days went smoothly. Water was never difficult to find, and as long as they drank it whenever they found it, they managed all right. The food, on the other hand, was rapidly disappearing. They went through a can of fruit a day, and had some oats as well. Despite this, Sammy was almost constantly hungry, and could not stop thinking about the food he'd abandoned in the lake.

They also had occasional bumps: like Toad throwing a rock at a beehive and getting stung six times, and Toad eating green berries off a tree during lunch and vomiting twice, and Toad insisting that he climb a particular tree and then falling out of it. Had it not been for Sammy's blasts, the fall may have been deadly.

He couldn't figure out where Toad got his energy from. Unlike Sammy, Toad seemed to be in a pleasant mood more often than not and always had to be doing something while they walked. Sometimes it was chatting, sometimes it was kicking rocks or throwing them.

Toad often boasted about what great aim he had. "I can hit anything—even better than my dad," he told Sammy as they walked passed an overgrown orchard. "My dad played in the minor league for two years until he was called up to pitch for the Jaguars."

"I don't know baseball very well," Sammy said. "Who are the Jaguars?"

Toad fixed Sammy with a confused look. "They're the best team south of the Rio Grande. Okay? They won the World Series two years in a row against the Dodgers. Anyway, my dad played for them a few games, but got injured. That's when he started working as an engineer for the air rail hub in Rio."

"And you throw better than your dad?" Sammy asked.

"Yeah. Not kidding. He said I'd for sure make it to the majors some day."

Sammy stopped in his tracks. He didn't buy it. Toad was reminding him an awful lot of his old friend Chuckles, who was known for making up some ridiculous lies. They stood a few meters from an apple tree with lots of unripe apples. Scouting around, Sammy found a couple dozen walnut sized rocks. He gave half of them to Toad.

"If you can hit more apples than me, I'll give you a quarter of my oats."

Toad grinned and sniffed. "Okay."

Sammy went first, knocking down six apples with twelve shots. He felt pretty good about himself, especially since he'd gotten lucky on a couple throws. Toad took his spot on the ground and made his first throw.

An apple hit the ground.

Toad threw again with the same result. And again. And again. With just twelve throws, Toad knocked *fifteen* apples out of the tree.

17 | Queen

March 9, 2086

IN THE EMPRESS' SUITE OF THE ROYAL HOTEL in Rio de Janeiro, the Queen stood in front of her bedroom mirror, a tall looking-glass adorned in ornate gold, hand-crafted and painted by Julio Strangewall, and one of only five in the world made by his hand. It stood exactly three meters tall and two wide. The glass itself was spotless and couldn't be touched.

Mirror, mirror on the wall, who's the fairest of them all? She silently asked her reflection.

The Queen loved mirrors. They were the purest way of mocking the most powerful force in the world: time. At nearly forty-seven years of age, she looked to be about twenty-five. Her porcelain skin was flawless, bearing no moles, scars, or blemishes of any kind. Her dark, rich hair was styled to perfection. Her unnaturally white teeth were straight and perfect. Of course, she had help. Beauty had a price. She let only the best cosmeticians touch her.

As far back as she could remember she'd taken pride in her looks. Her mother had once said that even when the Queen was two and three, she'd had particular tastes in fashions. Her father had told her the story of Snow White and every night before turning out her bedroom light, he would say: "Mirror, mirror, on the wall, who's the fairest of them all?"

The Queen, just a little girl, raised her hand each night. As she got older, instead of getting mad at her for spending too much time primping before school, he would announce: "Here comes the Queen! The fairest of them all!"

He hadn't been wrong. She knew from her reflection that her looks were superior to almost anyone's. Confirming her belief, she had been endowed the regal title *Queen* three times. The first by her teasing parents at age five. Second, in high school, voted as prom queen her freshman, sophomore, and junior years. The third and final time was in the Wyoming facility by the guards and her fellow Thirteens because of her prowess. None of them matched her skill in fighting. The title was their sign of respect. And she'd earned it.

She arrived in Rio on the ninth of March. Her first order of business was to scout the house and store of Floyd Hernandes. She also kept an eye on Floyd's nephew, Fernando. After three days of careful surveillance, she'd learned two things. First, the Hernandes family was gone. Second, Fernando wasn't. She broke into the Hernandes' home and searched through records, photos, notes, anything that might tell her where they'd gone. She compiled a list of family, friends, colleagues, and neighbors who the family might know well enough to seek out for refuge.

One by one, she checked names off her list. For those she had to speak to directly, she assumed the persona of an interested buyer of Floyd's business. Every last person claimed to have no knowledge of their whereabouts. Floyd's brother, who was running the shop in his brother's absence, claimed Floyd had decided to take his family on a badly needed vacation, an absurdly transparent lie.

She dug deeper.

A breakthrough came when the Queen discovered that Karéna Hernandes had kept in contact with a college roommate for more than fifteen years. The ex-roommate now lived in Sao Paulo. Something about it felt right to the Queen. A few hours' travel away, a close but not obvious friend, somewhere they could take off to in a hurry. Someone the wife trusted.

Yes, this is the one.

She hit the house at night. It was a large single-level home in the middle of a colorful, well-designed suburban block. Alarms were on the doors and windows. *Idiots.* A portable EMP took care of those. The pulse lasted only twenty seconds, but she jimmied the door and entered in less than twelve. Wearing a gas mask, she took a small remote-controlled car out from her duffle bag and set it down in the entryway. Taped to the top of the car was a canister. She drove the car at a pace that let her walk behind it. To the trained eye, a fine spray of white mist plumed out from the back of the canister while the car rolled silently along the carpeting.

Five minutes later, she put the car away and went to work. Using night vision, she went through the house and killed anyone who wasn't a member of the Hernandes family. Nothing fancy for these folks, just a knife. Into her duffle bag, she stuffed anything of value. Once she'd made it look like a robbery/murder, she dragged the Hernandes' drugged bodies into the living room. She bound their ankles and wrists, placed duct tape over their mouths, then woke them up.

The terror in their eyes was a real treat.

"You harbored a spy," she told them, standing above their prostrated and bound forms lined up neatly like graves in a cemetery. "He told you his name was Albert. In fact, it was Samuel. He is an operative in training for the New World Government. You have information on where he was headed. You will give it to me now."

Since the day her mind had been opened, she'd learned to savor the moments when people gave her power over them. Generally, that happened in the instant they realized she could and might kill them. And since she was smart enough to know that most people never get to relish in such a delicious exchange, she never lost her hunger for it. Fear, sadness, anger—those things she saw as cheap and common. Honest, vibrant, pulsing terror—that was a precious gem of human emotion.

Right now, she saw it in the eyes of every member of the Hernandes family.

"One of you is sixteen," she stated. A glance at each of them told her who it was. The sixteen-year-old paled and began to cry. "You are very pretty—the fairest of the family."

The Queen killed her first. Mom, Dad, and kids all screamed through the duct tape.

Now she had everyone's attention. The feast was just beginning.

"Sixteen is a special age, you know," she said to them.

⑤

Sixteen-year-old Katie Carpenter had her bedroom all to herself, and she decorated it very fashionably. She had a four poster bed with transparent curtains, a wooden vanity on the opposite wall, framed posters of Buster Keaton (her favorite actor), and a closet bursting with enough clothes to satisfy any mood she might be in on any given morning.

The Carpenter family wasn't rich, but with only one child, the parents could certainly dote and spoil.

It was a Friday morning in October of 2056. The bright fall sun shined brightly through her windows, illuminating her room and spilling several bright rainbows onto her west wall with the aid of the prisms hanging in front of the glass panes. The room looked the same, smelled the same, and the voices and movement of her parents hustling and bustling about sounded exactly the same as any other day before school. But Katie did not feel the same.

This new feeling seemed to have been sparked by the dreams she'd been having lately. Like, in last night's vision, the one still fresh in her memory, she had beaten her school teacher to death with a wooden ruler while her ex-boyfriend watched. Then she turned on him.

It was just one version of the same theme. For the last few weeks, blood, violence, and overwhelming pleasure had ruled her dreams in an unprecedented manner, more recently spilling over into her daydreams. At first she had been disturbed by them. She'd even considered going to her parents, but she didn't want them to think their "queen" was a freak. Besides, they were just dreams. And as she began to comprehend the endowment of power the dreams offered her, her self-disgust eroded.

Today the transformation was complete. What exactly that meant, she wasn't sure. *Liberated.* She tried the word on for size. *Is that what I feel?* She rose from bed and sat on the chair at her vanity, inspecting herself with a scrutinizing eye.

"Katie!" her mother called from the kitchen. "Get ready for school or you'll miss first period again!"

"Come on, Queen," her father added. "Listen to your mom."

But Katie stayed at her mirror, grinning with a bigger smile than she'd ever had before. She reveled in new sensations and ideas that blossomed like sunflowers in her mind.

I'm free.

She basked in some unknown sense of joy. Why should she have to get up? Why should she do what they asked? *Not now and not anymore.*

"I'm free," she whispered as she got back into bed. "Shut up, Mom and Dad. I'm free!"

"What was that, Queen?" her dad called from below. "I couldn't hear."

Her smile grew a little more. "Don't make me repeat myself."

Fifteen minutes later, her mother's voice repeated her call with more fervor.

Now Katie was annoyed. Her mother's infringement upon her newfound sense of liberty needed to be addressed. She had a choice to make. Give in to the fantasies in her head or not?

Throwing back her covers in a huff, she climbed out of bed, still in her underwear, and marched downstairs. The images and emotions from her dream still hadn't faded, blurring her sense of reality and imagination.

In the dining room, her father had his back to her. He held his favorite coffee mug with a Greek symbol for pi. Her mother flitted between the stove and the fridge, preparing Katie a hasty breakfast.

Katie saw the knife sitting on the counter next to a cantaloupe wobbling precariously close to the edge. As she picked it up, her mother turned and shrieked at the sight of Katie in her underwear, holding the knife. With the blade clutched in her fist, Katie rushed at her mother and stabbed her twice. The sense of freedom flooded her entire being, transfiguring her into something else—something greater.

Her father howled at her as he jumped up from his seat and yanked back Katie's arm.

"What have you done?" he screamed.

Katie's mom slumped to the floor with two red stains spreading on her blouse. A wheezing sound escaped her lips just before died.

Her father tried to pry the knife out of Katie's hand. When his efforts to get the weapon from his daughter proved vain, he landed a blow to the back of her head. Katie hardly felt it and answered his punch with a kick to his groin. As he doubled over, he looked at his daughter with a grimace that expressed more than physical pain. Tears and confusion were on his face.

Katie stared back with withdrawn interest. No sooner had he bent over in front of her and exposed his back, she put the knife into it.

"Queen . . ." he grumbled and joined his wife on the linoleum tile of the kitchen.

Satisfied, she went about making more of her dreams a reality.

When she happened to glance at the clock much later, she realized she was already over an hour late for school. She showered and dressed, deciding during that time to take her dad's car to school. Despite having her license, she'd always been too scared to drive on the roads. That wasn't a problem anymore.

Never in her life had freedom been so tangible. It made her giddy. But she still had to go to school. An absence would be noticed. Her parents would be contacted. If they didn't answer, consequences would follow. School wanted to take her freedom away.

Today's my last day of school. I should make it fun.

Her father had thought of himself as a handyman, and kept many tools in the garage. Katie emptied her backpack and filled it with the most interesting tools and hopped in the car.

School kept her very busy. Unfortunately, the police caught her setting fire to the building and put it out before the flames really got going. It was her own fault. She'd wasted too much time killing girls in the bathrooms.

⑨

"You shouldn't have taken in that boy." She addressed the Hernandes family like a lecturer. "He was a very bad boy. And I have to find him."

Mrs. Hernandes' eyes darted back and forth between the Queen, her husband, and her dead daughter. Tears leaked steadily from her eyes.

The children don't know, the Queen thought. From there she realized the order she needed to kill the rest. Mr. Hernandes was keeping his wife from spilling the information. So he died next. Mrs. Hernandes began to howl.

"You know where that young man was headed," the Queen said. "How many children do you want to have left when you wake up from this nightmare?"

She killed another daughter next. Mrs. Hernandes closed her eyes and screamed.

"Topeka!"

Thirty minutes later, the Queen stood in the master bathroom washing herself of the Hernandes' blood. The terror had been a plentiful meal for her ego.

- 237 -

That reminds me . . . She dug into her bag and removed her com.

"Call Diego," she stated into it. When the familiar voice answered the call, she spoke quickly and clearly, "Send a cleaning crew to my coordinates. Multiple bodies, very messy. Better be a good crew."

"You get what you needed?" Diego asked.

"Yes. He's going north. Deploy the night drones for initial sweeps between Dallas and Topeka. I don't want him to know we're watching. Meanwhile, see what satellites are available over the next few days. We'll use those, too."

She stowed the com and went back to the mirror. The blood spots on her face were gone. She took three bottles of cream from her bag and applied them to her skin. As she gently rubbed them in, she daydreamed about what she might be able to do when she caught little Sammy.

She detested being told to bring someone in unharmed, but sometimes her orders were just that.

Not this time.

No, she could do all kinds of fun things to him. Though she'd already had time to think it over, her ideas kept changing. This would be an important kill. *Maybe something similar to what I did to my parents?* Her tinkering had been rudimentary and unpolished. Her skills had grown since then.

She relished the anxiety. The cocktail of emotions made the hunt joyous. Would she catch the boy? Yes. No prey had eluded her yet. She was the Queen, the Eve, the first Thirteen. Most of the Thirteens revered her for that fact alone.

But why Topeka? The question lingered. *Is something else going on that the fox doesn't know about?* The thought bothered her. Not much went on in the world that the fox wasn't aware of. She left the house and started the drive back to Rio where she'd be picked up and taken to Topeka. During the six hour drive, her thoughts dwelled on the situation in which she'd been placed. Years in the Wyoming prison had taught her much, like how to focus her mind to think more clearly.

Something isn't right. As someone who'd been involved in almost every CAG-NWG battle since the prison break, she knew the strengths of the Fourteens. She knew how to beat them. An entire cell of Brothers and Aegis should be able to handle a platoon of kids.

Either the Rio cell had completely botched the job or she was dealing with something particularly dangerous. She'd visited several interrogation centers in Brotherhood strongholds. They were secure, usually deep underground or underwater. *A single kid couldn't escape that, could he?* Would having Anomaly Eleven make that much difference?

Perhaps a true savant, a rare wunderkind that comes along only once a generation. The fox wanted all the anomalies handled in some way or another. For most Elevens, and all Fifteens and Fourteens, they had to be extracted. For Thirteens, collected and trained. But for the Fourteen named Sammy, the fox was very, very direct: his DNA had to be utterly destroyed.

She would find him. It was only a matter of time.

18 | North

SAMMY AND TOAD SLEPT OUTSIDE each night, taking what little shelter they could find in the wild. The days ranged from cool to mild, and the nights were always cold. Most mornings Toad woke up hysterical from dreams of his parents dying. Once he realized where he was, he could calm down, but it unnerved Sammy to see someone so near his own age lose all mental stability in his sleep.

As much as Sammy wanted to empathize, he could only watch Toad as a cold observer with a faint memory of a similar experience. When he heard Toad quietly crying out in the night, his brain told him he should be weeping, too, but his eyes were as dry as the dust on his hands, and his heart felt nothing for his travel companion.

During the days of walking, they talked for hours at a time. It helped Sammy come to think of Toad less as a burden and more as a friend. He opened up to Toad and told him about his family, his friends, his abilities, but never about headquarters, the mission to Rio, or about what Stripe had done to him.

Talking about himself to Toad made Sammy aware of another strange thing going on inside his head. When he recounted some of his memories, he'd sometimes reach a point where part had been rubbed away leaving a white spot—a block. Whenever this happened a sensation of total helplessness hit him, and when the moment passed, he was left feeling despair like he had in the building with Stripe. The depression would last for a few hours, during which time he had no desire to talk or listen to Toad.

One time, in the middle of the night, Toad tried to wake Sammy up because he was yelling in his sleep about crocodiles. Still in a sleepy haze, Sammy thought Toad was a Thirteen sneaking up to kill him. He reacted by seizing Toad around the throat, and throwing him to the ground. Just when he was about to bash Toad's skull into pieces with a rock, he recognized the face and remembered Toad was his friend.

Toad never woke him up after that.

On their fifth day past Lake Texoma, they came to another ghost town: Stillwater. This one was much bigger than Cedar Mills, but just as cleaned out. Their provisions were all but exhausted. They had only a handful of oats remaining, and the last of the canned foods had been eaten yesterday.

Knowing they couldn't go five or six more days with a handful of oats, they were forced to spend a day searching the town for food. As they explored a neighborhood of homes, Sammy finally convinced Toad to tell him how he'd been caught by the Aegis.

"I already told you my dad works at the hub. Every year his work pays for all the kids of employees to go to this summer camp. I go so I can hang out with my best friend, Braden Barreiro. His dad is the chief engineer."

"I don't suppose they taught you canoeing at the camp?" Sammy asked darkly as he closed another set of empty cupboards in a desolate kitchen.

Toad glared at Sammy, then followed the look with a long sniff. "No. There's a pool, but no lake. We do archery, obstacle courses, sports . . . all those things. If you're on the yearly program like me, they keep track of all your progress so you can see if you're getting better."

"Wow," Sammy replied in a dry voice. "Just skip to the part where you used a blast. I've heard about two dozen of these kinds of stories."

"What do you mean?" Toad asked. "Blasts are what you do, right?"

Sammy nodded.

"I've never done anything like that."

"Then how'd they get you? How'd they even know you were a—" Sammy almost said a Psion, but he stopped himself. "What'd you do?"

"I was getting to that part!" Toad exclaimed as he slammed a pantry door shut. "It was my stats, I think."

Sammy wore a confused expression, but waited for Toad to continue.

"I killed everyone's record in archery. I mean it wasn't even close. I beat everyone but the oldest kids at the obstacle courses and races, too. Someone must have noticed that I did something unnatural, so they called the Safety Agents. When they came for me, Braden tried to stop them. They shoved him down so hard his head was bleeding. I don't even know if he's okay."

"You never shot energy out of your hands or feet?"

Toad shook his head.

Then it dawned on Sammy. "Holy crap! You're an Ultra!"

"What?" Toad asked as he sniffed.

"You're an Ultra! Anomaly Fifteens are Ultras. I learned about your anomaly in my training. Ultra-kinesis, they call it. See, I can shoot energy out because I have Anomaly Fourteen. You have Fifteen." Sammy wracked his brain for more information about the anomaly, but he could only remember bits and pieces. "Did you have trouble concentrating when you were in school?"

Toad nodded. "When I was younger they said I was hyperactive. A doctor wanted to put me on meds but my dad said no way."

Sammy pointed at Toad excitedly. "That's one of the earliest signs, if I remember it right, because your body processes more energy from food than the average person. It gets better—"

"As I get older?" Toad finished. "I don't have that problem as much anymore. My mom's really glad about it, too. Especially when we'd go to mass. Sometimes I just couldn't sit still no matter how hard I tried."

"This house is empty." Sammy jerked his thumb to the door. "Let's go to the next." They crossed the lawn and checked the door. Locked. They broke the window and went inside. As they searched, Sammy tried to recall more information about Anomaly Fifteen. "So you say you're fast, huh?"

"Yep. I ran the hundred meter dash in nine point nine seconds."

Sammy swore quietly. That was a pretty darn fast time, amazing for someone Toad's age. "Where were your parents? Were they there, too?"

"No, they weren't at the camp. My little sister was—"

"You have a sister?" Sammy asked, embarrassed he hadn't already known that.

"Two," Toad answered. "Both younger. I already told you that, remember?"

"I'm sorry. I guess I forgot."

They went through the next kitchen in an awkward silence. Sammy recognized the feeling of depression coming on whenever a hole in his memory appeared. He tried to fight it by keeping the conversation going. "Why would someone get you in trouble? It was a camp for kids. I mean, I know the signs: *KEEP THE PEACE! CALL IT IN!* But that doesn't mean people have to do it."

"Don't you know?" Toad gave a loud sniff as he looked over at Sammy skeptically. "About Safe Homes and Schools?"

"What's that?"

"Okay, where did you grow up? The moon? It's for terrorists—a law to catch terrorists, but I guess it's for people like me, too."

Sammy shook his head. He still hadn't told Toad about his NWG citizenship. "Why would anyone call it in, though?"

"They advertise it on TV," Toad said. His look of skepticism had changed to sheer disbelief. "You can get a reward if it leads to catching a terrorist."

"Really?"

"Haven't you heard it?" Then he started singing a little tune that sounded as if it were written for kids: "*If you see something strange, or something you can't explain—You gotta be safe—oh yes, you gotta be safe! So call Safe Homes and Schools . . . they'll protect your home in a hurry, so you don't have to worry!* Okay, are you serious? You haven't heard that? The signs are just the newest

- 244 -

thing. They're a year old, maybe a little longer. My mom says they're an eyesore."

Something on the top shelf of the cabinet next to the old stove caught Sammy's eye. He reached up and grabbed it. "Check this out!"

He tossed Toad a sealed pack of spaghetti noodles.

"Can we eat these?" Toad asked.

"You don't have to, but I will."

Unfortunately, the bag of noodles turned out to be the only thing they found in their search. Sammy figured they couldn't afford to spend another day in one place, so they took shelter in a different house that night. Sammy thought about using one of their three good matches to light a fire, but decided against it.

The journey turned less pleasant after Stillwater. The temperature dropped again and frost stayed on the ground each morning for three or four hours past sunrise. The oats were gone, and if they were to make the noodles last until Wichita, all they could eat was a few noodles apiece each meal. Being constantly cold and hungry put Sammy into a foul mood. Toad, on the other hand, seemed much less affected.

They would talk for a few minutes, then walk in silence for much longer after one of them said something that brought back too many memories for the other. On the second day out of Stillwater, Toad reached his limit with Sammy's depression. Without warning, he sat down on the ground and folded his arms. "Okay, I'm not going any farther until you tell me who you are. There's no way you haven't heard that stupid song on TV! Everyone I know makes fun of it."

"Fine." Sammy looked at Toad with a large measure of indifference. "Good luck." He took a few noodles out of the pack, set them on Toad's lap, and walked away.

"Wait!" Toad called out, sniffing rapidly. "You're not going to just leave."

"Watch me." And Sammy meant it.

Panting and huffing, Toad came jogging up from behind. "I wish—you would tell me—why you're so—"

Sammy had only to look at Toad to cut him off.

"You fight like . . . a ninja, but you don't know anything about what's going on around here! And you don't talk like—like a normal kid."

When Sammy said nothing, Toad kept going.

"And you almost killed me outside that building when we got out. Remember?" Toad paused and stared at Sammy's face from the side. Sammy could almost hear the wheels turning in Toad's small brain. "Did they hurt you?"

"YES!" Sammy screamed so loudly and suddenly that Toad fell back to his butt. He got up quickly and brushed himself off. Sammy wanted to run at Toad, knock him back to the ground, and beat him senseless for asking such a question. Instead he asked, "Didn't they hurt you?"

Toad turned pale and shook his head. Then he whispered something very quietly, but Sammy still heard it. It was laced with anguish. "They already knew who I was. And I told them what they wanted."

"Then it's a good thing you got out when you did," Sammy continued, "because you would have been dead real soon!" He allowed himself to breathe and felt his anger drop, along with his volume.

"I know," Toad mumbled, "but I wish you'd trust me."

Sammy snorted, not because of Toad, but because he suddenly remembered Brickert saying almost the exact same words about trust several months ago. Perhaps he hadn't fully learned his lesson.

He sat down on the ground and looked up at Toad with open arms. "What do you want to know?"

Toad seemed wary about Sammy's sudden willingness to talk.

"I'm not joking," Sammy said. "What do you want to know?"

Toad pointed to Sammy's hands with interest. "How do you know how to use those—those things you can do?"

Sammy answered in a very plain tone, "I'm a Psion, a soldier training for the NWG. I was accidentally left behind on a surveillance mission in Rio by my team."

Toad stared at Sammy, his expression slowly souring. "Okay. If you're not going to be serious, then let's just keep going."

It took time, but Sammy convinced Toad he was telling the truth. After demonstrating more blasts and some basic maneuvers, Toad became fascinated with Sammy's abilities.

"Can you teach me how to use my anomaly?" he asked.

Sammy told Toad he couldn't. "I don't know much about it."

"I'm sure the principles are the same, right?"

Sammy just shrugged. "Like I said, I don't know."

"Well, that's terrific! How am I supposed to learn to defend myself if you can't teach me?" Toad picked up a rock and expertly threw it at the tip of Sammy's shoe.

The rock didn't hurt Sammy, but a deep and sudden urge for violence flooded his body. It rose up from that darker half of him that had been born of Stripe's cruelty. He forced himself to think of something—anything to get his mind off it. He thought back to Byron's earliest sim instructions and recited them over and over until he calmed down.

What's wrong with me? He asked himself once he was under control. *Why do I feel like this?*

Toad seemed to realize that he'd gone too far and immediately apologized.

Cold winds swept across the flat plains and deserted farmlands of Mid-American Territory, dropping the temperature even at noon to cool levels. Sleep was difficult during the windy night. They walked long after dusk, following the North Star shining brilliant and high in the cloudless twilight, trudging along until their legs nearly gave out in exhaustion. Only then were their bodies so tired that even the cold could not keep them awake.

Sammy's faith, meanwhile, was stronger than ever. It had to be. If ever he had a chance of getting home, it was in Wichita. He just knew it. Deep down, he felt a resonating assurance that the resistance would be waiting there. The fantasy of getting home became sweeter the hungrier he grew. He couldn't perfectly remember his friends' faces anymore without glimpses of Stripe poking in, but he wasn't worried. Home was happiness.

By the start of the third day from Stillwater, Sammy knew they weren't going to make it to Wichita. Their precious bag of spaghetti noodles was diminishing faster than he'd expected. Sammy blamed Toad. Twice he'd caught Toad sneaking extra noodles. Not a lot, but it didn't matter. It really pissed him off, and all Toad had to say about it was that he couldn't stand the hunger any more. But Sammy couldn't complain. He'd sneaked extra noodles, too.

It was impossible to keep his mind off food. His energy was low. His stomach never seemed to stop growling, even after his small portion of noodles. The temperatures dropped even further as they walked farther north. It didn't help that the only thing Toad wanted to talk about was the amazing Robochef at headquarters. Sammy wished he'd never mentioned it.

He kept track of how far north they were based on the highways they crossed. He knew the farther they kept away from I-35, the better off they were, and the less chance they'd come across unfriendly eyes.

That night, Toad spotted a house alongside the highway. The back wall had been torn off, probably by a tornado, exposing almost the entire interior. He pleaded with Sammy through trembling lips that it was as good a shelter as any they'd find. Sammy was compelled to agree. They hiked over to the house and found the least drafty spot to sleep.

"Can we start a fire?" Toad asked through trembling teeth and a loud sniff. "Please? We still have two matches left."

Sammy was too tired and cold to argue. The condemned house had a fireplace, and the boys shoved anything they could find that would burn inside of it. The kindling caught well, and soon they had a crackling fire.

"If someone is following us, this might make it easier to find us," Sammy muttered to Toad as he put his hands and feet close to the flames. "But you know what? I don't even care right now. I'm warm."

They munched on a few noodles while Toad told camping stories. When they'd settled down and brushed their teeth (Sammy saw no need for their supplies to go to waste), Toad quickly fell asleep. Sammy, however, did not. His mind was elsewhere.

Wichita is so close . . . Just a few more days.

With this musing came daydreams of his friends at headquarters. His heart longed to laugh with them again. His stomach ached to eat real food again. His body yearned to sleep in a real bed again. *And a shower would be great too.*

He chuckled silently to himself—an old man's laugh—about the first time he had taken a shower at headquarters. He remembered something funny had happened then, but couldn't remember exactly what.

His thoughts were interrupted by a soft rustling noise coming from the damaged section of the house. It was so faint that he thought he'd imagined it. Then he heard it again.

"Hello?" he called out in a subdued tone. Toad stirred nearby, but Sammy heard no other sounds.

In his weary, lazy state, Sammy wanted to pass the event off as just some rubbish blowing in the wind. He lay on the floor, comfortable for the first time in a long while, wondering if he should investigate the noises.

Just when he decided he didn't need to, footsteps crunched some debris across the room, alerting Sammy instantly. His movement roused Toad, who sat up like a jack-in-the-box released from its prison.

"Butterscotch!"

A gun went off in the darkness, but the bullet struck somewhere unseen. Sammy moved into a crouching position, using both hands to shield himself.

"Get behind me!" he told Toad.

The crunching steps came closer until Sammy could see puffs of breath briefly warming the air far across the room.

"Stop where you are!" Toad cried out with plenty of fear in his voice. "Okay? You don't know what you're doing. My friend here is deadly . . . and—and pretty crazy. Okay? It'd be best if you just turned around and left us alone."

Into the firelight came a grizzled man dressed in a worn button-up shirt and patched jeans. His boots showed parts of his socks. He wore finger-less gloves, and both hands were clutched tightly around a small pistol. Sammy had already decided to kill him. The darker half born of Stripe was firmly in control.

He stood up and walked toward the man.

"Hold it right there now, boy!" The man's voice wavered as he took a tenuous step backward. "I didn't mean to fire a shot earlier. Wasn't trying to hurt no one . . . I'm just looking to see if you have anything valuable."

"Put the gun down or you're going to get killed!" Toad screamed.

Sammy had one hand outstretched, generating a blast shield protecting him from any gunshots.

"I'm serious!" Toad said. He got to his feet and moved toward Sammy, but Sammy sensed this and gently blasted Toad back to the floor with his other hand. "Listen to me! Sammy, don't kill him!"

"Stop there, kid," the grizzled man warned. He cocked the hammer back and licked his beard-covered lips. "I ain't messing around. Like I said, I just come to see if you have anything of worth. I got grandkids who need to eat. Can't grow everything in a garden."

Sammy ignored all this and kept walking toward the man who now appeared quite uncertain of his position of power. The man cursed and lowered his gun, but Sammy didn't care. He meant to kill. Toad was yelling at him. The shabby-looking thief was now retreating like a cowardly dog. Sammy only had to decide if he should use blasts to incapacitate or just use his bare hands . . .

Just then something struck him in the back of the head. He turned and saw a small block of spare wood rolling along the floor. Toad raised another block, waiting for Sammy's next move. Sammy turned back but the thief had fled. He glared at Toad, who glared right back.

They tried to sleep, but Sammy's rest was fitful at best. Anytime he closed his eyes, he saw Stripe and creams and spinning lights. Then he had to fight down the urge to track down the thief and kill him slowly. On top of all that, a dull ache emanated from his stomach.

The sun had barely risen when they decided to push on. Sammy spent several minutes watching out the windows to make sure no one was waiting around the house. The early hours of the morning were quiet and still. The only sounds came from their own feet and Toad's occasional sniffs. When they climbed out of the house and hit the ground, Toad noticed a little picnic basket in the grass.

Sammy was certain it hadn't been there the night before. Cautiously, they approached it. Sammy used a well-aimed blast to open the lid. Inside was four slices of bread, a small square of cheese, an apple, and a plastic bag containing two strips of dried meat—about enough food for one modest meal. Taped to the underside of the basket lid was a note.

I am sorry.

"See?" Toad said with a giant grin. "When you don't kill people, God helps you."

They ate half the food right away. Toad compared it to manna from heaven.

Using the map as his guide, Sammy steered their route away from the highways, away from the ghost towns, away from any more delays. *Wichita.* All that mattered now was Wichita. The Thirteens wouldn't matter there. The hunger wouldn't matter, either. He just had to get to Wichita. The small meal and the thought of Wichita kept his mind off his stomach for most of the day, but as night fell, the hunger set in again—and set in deep.

After an hour or so, it went away, only to return again more vicious and demanding. Fatigue hit him hard that night. After munching on a few noodles, he fell asleep in a ditch covered up by an old curtain.

He woke feeling sicker than he'd ever felt. He was sure someone had come along in the night and scraped out his midsection with a spoon because the word hunger now had a new meaning. It was also the first thing Toad mentioned when Sammy shook him awake. As they munched the last of their noodles for breakfast, Toad went on and on talking about how much he wanted to eat the rest of the food in the picnic basket.

Sammy cut him off. "Did you hear me take off in the middle of the night to hunt for food? It's all we have left. We can't eat it yet."

Their pace slowed. Sammy just didn't have the energy to push it. By noon, they had to stop and take a long break. They each got a slice of dry bread to eat.

Sammy stared at the map blankly, thinking only about how much farther they had to go to Wichita.

"You know anything about wild plants we can eat?" he asked Toad.

"I know we can eat wild pizza," Toad said dryly. He stared until Sammy got the joke.

All they could muster was a weak chuckle.

Fresh water from a stream helped revived them a little, but the day went on slowly. Twice, Toad asked if they could stop again, but Sammy forced them onward. His mind had reverted to daydreaming for comfort.

Wichita. The resistance. Returning home to headquarters in glory.

The only part of him grounded in reality was his feet. That was why Toad noticed the freeway first.

"Look!" His shouted tore Sammy's mind away from Capitol Island and onto a six-lane road running north to south.

After fumbling with the map, Sammy saw where they were headed. "That's I-35. If we follow it, we'll head straight into Wichita."

Thirty meters up the road was a sign. From their vantage point, Sammy could just barely read it: Wichita 89 km/55 miles

That's about two days' walk, Sammy told himself. *We can do that. If we keep finding water, we can do that.*

So the journeyers stumbled on, slowly going through the last of the food. Toad and Sammy often had to encourage each other with kind or stern words, other times with a hand literally pushing on the other's back. Although he'd never admit it, Sammy realized what a blessing Toad had become.

"You're the one who's supposed to have all this extra energy," Sammy complained to his friend. "How can you be tired?"

"I'm not a solar panel!" Toad retorted.

They stayed less than a kilometer east of the freeway not wanting to be seen by any passing cars or trucks. Sammy thanked whatever higher powers controlled the weather for a warmer night as they curled up in the grass and slept soundly.

His legs felt like two thick logs when he woke. His head buzzed like a thunder cloud had been shoved inside his ears. They stopped at a stream for water three times, just so their stomachs would feel full. Pacing themselves as best they could, they finally came to the outskirting neighborhoods of Wichita in the early evening. After passing several streets, Sammy stopped.

They were on the corner of a little shopping center. A gas station with a repair garage stood on one corner and a coffee shop on another. Across the way was a five-store strip mall painted in a ghastly pink.

Empty suburbs, no cars, no electricity anywhere . . .

Wichita was a ghost city.

Panic and depression filled Sammy's mind. *How can the resistance be operating in a ghost city? With no power or running water or anything?*

Dark thoughts of failure welled up in his mind. His eyes stung as tears began to form.

"So how do we find Sedgwick C. or Plainpal?" Toad asked, cutting through the fog in Sammy's head.

Sammy held his stomach. He was weak. Tired. Helpless. "I don't know." His voice sounded like a drone. "I don't know. I don't know. I don't know."

"Don't you even know what this Plainpal is? I thought you at least had a clue!"

"It was the best thing I had to go with!" Sammy shouted.

"You walked all the way up here not even knowing what the heck for?" Toad yelled right back.

Sammy would have snapped right then. He would have given into the darkness inside him and done who knew what damage and hurt to Toad, but his energy tank was empty. No fumes. No spare liter in the back. Bone-dry empty. He collapsed onto the sidewalk, hitting his knees, then his hands.

His chest heaved as he breathed.

"Are you okay?" Toad asked.

With great effort, he spoke. "We should try and find . . . a tourist office."

Toad sniffed and sat down. "Why a tourist office?"

"Because whatever a Plainpal is, I'm sure not every city has one."

Toad stared at Sammy like he was the world's dumbest person.

"What?" Sammy asked.

"There's one across the street," he said gesturing to the closest pink store with a large glass window. Painted in large letters at the very top: "VISIT WICHITA!"

"Huh."

After a feeble attempt at forcing the lock on the shop, Sammy blasted the window apart. He felt even more drained after doing it. *If I don't get food soon . . .*

"I still think that's wicked cool," Toad said with a particularly loud sniff. They grabbed all the brochures they could find of the city and left. Neither of them wanted to stay in a building they had broken into, even if the city was deserted.

Using the last of the sunlight, they spread the advertisements out around on the sidewalk and searched them. There were dozens of brochures for museums, restaurants, parks, but mostly literature about airplanes.

"Okay, I had no idea Wichita was the Air Capitol of the World, did you?" Toad asked.

More brochures. Night clubs, sports teams, more museums.

Sammy swore as he threw down another brochure. "Who cares about all these stupid museums?"

Toad picked it up curiously.

"Plainpal . . . Plain pal . . ." Sammy grumbled over and over again, looking at his tenth pamphlet. "You gotta be kidding me. It's not in this one, either."

"You'd think it'd be a little more prominent if someone made a specific reference to it. Wait a min—" He stopped short and stared hard at the pamphlet that Sammy had chucked.

"What?" Sammy asked, "Did you—?"

Toad put a finger up to silence him, and sniffed several times in a row. Sammy waited in silence until Toad showed him the pamphlet with his finger pointing at something. "Palace of the Plains," he announced proudly.

A huge smile broke out across Sammy's face, and a feeling of peace came over him. "Downtown. It's downtown. We have to check it out."

Downtown was, in fact, over two hours away. Not wanting to call attention to where they'd been, they put the pamphlets back in the store and grabbed a city map. The sun disappeared as they headed for the historical district of Wichita where the Wichita-Sedgwick County Historical Museum sat, also known as the Palace of the Plains. The giddiness gave him energy for about two kilometers, but soon enough, every step took effort. His legs tingled and his shoes skimmed the pavement of the sidewalks as he moved. Toad seemed to notice this because he stayed abnormally close to Sammy, probably to catch him in case he fell. Several times Sammy felt his head get light and fuzzy, but he forced the faintness away.

Finally there it was. The Plainpal.

Sammy had lost track of days and time, but he'd wandered through a good chunk of a continent to get here. The Plainpal. He had made it. Tears leaked down his cheeks from happiness and exhaustion.

It looked like a castle, still in excellent condition. In the pale hours of early night with a big half moon shining down on them, they saw the tall stone building standing proudly. Its four corners reached skyward in symmetrical cone-topped towers. In the center of the roof, pointing high above the four towers was a single clock tower. A blend of doubt and hope swirled as he led Toad to the building.

From across the street Sammy heard a grumble and instinctively readied himself for battle. Toad turned, too.

A middle-aged man lay slumped in the doorway of a tall white office building across the street. His clothes were rags, and he had a large frayed red hat pulled over his face. His right hand rested on his chest, while his left clutched an empty bottle. He mumbled something again, smacked his lips, and fell silent.

Sammy and Toad exchanged a wary look. The homeless man was the first person either of them had seen since the thief. If there was anywhere the Thirteens would post a guard, it would be outside an old resistance center. A surge of pain throbbed up Sammy's leg as memories of Stripe intruded on his thoughts. He fought the urge to glance down and see the crocodile mauling his leg.

"What should we do?" Toad whispered.

Sammy shrugged. He was now very used to nothing coming to his brain when asked these kinds of questions. He didn't like it, but he hated being frustrated as he waited for something that simply wasn't coming. Combined with his state of exhaustion, it was hard to worry about anything more. If he was to go on any longer, he needed food.

"It's too convenient that he's right there," Sammy said.

"Okay, except he's dead drunk."

"How do you know?"

"I saw my neighbor like that at our block parties. Looked exactly the same. I say ignore him."

Sammy shook his head "What if he's one of them?"

Toad sniffed, and Sammy wanted to smack him to make him stop.

"What if it's a trap?"

Toad chewed on his lips as he thought. Sammy felt himself teetering.

"You know what?" Toad stated. "It might be a trap. But you're gonna die if we don't get food."

Toad's decision made Sammy nervous. After all, wasn't Toad the impetuous one? "Just a second." Sammy tried to grab Toad's shirt and hold him back, but Toad had already moved out of range. "Let's play it safe for a minute."

"We've walked hundreds of kilometers, and now you want to play it safe. I'm starving! You're dying! If there's nothing here, we're going to die anyway." With that, Toad crossed the street to the Palace, walked right up to the main entrance, and stopped in front of the arched threshold.

Mustering the last of his energy, Sammy walked the same path and joined him at the sidewalk. He looked behind them. The drunken man stirred in his sleep, just enough to keep his face pointed toward them.

Sammy reeled again as he put his hand on Toad's shoulder. "Please . . . let's wait . . . until we've thought this through."

But Toad wouldn't hear it. He grabbed Sammy by the wrist and yanked him into the archway. Sammy turned back wearily to see the drunken man sit up sharply. Immediately he knew it was a ruse, but before he had time to react, solid metal bars sprang out of the arch and locked into the cement. The trap was sprung.

19 | Palace

March 21, 2086

THE QUEEN HAD SPENT the last few days in Topeka following various leads, including two at nearby juvenile detention centers. So far, everything had been a waste of her time. She had just begun planning to expand her searching radius when she received a call from Diego.

"I put one of our northern cells in charge of watching the drones and satellite feeds on your investigation," he told her. "They've found some things you might want to check on. I'm sending it to you now."

She accessed the data via her com, sifting through pictures and video feed.

"I see you, Sammy," she muttered as infrared from drones and satellites displayed images of two figures in the middle of the woods in Mid-American Territory. They were clearly headed north.

He's following I-35, but to where?

Perhaps he intended to walk all the way to Topeka following the freeways. She wasn't certain. But for now she had a starting point, and that was more than enough.

§ § § § §

With their last ebbs of energy, Sammy and Toad threw themselves against the thick bars, but the cage didn't budge. Fear of being tortured again exploded into Sammy's brain conquering every other thought and emotion. In a trance-like state, he held onto the bars with a vice-like grip and slammed his shoulder into them over and over again, screaming incoherently. His muscles ached and throbbed, but he paid no attention.

The bum slumped in the doorway swiftly crossed the street toward them. Both the bottle and pretense of drunkenness had been discarded. Now he carried a fully automatic pistol only partially concealed beneath his shabby coat. He aimed it at Sammy, but his eyes went back and forth between both prisoners.

At the sight of the gun, Sammy stopped attacking the bars. He didn't have the strength to blast—to stop bullets. He fell to his knees. Toad curled into a corner with his hands over his head, trembling and crying. The man came within two meters and held his weapon at the ready.

The man looked at Sammy with a calculating stare. He had a scruffy chin and neck, but clear brown eyes. No red around the pupils like the Thirteens. Judging by the lines around his face, Sammy put him at mid-forties to early fifties. He had an oval-shaped face and a crooked nose.

"Who are you?" His voice reminded Sammy of cowboys and horses.

Sammy didn't answer. Instead, he searched wearily into the depths of the man's eyes, looking for the cold, dark places that he'd seen in Stripe's.

"Who are you?" the man repeated with much more force.

Sammy gave him a piece of the truth. "My friend and I looking for some people here. Friends." His words were raspy, his throat swollen, from screaming like a caged monkey when the bars fell.

"Wichita's been deserted for over a decade."

"Apparently you live here."

The man adjusted his gun to remind Sammy it was there. "Who are you looking for?"

"*Friends* . . ." Sammy's voice came out as a weak scratch, ". . . who can help me get home." He watched the man closely to see if he understood his hints.

"Where's home?"

"I can't tell—" but Sammy's voice cut out before he could finish and he just shook his head.

The man lowered the weapon to get a better look at Sammy's face, then raised it again. As easily as any trained soldier, he flicked off the safety. "Unless you are an exceptional bullet dodger, answer my questions."

"Can't—sorry—friend."

The man fired once, just above Toad's head. Toad yelped, jumped, then sank lower. His crying changed to sobbing. Sammy swallowed hard but there was no saliva there. His throat was thick and hot. *I need a plan!* Nothing came. He'd brought himself and Toad to their deaths following a stupid notion that there might still be a resistance in Wichita, in the middle of CAG territory.

I'm a fool. A worthless fool.

The man pointed the gun at Toad, but looked at Sammy. "Tell me who you are or I'll shoot him."

"We're looking for a resistance!" Toad said in a whimper.

Sammy jerked his head toward Toad, but his friend's face was buried between his arms. "Shut up, Toad!"

"What resistance?" He pointed the gun back at Sammy.

"People—people resisting the government," Toad answered flatly.

It sounded so lame to hear it out loud.

Toad kept going. "We were taken prisoner in Rio de Janeiro by the . . ." He looked to Sammy for help remembering the names he'd been taught. "The Aegis! And he was held for weeks—me for days. But we escaped and made our way up here."

Sammy watched the man's face for any sign of malice or recognition, but he saw none.

"How did you escape and why did you come here?"

This was the question that Sammy could not let Toad answer without revealing everything. If the man was an enemy, they would be tortured for more information. Only this time, they had no chance of ever escaping. No lucky breaks. Sammy was already nearly broken. Toad cried again, looking to Sammy through squinting eyes. Sammy couldn't speak.

Toad continued to summarize their tale. "We came here because he found a map that said there was a Plainpal in Wichita that was part of the resistance. I didn't know what it meant, but I came with him anyway."

"Why?"

"Because—" Toad sniffed several times. "Because we're part of the resistance, too."

Sammy's brow broke out into sweat. Toad had done a marvelous job concealing their anomalies.

"There's something you're not telling me. But I think I'm good enough at reading people to know when I'm being lied to." He lowered his gun and crossed to the building wall nearest the bars. "We've been watching you since you came into the outskirts of the city. You make an interesting pair of characters. I wasn't sure if you were putting on a show. I thought you knew you were being watched."

He thumbed the safety on the weapon and stowed it into one of the deep pockets in his coat. A little smile appeared on his face. "Take them in."

The door to the museum opened and before Sammy had time to look around, a cloth sack was thrust over his head and he was dragged inside. Toad shrieked as the same was done to him.

Having no energy to resist, Sammy allowed himself to be carried. Another door opened, and Sammy felt himself set on a soft cushion. Several hands patted him down while someone else ran a scanner over him. He heard two beeps.

"He's clean," a voice said.

Then the door closed. Sammy grabbed the cloth and tore it off his face. Toad wasn't in the room with him.

Sammy panicked. He was alone again. He didn't want to be alone. His shoulder ached like it had been whacked with a mallet, and his throat still burned. Too tired to do anything else, he stared at the door. It took several seconds for him to notice there was no handle or knob on the inside. He yearned for food, water, and a shower.

The room was small, about the size of a small bedroom. He sat in the only chair, which was comfortable. A light shone above him, but the switch was not in the room. Other than the chair, there were no furnishings.

The door opened, and a familiar-looking man entered, shutting the door behind him. Sammy guessed the man to be in his mid-sixties. His hair was cloud white, his eyes so blue they caught Sammy's attention. He wasn't smiling, but he didn't look angry or intimidating, either. His clothes were simple: a gray and white flannel shirt and jeans. He wore leather boots, not sneakers. Sammy couldn't remember the last time he saw someone wearing cowboy boots.

"I have a man just outside the room. Don't get any ideas."

Sammy didn't respond. He didn't have the strength.

"What's your name, kid?"

The only thing that came out of Sammy's mouth was a croak. "Do I know you?" he tried to say.

"Do you know me? I don't think so, because I don't know you. And I don't forget faces easily. You gonna tell me your name?"

"Are you resistance?" Sammy asked. He found it easier to whisper as loud as he could than attempting to use his full voice.

The man stared at Sammy gravely, his lips tight and his face lined. Finally, he nodded.

Sammy fell out of his chair onto his knees. He didn't care how pathetic he looked. Nothing mattered but one thing. "Food."

The white-haired man knocked on the door. It opened and a head poked in. "Get him some refreshment."

"Like what?" the guard asked.

"Water. Crackers. Something he can easily eat."

Less than a minute later, a small plastic plate came back with crackers, cheese, apple slices, and clean, ice cold water.

Sammy reached for it, but the man shook his head. "Your name."

His eyes were fixed on the plate. His chest heaved and his mouth watered. "Uh—Albert."

"Your real name, please."

Sammy stared at the food. "Samuel Berhane."

Then the plate was in his hands. He touched the food. It was real. He put two whole crackers in his mouth and savored their saltiness. Before swallowing, he put two more crackers in, then two more.

"Slow down. You're gonna choke."

Sammy ignored this and ate again. The water helped everything go down easier. It also extinguished some of the fire in his throat. "Thank you," he remembered to say through a mouthful of cheese.

The older man smiled, then laughed. His laugh was familiar, too. "Not a worry. Do you go by Samuel or Sam or Sammy?"

Sammy nodded at the last.

"Sammy it is. My name is Thomas Byron."

A nuclear bomb went off in Sammy's stomach. His eyes got big, his hands went to his midsection, and he hurled everything back up: crackers, water, cheese and apple.

Thomas backed up to the wall, but Sammy wasn't thinking about the vomit. "Thomas Byron?" he repeated. His voice sounded only slightly better than before. "Thomas Byron?" If he had the energy he would have bounced up and hugged the man. All he could manage was a waning smile. "Walter Byron's father?"

This time it was the old man's turn to look shocked. The surprise turned to confusion, then to understanding.

Thomas supported himself on the wall and produced a white handkerchief from his back pocket. "You're from—?" his hand pointed weakly in a gesture Sammy interpreted as *over there*. "And you know my son?"

Sammy nodded his head as best he could.

"He's alive?" Thomas asked. "And well?"

"Yes."

"Oh me, oh life . . ." the old man said as he dabbed his eyes with the handkerchief. Sammy sat in the chair and watched him, wondering if he should say something. Without a word, Thomas stood, knocked on the door, and left the room, still wiping his eyes with his handkerchief.

Sammy decided to try to eat again, only this time to take it slowly. He'd hardly finished two crackers when the door opened. An older woman entered with Thomas, clutching his hand. Tears were in her eyes, too.

"Do you really know my Walter?" she asked.

Sammy nodded, torn between eating the food and talking about Commander Byron. The couple embraced.

"This is my wife, Lara." Thomas patted her on the back. "We haven't seen our boy in a very long time."

It was too much for Sammy to wrap his head around. Byron's parents? Here? But now that he thought about it, Byron was from Mid-American Territory.

"We have a lot to talk about, am I right?" Lara said. "Thomas, get him out of this room and get him cleaned up—and the other boy, too. We can do better than crackers and cheese!"

Sammy and Toad devoured a kilo of food each while the Byrons watched them with fascination and disgust. As they ate, Sammy noticed his strength returning, though his body needed sleep and time to heal. He also had the difficult task of trying to tell the couple everything he knew about their son while simultaneously putting as much food as he could fit into his mouth. Before all was said and done, they had talked for the better part of two hours.

The longer the discussion went on, the easier it was to see so much of Byron in his parents: their religious foundation, their impeccable manners and kind dispositions. Even Commander Byron's eyes were similar to Thomas'. He found himself wanting to tell them every last detail he could remember. It gave Sammy the feeling that in some small way he had reunited the family again.

He told them about the Rio mission, how he met Toad, and their journey north, but he said nothing about Stripe or the room with the black door. The Byrons asked many questions about the death of the commander's wife, but Sammy couldn't remember if he'd been told how she'd died or not.

"Shall we give them the grand tour, dear?" Thomas asked his wife, throwing his arms back in a great stretch. He was quite robust for a man in his sixties.

"Not right now." She pointed at Toad, whose face had narrowly missed the plate when he fell asleep. Sammy couldn't blame him. The only thing keeping him awake was the exhilaration of meeting the Byrons. "They just need a couple of couches to sleep on."

"Well . . . I guess the tour can wait."

Lara showed Sammy to a nearby sitting room while Thomas led a stumbling Toad behind them. Sammy remembered nothing after his head hit a pillow.

Eventually Toad's sniffing woke him up.

"What time is it?" Sammy muttered.

"I think it's morning . . . I can hear them eating breakfast."

Sammy's mind became a little clearer. "Breakfast . . . I want some of that."

"Do you think we should go in there? I mean, are we guests? We probably smell bad, too."

"I don't care. I want food."

He stood and entered the large dining area, where over two dozen adults sat around a very long wooden table. Toad followed. Lara played the part of hostess and ushered them to their seats. Several people glanced or even stared at them, but Sammy cared too much about his eggs and toast. Not long after his third helping, Thomas jovially entered the room and rested his hands on the boys' shoulders.

"'To dwell in presence of immortal youth, immortal age beside immortal youth.'"

Toad looked at Lara with a puzzled expression.

"Tennyson," was all she said.

"You boys can tell I'm excited to take you around, can't you?"

"You're going to show us the palace?" Toad asked since he had missed that part of the conversation. "And let us stay here?"

"Of course we are." Lara responded from the sink where she and a few of the men were now washing dishes. "Where else would you go? You're family now."

Sammy stole a glance at Toad and saw no objection. The notion of family seemed nice, but hopefully this "family" would help him get back home.

Lara excused herself while Thomas showed them where they could shower and change into clean clothing. Then he gave them the grand tour, more of a history lesson, in reality. The building was nearly two hundred years old, originally built as the Wichita City Hall. When the resistance took over the building, it was the Wichita-Sedgwick County Historical Museum or "Palace of the Plains." With all the adjustments the resistance had made over the years to fit the building to their needs, the Palace was much bigger than it looked, which was saying something.

From his time in the bunker in Rio, Sammy had imagined the resistance to be a broken-down, barely-surviving faction of rag-tag fighters. From Thomas' tour of the Palace, he got the sense that it was much more than that. Besides a well-run organization, they had a network of tunnels running under half of downtown Wichita, and from some of the hints Thomas kept dropping, some highly placed people in government, media, and business.

"At any given time, we're housing seventy or eighty people in the Palace. Only thirty of us live here permanently. But we could house hundreds if we had to. We've tunneled through to a hotel a block away."

"How do you feed so many people?" Toad asked. "Do you have a secret farm?"

Thomas smiled proudly. "We have enough in storage to feed five hundred people for twenty more years."

"Twenty years?" Sammy's face betrayed his shock. Even his addled brain knew what a staggering amount of food that would be. "Where is your storehouse?"

"We keep it in several adjacent buildings around a few city blocks."

"How . . .?" Sammy started to ask, but still could not fathom so much food.

"Part of it came from cleaning out ghost towns near and far. Pantries, stores—you'd be surprised how much food people left around. Some of it is just good old fashioned know-how. We also get regular shipments of new stock from our members."

"What else is here?" Toad asked.

"We have an infirmary, and above that, in the towers, we keep our surveillance equipment."

"Like what?" Sammy asked.

"We got all kinds of toys up there. Land-based transmission interceptors, long-range terrain surveillance, not enough to be terribly effective, but we get snippets of stuff. Right now we think we're onto something big."

Sammy's ears honed in on this. He wondered if it had anything to do with what he knew. "What big thing?"

Thomas looked blankly at him for a moment and then answered, "I'll tell you later. Let's look at the basement, and then you boys need to see the infirmary."

"Okay, why?" Toad asked with a glare.

Thomas smiled at Toad like he was remembering something. "Seeing as how you both have been on the lam for the last few weeks, half-starved, etcetera, etcetera, the doctor thought it would be best."

"The doctor?"

"Bryce Vogt. You met him earlier."

"That jerk who shot at me?" Toad asked.

"Cool it, Toad," Sammy muttered, but Thomas just laughed.

"Boys, let's go the basement. I think you are going to love it."

Sammy thought it strange how excited Thomas was to get them into the basement. He understood once they went downstairs. The basement was huge. Massive. So massive, in fact, that Sammy guessed it must extend far beyond the borders of the Palace walls and connect underground to several adjacent blocks to their storehouses and who knew where else. He'd need a map just to get around. One thing was certain, if members of the resistance didn't want to leave the Palace, they didn't have to.

"There is one other resistance center," Thomas said. "Not all the resistance even know where that place is. Wichita is our base of operations."

The "base of operations" was a giant cavern filled with gadgets, machines, weapons, maps, holo-projectors, blueprints, records, generators, nitro-computers, and many other things Sammy didn't have a name for.

"It looks a lot cooler than it actually is," Thomas informed them when he saw the look of wonder on Toad's face. "We have some extremely talented people working on our side. They helped us get all this stuff. When the resistance first began we were in the technological dark ages, so to speak."

"How did the resistance begin?" Sammy asked.

Thomas ran his fingers through his hair, rumpling it like a kid would. "Shoot. You really want to hear that whole story?"

"Yeah," Toad answered for both of them.

Thomas stood for a second, looking around. "Well, let's sit."

He led them to a group of desks. After gesturing for them to take their seats, he pulled a mug full of pencils toward him and grabbed one. Leaning back in the chair and twirling the pencil between his fingers, he began.

"Either of you ever hear about the Mexico City bombing? Lark Montgomery?"

"Of course," Toad said, but Sammy was pretty sure Toad had not.

The history instructions had covered Lark Montgomery in detail. He was a nut job, part of a militant reactionary group resisting the formation of the CAG. Sammy tried to remember the exact date of all those events, but couldn't.

"The lawyer assigned by the state to defend Lark Montgomery was Crestan DeFry. Does her name ring a bell for either of you?"

Sammy and Toad both signified that it didn't.

"Figures. Well, one day, mark my words, there'll be volumes written about her." To emphasize his next words, Thomas tapped his pencil on the desk. "Brilliant woman."

The seriousness in Thomas' face reminded Sammy a lot of Commander Byron.

"Anyway, back to Montgomery—everyone thought he was mad as a hatter. In court and in press conferences, he raged on and on about how he hated the CAG, how the NWG was going to take everything back with force. His trial was famous for his long rants about the CAG being an abomination before God. It scared a lot of people—me included. In those days, terrorist acts were too common. People like him were burning government buildings, sabotaging the air rails. The prosecutors were willing to cut a deal with Montgomery if he'd give information on some of these groups, like where they got their funding from, who was running them, stuff like that.

"Montgomery refused. Crestan tried and tried to convince him to cooperate, but he was adamant that he wanted the death penalty to complete his martyrdom. About two days before his sentencing, Crestan visited him in prison. She'd set her mind on persuading him to talk. What she found was a completely different Montgomery than the one she'd come to know. Instead of the uncooperative braggart, he was quiet and soft spoken—Crestan thought he even seemed scared.

"Naturally, she interpreted this as willingness to cooperate, so she pressed him on the issue, but Montgomery still wouldn't budge. In the end, he was sentenced to death—it was what he wanted—even though Crestan did everything she could to prevent it. But he stayed his mad, crazy-talking self, right until the end when he rode the electric chair to hell."

The pencil did a little dance across Thomas' fingers. Sammy was impressed with how well he could make it move. Everyone watched the pencil for a moment while Thomas chose his next words. It reminded Sammy of the commander, who often seemed to carefully pick the best word to say in a conversation.

"Even after Montgomery's execution, which happened in record-breaking speed, I might add, that day stuck with Crestan. She got to thinking that maybe there could be more to him than just a psycho. She contacted an old friend from law school. Henrico Garcia. They started looking deeper into Montgomery's association with pro-NWG groups. None of them had taken credit for the bombing. They started to wonder how Montgomery had financed his terrorism. When Crestan and Henrico confronted Montgomery's widow, things went from strange to crazy.

"She lived in the same house she'd been at before her husband got arrested. Six kids, ages ranging from two or three to thirteen, I can't remember the details. She didn't work, but the kids were all wearing decent clothes and looked fed. Where was she getting the money from? Crestan already knew Mrs. Montgomery from handling her husband's case, but the widow had refused to testify for or against her husband. He'd wanted it that way."

Sammy could tell Thomas was getting excited by the way the pencil waltzed around his fingers in a near blur. Thomas didn't seem to notice it at all.

"When Crestan and Henrico went down to Santa Fe to visit the Montgomery's, they almost weren't let inside. It took every bit of persuasion they had just to get her to open the door. Crestan told me the widow looked terrible, like she'd aged twenty years in just two. She let them in with a cigarette in hand, and smoked every moment they were there. Crestan told Mrs. Montgomery everything: her suspicions about the funding of Lark's terrorism, his breakdown before the sentencing, everything. Crestan didn't tell Mrs. Montgomery this, but she believed the NWG had somehow directly contacted Lark and used him as a lone wolf, promising him money for his family.

"Boy was she wrong! When Crestan spilled her guts to the widow, Mrs. Montgomery got up and closed all the blinds in the room. Then she sat back down right next to Crestan and Henrico so she could whisper in their ears.

"'They're watching me . . . always,' she told them. 'They must be watching you now, too. Don't come here again.'

"Crestan was skeptical and asked the widow to be more specific, but the woman just shook her head like a frightened child."

"Weird," Toad said.

"Crestan couldn't leave it alone. Their investigation focused on proving Lark had been funded by NWG operatives, but the deeper they went the more they learned about Lark's past. When Lark Montgomery had attended the University of Utah, he had a roommate named Jeffrey Markorian, a strange man well-placed in the Continental Security Department. Flight manifests placed Markorian in Santa Fe six months, three months, and one month before the bombing in Mexico City. He also visited Montgomery in prison the day before Crestan had noticed that strange, reserved behavior."

"Did they go public with their knowledge?" Sammy asked.

"They never had a person to pin it on. Coincidental evidence only, but no traces of money. How Mrs. Montgomery was feeding and clothing her family, Crestan never found out. Nine months after they visited the widow, Henrico's house blew sky high with most of his family in it. Gas leak, they called it. Always a gas leak. Henrico would have been in there, too, except he'd gone outside to feed the dog with his oldest son. He immediately went into hiding, and Crestan's family joined him with some extended family and friends. Those thirty people were the spark of the resistance. It started in Mexico and spread north and south."

"Why put the headquarters in Wichita?" Sammy asked.

"It was practically a ghost city by then. Isolated. People travel through it, but almost no one stops."

"But you—I mean, Commander Byron grew up here. He told me so. And the Scourge was fifty years ago!"

"Right—right. You gotta remember, some places just . . . emptied out. Other places suffered slower deaths. Wichita tried to hang on, but it was a losing battle. Most of the Mid-America is ghost now. It's cheap farmland. Those empty towns you walked through, they'll be knocked down someday to grow more crop."

"But what you were talking about before . . ." Toad said, "Are you saying the CAG bombed itself?"

Thomas wasn't smiling now. He dropped the pencil onto the desk where it rolled until it hit the mug. Several other resistance fighters walked by in a group talking about basketball. Two of them said hello to Thomas and went on.

"You weren't alive then. It's hard to explain why it makes sense."

"Try us," Sammy said with a touch of annoyance that Thomas heard.

The older man didn't hesitate to apologize.

"I don't mean you boys are dumb!" He laughed, but it felt forced, as if he wanted to be happy, but just couldn't make it. "I think the CAG hired Lark Montgomery. He studied acting, of all things, at college. Add to that he'd racked up lots of debt with his gambling addiction and couldn't get good work because of his conservative political leanings . . . Yeah, I think the CAG hired him for three reasons: to unify the country's resolve, to make everyone afraid of the NWG, and to consolidate power federally.

"By the time Crestan and the others went into hiding, they'd already made contacts through online forums and groups. Some of them were conspiracy theorists or others who had written about similar things happening. Not many, but a few. With those people making new contacts and networking through trusted family members or friends, they had almost a hundred people after their first year. Some joined the group by going into hiding, others stayed home and went about their normal lives. It just depended on their situations.

"The resistance peaked in 2075. Lara and I joined that year. Five thousand members, eighteen branches. Crestan and Henrico turned out to be geniuses when it came to operating something that big completely under the radar. They had people above ground networking through jobs and neighbors and family. Those in hiding were underground, not always literally, of course, but you get the idea. It was too risky to be communicating from branch to branch through any traceable routes like coms or internet, so they used pigeons with messages implanted under the skin.

"One of the resistance's goals was to reach out to the NWG, but in 2074 Congress passed the Safety Laws, making travel and communication out of America extremely difficult."

"Weren't people bothered by that?" Sammy asked.

"It bothered me and Lara." Thomas shrugged and picked up the pencil again. "Others? Not as much as you'd expect. By then there'd been so many terrorist acts, or attempted acts by so-called terrorists, people were scared out of their minds. You'd be surprised how many folks will trade their freedom to feel safe."

Sammy had heard enough. He wanted to talk about getting home. Before he could bring up the subject, Bryce Vogt walked into the area. His clothes were different. Instead of the poor man's garb, he wore a long white coat over a dress shirt and pants. The scruffy beard was gone.

"What's up, Doc?" Thomas asked, replacing the pencil in the mug.

"Time for the physicals," Dr. Vogt said to the boys. To Byron he added, "You also need to see about cleaning up that tourist shop they broke into. They're wanted by the CAG and their prints are all over that."

"Physical?" Toad repeated, straightening up in his chair. "I don't need a physical."

Thomas waved his hand at him to calm down. "Just a precaution like I mentioned earlier. For our own good as much as yours."

"Come with me, Toad," Bryce called over his shoulder as he walked back to the stairs. "I'll see you first."

Toad shot Sammy with a questioning look, as if he needed Sammy's approval.

"You better go," Sammy told him, "or they'll make you."

Toad rolled his eyes and hurried after the doctor.

"See if they can't figure out what's wrong with your nose!" he called after him.

Sammy watched them go, then gave his attention back to Thomas. "Is there any chance you can help me get back home?"

Thomas leaned forward, and made a sort of grimace. "I'm not surprised you asked. I figured you would. Truth is, I don't really know. Things have changed a lot since the seventies. Everyone here is afraid; afraid to act, afraid of getting caught, afraid of what happened to our resistance in 2075. Crestan, Henrico, and many, many others . . . all dead. We all know what happened to the ones who were caught. It's how the CAG brought down most of the old organization. Tortured until they got everything they could get."

A chill ran through Sammy's body, and he felt like he was on fire. An icy fire. The pain in his leg flared up again until he closed his eyes so he wouldn't see the crocodile biting his leg.

Thomas must have misinterpreted Sammy's expression for disappointment. "I swear, Sammy, I'll do what I can, but you'll need to be patient with us. Okay? Things happen here, just more slowly than I'd like."

"Sure. And I'll do what I can for you and the resistance."

Thomas drew very close to Sammy as though he wanted to say something very private, then he pulled away. For a moment, his eyes were full of pain and the lines in his face seemed to go much deeper. The emotion present between them was intimate and unspoken, but it connected Sammy to Thomas in a similar way he'd felt connected to Commander Byron. He sensed that Thomas was carrying a very heavy burden and was unwilling to share it.

"Well, there's one thing you can do for me, at least. I hope I'm not asking too much . . ."

"What's that?"

Thomas smiled wistfully with tears in his eyes. "Could you show me some of the stuff my son taught you to do? It's been ages since I've seen it."

Sammy smiled, then laughed. And laughing felt real good.

20 | Hollow

March 25, 2086

"GOOD MORNING, PSIONS. Good morning, Psions. Good morning, Psions."

Jeffie heard Strawberry stirring above her.

"I hate Mondays," Jeffie said into her pillow. "Why am I such an idiot?"

She and a few others, including Kobe, stayed up past 0200 playing *Pistols of Fury*, a virtual first-person shooter. It was fun, and she liked winning. That was her excuse. It seemed no matter how many times she awoke regretting those late Sunday nights, she found a way to justify doing it the next weekend.

Last night, after everyone else had left for bed, Kobe tried to talk to her again. It wasn't like she did not enjoy talking to him, but he wanted to have serious discussions. Her solution was to avoid the subject until she was too tired to think and had no problem telling him that she needed to go to bed. It was a cycle that repeated itself weekly.

Stumbling on shaky legs across the room, she rubbed her face and combed her fingers through her hair. When she flipped on the light, the voice stopped.

"Good morning, Psion!" Strawberry said in an overly-bubbly voice, hanging over the side of her bed.

Jeffie laughed even though Strawberry said it to her almost every morning.

The morning routine was so ingrained, Jeffie didn't even think about it. She grabbed her com and checked for messages. After three weeks of no word about her and Brickert's request to have access to Sammy's holo-records she was beginning to think that the commander either forgot or didn't want to tell them no. This morning, however, she saw a message in her inbox. She wasted no time opening it.

```
Gefjon,

Please see me during lunch. Sim room four.

CWB
```

Great, she thought, *now I won't be able to concentrate on instruction.*

While Strawberry went straight upstairs to breakfast, Jeffie was scheduled to exercise. Kobe watched her come in as he jogged next to Kaden. She considered ignoring him, but couldn't bring herself to do it. She flashed him a friendly smile and gave him a sign to wait a minute. After scanning in, the computer gave her a recommended workout, and she joined Kobe on the treadmills.

A screen in front of them showed the world news. The big reports of the morning revolved around more rumors of a possible moon colony and an upcoming address by the NWG president about new regulations on stem cell research and cloning.

"Morn . . . ing . . ." Kobe puffed out as he sprinted.

"Good morning." She started out with a brisk walk to get her blood flowing. "I don't know how you get up so early after keeping me up so late."

A wry smile grew on Kobe's face. "I sleep better . . . after late nights . . . with you."

Jeffie blushed and closed her eyes. While she enjoyed Kobe's attention and certainly recognized his good looks, she hated the guilt she felt when she was with him. They exercised side by side in silence for a couple minutes as her walk turned into a jog. Not long after she reached full pace, Brickert entered the room and took the empty treadmill on her left.

"What do you think?" The excitement in his voice told her exactly what Brickert was referring to.

Jeffie silently told Brickert to say nothing more by shaking her head with wide eyes, but it was too late.

"Think . . . about . . . what?" Kobe asked. Kaden seemed interested, too.

"Oh—nothing." Jeffie response came too quick and she immediately regretted it.

After an uncomfortable pause, Brickert replied in a cool tone. "Don't worry about it. It's personal."

"Oh . . . sorry," Kobe responded.

Brickert wouldn't say anything else. The tension between Kobe and Brickert was evident. When Jeffie tried to make conversation, it felt strained. She didn't like being secretive around Kobe, and she liked Brickert's blatant rudeness even less. The awkwardness made the workout session pass slowly enough that she actually looked forward to her instructions.

After grabbing a protein shake—something Kobe had gotten her to start eating—she hit the showers and went to instructions.

Four hours of physics.

Trying to master the basics of special relativity and four-dimensional equations was the absolute worst. It required her full attention, but with the impending meeting with the commander, she was unable to give even half of it.

Brickert stood outside her classroom door, startling her when she exited.

"Sorry. Ready?"

She nodded and walked with him to the stairwell.

"And I'm sorry about earlier," he added, "but aren't we supposed to keep quiet about what we're asking from Commander Byron?"

"Oh please, Brickert," she answered. "Do you really think I don't know why you said what you did?"

"I'm not answering that," he said with his face pointed at the floor.

"Brickert . . ." She had a pleading note in her voice.

"No! I'm not getting into that conversation with you again."

"Fine!"

"Aren't you worried Kobe's going to find out what you're doing with me?"

Jeffie tripped and banged her knee on the next highest step. "Ouch!" she cried out. Then, through gritted teeth, she said, "I'm not worried about him."

"Jeffie," Brickert said, cutting off her thoughts with a placating voice, "I know Kobe's got the hots for you. I'm not blind, I tell you."

"I'm not worried . . ."

Brickert's blue eyes reproached her halfway through her sentence.

"Really!" she insisted. "Sheesh . . ."

Brickert was a lost cause when it came to Kobe. Not only did he seem to blame Kobe for Sammy's "absence," but he also nursed a deep grudge for being teased incessantly when they had been "pukes." Even though Kobe wasn't like that anymore, Jeffie couldn't get Brickert to see it.

They continued up the stairs and through the chalk white halls to sim room four. Byron was waiting inside. He'd set up the room just like their last meeting.

"Have a seat."

Jeffie couldn't tell by the expression on his face whether he had good news or bad, but her stomach lurched. *Why am I nervous?* She folded her arms across her lap, trying to appear indifferent. Then she thought it might not be in her best interest to look indifferent, so she put her hands at her sides until finally settling with linking her fingers back in her lap.

"I am sorry it has taken so long—" Byron began to say.

"It's okay," Jeffie responded, while Brickert said at the same time, "No big deal."

The commander gave them one of his knowing smiles that always frustrated Jeffie. Still, she took his smile as a good sign.

"It took some convincing at Command, and then again with General Wu, but . . ."

Jeffie gasped. "You got permission!"

Commander Byron's face told her he had.

Brickert and Jeffie high-fived each other.

"A couple of stipulations first. Anyone can use them as long as it is for training purposes, and it must be done in your free time, not during your sims. Now, I am not going to advertise this news, and neither should you. But if someone comes to me I will send them your way. Okay?"

"Okay," they both answered.

"I have to go," Byron said, handing Brickert a small piece of paper, "but I hope it helps you both. That is his password. Make sure you wear zero suits while you watch." After giving them both a long and solemn look, he left the room.

Jeffie huddled close to Brickert who was already examining the paper. Before she got a chance to see it, Brickert let out a loud laugh and passed the paper to her. She snatched it to see what was so funny.

She read the words aloud: "User Name: Samuel Harris Berhane, Jr. User Password: fjords." She couldn't help but smile. As they walked to lunch, Brickert chatted animatedly to Jeffie, but she was oblivious to it. All she could think about was how she would see Sammy again after her sims.

As always, she took a minute before launching her first trial to remind herself why she was training. Sometimes she remembered Martin's memorial service or the way Cala looked when she got back from the hospital. Mostly she thought about her family and Sammy. Doing this helped her push herself harder and longer in the sims.

While she still hadn't completely accepted Sammy's death, there was an ever-enlarging part of her that believed she wasn't going to see him again. Her best friend had been cheated of his best years of life. Each time she thought about that, she found a deep reserve of anger to tap into and channeled it into her sims.

Two Thirteens appeared, one in front of her, one to her side. She raised her blast shields and blocked their first volleys. With a jump-blast, she flew straight into one Thirteen, her hand blast bowling him over. Her other hand was extended to shield the bullets at her flank.

She landed neatly and kept up her shield. Three blasts in short bursts kept the fallen Thirteen off balance. When his face was exposed, she hit him with another powerful blast. His head slammed back against the floor, oozing liquids. The kill fed her fury, which she, in turn, fed into her aggression on the remaining Thirteen.

Spinning quickly, she fired at him with left and right-handed blasts, keeping him moving. He responded by using random levels of attack, forcing her to adjust her hands and second-guess her assaults. All she had to do was wait for him to reload.

There it is!

The Thirteen dumped his clip just as Jeffie ran at him. He bared his teeth, dyed black and ground into points, and sprung off the wall trying to avoid her blasts by landing on top of her. Jeffie used a jump-blast, flipped her body backwards mid-air, and connected with the man in the neck. He collapsed to the floor, and she landed neatly, watching him disappear with a hate-filled grimace.

That night, she and Brickert met outside sim room four wearing their zero suits. Jeffie hated wearing hers. The suits were skintight and even had to cover the face with a thin netting. Not wearing one could be deadly in an interactive hologram simulation. Her hands twisted around each other as Brickert opened the door and led the way. Her breath caught in her lungs as she expected Sammy to be waiting inside.

The room was a dark, empty tomb with ghostly white walls. The panel on the wall glowed with life as the motion sensors in the room detected their presence. She had the simulator create two chairs for them, and then, with shaky, sweaty fingers, entered Sammy's name and password into the computer. Only a half second passed before the entire list of Sammy's holo-records displayed along with dates and times and outcomes. She narrowed the list down to records of Sammy fighting four Thirteens or more. A blink of light and a new list appeared.

"Start from the beginning?" she asked Brickert over her shoulder.

"Sure."

Jeffie selected the first item on the list and took her chair.

"I feel like we should have brought popcorn or something," Brickert commented.

She tried to smile, but her heart was pounding a techno beat in her chest. And then he was there—right there inside the room with them. The beat of the song picked up ten points on her internal metronome while Brickert grinned goofily.

"Cool."

Jeffie nodded. She stared at the face she thought she'd memorized perfectly.

So many things I've forgotten.

The four Thirteens took form in various spots around the room. Jeffie noted Sammy's apprehension by the way his eyes shifted faster than normal and his face took on that stony appearance. She also saw the same shrewd, calculating look he wore in the Arena as a seasoned honcho who'd never known defeat. The silence of the recording was punctured with gasps or utters of surprise, mostly from Brickert. All in all, the battle lasted well under two minutes, ending when Sammy sacrificed too much of his backside. In a desperate attempt to take one of them out, he received a volley of shots in his back.

"Can you believe how fast he was?"

Jeffie didn't answer. She'd just seen Sammy for the first time in months.

"I knew he put himself through a strenuous exercise routine," Brickert continued, "but . . . wow!"

"Yeah . . ." She was eager to watch another one. In fact, she felt like she could sit there all night. "Did you know he was that fast?"

"Kind of. I know he focused on long-distance sprinting, different kinds of things to build up his white muscles."

"His what?"

Brickert chuckled with a half-shrug. "I don't know. He explained it to me once. There are different types of muscle fibers, slower ones and faster ones. Fast ones are white and help improve short bursts of speed."

"How come I never knew about this?" she wondered aloud. "All our time talking, and I didn't even . . ."

Brickert put his hand on her arm in a way that communicated his sympathy. "I was his roommate. I took him for granted, too."

Another holo-record started and ended with similar results. Brickert and Jeffie took verbal notes about what they needed to improve. Jeffie still couldn't believe the quickness of Sammy's reflexes, the perfect timing of his jumps, and his sheer recklessness. Sometimes she and Brickert caught themselves groaning or cheering along with the sims.

After an hour of the same result, Jeffie got up to pick a different record. "I want to see his first victory. It took him a month before he won. Let's watch it."

"Okay," Brickert said with a shrug.

This victory had special meaning to her. The night he told her about beating the four-Thirteen sim was the same night she'd forced him to play six hours of Star Racers until she beat him. The spontaneous embrace they'd shared in that moment had left her wanting more. Jeffie had experienced a few flings, all of them squeezed into a busy life of sports and other activities. She'd had kisses and romantic moments during those brief relationships, but being in Sammy's arms felt better than anything else.

She wanted Sammy.

In a huff, she broke her thoughts away from the memory and turned her attention back to the holo. Sammy sped toward the ground faster than anyone Jeffie had ever seen before, breaking the neck of a Thirteen with a loud and quite gruesome *SNAP!* Then, after removing the Thirteen's finger, he used the gun to finish the other three.

"I know I'm starting to wear the word 'wow' out, but the only other ones that come to mind are too obscene."

Jeffie nodded in agreement.

"You think we can fight like that?" Brickert asked her.

"He taught Al to beat the four Thirteen sim, didn't he?"

"But that's Al . . ."

"And I'm Jeffie. And you're Brickert. So what? Start the next one."

Brickert started to respond, but Jeffie got a text from Kobe.

Hey J. Where are you? Wanted to hang before bed.

She wrote him back a short message saying she was too busy. Brickert tried to act oblivious, but his small, annoyed snort was enough to tell her that he knew what was going on.

Please don't come looking for me, Kobe, she begged silently. But about five minutes after she sent the text, the sim room door opened, and in walked Kobe with his brother reluctantly following behind, both in their own zero suits.

"Is it okay if we watch?" Kobe asked them.

"Err . . ." Brickert slowly glanced over at Jeffie. His eyes told her plainly the answer was *No, not okay.*

Kobe noticed this and turned to her. "Do you mind?"

"No," she answered. She kept her eyes on the action in front of her. And though she tried to concentrate on what Sammy was doing, her mind kept thinking about Kobe's presence, wishing he wasn't there. Perhaps she wasn't alone in her feelings, because as the four of them watched, no one spoke. She had a pretty good idea why Kobe had come, but hoped she was wrong.

Brickert stayed another hour before announcing that he was going downstairs for a late dinner. She begged him with her eyes not to leave her with Kobe and Kaden, but his own silent reply was, *You said he could stay, not me.*

"And I think I'll go with him," Kaden said without hesitating. "Later, guys."

Jeffie closed her eyes. *Wonderful. Just wonderful.*

Kobe moved over and took the holo-seat next to her.

Please don't do this, Kobe. Please don't make me talk right now.

His first words were: "Can we talk?"

She knew she was doomed. She swallowed hard and said, "Do we have to do this?"

The room was silent for a moment. The holograms of Sammy and four dead Thirteens slowly faded away. Jeffie wanted to take off her zero suit now as the room seemed to have gotten very warm very quickly. Kobe watched her with a nervous expression, which for him was rare.

"Are you watching these recordings to get better in the sims or just to see him?" He nodded toward the empty space in the middle of the room as if Sammy were still there.

"I—I don't know why you're asking that." It threw her off balance that he had gone right for the point. She'd expected him to build up to this moment. "You know how much I want to be better."

"It's been months now. Don't you think you should consider moving past it? I mean, you weren't married . . . or in love. You know?" He laughed, but without his usual gusto. "We're too young for that stuff!"

"None of us feel our age here." Her tone told Kobe that he should know exactly what she meant. "Look at Al and Marie! When they were seventeen they were already practically engaged."

"So you're saying you were in love with him?"

"How could—I don't know, Kobe!" she answered. "I never really had a chance to find out."

"How do you feel about me?" he asked, putting his hand on hers. "I know I blew it before, but we've had great times together."

"I've had great times with Strawberry, too." Even though she wanted to move it, she left her hand under his. She liked the touch.

Kobe snorted and that wry smile crept back on his lips. "Funny," he offered. But then he was serious again. "Do you feel like you're ready to—I don't know—date someone else?"

"Do I have to answer that? Can't we just do what we've been doing? I can tell you've got . . ." She searched for a word that didn't sound like something she'd just heard Brickert say, but failed, " . . . the hots for me. You make it pretty obvious, and it hasn't stopped me from hanging out with you every weekend."

"I know. I'm glad, but I feel like the memory of Sammy is keeping us from being more than friends. I miss him, too. I was there. He saved my life."

"I know!" Jeffie said much louder than she meant to.

"Do you blame me?"

"NO!" she shouted, then caught herself and calmed down. "No. Not at all." And she meant it. "But what's the point if I'm so mixed up right now? Can't you give me some time?"

Kobe's face was now more serious than she had ever seen it. "Jeff, I was there." His eyes were fixed on the wall opposite them, unblinking and lost in its perfect whiteness. "I took two bullets near the end of the battle. It was all on Sammy to get us out of there. He fought . . ." Kobe cleared his throat and looked up at all the micro-projectors hanging in the ceiling. "You had to have been there to believe how he fought. I was slipping out of consciousness, but I still knew I was seeing something special. Then a bomb went off, and he threw himself in front of me to—you know—to save me. That blast knocked me out. I can't imagine what it did to him. I—

I don't think he's coming back, not after what happened in there. And I'm not saying that for me. I got over it. It took time, but I did. I'm saying it for you. I'm sorry. I'm very *very* sorry."

Jeffie folded her arms across her chest. "If anyone could have survived, it's Sammy. After what I just watched, I know that now more than ever." Her tone had an icy temperature that made Kobe look away again.

"I agree." His voice was quiet, maybe even embarrassed, but Jeffie couldn't tell for sure. "I'll give you all the time you want."

Jeffie whispered her thanks with closed eyes. She wasn't sure she could handle all of this. Suddenly Kobe's warm lips pressed against her cheek.

She opened her eyes and looked into his. "Thanks for telling me that stuff, Kobe."

As soon as Kobe was gone, Jeffie started the next recording. She paused it just as it started so there were no Thirteens in the room. She stood next to the three-dimensional image of her best friend and looked into his eyes. The holo-record was so perfect that it was easy to pretend he was right there with her, looking at her.

No, she corrected herself, *looking through me.*

She couldn't smell him, couldn't touch him, but he was there. She put her hand above his shoulder, pretending it rested on his jumpsuit. Her hand hovered in place, shaking barely enough that her skin dipped in and out of him. An ache so deep and strong for him rose up that she had to touch him. Had to. She lurched for him with her arms and fell forward through his image. When she hit the floor, she knew he was gone, and allowed herself to have a good cry.

The next morning, she and Brickert told the computer to tailor their exercise routines to helping them increase their speed and bursts of power. The first day almost killed her.

For a week, the only difference she noticed was exhaustion, and consequently, how poorly she performed in instructions and sims. The electronic trainer assured her she would feel a difference in her performance in three to four weeks, and that gave her hope.

Nothing more was said between Jeffie and Kobe about their conversation in sim room four. She treated him no differently than she had for the past several weeks, and he continued to be his usual, flirtatious self around her.

Friday night, she went to bed earlier than normal. A week of rigorous daily workouts and fighting two Thirteens in the sims had taken its toll. She skipped her usual nighttime shower and collapsed on her bed only to find something bumpy in her pillowcase. Annoyed, she reached inside and pulled out a scarlet envelope with her name decorated in loopy gold ink.

Jeffie first thought that Kawai, known for doing things just like this, was planning another girls' night. She was sure her guess was right when she opened it and removed a very fancy invitation. But Kawai was not the type to invite another girl to a picnic. It was from Kobe. The date was set for the upcoming weekend. Suddenly, sleep was far from Jeffie's mind as she lay back on her bed twirling the envelope and card between her fingers.

She heard a snap and the door opened. It was Strawberry grinning like she'd just seen Antonio working out with his shirt off.

"Oh good. You found it."

"This?" Jeffie asked holding the envelope.

- 295 -

"What else?" Strawberry never bothered containing her excitement. "Are you going to say yes?"

"I don't know," Jeffie muttered. "That's what I was just thinking about. You put it in my pillow?"

"Naturally." Strawberry gave a short bow and sat down on the bed next to Jeffie.

Jeffie exhaled hard and said, "Do you think I should go?"

"Yes!" Strawberry said breathlessly. "Kobe is so cute. Antonio likes him, too. Well, everyone likes him except—"

"Brickert," they finished together.

"But you can't do everything to please Brickert!" Strawberry pleaded.

"Trust me, I know." Jeffie laughed but not in a mirthful way.

"You don't owe anyone anything. You're allowed to go on dates. Especially with stunningly cute boys with stunningly cute dimples."

"But I told him to slow it down and give me some time. He gave me a week. I'm supposed to reward him for that?"

"He's a boy, Jeffie. You're lucky he waited a week."

Jeffie knew her roommate was right. And after all, it was just a date. She'd never even gone on one with Sammy. "Okay. You're right. I'll go."

"Yay!" Strawberry cheered, bouncing and clapping in place.

Jeffie looked at the envelope again with a half smile. *So he can be thoughtful,* she mused to herself as she pulled her com off the charger and sent Kobe a short text accepting his invitation.

21 | Talking

March 25, 2086

SAMMY AND TOAD SPENT TIME RESTING from their travels. Thomas and Lara gave them a bedroom, three square meals, and tried to keep them involved (or at least informed) with what was going on around the palace, but Sammy didn't like sitting around doing nothing. Too much time on his hands left him with bad thoughts of home, Rio, Stripe, and walking forever with horrific hunger pains.

During this time, Sammy noticed that Thomas and Lara acted differently around him than Toad. Lara instantly liked Toad and established a matronly bond with him, but with Sammy she spoke very softly, as though he was delicate. Meanwhile, Thomas would often ask Sammy if he was happy and comfortable, if he was okay with the food and living arrangements, or whether he needed anything that hadn't been offered.

They had pancakes for breakfast on Monday the 25th. Sammy noted the date because Brickert's birthday was only a week away, and he had hoped to be back in time to celebrate it. Toad ate like he wanted to break the world record for most pancakes downed in one meal. Lara watched him with a bemused expression. Twice during the meal Sammy caught Thomas glancing nervously in his direction. Each time he met the older man's gaze, Thomas's eyes returned to his holo-tablet where he read the morning news.

It was Lara who spoke up. "You know, Sammy, I think Dr. Vogt wants to examine you again."

Sammy noticed that soft tone in her voice. *Careful*, he thought, *she's being careful.*

"Oh yes," Thomas added in a similar tone. "He's been out of town, but he should be back sometime today. I think he did mention that."

"What for?" Sammy asked.

Thomas shrugged. "Just to check a couple things." The look in his eyes told Sammy that Thomas wasn't being completely truthful.

"I—uh—I told the doctor about what happened to you in Rio," Toad admitted.

Sammy threw down his fork. "What did you do that for?" he yelled. Thomas stood up quickly, and Lara moved closer to Toad.

"Toad did the right thing, Sammy," she said.

"It's not his place to say anything about me!" Sammy stared at Toad, who would not look back at him.

Lara and Thomas exchanged a wary glance, and this made Sammy even madder.

"The doctor's not here," Thomas reminded him, "no need to worry. You can see him after lunch."

Sammy stared at Toad, who, in turn, stared at his plate, occasionally sniffing. Again he had to fight back the darkness inside of him that wanted to do violent things to those who made him angry.

"Excuse me," he said. "I'll be in my room."

The afternoon came quickly. Sammy read *Great Expectations* on his bed until Dr. Vogt came for him.

"Ready, Sammy?" the doctor said with a light tap on the door. He was wearing neither a doctor's coat nor a stethoscope, just a pair of relatively new jeans, tennis shoes, and a maroon and gold t-shirt with the word MONARCHS printed across the chest. "Back upstairs we go."

"What's this all about?" Sammy asked when they sat down in Dr. Vogt's office.

"I want to talk some more about what you went through in Rio. Not just what the Aegis did to you, but the time you spent in isolation before that. You must be pretty messed up inside." He tapped the side of Sammy's head.

"I'm fine." Sammy's statement came out monotone and unconvincing.

Dr. Vogt put his hands in his lap and stared at Sammy for a good ten seconds. "To be perfectly honest with you, I'm a medical doctor. I have a degree in psychology from Hastings College, but that was almost twenty years ago. After that, I went to Johns Hopkins Medical School."

"So, you're a psychiatrist?"

"No, I was an internist. So I'm about as qualified to treat whatever is going on in your brain as you are to treat my ulcers."

Sammy saw the smile in Vogt's brown eyes, even if it didn't reach his mouth.

"Then how are you supposed to help?" he asked the doctor.

"I thought you said you're fine."

"I am."

"I didn't bring you up here to waste time, Sammy. Just admit you have a problem so we can get on with it." Dr. Vogt's tone of voice wasn't harsh, but frank.

It angered Sammy to be spoken to that way. Fresh memories of his time spent with Stripe played in his mind like an out-of-focus holo-film. Tears crept into his eyes, and he had to bow his head to hide them.

"You were tortured, Sammy," Dr. Vogt said in the same, frank voice.

A barrage of emotions slammed into Sammy, and he found himself reeling from betrayal, fear, anger, and shame all at once. Each emotion was like a different anvil pressing down on his chest and shoulders. It was so much that he didn't know how he could cope with it.

"You don't know anything about it!" He glared at the doctor as he spoke.

"Do you want help?"

Sammy tried to gain control over his emotions but couldn't. A pump inside him was regurgitating up his darkest feelings, and he couldn't find the off switch.

The tears kept flowing.

"Because if you want help, I'll try. It's got to be better than having all the junk stewing in your brain. Right?"

An old wooden clock on the wall ticked the time away and rain pellets tapped on the window panes. Sammy hadn't noticed until now, but a big storm was rolling through.

"Have you suffered any hallucinations? Any distortions in reality? Anything odd or upsetting?"

Sammy mumbled a few words about a crocodile and his leg.

"I didn't catch that."

It sounded so stupid to Sammy that he wouldn't repeat it.

Dr. Vogt folded his arms across his chest and sighed impatiently. "Look here. From the short time I've been observing you, I've been very impressed. You seem to be extremely emotionally stable and—"

This time Sammy shook his head madly.

"What?" the doctor asked.

"I'm not—I'm not . . . stable." The things he wanted to say were humiliating, but he wanted to be rid of the demon inside him. He'd managed to bury the memories by focusing on making it to Wichita and fighting off gnawing hunger, but over the last few days they had been resurfacing. Reading had helped a little. "I—I'm—I wake up from horrible dreams every morning scared so badly I think I'm going to pee on myself. Sometimes Toad annoys me so much I want to kill him . . . and I imagine ways of doing it. He sniffs all the time!"

The doctor looked up from the paper he'd been scrawling on as Sammy spoke. "He has a badly deviated septum and it clogs his nose. Combine that with his ultra-kinetic anomaly and it's a recipe for a Tourrettes-like tick."

Sammy shook his head in the same irritated way. There was one more thing he had to say. Swallowing hard, he forced himself to tell the doctor the most embarrassing thing of all. "And I'm not smart."

"Oh? I beg to differ. Just getting here proves you're very smart."

"No! I figured out all that stuff before I was—before everything happened. I used to be able to—to see!" He shouted the last words and banged his fist on the arm of his chair. The chair trembled lightly. Tears flowed again, but he wiped them away as if they were acid.

"See what?" the doctor asked, jumping slightly in alarm at the unexpected outburst.

"I don't how to describe it. My brain," he explained, tapping his head just as the doctor had. "It figured things out so clearly that I could see it sometimes."

"You mean your Anomaly Eleven?"

Sammy nodded slowly.

"And now you can't? You can't see?"

Admitting it made Sammy feel naked, even more than when the doctor had examined his skin from head to toe and every part in between. He wasn't the same person anymore, and a part of him he'd loved so much—a part he'd come to depend on—was gone. And the idea that he might never get it back was unbearable. All because of Stripe, because he had been stranded in Rio, and because all the Psions back home thought he was dead. Sammy wished now that he could go back to Rio and do worse things to Stripe than what he had. He wished he had fought the Aegis in Floyd's store, and even if he'd died, at least he wouldn't have suffered through all this crap.

The doctor's hand gently rested on his shoulder. "I'd like to help you, Sammy."

"How?" Sammy cried. "I'm so screwed up! Even if I make it back home, no one's going to know me."

"Half of that is right. You are messed up. But your youth and your intelligence will help you heal. Are you willing to try?"

Sammy gave a great sniff.

"Who's sniffing now?" the doctor asked.

An abrupt laugh came from Sammy, and he felt a little better.

Dr. Vogt left his hand on Sammy's shoulder and continued speaking. "It's funny because I was fascinated by psychology in college. It was my major. Then I went to medical school and never got to use it. I fell in love with surgery, and it was more exciting. Now all I ever do is give people stitches or antibiotics. I'd love to help you. We can work through this. I'm not saying I can cure you, but I can help. Since you got here, I've been looking through different resources and studies on torture victims, abused children and spouses. Things to help rebuild the psyche."

"What's a psyche?" Sammy asked.

"I'll teach you all of that. But the kind of therapy I have in mind is intense, and it'll last about a month. You'll have only limited contact with Toad and Thomas and Lara. You and I will have very involved discussions about yourself and what happened to you when you were tortured. It may very well be as hard to go through as what caused the damage to your mind. Do you think you can handle that?"

"I guess."

"Don't give me an 'I guess' answer, Sammy. I need a commitment. A month is a long time, and I know how badly you want to get back home—"

"NO!" Sammy rose out of his seat. "I want to be whole again before I go back. I want to feel . . . like myself. And I'm not myself."

The thought of his friends whispering behind his back, knowing they thought of him as a psycho . . . If he went back to headquarters, he needed to be the person that they knew, otherwise he would never really be home.

"You're okay with beginning right away?" Dr. Vogt asked.

Sammy didn't answer. He was still absorbed in daydreams of his friends staring at him with frightened expressions.

"Did you hear me?"

Sammy jerked out of his reverie. "Huh? No."

"I said we'll start right away. Again, I'm no psychologist. I'm not trained to do this, but I'm as qualified as anyone you're going to meet around here. And I want to see you through this."

Outside the window, rain and hail came down in sheets. Wind blowing off the windows and walls of the building howled like ghosts. A tiny sliver of sunlight broke through the vast cover of gray-black clouds in the sky.

Sammy sighed. "Okay. Let's do it."

Dr. Vogt got up from his chair and went to his bookshelf. "I sleep here, you know. The infirmary is my apartment. You'll be here with me after breakfast until dinner every day. I'll give homework to keep you busy at night."

"Oh, great." Sammy tried to grin, but his face felt tight as though he hadn't smiled in ages. He watched Vogt pull several books down off his shelf. Nine total.

"These are for you," he said, carrying the pile to Sammy. He handed the books to him one at a time. "Freud, Skinner, Lacan. You've heard of those guys, right?"

"I think so. Freud for sure."

"Here are some more names. Freud Jr—his daughter, not son. Rogers, Bandura, Chin. Chin is still alive, I think."

"Am I going to read all these?" Sammy asked with wide eyes. The books were not small. Not small at all.

The doctor smiled and handed Chin's book to him. "Not cover to cover, but much of this you're going to learn."

"How will it help me?"

"The platform of the theory I'm going to use revolves around combining several different psychological thoughts into one. That's what Chin's books teach. You have to learn to apply the therapy, which means you need to have a decent understanding of psychology. Education begets implementation. Since you're the one who needs the help, you have to fix yourself. I'm going to guide you and give you the tools to do it."

Dr. Vogt was true to his word. He sent Sammy home with a reading assignment and the next day they met from breakfast 'til dinner. For the first few days he taught Sammy psychology: psychoanalysis, behavioral psychology, brain function, humanism, classical and operant conditioning, personality construction and deconstruction, abnormal psychology . . . they touched on everything and delved deeply into many subjects.

The schooling frustrated Sammy. For someone used to picking things up so quickly, he struggled to grasp some of the concepts, and often needed Vogt to explain things two or three times. After they finished each day, he'd eat and spend time with Toad and the Byrons. Then he studied late into the night after Toad fell asleep, snoring from his deviated septum.

Dr. Vogt didn't have patience for Sammy getting distracted or being sarcastic. He didn't chit-chat much, either. Occasionally he had to leave for other duties involving his medicine. In these instances, he gave Sammy chapters to read or documentaries to watch on famous psychological experiments.

Their lessons went on for ten to twelve hours a day, breaking only for lunch and restroom visits. After their tenth day, when Dr. Vogt called it quits, he stopped Sammy at the infirmary door.

"Get a good night's rest, Sammy. The easy part is over." He scrawled something down on his notepad and tore the paper from it. After crumpling the sheet, he threw it at Sammy. "Read that."

Sammy read it.

Who are you?

"Okay." He looked to Dr. Vogt for an answer. "I don't get it."

"We're going to have a truth talk."

"Truth talk?" Sammy repeated. "You mean I'll lay on a couch and talk to you about my mother?"

"Not quite." There was no indulging smile on Vogt's face. "Think about the question. You're going to spend the entire day answering it."

Weary, worn, and with heaps of undigested information floating around in his brain, Sammy went to bed. Toad asked a few questions about how the lessons had gone and told Sammy about how he'd spent another day eavesdropping with Thomas.

"It's boring," he explained. "I'd rather be in class with you. Really. But when our shift finished Thomas and Lara started working on my Ultra skills with me. They're going to try to help me start learning what I can do. Lara thinks that if I'm good with a bow and arrow, I'm probably good with a gun, too."

Sammy wasn't listening. *How am I going to spend an entire day answering that one question?*

He doubted it would be as hard as Vogt said. After all, he'd accomplished some amazing things before and after leaving Beta headquarters. Telling the truth seemed rather low on the scale of difficulty.

That was what he thought . . .

"You must talk the entire time we're together," Dr. Vogt explained the following morning. "If you can't think of anything more to say, I'll prompt you from the notes I will be taking. You can have all the water you want during our sessions, but you're only getting two bathroom breaks. Don't drink too much."

The doctor pulled out a thick notebook and five pens, laid four of them above the notebook, and kept one in his hand.

"So . . . who are you?"

Sammy dragged out his answer for twenty minutes before he ran out of things to say. He stared at the doctor with a blank look, silently asking what more he wanted from him, but the doctor continued to scribble notes down onto the notebook. After a bit of pondering, Sammy talked about his favorite foods. From there he moved to other preferences and dislikes. Those took another twenty-five minutes. His forehead began to ache from searching for things to say.

After an especially long pause, Dr. Vogt commented, his eyes still on his notes, "So far everything you've told me is superficial. Who are you?"

Sammy's mouth opened to answer but all that came was "deh—ah—mmh . . ." and then a long sigh.

It was the longest day he could remember. Longer even than his days walking through the plains of Mid-American Territory. Anytime he stopped for longer than a minute, Vogt prompted him to expound on something he had said. The talking took unusual turns. Sammy discussed aloud his lack of conviction of anything spiritual, mentioning how some of his friends had firm beliefs in God and an afterlife, but he had none. His parents had raised him that way, believing that if he relied on himself rather than a god, he'd be more likely to succeed. But on the other hand, he knew people like Al, Marie, and Kawai who were very spiritual and also successful.

His oratory then dipped into shallow philosophical waters and skimmed the surface of the more sordid details of his personal history, intentionally omitting some things. He knew he'd talk about them sooner or later, but preferred later. To stall for more time, he drank sips of water. After using both his bathroom breaks, he had to go again. He bore the pressure for about an hour before begging Dr. Vogt to let him go.

"You can use the restroom," Dr. Vogt said, "but I'll start rationing your water if you do."

When their day came to a close, Dr. Vogt packed away his things with a satisfied expression, and gave Sammy his homework and another question. With a scratchy voice and a throbbing headache, Sammy ran for the bathroom. Later in the evening, Toad tried to talk to him through dinner about figuring out a way to teach him how to use his Anomaly Fifteen, but Sammy had no desire to speak. He excused himself and went to bed.

After reading two chapters from *Abnormal Psychology* by the light of his bedside lamp, he unfolded his little piece of paper and read:

What do you want?

He whispered a silent swear word, tossed the paper into the waste bin, and turned off the light.

He woke early the next morning so he could do his exercises. Toad usually joined him, but Sammy decided to let his friend sleep. Toad knew where Sammy would be, anyway.

Dr. Vogt took breakfast with the group, but he never spoke to anyone about his work with Sammy. He ate quickly and then asked Sammy to join him upstairs.

Sammy sighed and got up.

He talked about wanting to be whole again, wanting to be home, wanting to win a war that he didn't even fully understand. He told Dr. Vogt about his friends in Johannesburg who were locked up in the Grinder and how he wanted them to have good, productive lives. He wanted a family again. He wanted to make sure Stripe was dead. He discussed more intimate thoughts like how he wanted to know if there was a god. To lose his virginity before he died. To go into space. To own a dog. To live by a large body of water. He even mentioned how he wanted Toad to be able to train with other Anomaly Fifteens since he, Sammy, didn't know how to help him.

The next several days went by with almost no variation. *Who do you want to be? What have you learned in life? What are your regrets? What are your strengths? Weaknesses?* A new question. Day after day. Each one presented different challenges. The more he relived his past, the more his memory seemed to improve. However, it was difficult speaking about his role models, many of whom were no longer in his life: his parents, his foster father, Commander Byron, and Al. He still wasn't sure he'd see any of them again. When he told Dr. Vogt about his parents' death, he became very emotional because he'd never mentioned before how much he regretted not being there to help them. But he got better at talking. Sometimes he went for a whole hour, and the only thing to stop him was a dry mouth or a hoarse throat . . . or tears. The longer the therapy went on, the more he grew to believe that the point of the exercise was to understand himself better. But he never got to ask because the doctor never afforded him the chance.

The questions Dr. Vogt asked became more difficult to discuss. His homework assignments had quotations of his own words matched up with chapters to read. There were rare but beautiful moments in his monologues when Sammy discovered nuggets of truth—when the things he said startled even himself. Sometimes they were dark and ugly, sometimes they were pleasant and uplifting.

When Sammy got the question that asked *What was the torture like?* Everything changed.

It was like starting all over again. He couldn't find words to accurately express what he wanted to say. The frustration mounted until he was screaming at Dr. Vogt. The demon that Stripe had created (or worse, unleashed) inside him had lain dormant for many days, but now it wanted control. On that day, he hated Dr. Vogt more than he'd ever hated anyone. He wanted to lash out and break the arm writing those endless pages of notes.

That day nearly broke Sammy's belief that he could be fixed. He didn't cry at all during the therapy session. His jungle safari of emotions never explored that terrain, but it came close. When the day ended, his leg ached as if it'd been an all-day buffet for reptiles, his head throbbed, and his skin experienced hot flashes every few minutes. He received his next question at the end of the day. He didn't look at it until he was in bed. Waiting until bed had become his ritual of sorts. When he did finally look at it, he broke down bawling.

What was the torture like?

This was his topic for three days. The second day was the worst. He hated Dr. Vogt even more for forcing him to do it all again a second time, and spent half of the session yelling until his voice went out. The rest of the session, he whispered his anger. Then, halfway through the third day, he had a breakthrough. And he knew if he hadn't sat and talked to Dr. Vogt for all that time, it would have taken him much longer to receive the revelation.

"Stripe hurt me in ways I never knew were possible. I wanted to die, but I didn't want to die at the same time. And I don't know if it is because of fortune, or God, or luck, or fate that I was spared. I don't know. But I don't want it to have more impact on my life than other things. I want my life to be about the people I love, the girl I want to be with, you know, that stuff. Not what Stripe did to me."

Dr. Vogt made a rare comment. "Perhaps not said very eloquently, but that's a very mature thing to say, Sammy. Especially for someone your age."

"I still worry if I'll ever be smart like I used to be. I guess if not, I'll deal with it. But my body works fine. And I don't want to kill Toad anymore."

"For now . . ."

He and Dr. Vogt shared a laugh.

"I feel better. I mean, my dreams still suck and I still get emotional when I think about things, but that will get better, too, I think. I hope. I guess that's it, though. You know? I have hope."

Their work continued for a few more days. The kinship he formed with Dr. Vogt was unique to any other relationship he'd had. Through the kaleidoscope of emotions he experienced in that small infirmary sitting across from the same face, Sammy felt a great sense of respect and gratitude for what the doctor was doing.

Then one day the doctor brought Sammy upstairs at the normal time, but did not take out his notebook or pens. Simply by looking at Vogt's face, Sammy knew their time together was over.

"I had every intention of discussing your next question today, but something's come up."

It was like icy water had been splashed on Sammy as he remembered he didn't belong here. Not in the infirmary, and not in Wichita. Not with the resistance. Out there was Toad and the Byrons working, and even farther beyond were the Betas—Betas and Alphas who might be in danger. He was meant to go home and warn them about Commander Wrobel. None of that changed the fact that something special had happened in this room— something important to Sammy.

"You already know Thomas monitors the surveillance equipment up in the tower and down in the basement," Dr. Vogt explained. "Right now conditions are just such that they've had a major breakthrough with the decoding—this new lady from Alberta managed to do it. Anyway, they need all the hands they can get to help man the headphones and decoding machines. He asked if we could finish early."

"What do you think?" Sammy trusted Vogt's judgment more than his own.

"You've shown more progress than I expected. You're not out of the woods yet. You should probably expect to have your bad days and good days. Emotional relapses are normal. But I think you're okay. If okay can be applied so generally to anyone, then it can be applied to you."

"Really?"

"Yeah. You're a bright kid and very down to earth. Honestly, if what happened to you happened to most other people, they'd be a lot worse off than you. Part of that is you've already dealt with tragedy, but another part is that you're made of tougher stuff than you think."

Warmth and happiness surged through Sammy when Dr. Vogt said this. No one had paid him a compliment since Floyd in the butcher shop. The words fed his starved spirit.

"Thank you," Sammy told him. "You saved my life."

22 | Secrets

April 27, 2086

JEFFIE STOOD IN FRONT OF HER CLOSET MIRROR holding two different outfits in front of her. The Game was minutes away from starting, and knowing she wouldn't have time to decide later, she tried to choose which she should wear on her date with Kobe. Tonight would be their third date in a month.

All of a sudden, Strawberry burst in the door. "Hey!" she shouted. When she saw the clothes Jeffie held, she stopped and her eyes got big. "Wow! I like it! Getting some smoochie smoochie tonight?"

Jeffie rolled her eyes. "What's got you all excited?"

"Hasn't anyone told you yet?"

"Told me what?"

"Brickert's the honcho!" Strawberry squeaked, then ran back out of the room.

Poor Brickert, Jeffie thought. *He must be a wreck.*

She tossed the clothes onto the bed, undressed from her pink and baby blue jumper, and put on her noblack suit. Upstairs in the cafeteria, Brickert had made good progress on a hamburger, far from the nervous basket case she'd expected. He waved when he saw her. Kawai and Natalia were with him.

Actually, Jeffie decided, *he looks downright excited.*

Just a week ago, Kawai had been honcho for her first time. Byron had pitted her against Li and Levu. Li had won. Now Kawai seemed intent on stuffing Brickert's head full of as many helpful tips as she could think of. Natalia, on the other hand, looked nervous enough for the whole group.

Jeffie helped herself to a glass of juice and caught a look at the panel:

Team 1: 5th floor
Ivanovich, Natalia
Petrov, Ludwig
Plack, Brickert(*)
von Pratt, Parley
Tvedt, Gefjon
Zheng, Li Cheng

Team 2: 5th floor
Alanazi, Cala
Covas, Miguel
Covas, Rosa
Enova, Levu
Morel, Brillianté(*)
Reynolds, Kaden

Team 3: 5th floor
Ndumi, Hefani
Nujola, Kawai
Otravelli, Antonio
Plack, Strawberry
Reynolds, Kobe
Yoshiharu, Asaki(*)

Victory: 2 wins
Maximum Game Length: 20 minutes
Start time: 16:30

"I must say, good woman," Kobe commented from behind, "rarely have these eyes seen such well-designed teams."

Jeffie turned to see him peering right over her shoulder. Kobe looked very, very good in the noblack. The dark cloth contrasted well with his blond hair and lightly-tanned skin. His angular, strong body was well defined by the tight cloth.

"I find myself compelled to agree with your assessment, young sir."

Kobe drew a little closer and leaned into her ear, whispering, "So are you excited?"

Jeffie put on her most serious expression. "Of course. I'm always excited for the Game." Then she walked over to Brickert.

As Jeffie had previously experienced, everyone had advice for a new honcho. Many were pleasantly surprised that Brickert had been tapped at such a young age. At one time, it had been widely known that Brickert dwelt at the bottom of the personal statistics. Even though the stigma still stuck, Jeffie knew it was no longer true. In reality, she and Brickert had steadily climbed the ranks for weeks. Both of them were now ranked in the top ten in all four categories.

"It's too bad your brother has to lose his first Game," Antonio told Strawberry from a few seats over.

Kawai sent a withering glare to Antonio. "You seriously need to get over yourself."

Jeffie winked at Kawai in approval. Antonio knew everyone thought of him as the cocky new kid, but he seemed happy to fill the role. He did it so well, it was almost endearing.

"I'm trying. I'm trying. But my team's won the last four of six. That should tell you something right there, darling."

"I was on your team three of those Saturdays," Kawai pointed out, " and you were the first to be deactivated at least twice."

"But not before taking out several other players," Antonio said emphatically.

Jeffie looked at Brickert and rolled her eyes. Brickert smirked but said nothing.

"I know! I know!" cried Antonio. He waved his arms in the air like an evangelical preacher. "You all think I'll never be as good as Sammy . . . but I'll prove you all wrong."

Jeffie wasn't bothered by Antonio. She'd learned a while ago that he didn't mean to trash on Sammy's memory by wanting to beat his records. It was just in his nature to be loud and abrasive.

"I used to think the same thing," Kobe called over to Antonio. His tone was friendly, but restrained.

"And?" Antonio asked.

"I played against him . . . and he beat me in everything." Kobe's statements surprised Jeffie; he still rarely spoke about Sammy.

Not deterred for long, Antonio collected his ego and talked on about his stats and performances to the only people who would listen: Strawberry and Hefani. However, he didn't have time to get a full head of steam going because the lights dimmed, telling the Psions to go to their starting points.

"Let's go team!" Brickert called out. His voice cracked badly, but Jeffie suppressed her urge to laugh.

Strawberry was not so generous, "Let's go team!" she mimicked, doing a very good job of it, too.

Everyone laughed at Strawberry's imitation, even Kobe, but he stopped when Jeffie shot him a warning look. Brickert ignored all of it and pushed passed the crowd. By the time his team had reached their portal on the fifth floor, Brickert's determined, confident exterior had worn off. His face was a touch whiter than normal and his voice had an edgy quality. The subtle change in his demeanor had happened in mere minutes. Jeffie could relate. She'd gone through the same thing weeks ago. The oldest boys on the team, Li and Ludwig, tried to engage him in a discussion on strategy.

"The Games are going to be short, we should probably blitz," said Li. "What do you think?"

Brickert looked at him for a moment, and then his face went in his hands. "Uhhh yeah . . . sure."

"You alright, Brick?" Ludwig asked.

Brickert let out a long groan. Jeffie exchanged worried glances with Natalia.

"Can't one of you take over for me?" Brickert moaned. "I'm not ready for this."

"Just give it your best," Natalia said in a soothing voice, gently rubbing Brickert on the shoulder. "You'll be fine. Even if you don't win."

Brickert peeked through his fingers at Ludwig. "You think we should blitz?"

"We've got the two most reserved girls as the other honchos. We're going to see some conservative strategies. You dig?"

"You have to call the shots in there," Li told him. "We're only going to do what you tell us."

"Okay," responded Brickert, taking short, rapid breaths.

"Game one, begin," announced the mysterious female voice.

Li and Ludwig grabbed Brickert under each arm and hauled him to his feet. Ludwig stuffed the helmet onto Brickert's head and smacked him on the behind.

"Lead us, fearless one."

Every member of the team put his or her helmet on and walked into the darkness.

The setup was one that Jeffie had seen only a few times before. It reminded her of an upside down, three-legged stool. Each team started at the top of one of the legs, and met in a circle suspended high above the Arena floor. With only twenty minutes allowed in each Game, the action had to be fast and furious. If time ran out before all members of two teams were eliminated, the team with the most players won. If at least two teams were tied, play resumed until the ties ended.

"Me and Jeffie and Natalia will attack by air, the rest on the floor," Brickert said. "Let's beat them to the circle!"

"Brickert . . ." Jeffie started to say, but then cut herself off. With the stairs being so steep, getting there first meant putting themselves at a tactical disadvantage. Li and Ludwig had told him to blitz before they'd seen the setup.

Brickert should know he has to adjust.

"What, Jeffie?" he asked

"Nothing," was her answer. *Better to let him learn for himself.*

- 319 -

The team rushed down the steps, and Jeffie followed. Brickert was the first into the air, using one palm in a high hover and using the other to blast and shield. Natalia followed shortly after. Jeffie, in the back of the group, was last.

Brickert's plan ended in a spectacular rout of his own team. When his six reached the platform, both opposing teams were still on the stairs. No doubt realizing his mistake, he changed orders to have everyone rush Brillianté's team. It wasn't a terrible idea. The attack gave them the element of surprise, and they managed to take out two of her team before the positional disadvantage inevitably turned the tide against Brickert. But when Asaki's team came up from behind they stood no chance.

Asaki's team had won.

Brickert never recovered from the first loss. As the Game went on, he was more and more on edge. His instructions grew increasingly complicated, leaving Jeffie and others with no idea what they were supposed to do. By the end of the fourth match, when Asaki's team achieved victory, Brickert had given up.

"You should have seen me in there," Antonio said to Natalia and Strawberry as the Betas exited the Arena. "I practically took out Brillianté's team by myself."

Jeffie looked around for Brickert, but saw only Kobe, Kaden, and Miguel, all laughing hysterically at something Kobe had just said. Seeing Kobe reminded her of her date and how she didn't have much time to get ready.

At the bottom of the steps, Brickert walked by himself. Jeffie recognized in his face the same frustration she'd felt when she'd lost her first round as honcho. It had taken a long time for the sting to go away. His face scowled up in the direction of Kobe and his friends' lingering laughter, but when he saw Jeffie coming back down the steps toward her, he gave her his attention.

"What did I do wrong?" She wasn't sure if he sounded hurt or confused. Maybe both, but it only made her feel worse.

"I'm sorry, Brick. I know how it feels." She didn't feel like she was saying anything helpful.

Brickert just shook his head and glanced up again at Kobe, who was still laughing. He mumbled something that Jeffie couldn't hear.

"What did you say?"

"It doesn't matter." Then he punched his other hand angrily. It was very unlike him to take a loss so seriously.

"Really?" Jeffie asked with raised eyebrows. "Because it looks like it matters. Are you mad at me? I tried hard. Really, I did."

But he shook his head even more and quickened his pace up the steps. "It's not that."

Jeffie reached up and grabbed his sleeve. "Hey, talk to me. Then, what is it?"

He shot another reproachful glance back up the steps, and turned to her. "It's your friend."

"What about him?"

"He was laughing after I lost."

"At you?"

"I don't know, I think so," Brickert explained. "He was laughing when Strawberry made fun of me. Seems like he's becoming more and more like his old self again. You remember how he was. To me."

He looked her in the eyes with a searching expression, but Jeffie felt only a wave of relief. At least Brickert wasn't mad at her. She relaxed her grip on his sleeve and touched him gently on the arm.

"Maybe you shouldn't jump to conclusions. Everyone laughed at Strawberry."

Brickert pulled back. "Why are you taking his side?"

"I'm not taking—"

"He's the same as he was! He doesn't care about Sammy! He's using Sammy to get to you. And I'm not going to take his crap anymore, I'll tell you. I'm not a pushover. You watch, Jeffie, I'm standing up for myself."

Jeffie opened her mouth to say something back, but Brickert ran up the stairs. Part of her wanted to go after him and explain her feelings, but she knew she needed to get ready for her date. Besides, he would be in a better mood later.

After showering and dressing, Strawberry insisted on helping Jeffie apply her makeup. Giving her consent proved to be a mistake because Strawberry interpreted it as having the final say in Jeffie's total appearance. Jeffie went through three outfit changes and two complete overhauls of her hairstyle. All of this put her twenty minutes behind schedule.

On the other hand, when Strawberry finally let Jeffie see herself in the mirror, all she could say was, "Wow!"

"It helps having so many older sisters. And I'm telling you, you look beautiful!"

Looking beautiful only made Jeffie nervous. She liked looking good, but she couldn't remember ever looking this good.

"Go get him, girl," Strawberry told her with a wink.

Jeffie met Kobe in a shady spot on a blanket he'd laid out and decorated with candles and dinner. The sun cast pink and lavender splashes across the sky as it dipped below the pine trees. The air was perfect for the spring and smelled wonderfully fresh.

It only took a moment for Jeffie to recognize the location as the same place where she and her fellow recruits had planned Sammy's birthday party. A strong jolt of guilt hit her stomach, but she forced herself past it before she lost her appetite. The blanket was full of things she liked: smoked salmon, fries, orange salad, and butternut squash. Kobe had obviously asked around to find out her favorite foods.

"Is it good?" he asked her just as she put some more salmon in her mouth.

Jeffie smiled and with her mouth full answered: "Delicious." Then she laughed.

"Gross," Kobe said with a wrinkled nose and grin. "I've never been a fish person."

"Really?" she responded. "Because your eyes are kinda fishlike." She puckered her lips and widened her eyes.

Kobe smirked at her. "Salmon and halibut are okay, but still . . . I have to put a lot of tartar sauce on it." As he said this, he put another spoonful of sauce on his fish.

"Then why'd you get it?" she wondered as she put some on her plate.

"I don't *dislike* it. Besides, this is smoked. It's pretty good smoked." As he said this, he put a big bite in his mouth and chewed it slowly with a face exaggeratedly in love with the food. "Mmm. So good."

Jeffie giggled loudly. "I like pizza, too, you know."

"And then afterwards we drink root beer and have a burping contest!" Kobe offered in jest. "Come on, I wanted it to be a nice night."

"It is nice," she said sincerely and flashed him a confidential smile. "Thank you."

He winked at her and took another bite of his food.

"I hope this doesn't mean that we're . . . together now?"

"Of course not," Kobe answered quickly. "Kaden and I do blanket dinners all the time. No big deal."

Jeffie burst into laughter and Kobe joined her. "You're a nerd."

"Thanks."

Even after they finished eating, several minutes passed in conversation. Both followed basketball, so they talked about their favorite teams. Then they got into a friendly argument about whether football or American football was better.

"You can't use your hands!" Kobe said. "It's not a real sport!"

"That's like saying running isn't a sport!" she shot back. "How many football matches have you even watched?"

Kobe opened his mouth to answer when footsteps dragging through the leaves interrupted him. It was too dark to see who was making the noises, but the sounds came closer.

"Hey!" Kobe called out. "Can we have some privacy?"

The footsteps stopped and then crunched right toward the picnic area.

"Guess not," Kobe muttered.

A figure emerged from the shadows and into the dull illumination of the candlelight. It was Brickert. His chest heaved, his hands shook, and his face had turned ghostly white.

"Can you please leave?" Kobe asked hotly.

"NO!" Brickert shouted, his voice cracking again like it had before the Game. "Jeffie! What are you doing with him?" As he asked this, he glared at her fiercely. "What about Sammy?"

Kobe got to his feet. "We're on a date. She doesn't need you here bringing that up right now."

"Oh, I'm sorry!" Brickert spat. "You're only moving in on the guy-who-saved-your-life's girl! But I guess to some people that doesn't merit any respect, I'll tell you!"

"You don't have a clue!" Kobe yelled. "You weren't there. He was my friend, too."

A harsh laugh came from Brickert's throat. "Yeah, right. And I'm engaged to Commander Byron. Didn't you get an invitation?" He turned to Jeffie, who had been unable to find her voice in the conversation. A blend of shame and hostility swirled inside her when she saw the accusation in his eyes directed at her as well. "What's your deal? You were the one trying to convince me a few months ago that he's still alive. You were crazy about him!"

"I—" she started to say.

"No, don't answer that, Jeffie," Kobe told her. "Sammy's dead, Brickert. Two bombs went off not more than a meter away from him. And you being here trying to convince Jeffie otherwise isn't helping things!"

Brickert's chest heaved one final time and a pathetic, strangled yelp escaped his throat. Jeffie watched him with pity, still not knowing what to do or say to help the situation. Then Brickert launched himself at Kobe, ramming his head into her date's stomach.

"Brickert—no!" She jumped up to separate the two.

Brickert's weight took Kobe down to the ground spilling candles and dishes and food everywhere. Half-sitting and half-laying on top of Kobe, Brickert pounded at Kobe's face while yelling at him. Jeffie tried to pull him off, but Brickert held onto Kobe so tightly with one hand that he couldn't be budged. Kobe raised his arms to block the blows but did nothing to hurt Brickert. Smelling smoke, Jeffie saw the blanket had caught fire, the flames spreading fast toward the two boys.

"Help!" she yelled. "Stop it Brickert!"

But Brickert did not stop.

In response to her cries, several more footsteps crunched down the path from headquarters. Kaden, Strawberry, and Antonio came sprinting onto the scene. Antonio tackled Brickert clean off Kobe whose face was bleeding and bruised. Strawberry helped Jeffie stomp out the flames. Next came Commander Byron looking bewildered and harried.

When he saw that the flames were extinguished, he crossed over to Brickert in two steps and yanked him up by his shirt collar.

"Get to solitary, Brickert!" he said in the sternest voice Jeffie had ever heard and then dropped Brickert down to the ground. He knelt down by Kobe and helped him to his feet while Brickert ran off in the direction of the building. "Are you alright?"

"Yeah. I'm fine." Blood from his nose and mouth made his voice thick.

"Did you do anything to warrant Brickert's anger?"

"No, sir," Kobe said instantly. "I swear I didn't."

The commander stood up and surveyed the scene. Jeffie watched him, still shocked.

I should have talked to Brickert sooner. I should have told him I was going on a date.

"Kaden and Antonio, will you help Kobe back to the cafeteria?" Byron asked. "I will call Dr. Rosmir and ask him to meet you there shortly."

Kobe seemed too dazed to worry about Jeffie or the picnic, so after everyone left, Strawberry stayed behind and helped Jeffie clean up the mess.

"I'm sorry," she blurted out, her voice even higher than normal. "This is all my fault."

A soft snort of air came out of Jeffie's nose. "How is any of this your fault?"

"Brickert was looking all over for you. He wanted to watch something with you, but wouldn't say what. Then he noticed Kobe wasn't around either. So he pestered me until I let it slip that the two of you were on a date. He ran out as soon as I said it."

"Oh," Jeffie responded quietly. Her mouth froze in surprise for almost two seconds. "I still missed the part where you had some fault in it."

Strawberry stood silently for a moment, shrugged helplessly, and then finished gathering up the rest of the picnic supplies. The blanket was ruined, so were the broken dishes. They disposed of those things in a dumpster before going inside, the rest they carried up to the kitchen. Along the way, several Betas stopped them to ask what had happened. Natalia looked furious and ready to unload when Jeffie stopped her.

"If you accuse me of doing something with Brickert behind your back, I'm going to smack you."

Natalia stamped her feet haughtily and marched back down the hall, pale blonde hair swishing behind her. Strawberry followed Natalia to explain the situation.

Jeffie peeked into the cafeteria and saw that several Betas, mostly females, were gathered around Kobe, checking to see if he was alright.

Antonio was over in a corner talking to Hefani under his breath. Ducking out before anyone saw her, she went to the exercise room and sent a text:

Commander,

I know it's called solitary for a reason, but may I please go visit Brickert? I think I can relate to what he's going through better than anyone else. What happened is partly my fault.

Gefjon

She knew he would tell her no, but sent it anyway. Kaden stepped into the room just after she finished.

"Hey." His voice was a little too calm, and he looked as though he felt very awkward being there. "You got a minute?"

Jeffie checked her inbox, which showed no new messages. "Sure. What's up?"

Kaden chuckled. "Nothing. It's just funny, is all. Usually in times like this I end up apologizing for something Kobe's done. I had to do it a lot when Sammy was around. But even before that . . . I don't know. Kobe's always been doing crap."

Jeffie stared at Kaden's shoes for a moment, then answered him. "You don't have to apologize, though. Kobe didn't do anything."

"Oh, I know. I just came to make sure *you* know that. Has he ever told you he's older than me?"

Jeffie shook her head.

"It's true. By a whole five minutes. But I've always felt like the older one until recently. Kobe's changed so much for the better ever since . . .

Rio. I'm really impressed. I just wanted you to know that even if Brickert doesn't know it."

"Kaden, I know that. And you know I know that." She looked him in the eyes now. "What do you really want to say to me?"

Kaden grabbed a basketball and put it on his hand, then he spun it as it hovered over his palm on a blast. Jeffie watched him, mesmerized. He kept the ball spinning as he spoke. "Why are you dating Kobe?"

"I don't know."

"Is it because you like him or because you miss Sammy or because he was the last person with Sammy?"

"I—I like him. I mean, of course I miss Sammy. Everyone misses Sammy."

Kaden changed the strength of his blast, letting the ball keep spinning while he did it.

"You're better than Kobe at that." She meant it to be a statement, but it came out more like a surprise.

The ball hit the floor and Kaden let it bounce away. He finally looked her in the eyes again and asked, "Can I ask you a very personal question?"

Jeffie gave him permission with a look.

"Do you believe Sammy is dead?"

Of all the questions she'd expected to hear, that was not one of them. Jeffie reeled back from where she stood, bracing herself on the handle of one of the exercise machines. She couldn't answer. She didn't want to.

"Excuse me, please." She turned and ran to the ladies' restroom. It was there that Byron's response came. Jeffie was stunned. Not only did he give her his permission, but also authorized her vocal patterns to get into the room just once. After composing herself, she crossed the third floor to the solitary rooms and let herself in.

Inside, Brickert lay on his back on a restraining table with his hands over his face. He looked between his fingers to see who had come in. This was enough for her to get a good look at him. His face was puffy, especially around his eyes. He pretended not to see her.

"Hey," she said weakly, taking the seat by the table.

Brickert made no sign that he'd heard her.

"How long are you in here for?"

Brickert's shoulders shrugged, dropped his hands, but stared at the ceiling.

"You mad at me?"

Another shrug.

"Commander says you're going to be sent home, and they're going to make you take that pill. You know, the one that will take away your Anomaly Fourteen."

Brickert rolled onto his side. "You're extremely funny, Jeffie. Go away."

Jeffie grinned at her own joke, glad he would still speak to her. "If you're mad at me, why'd you go at Kobe?"

"It's wrong to hit a girl." Brickert snorted at his own comment and mumbled, "Come on, you know why."

When Jeffie had sent the text to Byron, she'd thought she knew what Brickert needed to hear. Now, sitting with her friend, she sensed a wide rift between them, punctuated by her loss for words. She knew it had to do with the same subject that Kaden had just asked her about. Her body tensed, and she hoped Brickert would say more. Finally, he did.

It came in a quiet question—almost a whisper. He still didn't look at her, preferring to stare straight up at the white ceiling. "Do you still think Sammy's alive?"

Jeffie couldn't believe he asked her the same question. However, she was more prepared for it this time. "I used to have dreams about him being alive. I used to think I'd see him in the mornings, and that him being gone was a nightmare. Those have all stopped now."

Brickert shuffled his body slightly. Even in little movements like that, his body language indicated how upset he was with her.

"I want to, Brickert!" she added quickly and perhaps even less truthfully than she realized. "Part of me wants to never let go. I—I guess part of me also wants to let go. I'm tired of waiting." Hearing the frustration and resentment and fatigue in own her voice surprised her. Some of this she directed at herself, but some she directed at Sammy, too. In a way—and she'd never voice it to Brickert—she wished she'd never met Sammy because that would mean never going through any of this drama.

"Like it would have been so hard for God to have just let Al and them find—or even see—his dead body so we could know for sure! Right, Brickert? I mean, he—he never even had a real funeral!" She stopped before her emotions ran too high for her to control.

Brickert finally turned over and faced her. His eyes stared hard into hers. Something passed between them, Jeffie did not know what, she would have called it a ball of invisible light if she had to give it a name. The invisible light went deep down inside her soul and warmed her. When Brickert closed his eyes the connection was broken, but something stronger stayed inside of her.

"Just have faith, Jeffie," he told her softly.

Jeffie put her hand on his arm and he opened his eyes again. In them, Jeffie saw that Brickert did not just believe Sammy was alive. He knew Sammy was alive. Somehow, he knew it.

"What did you say?" she asked.

"Just have faith," he repeated with a simple smile. The puffiness in his eyes was more pronounced than ever, but he had command of his emotions. "Sammy's not a god or an angel, but . . . he's smart. He's dang smart.

23 | Eavesdropping

April 28, 2086

SAMMY WAS BORED OUT OF HIS MIND. He'd spent almost a week sitting next to Thomas Byron in one of the towers of the Palace, huddled over a table with a pen in his hand, a piece of paper in front of him, and wearing a pair of earphones. Surrounding him in the cramped room, packing almost every spare centimeter of space, stood more surveillance and recording machines than even Thomas had a name for. Right now Sammy was listening to two women discussing plans for their children's playgroup.

"I don't mind if Lissa brings Ethan, but he's a scratcher," the woman named Nanette said. Her voice sounded like her nose was pinched, and it grinded on Sammy's nerves. He'd been listening to her for over ten minutes.

"You're right, he is a scratcher. Last time he drew blood on Suzette's cheek!" her friend, Dana, complained. "She's thirteen months old, for crying out loud! She can't defend herself. And Lissa doesn't do anything about it."

"She thinks it's just a phase. Lana had the gall to agree with her."

"Well, at least Kinsie's not coming," Dana said. "Do you want to know what Jill and Charlene call her?"

"Let's hear it."

"The Kinsanator!"

The two women screeched into the phone so loud Sammy jumped in his chair.

"Everything okay, Sammy?" Thomas asked.

Sammy pulled off his headphones and rubbed his aching ears. "Fine. Just loud."

Thomas took off his own headphones and looked at his watch. "The others will be back from lunch soon. We'll go then. You're used to all the excitement of fighting. Not the boring work. This is where intel comes from."

"I know," Sammy grumbled. "Believe me, I've been told it before."

Thomas chuckled with his whole body. Sammy glanced up at the transmission signal, which now showed three red lights. Nanette had finally hung up with Dana.

"So, how are you faring, Sammy? We never really spoke about your therapy. Well, Dr. Vogt said I wasn't supposed to talk about it while it was going on. He never said if I could bring it up now that y'all are done with it."

Sammy shrugged casually. He had wondered how long it would take to get to this question.

"When you first got here, you seemed, well, out of it."

"I don't know. I'm okay. Better than I was."

"But still not yourself?" Thomas asked.

Sammy shook his head.

"Well, give it time. From what Toad told me, you've been through fire and brimstone," he said with a grandfatherly air. "You must be a real strong boy. I'm sure Walter saw that, too."

"Um—thanks." Sammy looked away while trying to think of a new subject to discuss. "So, why aren't we picking up anything from the Thirteens?"

"It's like sifting sand for gold," Thomas frowned at the transmission signal. "You might be sifting in the right place, but it takes time even to find a few small kernels."

"How does all this stuff work?"

"Well, we recruited this new lady, Darnee—Marnee—yeah, Marnee . . . or something like that. She's been working in the communications field all her life. When we located a Thirteen cell, we started planting taps on the nearest BSCs."

He saw Sammy's puzzled expression and smiled as if he had been trying to confuse him. "Sorry, but you should see your face when you don't understand something. It's the funniest thing. I can tell you're not used to it. When you make a call from a com, it goes to a tower and from there to a big box called a Base Station Controller or BSC. That's the box that does the thinking for the whole system. Marnee, or whatever her name is, has been putting transmitters in these BSCs and the transmitters send us copies of the signals."

"That's a whole lot of calls, right?"

"No, the transmitters are wired in. They listen for a big list of pertinent words. 'Thirteen', 'NWG', 'attack', stuff like that. Even your name is on there now. If something hits, we pick it up and keep the data file."

Thomas's excitement was visible even in the dim lighting of the tower.

"And you're sure we're looking in the right place?" Sammy asked.

"We've known about the Thirteen building in Orlando for a while. I'm pretty certain we can intercept their communications."

"Do you know exactly where they're—the cell is based?"

"We do now. Using Toad's information about the building you were kept in, we looked for someone who owned a large office building in both cities. Bada-bing bada-boom! In fact, we've managed to locate seven Thirteen cells now. Well . . . seven unconfirmed cells. That's a pretty big breakthrough, Sammy."

"What's the likelihood of us hearing anything?"

"Beats me. But at least we're doing something useful."

One of the three red lights turned green, and Sammy hurried to put his headphones back on.

"Hi, is Robbie there?" a girl's voice asked.

"Just a second," came an older, male voice.

There was a pause and a "Hello?"

"Hi Robbie, it's Keira. Have you looked at our homework? Kaylin and I couldn't figure out number thirteen—"

Sammy sighed and listened on. Minutes later he heard a conversation regarding a delayed order for thirteen hundred dollars worth of gym equipment.

They had another lull in calls. Sammy leaned back in his chair like a seasoned veteran and threw questions at Thomas about the resistance. He listened to a long narrative on the effectiveness of pigeon communication and how Crestan and Henrico were killed.

"So how did you get involved? When did you join?"

The bright and animated look on Thomas's face that always accompanied his enthusiastic stories for the resistance melted away. Sammy instantly wished he hadn't asked the question.

"'For deeds undone rankle and snarl and hunger for their due'," Thomas muttered solemnly, fiddling with his headset as he spoke. "'Til there seems naught so despicable as you in all the grin of the sun.'"

Sammy had no idea what Thomas was talking about, and was about to ask him when Thomas put his headset back on and turned away.

"I'm getting something on here," he said as he tapped on his earphones.

Sammy knew Thomas was lying, but he didn't call him on it. *What did I say that was so offensive?*

Before he could dwell on it too long, he got another call. Their relief came soon after to spell them for a lunch break. Thomas didn't say anything as he left the room, and during lunch he seemed sullen, even to his wife. Lara gave Sammy an inquisitive glance when her husband was short with her, but Sammy just shrugged. Lunch went by too fast and Sammy was back upstairs in the tower wearing headphones again.

The day dragged on: a housewife complaining about a defective vacuum, her language so coarse it embarrassed even Sammy. An emergency call from a boy in college asking his dad for money to fix his car. Several boring business calls.

He let a long sigh go quietly. He did not want Thomas to think he was uninterested.

Why won't he talk to me? Sammy wondered. *Maybe I should just apologize.*

His light turned green again.

"Go ahead," a very deep male voice said. There was a sense of authority that Sammy had heard before. It reminded him of some of the workers at the Grinder, the ones that really got off on ordering people around.

The second voice had an edge to it, like he was a little nervous. "We crunched the numbers. Three times. We simulated them on multiple programs and reached the same conclusions. You need more people in the operation."

Sammy's ears pricked up at these words.

"How many do we already have?" the deep voice asked.

"Sixty at my last count."

"What's the breakdown?"

"Forty-five Aegis and fifteen Brothers," came the answer slowly, as if the nervous man had read the numbers from a list. Sammy sat up straight in his chair and gripped the arms tightly. He'd gone from sheer boredom to high alert with one word. Thomas, not looking in Sammy's direction, did not notice this change.

"Who thinks we need more?" the authority-voice asked.

"The entire tactical team."

"How many more?"

"Ten more Brothers. We calculate seventy people in that ratio is the most efficient number to best guarantee success."

"What's the difference?" the voice growled.

"Based on all our data we see the likelihood rising from seventy-two to ninety-one percent likelihood of success."

The deeper voice grumbled in the background. "I'd gamble on that."

"With a liberal appraisal we expect thirty Elite and two squadrons of Fourteens."

"All on site?"

"Either at the launch or in the Baikonur control tower."

The deep male voice barked, "Have the team run the numbers again and call me."

Then the line went blank.

Sammy took a deep breath. His hands still gripped the arms of his chair. The tips of his fingers had turned bone white. He put the headphones down on the table and tapped Thomas lightly on the shoulder.

"I think I heard something you might want to hear."

Messages were sent out immediately. Days later, a meeting was held. Something about seeing hundreds of people assemble at the Palace helped Sammy understand just how large and well-organized the resistance really was.

"Won't having all these people here run the risk of being discovered?" Sammy had asked Thomas as he sent out messages.

Thomas, who had regained all his optimism and energy the instant he had listened to Sammy's call, wasn't worried. "I've told you already, this city is tunneled for just such things. Everyone knows to use extreme caution. People still travel through Wichita going all directions."

"And you're still not going to let me in?"

"Sorry, kiddo," Thomas said with genuine regret. "Members only."

Sammy was beyond annoyed that he couldn't go to the meeting. But when he saw that Thomas was firm in his decision, he didn't argue.

He and Toad decided to use the time to work on Toad's anomaly. The Palace had a large exercise room, so they went there. Toad was eager to show Sammy some of the stuff he'd been practicing. He had Sammy blast baseballs at him while he deflected them by throwing his own baseballs. While they messed around, they discussed the intercepted transmission and hypothesized what would be done about it.

Just when Toad was about to show off his shooting skills, Thomas came into the room.

"Sammy," he called out from the doorway, "we need you in here."

"What about me?" Toad cried out in unmasked jealousy.

Sammy looked back at his friend apologetically, but was eager to be involved with the meetings. He followed Thomas up to the fourth floor where a large meeting hall was packed with people; men and women of different ages, races, and statures. Many of them were turned facing each other in conversation—so many, in fact, that the sound from the room was a low roar.

"We spent most of the morning discussing one thing, Sammy," Thomas told him just outside the hall, "getting you home. I told them you have information about a possible mole in your organization. I also told them it's a remote but real possibility that there are Psions in CAG territory searching for you. They've heard the intercepted conversation between the

- 340 -

Thirteen cell in Orlando and the tactical team. So everyone in there knows that it's important we get you back. The only question now is whether they'll be talked out of it."

"How? What do you mean?"

Thomas put a hand on Sammy's back and steered him into the hall.

The instant the door closed behind them, the chatting in the hall stopped, heads whipped around in Sammy's direction, and every last member of the audience rose to his or her feet. Someone, somewhere began clapping; two strong, sturdy hands rhythmically pounding into each other. Another pair joined them. Then two more pairs. Like rainfall transforming from a gentle shower into a mighty storm, the hall erupted in applause and cheers.

Thomas's hand fell on Sammy's shoulder. The old man leaned over to whisper in his ear: "They're standing because of you. For what you represent."

For a long time Sammy just stood there, rooted to that spot just inside the door. He looked into the eyes of the resistance as they looked back at him, cheering and clapping. It must have gone on for minutes.

At that moment in his life, he understood what it meant: the oath he had taken, the battles he had fought and might yet fight. In that room, with all those people, it all made sense. Sammy knew why he was a Psion.

Another hand on his other shoulder pushed him forward. As he walked toward the few chairs that faced the crowd, the noise came to a crescendo and held there. Sammy put up a hand and awkwardly waved in acknowledgement of their praise, then sat down.

Slowly the applause died down.

Thomas stood up to speak. "I think Sammy's a little overwhelmed."

Polite laughter rippled through the resistance members.

"I think I've taken up enough of the morning explaining why I believe we need to get Sammy back home—whether we can reach out to the NWG or just get him there ourselves. However, I promised our ombudsman some time to speak his mind and give his thoughts on the matter. So let's hear from him."

The ombudsman sat in a chair on the opposite side of Thomas. He was a tall, thinly-built man wearing a respectable business suit. His dark hair was thinning on the top and graying on the sides. He had all the signs and lines of a chronic smoker. As he spoke, he licked his lips often.

"About eleven years ago, most of our organization broke down because of unneeded risks. We lost over ninety percent of our manpower and many of our properties. It was a huge setback. Since then, we've been on a course of extreme caution. We haven't done much to advance our cause other than collect data, move people into strategic positions of opportunity, and grow our numbers again. That strategy has worked, I believe. We've gone from three hundred members to almost two thousand.

"I think we need to ask ourselves several questions before voting on these decisions. First, are we sure we want to attempt to steal a ship? Thomas has suggested looking at Offutt as the site for the caper. This may possibly bring on unwanted attention. Do we want to risk lives—manpower—if things should turn ugly? Next, is there an easier way to contact the NWG to inform them of what we've discovered? Thomas suggested our member in Los Angeles who works with GNN. He's referring, some of you probably know, to Ty Robbins. We have few people as well placed as he. We all need to ask ourselves this question: is what Thomas has proposed too risky or even counterproductive?"

"In what way is it counterproductive, Doug?" Thomas didn't look happy as he spoke. In fact, he looked downright pissed off. "We sent people down to the old Rio compound to investigate. They found plenty of evidence to suggest someone had been there looking for Sammy!"

Doug licked his lips twice more before responding. "Well, you know, we're not absolutely certain how important this operation is. Is it worth risking exposure to what we're doing here? Is it worth putting the lives of many people at risk. I'm not against striking out if this is worth it, but we need to be sure it is."

Thomas spoke again. "Come on, Doug, you heard the recording!"

Doug turned briefly to Thomas. "Please, it's my turn to speak. You've had your say."

Thomas became silent, but seemed to take great effort in doing so. Sammy could sense something of a rift between the two men.

"Are we overreacting?" Doug added. "I don't know. We've worked very hard to build ourselves back up since the CAG caught, tortured, and killed so many of us. We must make sure that we're practicing both prudence and responsible resistance."

A general murmur broke out in the crowd. Thomas looked at Sammy and shook his head.

"So let's stop yammering and take a vote!" he called out over the noise, which grew quiet at the sound of his voice. Sammy smiled to himself as he remembered the way Commander Byron could take control over a large group.

"We'll vote on both items separately. If either item passes with popular consent we'll form a committee of seven to determine how it will be carried out. All in favor of attempting contact with people who might be searching for Sammy say 'aye.'"

A loud burst of 'ayes' rang across the room. Sammy was almost positive it had been unanimous.

"Any opposed with 'nay.'"

There were no 'nays.'

"That decision passes unanimously. All in favor of stealing a cruiser for Sammy to fly home say 'aye.'"

This time there were noticeably less 'ayes' from the crowd. Sammy saw Doug had not voiced in favor. Thomas looked both nervous and disappointed at the response.

"All those opposed?"

A similar sound of 'nays' echoed.

"The vote is undetermined." He shot a glance at Sammy. "I motion for a hand vote."

"Seconded," Doug said from his chair.

"Then let's have a show of hands."

This time members of the leadership counted hands. The total was one hundred eighty seven for, and one hundred thirty seven against.

The motion passed.

Late that night, Sammy sat in a room with seven members of the resistance. One of the seven was Doug, the ombudsman. He told Thomas if the resistance was going to go through with the crazy notion of stealing a cruiser, he wanted to be on the committee to plan it. Things around the Palace were manic with people scrambling everywhere to get stuff done. No one really knew what the timetable was for the CAG's impending attack on

Baikonur, or what it really meant, but the decision was that the sooner they acted to prevent it the better.

Thomas roamed between the two committees trying to keep everyone on task. Permanently attached to his hand all night was a steaming mug of what smelled to Sammy like hot chocolate. When Thomas came back into the room to check on the "Cruiser Caper Committee," as he dubbed it, he was beaming.

"We've wrapped up plans for the GNN message. Ty says it will go out on the morning broadcast. If Walter is looking for Sammy in Rio or wherever, he should get the message."

"How's it going to happen?" Doug asked.

"Ty's slipping it into the prompt. Says he'll claim they were hacked. It's happened before."

"Won't the news producers see it on the prompt and stop the feed?" Doug wondered aloud.

"No. GNN uses those—what do you call them—contact prompts. Puts the prompts right in front of the eye. They won't know it's coming until it comes out of the newscaster's mouth."

Dr. Vogt spoke up next. "We've already taken precautions in case something goes awry. His family is on the way here as we speak, and he'll be joining them as soon as he's loaded the prompt. If it all blows over, he'll go back to work."

Doug nodded, satisfied.

"And this will be heard all over the continent?" Sammy asked.

"All over North and South America," Thomas answered. "We're banking on the idea that if they're here, they're watching the news. If so, they meet us at Offutt and pick him up. If not, he flies himself and Toad out."

"Fine. What's the message?" Doug asked.

"You'll love it, Sammy," Thomas chuckled as he pulled a handwritten draft out of his shirt pocket. He cleared his throat dramatically and read: "An Omaha librarian searching through antique books found an unpublished and unread poem co-written by Walt Whitman and Lord Byron titled 'The Brains of Samuel'. Scholars say it is the first of its kind, and if testing confirms its authenticity, it's estimated worth would be in the millions. It will be flown out of Omaha early Friday morning to the Smithsonian Institute for age analysis and verification."

Sammy laughed hard when he heard it, but Doug didn't seem sold. "How on earth is that going to clue anybody to anything?"

Thomas explained, "Anyone who knows my son knows who he was named after. And anyone who bothers to fact-check it will know that Lord Byron died when Walt Whitman was five years old."

Doug smiled broadly. "And Whitman wasn't a prodigy like Mozart, was he?"

"Not that I know of," Thomas laughed and took a long swig of his hot chocolate. "So what have we got so far on the cruiser caper?"

24 | Plans

May 2, 2086

"REALLY? SHE WANTS PURPLE FLOWERS?" Byron asked Albert. He sat in his office talking to his son over video conference, taking notes on the young couple's wedding plans. Since Emily wasn't alive to help, Byron was determined to do as good a job as two parents would. He'd even gone so far as to order wedding catalogs to help him understand what it meant to plan a wedding.

"Yeah, she's got it all listed right here." On screen, Albert tapped his holo-tablet. "She's very organized."

"I do not want to intrude on your plans, but . . . purple flowers?" he asked again. "I have never seen any purple flowers in these catalogs, have you?"

Albert laughed hard. Byron joined him. "You've been reading up, huh, Dad? Well, remember, her wedding colors are purple and white."

"Wedding colors, huh?" Byron repeated. He flipped to the glossary of one his books. *Wedding color(s): A color or series of colors around which the wedding decorations, flowers, and ceremonial clothing is arranged.* "Yep, wedding colors."

"Oh, come on!" Albert said when he saw his dad look up the term. "You act like you've never planned a wedding!"

"I never have."

"Yeah, well, at some point you must have done something . . ."

"I like planning parties as much as I like bowling. And my best bowling score—"

"Is ninety." Albert rolled his eyes. "Great joke five years ago. But Marie and I aren't getting married on a whim—"

"It was not on a whim. Emily and I—we just saw no need to go through all these . . . preparations."

"It was a whim," Albert said, still chuckling.

Byron let the argument slide. "So where am I going to find purple flowers?"

"Marie said you could order them from the floral shop down the street from the history museum."

"Do they handle large orders like that?"

"Oh yeah. All the time."

"Then I will look into it," Byron told his son.

"Thanks. Do you have anything new on the other thing?" Albert's tone implied that he was referring to Byron's secret investigation into a possible mole in the Alpha hierarchy.

"Nothing. I checked transmission records of everyone. I saw no suspicious records. No unusual expenditures or income. We have no record of anyone except aircraft engineers visiting that hangar where the stealth cruiser was kept. Whoever did this has been very careful."

"No one with ties to the CAG?"

"Honestly, Albert, I have the closest ties to CAG of anyone in Psion Command. However, I have no plans of giving up. Rest easy on that."

"And no word on Sammy, right?"

Byron folded his arms across his chest. "You already asked me that. Do you really think I would forget to tell you if I heard something?"

Albert rolled his eyes. "I know, I know. Thanks for the chat. I got to go."

"I am excited for your wedding, son. You know that, right?"

"I know, Dad, really. But I've still—"

"Got to go. Talk to you soon."

Albert's face disappeared as the screen on Byron's wall went blank. The commander leaned back in his chair and enjoyed the moment of being able to help his son with wedding plans. It was true, he had not gone through the same process with his wife because of the hurried nature of their wedding.

His screen flashed again. At first he thought his son had forgotten something, but it was not Albert. It was Victor. He looked at the clock and realized it was almost midnight.

What could he want? "Accept."

"Walter," Wrobel said right away. His face appeared on the screen, looking more tired and drawn than Byron had seen him in quite some time.

"Victor, to what do I owe the pleasure?"

"I need a favor, Walter. I'm absolutely swamped."

"You look swamped," Byron said with a gentle smile.

Wrobel took the joke in stride with a friendly smile of his own. "You haven't lost your charm." His face turned serious again. "Have you read through the latest briefing for the moon launch?"

Due to the lateness of the hour, Byron had to take a moment to pick his brain. "Sent by you two days ago?"

Wrobel nodded. "General Wu didn't like it. He wants two squadrons at the launch. Along with three dozen Elite."

"And you would like my help . . ." Byron finished.

"My plate is full just working with the Elite. Plus, I've got two upcoming Panels to organize for your Betas."

"My son is getting married in a month, not to mention I run this entire complex," he said with an implying tone of voice. "Are any of the other commanders able to pick up some slack?"

"Believe me, Walter, I've checked. I really need your help on this."

Byron suppressed a small sigh. He knew that he was going to say yes, and decided to do so just to have the conversation finished. At least this was a very short-term project.

"Okay, send me the info."

Wrobel looked as if a huge burden had been lifted from his shoulders, and his boyish charming smile returned. "Much thanks. I'm sending you a file with everything you'll need."

"I look forward to it," Byron responded with his best not-excited smile.

"Let me know if you have questions."

"Will do, Victor."

Commander Wrobel's face disappeared, and Byron downloaded the file his friend had just sent. A strange feeling passed over him as he looked at the file waiting to be opened, perhaps he should have thought twice before accepting Victor's request. He'd felt similar promptings before, and usually listened to them. Maybe it was the lateness of the hour, or maybe just loyalty to his friend, but he opened the file and went over the maps and mission data Victor had sent.

Dear Moon Launch . . . how do I hate thee? Let me count the ways, Byron mused to himself.

The Alphas had nothing to do with the upcoming launch, code-named Artemis, except to serve as a precautionary security measure against an attack. Byron remembered ten years ago when they'd gone through a similar hullabaloo over the first moon launch, Pioneer. The Pioneer had carried the seeds of the first moon station. Over the last decade, astronauts assembled and tested it meticulously to ensure its safety for living.

Apparently the Pioneer was a success, because the upcoming Artemis shuttle would carry even more cargo and two hundred fifty passengers to the moon. The first moon settlers. The moon colony, the Pioneer and Artemis launches, all of it was top secret until the big announcement the day before liftoff. Rumors had been out there for many months, but so far the secret had stayed well-kept. According to General Wu, special media invitations had been extended to cover the event, and its announcement would happen only hours before the Artemis shuttle took off.

The Alphas and Elite would be nothing more than babysitters with front row seats to the launch. After re-reading the brief and looking through all the squadron schedules, he sent emails to two squad leaders telling them he'd assigned them for the task, and that they were to meet to discuss specific assignments. All of that took about an hour.

A glance at his clock told him it was time to retire. He stretched as he got up from his desk and felt his knees groan. Just as he was about to turn out the lights, something stopped him. It was another call.

"My goodness," he grumbled. "Who is calling now?"

His screen showed an unidentified number incapable of video feed.

Tango squadron.

It had only been two days since their last check-in, and another wasn't scheduled for another five days. Risking too many calls was dangerous—this unexpected contact must be important.

He accepted the call and heard screaming in the background.

"Commander! Commander! Can you hear me?"

"Hello?" His eyes went wide as he gripped the edge of his desk. "I hear you. Are you all right?"

"Commander, this is Shamila. You're not going to believe this!" the voice shouted. The connection was poor and there was the occasional break up with static, but Byron realized the screaming was celebratory. "You're simply not going to believe it!"

"Well, what is it?" Byron asked. He felt his own excitement climbing. "Did you find him?"

"Just listen."

After those two words came a perfect feed of a news broadcast from Los Angeles. Byron sank down into his chair as he listened, not knowing how Sammy had done it, but absolutely certain those words were meant for him.

"If I'm not mistaken," Shamila said, "somebody's trying to tell you something. Don't you agree?"

Byron tried to laugh, but emotion choked him. He gripped his desk hard as a silent prayer escaped his lips. "Thank you, God. This is a miracle."

"Are you there, sir?"

"Yes."

"What are our orders?" Shamila asked.

"Get to the coast. I will clear everything with Wu and meet you there ASAP. Be ready for my arrival."

The joyful shouting continued over the com link. Byron clapped alone in his office. "Good work. Tell your whole squadron that."

"Yes, sir," Shamila said through the static, "We'll see you, sir!"

The line went dead. Byron stood back up, rubbing the last of the sleep out of his eyes. After getting a long drink of water, he sat back at his desk and put through a call to General Wu on urgent status. Byron thought about what he would say. He had a lot of explaining to do.

25 | Doug

May 2, 2086

THE QUEEN DROVE HER MOTORCYCLE back into Wichita following the GPS coordinates to the last place Sammy and his traveling companion had been seen on satellite. Downtown Wichita. A ghost city. The trail had stopped here and no matter how hard she searched, she could come up with no sign that they'd left town. Unfortunately, she had no evidence that they'd stayed, either.

Come out, come out, wherever you are, Sammy.

She'd been here seven times in the last month. Each time, she grew more moody and restless. All she wanted was something to take her frustrations out on. Driving slowly on her bike, she rode through downtown, passing building after building. As she passed them, she aimed her infrared thermometer at the windows. All of them were the same: seventy-one degrees, virtually the same temperature as outside.

Something is going on here. She brought the bike to a stop and stared around the block. On her left was an old building that looked like a castle. On her right was a tall office building. A block away was a giant, round convention center. She revved the engine and shot recklessly toward it, pointing the device into these windows as well. Then something caught her eye.

One of the doors moved just slightly, as though she had barely missed someone going inside. She wasn't even certain it hadn't been a trick of the light, but checking it out seemed better than driving around the city. She pulled the bike to the curb and hopped off, jogging up to the door.

There was a scent in the air. Then she spotted the source on the ground. A cigarette butt, hastily snuffed and kicked, but not well enough.

The interior of the building was only dimly illuminated by the natural sunlight streaming in from the large street-side windows, and opened up to a large foyer with yellowed signs pointing visitors to different halls, theaters, and an adjacent hotel. A thick layer of dust covered the faded carpets. Footprints ran through them. Fresh ones.

"Sammy?" she called out as she examined where the prints led. "Don't you know that smoking can kill you?"

The Queen stalked after her unknown prey, flashlight in hand. The tracks led around the circular building and into a giant exhibition hall. Inside, it was completely dark. *The prey runs blindly.* The thought made her smile. She put away the flashlight and retrieved a gun with a mounted light.

The tracks cut straight across the hall. She hurried onward. The air was so still that the smell of sweat mingled with nicotine and tar hung in the air.

A door in the back took her into an adjacent hallway. This one had hundreds of chairs facing a stage. She kept her light trained on the floor several paces ahead of her, shining it upward every ten steps to see if her prey was in sight.

The steps went across the room, around all the chairs, and toward another door. She set her sights on it, but something told her to stop.

Either she heard it or felt it. Sometimes her intuitions were basically the same, but she sensed the faintest movement near her, behind a row of chairs. To a mind trained as well as hers, even the smallest of movements was too much.

The boy had tried to lay a trap. He had retraced his steps through the dust, and hidden like a cornered cowardly snake.

No snake was fast enough to bite her.

She whipped her body around just in time to see a tall, middle-aged man rushing at her as fast as stealth would allow with a large wooden chair raised high above him. He brought the chair down at her head, but she deftly maneuvered away and kicked him in the stomach. The chair slipped from his hands, crashing to the carpet. The man doubled over, and she sent an equally vicious kick to his face.

SNAP!

Blood gushed from his nose as his head jerked back sending him into the air and landing hard on his back. The Queen pressed her foot down his throat, closing off his windpipe. The man's large hands wrapped around her foot and tried to push and pull it off as his face grew redder.

"Your efforts are a waste. You know it. I know it."

Her words had no effect on him.

"What's your name?" she asked, relieving his windpipe of just enough pressure to allow him to speak.

The man choked out several colorful words, none of which could possibly be his name. She pulled a tube from her belt and withdrew a needle from it. The man saw it and shook violently.

"Futile," she said as she injected its contents into his shoulder.

A small burst of joy erupted in her mind, accompanied with a slow sigh of relief.

Today is going to be a wonderful day . . .

"Hello."

Twenty minutes later, the man opened his eyes and looked directly into the Queen's. She saw his pupils dilate from fear-induced adrenaline.

"I gave you a small paralyzing agent so I could undress you without trouble. Do you understand?"

The man gasped sharply, stammering all over himself. Slowly he realized he was bound like a hog, wrist to wrist, ankle to ankle, and wrists to ankles. She'd dragged him near the hall door and propped it open so that the light from windows could illuminate their pleasant scene.

"If you are wondering why it's cold, it's because you're naked." The Queen held up the man's wallet and he looked at it. "Is your name Richard Berkeley?" she asked, holding up his driver's license.

"Yes!" he cried. "Please, I don't understand what's going on!"

Lying.

"And you live in Papillion, Nebraska?"

He nodded and licked his lips.

Lying again.

The Queen noted his tells. *No training in lying. He will be easy.*

"I found your little pill inside there, too. And since you're not on birth control, I'm guessing it's a suicide pill. That, along with the fake ID of Richard Berkeley, tells me that you are a very naughty boy. Part of some silly anti-CAG terrorist group maybe?"

The man made no sign for or against it.

"I sure hope so. We had lots of fun with those resistance fighters from a decade back." She fished around in her bag and finally pulled out a small device about the same size as the metronome her mom used to put on top of the piano when she was younger. She held it up so the man could see it. "Do you know what this is?"

The man nodded again.

"Good. Then why don't you tell me your real name."

"You know I won't."

"Why?" the Queen asked. "Is it nobility or stupidity? I already have a sample leaking out of your nose!" she screamed, smearing his blood over his face roughly.

His nasal bones crunched with her hand's pressure, making him pale and groan from the pain.

"It will take about an hour to search the database for your record. Know what I'll do during the time I'm waiting for your name to come up? I'll hurt you. And then I'll have your name, and you'll be no better off than before."

The man's face was defiant. "Do it the hard way."

His screams went on for seventy-five minutes. Despite his pain, the Queen knew he wasn't broken. It didn't worry her, she hadn't played the trump card yet. When her device started beeping, she picked it up and read the display to him.

Doug Corri

With the name came all the information she could want to know. She removed her blunted instrument from the sole of his foot, and sat down on the floor near his head.

"So, your name's not Richard. You're not from Papillion. And I'm guessing you don't like long walks on the beach. Right, Doug?"

Doug's tear and blood soaked face jerked in her direction.

"I found this in your wallet," she said, brandishing a picture of his family and then dropping it on his bare chest. He raised his head just high enough to see himself standing next to his red-haired wife and three red-haired daughters all wearing Los Angeles Dodgers shirts and sitting perfectly arranged for a family portrait. "I'm betting this is real."

For the first time since he had woken naked, the Queen noted, Doug looked genuinely terrified. He sputtered a little, spraying flecks of blood, spit, and tears, but she quieted him with her own words.

"We've had some fun. You held out while I gave you a real strong dose of pain. But now that part is over, Doug." As she said this, she stroked his hair lovingly, the way her father did for her when she was sick. "I don't care about your family. They aren't involved. In truth, I didn't come here for you or your little band of Merry Men, either. But now that I've found them, I'm going to look for them. I'm being honest because there's no use in lying to you. You're already dead, and we both know that."

No look of surprise came over the man's features. His eyes stayed steady on hers.

"Right now you get to choose between your three beautiful daughters and a boy named Sammy Berhane. That's all I care about for today. You can either tell me where I can find Sammy, or I'll do the most evil, perverse things you can imagine to each of your three beautiful daughters."

Doug sputtered through the slime of his own fluids covering his face, but the Queen continued.

"I won't kill your wife, Doug, because I'll want her to live the rest of her life having lost her entire family. However, I will tie up each of your daughters after paralyzing your wife in her bed, and I'll do things you have probably never imagined to each of them." She spoke to him now as if she was telling him a bedtime story, still petting him in that soothing way. "And when your little angels finally realize, after screaming and begging for help, that no one will ever come to save them, I'll kill them. One at a time. In the most creative way I can come up with that day. Do I need to describe those three beautiful deaths for you?"

Doug shook his head frantically. "Please don't—please—they're innocent."

The Queen watched him. This was the most important part of breaking the person. It was imperative that he trusted her. He needed to know she meant it deep, deep, deep down. "I have no reason to go after your family. Your wife isn't involved in this little group here, is she?"

"No! Of course not!" Doug answered, but again she saw through the lies.

"I didn't think so," she whispered, but now, in her mind, the wife was already dead, too. "So it's your choice, Doug. And if you lie to me, the first thing I'll do is go to your home, do you understand? I know you can see your three daughters screaming and crying for you while I hurt them, can't you?"

"Yes!" Doug cried. "Please—I beg—please—don't hurt my girls. They've done nothing!"

"Look at me, Doug!" shouted the Queen, grabbing his face and holding it still. "I'm not ugly or cruel, am I? Aren't I beautiful!?"

Doug nodded, and the Queen noted with satisfaction that he did not lie.

"Does this look like the face of someone who would lie or kill because she enjoyed it?"

Doug hesitated, but finally answered: "No."

"I only want Samuel. Will you give me the information I need?"

Doug didn't answer for several seconds, and right before the Queen had to say something else, he said, "I'll tell you."

Late into the night, Doug finally died. The Queen tried reaching her NWG contact, Wrobel. He did not answer. She tried him again with the same results.

He put me on this job. He should be answering!

She slammed her foot into Doug's lifeless body and heard a satisfying crunch from his ribs. She thought for a moment about her options . . .

"Diego," she said aloud.

Her com screen flashed blue and white for a moment, and Diego's badly scarred face appeared. "Only you would call at this hour. What do you want?" His tone was a perfect blend of sarcasm and reverence.

"I want a team."

A curse in the animal-like language of the Thirteens ripped through his clenched teeth. His face formed a sneer. "Everyone's wanting a team these days. Why didn't your Newgie traitor ask me directly?"

Her mood was getting fouler by the minute. A perfectly good body lay at her feet and she wouldn't have time to do anything with it. Half the fun of a kill, gone. She now knew that the little bastard was somewhere in the city, but Doug wouldn't tell her, no matter what she threatened. Yet he'd sung about their upcoming excursion to Offutt Air Field, the hidden message in the news broadcast, and how the kid planned to return overseas Friday morning. Plus, Doug's people knew about the designed attack on Baikonur. As for Diego, right now she had no patience for him.

"I want a team. In Omaha. As fast as you can manage."

Fortunately, the exact location of some new resistance mattered little right now. Once she snagged the boy at Offutt, she could bring a dozens of Brothers and Aegis back to Wichita and snuff out the whole operation. For now her attention was on Sammy. She wanted to kill him so badly, the cost no longer mattered. All this time spent hunting him had made her slightly obsessive. She saw nothing wrong with that.

Weeks of foreplay . . . I'll have my big finish.

"Tomorrow?" Diego spat.

"In a few minutes it'll be today." She tapped her watch with a nasty smirk.

"Is this still about that kid the Newgie sent you after?"

"Does it matter?" she said, intentionally lacing her voice with warning. "I want a team."

"That kid killed more than a whole team already. Practically single-handedly. They weren't the best team, but—"

"Do you have a point?" she interrupted.

Diego dropped his reverential act. His whole face changed, and the Queen didn't care. "Yes! This kid fights better than anything I've ever seen, Katie. It's . . ." He paused to search for words, oblivious to his mistake.

He had crossed the line by using her name. And she did not like being warned about a juvenile Fourteen. "I WANT A TEAM!" she screamed for the last time.

Diego jumped and let a stream of curses fly from his disgusting tongue while his scars reddened and burned. "You can have your team . . . It's not very big, but they're available, six Thirteens, ten Aegis. Whatever losses you incur are on your head, and you make sure the fox gets a good word about me from you."

"Of course."

She sent him her sweetest smile and put her com away. There was nothing worse than having a pressure mark on her face from the stupid thing. She checked her watch again. It was a designer style by Favaracci. Nearly indestructible and priceless in value.

Twenty-four hours.

Time to sleep. In the evening, she'd meet up with her team. When this little band of resistance fighters showed up, she'd be waiting. Hungry. And there would be hell to pay for little Sammy.

26 | Caper

May 3, 2086

MOVING SIXTY-TWO PEOPLE out of Wichita proved to be quite an operation. Thomas insisted that they take great care to avoid drawing any attention to the ghost city. During the night before and the morning of the caper, cars were positioned throughout downtown Wichita by means of underground tunnels excavated over the last decade. The tunnels were few and crude, but useful. Between the twelve different vehicles, they had ten different exit points. Sammy was impressed.

One car left every twenty minutes or so. By noon, the last of the ten cars reached the freeway heading north. Sammy and Toad rode in a van with Thomas, Lara, and two other men: Dr. Vogt and a man named Stewart.

It was the largest operation the resistance had carried out in over ten years. Sammy tried not to think too much about stealing the cruiser. Each time he did, his arms and chest began trembling, and he had to grip his knees to keep them under control. And every time the thought *I'm finally going home!* Popped into his mind, he couldn't help but grin from ear to ear. Whenever Thomas saw it, he shook his head and laughed.

The older Byron was in rare form, too. He chattered almost non-stop, whether reviewing plans over his com, discussing tactics, or simply quoting more of his favorite poems, he did not stop talking. Lara warned him to stuff it or she'd drop him off on the side of the road, but Thomas' mood was infectious to all but Toad.

Toad wouldn't say a word. He and Sammy had talked late into the night about stealing the cruiser and flying to Capitol Island.

⑤

"What if something goes wrong in the hangar?" Toad had asked Sammy once the adults went to bed. "I'll be in the thick of it. You've only given me basic combat lessons."

"You'll be fine," Sammy reassured him. "I'll watch out for you."

"And I hate flying! What if we get shot down?"

"We won't. I know how to fly."

"I'm not even sure about moving to the NWG and becoming an Ultra. Maybe I should just stay here with Lara and Thomas . . ."

"They are really nice," Sammy agreed.

"Lara even hinted that I can stay with them if I want."

Sammy had been playing with a tennis ball, blasting it against the wall and catching it, then blasting it again. "You can do that. I bet they would let you."

His words hung in the air. Toad looked at him expectantly. "Okay . . . And? What do you think?"

"It's your choice, Toad. Not mine. I chose to become a Psion because I didn't want to go to prison. Some people choose it because they want to become a superhero. My friend Brickert did it to get out of his family's poverty. You . . . I don't know. Do you want to stay here and wonder forever what it'd be like or will you not care?"

Toad fought back his tears, a reminder to Sammy of just how untrained this kid was and how recently he'd been traumatized. "I miss my family. I don't know what to do."

"At Psion headquarters, Thomas' son is in charge. He's a very good commander. I'm sure whoever is in charge at Ultra will be someone like him. And even look past that. When you graduate, you become an Alpha. So do I. We could possibly be in the same squadron. Maybe even roommates."

Toad calmed himself down.

"There will be girls there your age, Toad. Don't forget that, too." He gave Toad a wink, which made Toad laugh, then sniff.

"Cute ones?"

Sammy laughed, too. "No doubt."

Toad smiled, but Sammy could tell he still wasn't convinced.

"Look, Toad. I will watch out for you in Omaha. I promise. There's going to be a lot of us there. All of Thomas' people will be armed. I think we'll be fine."

"Okay," Toad said, nodding. "Okay. You're right." He took a hesitant step forward, then hugged Sammy. Sammy felt awkward at first. He couldn't remember Brickert ever hugging him. At the same time, it felt good. "I know it hasn't been easy traveling with me and stuff. I thought you were going to kill me a couple times."

Sammy chuckled. "Me, too."

Toad got into his bed and lay down. "Yeah, so, thanks for not killing me."

⑤

The caravan took variations on the same route until they all reached the freeway. The middle of America, beautiful in its own way, wasn't necessarily interesting to watch through the window of a van. Sammy counted cows for a while, then horses. He lost count several times, something that would never have happened before he met Stripe.

Don't think about that right now, he told himself as a familiar ache crept up his leg.

Around 1900, they exited the freeway. Twin missiles towered over the landscape, proudly announcing their arrival to the base. Sammy blew out a big puff of air. He could hardly wait to stretch his legs. Security booths stood at every entrance housing guards who checked ID on each vehicle and eye-scanned each driver. Fortunately, the team would not be entering the airfield grounds by the gates. Instead, they drove to a city park in nearby Bellevue for an informal picnic dinner. While Sammy and Toad set up the picnic with Lara, other resistance members reported to Thomas that their groups had arrived without trouble.

They had only one glitch: the last group called in from the road and reported that Doug had never arrived back at headquarters. After waiting as long as they could, another assignment had been made, and the group had left without him.

"It's not like Doug to miss an assignment," Thomas commented to his wife, Dr. Vogt, and Stewart. "And something this big—something he helped plan . . .

"Could be a family emergency," Stewart suggested.

Thomas shook his head. "Sheesh. I hope he didn't get hurt or take a fall somewhere."

"He smokes like a chimney," Dr. Vogt muttered. "May have had a heart attack for all we know."

"Call his family," Thomas said. "We have to follow protocol. Tell them to get to a safe house until we know where he is."

"Is there a chance we've been compromised?" Lara asked.

Sammy and Thomas exchanged looks. *You know I have to get back,* Sammy silently told him. The understanding passed between them. "It's possible," Thomas said finally, "but we've come this far—we've sent the message out. No turning back."

Lara accepted Thomas' decision. The picnic was casual but quiet. Ten people were assigned to eat at that particular site. Similar picnics were held in other parks across a radius of six kilometers. Thomas stayed busy handling questions and protocol about Doug. Word came back that Doug's wife couldn't reach him, either. Thomas was still resolved to go forward with the plan.

As the evening wore on, Toad's anxiety returned. Sammy didn't know what to do or say to help his friend. Thankfully, Lara noticed and invited Toad to take her on a walk. With an hour remaining before the groups had to move to positions, Sammy thought she'd made a wise decision. Better to calm Toad down now than deal with him during a crisis. As the two walked away, Sammy could faintly hear Lara speaking to Toad in a soothing, matronly voice.

"And you?" Thomas asked Sammy. "Are you nervous?"

Am I nervous?

The response came quickly. Nervousness was trying to act normal around Jeffie or facing Thirteens in a death match. It was not stealing a plane.

"No," he answered. "I'm not. Are you?"

"Just a little." Thomas chuckled, but without his usual bravado. "I haven't saved the world like you and Walter."

"I haven't saved the world, either. Why are you nervous?"

"There's a chance I might see my son. First time in—well—in a long time."

"How long has it been?" Sammy pushed.

"A long time," Thomas croaked. That look of anguish reappeared on his face, making him look much older than before. "Too long."

Sammy watched as the deep lines on Thomas' face formed a frown, then a grimace. Thomas was struggling to keep his emotions in check. He put a shaking hand to his mouth.

"I'm sorry." It was all Sammy could think to say.

Thomas cleared his throat as he waved a dismissing hand. "Nuts and bolts, kiddo. You don't want to listen to my sap stories. You're probably thrilled to go home."

"I am," Sammy agreed, unable to stop another grin from spreading on his face. "You can tell me what's on your mind, though."

Thomas picked at some grass absentmindedly, long enough for Sammy to wonder if the old man had heard him.

"Ever been completely wrong about something?" Thomas looked directly at him. It unnerved Sammy to see the beginnings of tears in Thomas' eyes. "But you thought you were right and refused to see it any other way?"

"Yeah." Sammy thought of the first time he'd stolen food after his foster father died.

"Well, I had a wallop of an argument once with Walter."

"Really?" Sammy couldn't imagine the commander arguing with anyone, especially his own father. Both Byrons seemed like candidates for World's Nicest Man.

"Worst thing is, even after I realized he was right . . . and I was being the jackass, I couldn't do anything about it. Walter Byron doesn't exist anymore—not on paper. So I can't just look him up and call him. I think that hurts the worst."

"I doubt—" Sammy started to say, but Thomas cut him off.

"No. You don't understand." Thomas pulled a handkerchief from his pocket and blew his nose. "My son tried to warn me about the war. He and Emily flew here at great personal risk to take me and Lara overseas. But I stuck my hooves into the ground like the most stubborn mule. Lara thought we should consider it—but me, I was just too . . ."

"Why were you so against it?" Sammy asked.

"I don't know. I'd grown up an American, and I'd always had a chip on my shoulder about the NWG. I guess I just didn't like change. There was lots of talk about cloning bans and gun restrictions and people were worried about losing their freedoms in a world government. I had unpleasant pictures in my head of what the future was like."

"And that's what the fight was about?"

"Just after Lark Montgomery was executed, Walter came to see me. He tried to tell me that the CAG had invaded Quebec and had plans to invade the other American territories that hadn't seceded. I threw him out. Told him if anyone invaded, it'd be the NWG."

"Yikes," Sammy whispered.

Thomas nodded his head, but wouldn't look at Sammy. "It wasn't until later I saw the signs. The remaining NWG territories went to the CAG. There were signs of battles, rumors of a secret prison break in Wyoming in '63, but no one had reported it. Traveling to the NWG became nearly impossible. Then came the embargoes, and communication was cut off. Internet firewalls. The longer I watched, the more it became clear I'd picked the wrong side.

"Just over a year ago, the CAG bombed five city buses in Lima and blamed it on NWG terrorists. As long as people are more afraid of the NWG than they are of their own government, nothing will change. You saw it in Rio, didn't you?"

"How'd you find out about the resistance?" Sammy asked. The sky grew darker as the sun sank below the horizon like an ominous countdown to darkness. It would not be much longer before it was time to go.

"I've lived in Wichita almost all my life, so I know the area well. After it turned ghost, I stayed behind to farm the land. There are so few farmers needed now, but it's very profitable for those who do it well. It didn't take long for me to figure out there was something strange going on in town. Lara thought I was going crazy, but I managed to track the center of movement around an old warehouse. Now that building's just another storehouse for food, but it used to be the center of their operations. Boy, they about flipped all their hats off when I showed up. Of course, I didn't have a clue as to what was going on, but Lara and I signed up real quick when we met Crestan. Then most of the resistance came crashing down a few months later. Everyone the CAG caught was labeled as a terrorist—another coup for them to use to solidify power. "

Thomas seemed swallowed up in the memories he was reliving.

"I've been part of all this for a long time now. In fact, I've sort of taken over things since most other leaders either died or fled. But I've never had a chance to make a real difference. The powerful play goes on, and I want to contribute my verse, Sammy!" He gestured all around them. "The resistance has been too scared to do more than gather information or get together and talk about how much they hate the CAG. When you showed up, Sammy, things changed. We're doing something. That's a big deal."

Sammy nodded in the silence. He heard Lara and Toad's voices floating over on the wind. He looked up to see them returning down the same path. Thomas leaned in close to Sammy.

"Listen, Lara will skin me if she knows I've given you this, but take it and give it to Walter, okay?"

Sammy glanced down and saw a small envelope with the commander's name on it. He took it and slipped it into his pocket. Lara and Toad walked up moments later. Toad was much more relaxed. Lara wiped something from her eye and rubbed his hair in a friendly way. Toad smirked.

"How are you?" Thomas asked Toad.

Toad gave a thumbs up.

"It's pretty dark, Thomas," Lara said.

She was right. The last of the sun's violent orange rays were long gone. Now returning were Stewart and Dr. Vogt, deep in conversation. They cleaned up all traces of the picnic and stowed them away in the van.

Everyone but Lara grabbed a shoulder pack. Thomas took a moment to tenderly kiss his wife and tell her goodbye. Before she let him go, she told him in a voice so low that Sammy almost couldn't hear it: "'Now set the teeth and stretch the nostril wide. Hold hard the breath and bend up every spirit to his full height. On, on, you noblest.'"

Thomas hugged her once more. "How pure, how dear. I love you, Lara."

Lara also gave grandmotherly goodbye hugs to Sammy and Toad. More tears came as she let go of Toad. Toad was emotional as well.

"I'll be waiting in the car, ready if you need me," she reminded Thomas.

From the way Sammy understood it, each car would take different indirect routes home, some routes lasting as long as two full days. As Thomas explained, if everything went as planned "our trails should be harder to follow than a good politician's speech."

Under the cover of darkness, the men of the resistance took off their top layers of clothing, wearing black shirts and pants underneath.

Two security walls, four meters high and spaced four meters apart, surrounded the entire base. Both walls were topped with razor wire. In silence, the five rebels hiked to the point of the wall nearest the hangars. Somewhere off in the distance, just outside the base, an explosion sounded loudly. Noisy fireworks burst up high, illuminating the sky in red, green, and blue.

"'And yet the menace of the years finds and shall find me unafraid'," Thomas commented. His stoic expression lit up in colors of green and gold made him appear majestic. "The distraction is in place, gentlemen. Let's move."

With a good blast, Sammy launched himself to the top of the wall, delicately balancing on the edge. From inside his pack, he withdrew a small set of clippers and worked on the razor wire. After two minutes of snipping, he removed a meter-wide portion of the wire and threw it away from his team. Next, Thomas tossed him a length of rope, which he caught and took down with him to the other side. Bracing his feet against the wall, he used his own weight as a balance against the weight of the first man, Dr. Vogt, climbing the wall. When Dr. Vogt reached the top, Sammy released his end and dismantled the wire on the second wall. Meanwhile, the doctor became the anchor for the rest of the team climbing over the first wall. Twenty minutes later, all five were over the second wall, moving like foxes toward the henhouse.

Crossing the eleven square kilometers of the base without raising suspicion was a formidable task. Streets, buildings, and other obstacles had to be negotiated along the way to the hangar. Halfway there, Sammy could see several figures approaching them on the left. Thomas stopped the group in their tracks and let a long low whistle leave his lips. It was returned twice. Then, from the right, two more whistles responded.

"Looks like we're all ready," Thomas whispered, pointing straight ahead.

The building looked like a typical air hangar with its high, semicircular roof on top of a long low rectangular base. Gigantic metal doors lined the back and front of the building.

They came to a side door. Stewart took care of the lock using a small tube with a hollow spout. He jammed the spout into the lock and squirted copious amounts of blue goo into it. Then he waited about three minutes before turning the knob.

CRACK!

The door was unlocked. They were in.

Two or three football fields could have fit comfortably inside the hangar. Over a dozen cruisers and planes formed a neat row down the length of the cavernous room. Those currently under repair or reconstruction were gathered together in one section.

The team split up to fulfill their assignments. Sammy and Toad were responsible for removing the wheel stops. Once they had, they pushed the cruiser from behind with Stewart in the cockpit steering.

Thomas gave the nod, and Dr. Vogt raised the nearest hangar door. A green light above the door blinked on.

"Folks, they officially know we're here!" Thomas announced.

When the cruiser had cleared the hangar by several meters, Stewart fired up the cruiser's circuits, checking equipment and running diagnostics.

"No signs of base security yet," Dr. Vogt called out from behind binoculars. "Our boys with fireworks must be doing a good job keeping them busy.

"Give it time!" Thomas shouted. "They'll come."

Toad and Sammy entered the cruiser next. Sammy helped get the ship ready to fly while Toad strapped himself in.

As Sammy waited for more circuits to report back their status, he began strapping on his own belts. The power lights clicked on, and systems reported no malfunctions. Sammy flipped the switch on the engines. Dr. Vogt and Thomas were now in the cruiser, too.

"Everything looks good from what I can see," Dr. Vogt reported from over Sammy's shoulder.

"Yep," Stewart agreed. "Power is good. Engines are perfect. Energy cells are well charged. The only problem you're going to have is finding an NWG channel to communicate on when you fly into their airspace. Make sure you dump your weapons over the ocean so they know you're unarmed."

"No problem," Sammy told them.

"You're sure you can fly this thing, right?" Thomas asked.

Sammy smiled at him. "Yeah, I did some simulators and stuff at headquarters."

"Don't fly over anything important, like the Eiffel Tower," Dr. Vogt added with a pat on the back.

Sammy pointed to the dash. "Is the GPS—"

"Took care of it already," Stewart said, holding up a small chip. "Unplugged and offline. Remember, no auto-nav, no communication until you're well out of CAG territory."

"Can't you just disconnect all the stuff?" Toad asked.

"No time. This is the safest you'll be."

A long shrill alarm sounded through PA system.

"Security's on its way," Thomas said. "How much more time do we need?"

"Just a couple more minutes," Stewart said, tapping the console impatiently. "We'll be fine. The other two teams should be able to hold them off until then."

For an instant, a small burst of flame appeared in the night sky, far overhead and way in front of the cruiser. It quickly disappeared, but not before Sammy glimpsed it. He almost disregarded it as another firework until he remembered the fireworks were to the south of the base, not to the north where the small flame was seen.

"Did anyone else see that?" he asked, keeping his eyes fixed on the sky.

An instant later, with his binoculars, Dr. Vogt pieced it together. "GET OUT!" he screamed. "Missile! Get out!"

"Get out now!" Thomas urged them.

Sammy released his strap, and jumped out of the cockpit, running for the hangar.

By the time Thomas yelled his last word, he and Stewart were also outside the ship, hot on Sammy's trail. Remembering Toad, Sammy turned back to see Dr. Vogt still in the ship struggling to help Toad out of his seat. As he ran back to the ship to help, he saw the small missile streaking toward the cruiser, only seconds away from impact. At that point, everything slowed down.

Dr. Vogt wrenched the straps off Toad, grabbed him roughly by the shirt, and threw him bodily out the door. Sammy pulled Toad up and yanked him away from the cruiser. Seeing the missile approaching, Sammy rolled himself and Toad to the ground, kicked off his shoes, and shielded, using both hands and bare feet.

The missile slammed into the cruiser with a thunderous sound that seemed to rip the night into pieces. Dr. Vogt hadn't cleared the door of the cruiser, and was hurled through the air by the concussion. Sammy's shields held strong but he was shoved back several centimeters along the runway, tearing his flannel shirt and scraping his backside.

Stewart and Thomas ran to Dr. Vogt, but Sammy already knew the doctor hadn't made it.

He stared at the burning wreckage of their ride home.

"How did—how did . . . ?" Thomas asked, gasping for breath. He and Stewart stared at the charred, broken remains of Dr. Vogt.

"Thirteens," Sammy responded heavily as the weight of his doctor's death began to settle in. His eyes seemed locked on the smoldering form of the man who had done so much to save him. *Why Dr. Vogt? Why the man who fixed me?* He felt the demon stirring deep inside. "They're coming—they knew."

From his pack, Thomas produced a flare gun, which he raised high over his head and fired. The tiny red flame shot heavenward and erupted, sending a message to the other teams to either come for aid if they were near, or leave if they were too far away to help. Sammy tried not to think what panic would go through Lara's mind when she saw the beacon.

"What now?" Stewart asked, clutching his ribs. His palms looked like tenderized steaks, and his face was scraped and bleeding, too.

"The game's afoot," Thomas said grimly.

Toad shrugged off Sammy's help and hobbled quickly to the front of the hangar. Sammy turned back to see Dr. Vogt one more time, then looked to the sky and saw a cruiser swooping down, preparing to land.

Stewart swore angrily. "We don't happen to have anything that could shoot that bird out of the sky, do we?" he asked Thomas. He wanted to see everyone in that aircraft burn and die.

"Didn't bring any explosives on this fishing trip," came Thomas' response. "Can you take Toad behind one of those cruisers and do a patch up on both of you?"

Stewart replied in the affirmative and steered Toad into the hangar.

"Let's break out the toys," Thomas said as more resistance members arrived from other doors. "We need to set up a perimeter. Take position under cover."

Every person on the mission, with the exception of Sammy and Toad, had brought at least one firearm along for an extra measure of security. Thomas and Stewart had hand cannons, a few other men had automatic rifles, but the rest only had pistols. The biggest problem was ammunition. No one with automatics carried more than a few clips.

Next to one of the half-repaired cruisers was a pressure-driven nail gun. Sammy picked it up and tested it. In a tool box nearby, he found two more bottles of CO_2 and an extra magazine of nails.

"Toad, no offense, but I don't think you should have a weapon," Sammy told his friend. "Stay out of the way, and you'll be fine."

Toad looked anything but fine.

"Did you hear me?"

Toad nodded.

Sammy looked out the hangar. The cruiser would be landing in less than three minutes.

"What's our plan now?" one man asked Thomas.

Sammy, used to being the one to come up with great schemes, set his brain in gear but felt only the familiar emptiness he'd come to associate with the loss of his anomaly.

Thomas drew himself to his full height. "Close that door," he ordered with the same commanding presence and voice as his son. "At any moment our enemy is going to come through here along with who knows how much security from the base. Our goal is to get Sammy and Toad out of here. To do that we need to clear the runway. Clear the runway. Understand me?

This is kill or be killed. When you run out of ammo, which I'm sure you will employ sparingly, use whatever you can find. Throw anything you can at them. This will either be the resistance's finest or final hour. Do not let yourself be captured alive."

"Will the other teams be coming to help?" someone called out.

"We can only hope," Thomas answered.

Sammy took cover behind a small tool cart with Thomas and Stewart.

He saw a broken pipe with a sharp, broken edge and gave it to Toad. "Focus on defending yourself. Let me take care of the rest."

BOOM!

One of the big hangar doors gave a violent shudder and wobbled in its track. Screeches and yells muffled through the door and reached Sammy's ears.

"They're coming," he whispered to himself.

A small rush passed through his body. He hadn't felt this alive since the factory. As he gripped the nail gun tightly in his hands, every muscle and joint tensed itself, ready to spring into action the moment called upon. This was what Byron had prepared him for.

BOOM!

The door bent inwards but did not break. In the corner of his eye, Sammy saw something shaking. He turned and saw Toad's hands trembling visibly, tears leaking from his eyes.

"Just remember to take cover if they shoot at you," Sammy said. "Like I taught you. Use your speed to your advantage. None of them can match your speed."

BOOM!

Flame rose up through a great seam in the bottom of the door and rent the door in two, peeling inward along the tear. A small object no bigger than a golf ball flew in through the crack.

Dink.

It bounced once on the cement floor before Sammy recognized it as a round grill canister—a smoke or gas bomb.

Probably filled with nerve gas.

He took careful aim and shot a hand blast at the canister. It stopped mid-air and bounced again on the cement. He quickly blasted twice more, forcing the canister back out the crack. Through the door, Sammy heard a sharp yell and a foot kicked the canister down the runway. Then the battle began.

Two body-length plastic shields emerged through the breached door carried by two Aegis in their green-brown uniforms. A third Aegis crouched behind them. All three shot into the hangar. Any resistance fighter not already behind cover moved quickly to find some. The Aegis were virtually untouchable as they worked their way in with their backs to the wall, making room for others to enter the hangar.

It wasn't like the last time Sammy had battled the Thirteens. They had attacked swiftly and without warning, overwhelming them with their numbers. This was different.

Why are they making such a show of entering the building? Sammy wondered.

He remembered the sims, how the Thirteens always tried to surround him.

"Come with me," he told Toad.

"Where are we going?"

Sammy didn't waste time answering. He left his post and ran, still barefoot, down the hangar. Toad followed behind. An old bomber under reconstruction was parked not far from a door opening to a hallway extending toward the back of the building. A service ladder stood next to the plane. Sammy checked to make sure it was firmly attached at the top. Once certain, he sprang up the ladder and walked across the top until he came to the plane's vertical stabilizer. Toad climbed up with him.

Sammy crept along the stabilizer until he had a clear view of the door. Toad leaned over Sammy's shoulder to get a look.

"You think more will come through there?"

Sammy nodded.

Within a minute, the doorknob turned. A head poked out searching left and right, but not top to bottom. A man in a military police uniform came through the door, his weapon ready for assault.

"See?" he whispered to Toad. "The Thirteens will come in from the front, while security sneaks up from behind." Another man and woman came next. Sammy took careful aim with the nail gun.

Spit! Spit! Spit! Spit!

One guard received a nail through the ear, the next in the throat. The third guard reacted quickly, and Sammy missed. Sammy ducked down, lying flat on his belly. He shimmied slowly toward the end of the plane and fired again.

Spit! Spit!

A nail went into the guard's chest, close to his heart. The guard dropped his weapon and grabbed the wound.

"Take one of those weapons for yourself and take the other two back to the team," Sammy told Toad. "Stay under cover as much as you can while you move."

Toad nodded and turned to leave.

"I'll come find you as soon as I know this way is clear."

Toad climbed down the ladder while Sammy jumped off the edge of the plane and landed near the door. He threw open the door and pointed the nail gun down the hall. No sign of security. He ran back into the hangar, away from the battle, until he came to a second hall. Two more security guards were coming in. Sammy rendered one of them unconscious with a nasty blow to the side of the head, then dropped the other by blasting him into the wall. Gunshots rang out behind him as the resistance opened fire on the invading enemy.

He had one more hall to check.

Sammy opened the door and took a few steps into the dark corridor. A strange sensation crept over him, telling him he wasn't alone. It was like an awful restlessness starting between his shoulder blades and spreading over his back. He came to a bend in the hall and stopped at the corner. Leaning his back against the wall, he readied himself for his next move. In a whirl, he rounded the corner, shielding with gun at the ready.

A woman jumped back from him, screaming in alarm. Sammy froze in surprise. The woman was incredibly beautiful with long hair so dark it was almost raven black and naturally tanned skin—perfectly tanned, now that he thought about it. And she was tall, too, almost as tall as Sammy. Her body was flat against the wall and her head snapped toward him.

Her eyes, wide in fright, were a very dark blue, but devoid of any red coloring typical of Thirteens. Either she was an Aegis in casual clothes, or a civilian.

"What's going on?" she asked. "Who are you?"

He didn't answer right away. He was still caught off guard by the magnificence of the woman standing in front of him.

"Uh . . . who are you?" He lowered his gun, but kept his blasting hand ready.

"I'm . . ." she said breathlessly. "My husband works nights here. I heard shooting." She looked him up and down, and he realized he must look ridiculous with a nail gun.

"You'd better go. There's a break in." *And I'm the one breaking in.* He turned to leave, but she grabbed his arm.

"Can you walk me out?" Her voice had an overtone of pleading to it. He looked back into her eyes, which looked like the color of an ocean at night. He didn't see the same fear there that he heard in her voice.

He wasn't sure why, but he didn't trust her. "I'm sorry. I can't."

She tugged his arm again. "Come on, Sammy." Her phony scared face melted into a flirtatious smile. She puckered her lips at him. "Walk me out, and I'll make it worth your while."

Sammy ripped his arm from her grasp and brought his gun up to shoot. Her left hand emerged from behind her with a jigger.

"Mine's better than yours."

Sammy gazed back at her and found that the darker side of him did not mind bantering at all. "One Thirteen. That's child's play. You can even have my gun." He offered her the nail gun with a smirk.

The woman laughed. It chilled Sammy like putting his feet in ice water. He heard her confidence, and it made him nervous.

Why isn't she afraid?

"Keep it. I've studied up on you, buddy. You probably think you're hot stuff, but the ones you killed in that factory . . . amateurs."

"I doubt that." He pulled the trigger and sent a blast from his left hand; he wanted as much distance from her as he could get.

She fired, too. The braxel fell harmlessly to the floor, and Sammy's blast launched her down the hall. Sammy was impressed to see her neatly tuck her body down and make a graceful landing a few meters away. He expected her to retaliate, attack him as he had seen before, but she stood there calmly waiting for him to make a move. His muscles tensed—he prepared to launch himself at her. Then a thought struck his mind: *Toad.*

She's keeping me from the main battle, where I need to be.

He turned and sprinted back to the hangar, shielding himself from behind as he ran.

27 | Blood

May 3, 2086

THE HANGAR WAS CHAOS. Sammy mentally beat himself up for spending precious time away from the fight. He looked around the hangar frantically for Toad but saw no sign of his friend.

The resistance was pinned. A couple of Thirteens and several Aegis, with their large plastic shields, had taken spots around the perimeter of the hangar, trying to form a ring of death around Thomas' men. Many of the resistance members were hidden at strong defensive points near the legs of cruisers and jets, but Sammy saw two of their own on the floor motionless, with dark red puddles beneath them. This defense would not last long. Already the Thirteens were climbing up the hulls of aircraft, gaining superior positions of attack. One was atop the same bomber Sammy and Toad had taken refuge on only a few minutes ago. Sammy launched himself to the top of the jet, and the Thirteen turned to greet him. He was a short, tanned man with tiger stripes carved into his skin.

Sammy sent strong blasts at the Thirteen. He sidestepped them, but the ricochet off the vertical stabilizer spun him around. He quickly caught his footing and fired several rounds at Sammy from two automatic handguns. Sammy jumped over the spray of bullets and retaliated with more hand blasts, but they were just as easily evaded. Sammy stayed in the air as much as possible, using his nail gun and left hand as both offensive and defensive weapons.

He waited for the impending reload moment, when he typically took advantage of a toothless Thirteen. When it came, the Thirteen reloaded so fast that Sammy had no opportunity to strike. He sent a blast at the Thirteen, followed immediately by a nail. The Thirteen dodged the blast, but the nail got him in the arm. He jumped at the Thirteen with feet blasts, ready to shield should the Thirteen fire at him, but instead the Thirteen timed Sammy's attack perfectly and smacked him hard across the face with the back of his hand.

Off balance, but now too close to the Thirteen to be anything but deadly, Sammy fired his blasts at the same time the Thirteen fired his gun. His blasts blocked the bullets and knocked the Thirteen off the plane, still firing as he fell.

Sammy shielded the round of volleys aimed at his chest and head. Rolling low to a new position behind the cover of the vertical stabilizer, he took aim again and fired the nail gun.

Spit! Spit!

Two nails poked out of the Thirteen. One embedded in his stomach, the other in his groin. The Thirteen doubled over, clutching his crotch.

Sammy aimed at the Thirteen's head. The Thirteen smiled back as though Sammy had just told him the greatest joke in the whole world. The nail went into the Thirteen's eye and his head dropped to the floor.

Forgetting Toad for a moment, Sammy looked for the woman he thought of as "Beauty." Then, with a loud shriek, an Aegis spun around and faced Sammy. Two more followed his lead. They moved toward him behind their shields. From the other end of the hangar, Sammy heard noises and, at the same time, Beauty emerged from the hallway with four other Thirteens. Sammy cursed softly.

Where are you, Toad?

Then, in the cockpit of the cruiser closest to Beauty and her Thirteens, Sammy saw his friend. Behind the glass, Toad jumped and waved his arms like mad trying to get Sammy's attention. Sammy doubted that the Thirteens had seen Toad yet, but they were much closer to Toad than he was.

Small cheers erupted from the resistance. Sammy peeked around the stabilizer and saw more resistance arriving from the blown hangar door: at least ten more men and women, all armed. The three Aegis turned to meet the new wave of help.

Sammy jumped off the jet and raced down the hangar toward Toad.

⑤ ⑤ ⑤ ⑤ ⑤

Commander Byron sat in the co-pilot seat of the stealth cruiser anxiously patting his hands on his knees in a mindless rhythm.

"Prepare for evacuation," the Elite pilot announced, probably sensing Byron's impatience. Even now, en route to Omaha, it seemed too good to be true. But he knew Samuel was there. He knew the message was meant for him. No doubt in his mind.

But how?

He looked back at Tango Squadron, undersized for what could potentially be a combat mission, but all he could bring under the circumstances. General Wu had chewed Byron's backside for almost an hour. Byron had never seen him so angry. Despite all this, he still hadn't told the general about a possible mole in the Psion ranks.

Not now. Concentrate on the task at hand.

If anything else went wrong tonight, he would face a crucible of heat from his superiors, least of all being sanctions from General Wu.

"Evacuation in thirty seconds . . ." the Elite pilot said.

The Offutt Air Base runway stretched out in view of the cockpit window. Blue and red lights lined the pavement. The lights led the way to the hangar, which grew larger as they approached. One cruiser was already on the runway, not far from the building.

Behind it, light blazed through a crack in one of the hangar doors.

And there was something else.

"What's that thing right there, pilot?" Byron asked.

The Elite punched his console. "Nothing my scanners are picking up."

Byron kept his eyes trained on the unidentified object.

My goodness, he thought, *has Samuel already escaped?*

"Sir, that's wreckage of another cruiser down below," the pilot announced. "Looks like it was shot down."

Questions raced through Byron's mind. Had Samuel's cruiser been shot down? *Not now. Not after all our work.* His hand gripped his knees tightly.

"Okay, everyone," he said in a loud voice, "Something's going on down there. I do not want to take a single casualty tonight." He let the words sink in for a moment. "Hear me? Be smart." He tried to sound tough and hard, but he felt like they couldn't land soon enough.

With a stomach-lurching swoop, the cruiser suddenly dropped low enough for them to jump out and land comfortably on the ground using strategically placed blasts. The doors opened quietly and stayed open even after the team vacated it, leaving only the Elite pilot. As they ran toward the hangar, the cruiser landed two dozen meters away from the wreckage.

One of the Alphas checked the intact cruiser for enemies inside. When he gave the all clear, Byron signaled to hijack it. The rest of the team followed him to the gaping hole in the hangar door. Using blast shields as cover, he peered around the corner into the building. What he saw wasn't what he expected to see.

Thirty or forty men and women in civilian clothes were in a stand-off against several Thirteens and Aegis. He scanned the room and saw no sign of Samuel. He remembered the saying taught by Nicoletta Clardovic, his Elite combat instructor: "The enemies of your enemies are your friends . . . until they shoot at you."

"Who has more ammo?" one man in casual clothes yelled out to several nearby.

Shrieks came from several Thirteens in response to the man's outburst, and they moved in closer as a unified body. A hand signal brought Byron's team ready to move in and break the Thirteen's formation. Both Byron and the squadron knew their surprise appearance would throw the Thirteens off for only a moment.

Three fingers raised . . . two . . . one . . .

⑨ ⑨ ⑨ ⑨ ⑨

Sammy blast-jumped onto the top of the cruiser where Toad was hiding. Several gunshots burst below him. Instinctively, his hands fanned out, deflecting away any projectiles that could strike him from beneath. He raced down the length of the cruiser until he reached the cockpit. Firing several shots from his nail gun into the glass, he then used a blast on it. The glass gave, but not enough. Through the window, he saw Toad run into the cockpit looking up at him, relieved. Sammy gave him a nod.

Below, the shrieks and cries of the Thirteens told Sammy they were close. Lying on his stomach, he blasted the window again and again. Shards rained down into the cockpit.

"Can you jump out?" Sammy called to Toad.

"I don't know," was the response.

"They're coming. You gotta get out!"

Toad was pale and shaky, and Sammy feared the kid might lose his nerve.

"You can do it. Just don't jump into the glass."

"Will you catch me?" Toad asked.

Sammy glanced in the direction of the Thirteens. He could no longer see them.

They must be surrounding the cruiser.

"I'll help you," he told Toad, "but you've got to clear the glass. Those sharp edges will rip you open if you don't jump right."

"Okay . . . okay," Toad whispered as he readied himself to jump. "Three . . . two . . . one . . ."

Sammy grabbed Toad underneath the arms and heaved until Toad's feet landed on the edge of the glass. There was sharp crack, and the glass cracked loudly under Toad's weight. Sammy darted forward to grab Toad before he fell. His fingers wrapped around Toad's wrist just as the whole section shattered. The full force of Toad's weight hit Sammy, jerking him forward down into the cockpit. A grunt escaped him as he landed on Toad.

"Oof! You're heavy!"

They both got up. Sammy's hands and arms were bleeding in several places from small pieces of glass. Toad had gotten a couple cuts himself; a small one on his face and a long, thin one on the arm.

Several thumps were heard above.

"Here they come," Sammy muttered.

Toad brandished his pipe like it was a sword.

"Where's the gun you got?" Sammy asked.

Toad frowned. "One of Thomas' guys asked for it."

Sammy swore as he took the pipe from his friend. "You'll live longer if you use the nail gun. Don't worry about anything else. Just shoot Thirteens."

Toad nodded, but Sammy was worried. He handed the nail gun over to Toad and crouched to the floor holding the pipe in his right hand, steadying it with his left. When the first Thirteen appeared at the site of the broken glass, Sammy shot the pipe off like a rocket, impaling her face. She was thrown back from the glass out of sight.

As Sammy stood back up, Toad threw up behind him.

"What is wrong with you?" Sammy asked.

Toad retched again, but managed to hoarsely whisper, "That was disgusting."

Sammy understood. It had only been a few months since he'd first taken a life inside the factory in Rio. Now it didn't faze him at all.

"Just watch my back," he told Toad. "Don't let anyone sneak up on us."

"Okay, I know what it means to watch your back!"

Gunshots blared from above them, raining down through the hole in the glass. Sammy shielded, but couldn't see the gunmen.

"Stop them!" Toad shouted.

"I'm trying! Chill out!"

One of the gunmen turned out to be a gunwoman. The ugliest woman Sammy had ever seen, in fact. Her skin was a pale gray but only lightly scarred, and she had only half her teeth (and they weren't anything to brag about, either). Before Sammy knew it, she was in the cockpit with a gun aimed at his head.

While Sammy shielded, Toad fired at the same time she did. Both missed. Sammy blocked her shot, and she dodged Toad's, quite a feat at such a short distance.

The second, unseen Thirteen fired two more shots at Sammy. A shriek from the Thirteen in the cockpit told the other to stop.

Once Sammy focused on just shielding and let Toad take care of attacking, the fight ended quickly. Using one hand as a shield, he battered the Thirteen with his other elbow. Then he picked her up and half threw and half blasted her body back out the cockpit.

"What are we going to do now?" Toad asked as he held his position following Sammy's order. Bullets began pouring through the broken cockpit window again and the Thirteens stomped on the glass and the roof, creating tremendous noise. "Back through the glass or out the door?"

"I don't know yet," Sammy said. "I need to think."

"No time for that right now, Sammy," came a voice in the back of the cruiser.

It was Beauty's.

⑨ ⑨ ⑨ ⑨ ⑨

Sounds of gunfire, booms from hand cannons, and shouts echoed around the hangar. The Thirteens and Aegis reacted quickly, just as Byron knew they would. Only one Aegis died from their initial surge. Three more fell, injured. More importantly, however, their circle around the civilians was broken, leaving the enemy badly outnumbered and at a strategic disadvantage. The commander heard scattered shrieks and cries from the enemy, probably coordinating a new plan.

Byron held a syshée, his weapon of choice in most battle situations. Using one hand to shield himself, he fired at the nearest Aegis.

The Aegis ducked behind his body shield, but each time a syshée hit the shield, its barbed bullets tore softball-sized chunks out of the thick plastic. Most of the Alphas went air born, landing on the tops of jets and cruisers, drawing fire away from the civilians. The civilians were fairly well covered given their circumstances. Byron was impressed with their resourcefulness, despite many of them using only crude pistols.

Where are you, Samuel?

The Alphas' attack turned into an effective wedge through the enemy formation. The few remaining Thirteens and Aegis gave up ground, seeking shelter from the aerial attack of the Alphas. Not one Thirteen looked afraid or defeated, there was only the recognition of a loss of the advantage. If the beasts had a card up their sleeves to change their odds, they would have used it. Byron suspected that they had anticipated coming here to mop up a riff-raff band of civilians and one Psion.

Two more of them went down.

"All Alphas," Byron broadcasted from his com, "push the Thirteens to the east side of the hangar. Force retreat through that exit."

As fast as anyone could move, the enemies were out the door and gone. Several armed civilians left their defensive cover to give chase.

"Shamila," Byron announced to his com. "Get a visual on Samuel."

"Yes, sir," came her reply.

Byron directed his com link to the pilot. "Are the Thirteens headed to their cruiser?"

"No, sir," the pilot answered. "Not one, they've disappeared into the dark. I can't get a visual on more than two or three from here."

Byron was not surprised. "Va'pua, tell whoever these men and women are that the Thirteens are too dangerous to follow. They should retreat a separate way." He'd seen in the past when the Thirteens had fallen back only to set new traps and reengage under more favorable conditions. "Shamila, any success?"

"We've spotted a cruiser at the far west end of the hangar," Shamila reported. "Just found it, sir. At least three Thirteens there, too."

"On our way. All Alphas to the far west end of hangar. Full attack on the cruiser!"

He sprinted down the hangar with his team. The cruiser Shamila had mentioned came into sight quickly. Three Thirteens were gathered on top of the cruiser, all around the cockpit window, all shooting and stomping at the glass. Byron fired his syshée at the nearest of them. It was a large black woman with wild hair. She grabbed her shoulder, soaking her hand in blood. The syshée had turned it into a bloody mess. All three Thirteens had turned their attention to the approaching Alphas. From the fires blazing in their eyes, Byron knew he was in for a battle.

Hold on Samuel . . .

⑨ ⑨ ⑨ ⑨ ⑨

Aside from the oversized hand cannon in her right hand, Beauty was unarmed. Even now, Sammy found her to be an imposing sight: tall, strong, and thin, utterly beautiful. But she had an intangible quality that Sammy also noticed. A cloak of invisible evil that she wore. It permeated the air around her and unlocked more of the darkness still inside Sammy.

This woman was death.

"You must be important, Sammy," Beauty said. "But from looking at you I wouldn't know why."

"Hold that window, Toad," Sammy muttered. "Don't let them in."

"Maybe I should kill your boyfriend first," she offered, with a grin that showed off her perfect teeth.

Sammy attacked. Beauty shot off her cannon. Sammy easily shielded the shrapnel before it could spread. He threw a punch at her jaw, but she was already too far away before his fist was even close. Her legs landed on the cruiser wall, and he aimed a blast at her chest. She jumped over him, directing her cannon point blank at his body, too close for him to use his hands. He used a foot blast to jettison himself out of the way.

Beauty immediately changed her aim to Toad's backside. Sammy caught it just in time. With one powerful blast, he turned her weapon away, blowing the passenger seat of the cruiser into chunks of leather, stuffing, and tearing small holes through the cruiser's side. The frame of the chair hit the floor. The cushioning smoldered, making the air reek of burned plastic.

Beauty charged into Sammy, faster than he had time to react, sending him crashing into the wall of the cruiser with a dull thud. He returned her the favor, blasting off the wall, turning himself into a projectile. She sent another round at him, then crouched low like a spider, allowing him to sail harmlessly over her. While mid-air, another blast from his hand forced her off balance, driving her face into the floor. Sammy heard a sharp snap.

A grunt escaped her.

Sammy landed on the other side of the cruiser. Toad had turned away from the window. His face was pale and sweaty. The Thirteens had stopped trying to shoot into the cockpit.

"Take whatever cover you can find," Sammy told him.

Please, brain, I need your help. I need to see how to beat her.

Beauty screamed and shrieked a string of vile curses at Sammy, shoving herself off the floor. Her nose had broken, and blood flowed freely from it. Her cannon shot again. Sammy shielded himself, but the shrapnel had enough spread to rip into the sides and paneling of the cruiser. She shot again. As Sammy shielded himself, she rushed him. He focused the concentration of his next blast, but she anticipated it, flipping her lower body over the blast. Sammy ducked and rolled under her. In the corner of his eye, he saw Toad hiding himself behind the one remaining pilot's chair. He was aiming the nail gun, but his hands were shaking badly.

Come on, brain! WORK FOR ME!

Beauty used her hands to rebound off the wall and doubled off the ceiling to aim her body at Sammy. He tried to blast her again, but she whipped herself around too fast. The toe of her shoe caught Sammy in the ribs, but he rolled out of the way as her hand cannon tore a large chunk out of the flooring where he had just been. He used his foot to kick out at her, connecting with her knee, bringing her down to the floor in a tumble. As she fell, she whipped her cannon down on Sammy's shoulder. He yelled in pain, as a sharp crack of lightning spread from his shoulder to the tips of his fingers followed by a tingling numbness.

Sammy heard Toad pull the trigger of the nail gun, but all that came was a puff of air. Toad cursed. He was out of nails, and the spare cartridge was in Sammy's pocket.

Beauty got up first, leaping to her feet. In that moment, Sammy knew he had lost. Beauty had only shocked the nerve with the blow to his shoulder, but he couldn't move his arm. His other arm was caught underneath the damaged frame of the chair Beauty had blown apart only a minute ago.

She was too fast. Too strong. Too smart.

He knew there wasn't enough time to react. He tried to lift his legs so he could use his feet as shields, but he wouldn't make it in time. Her weapon was already pointed straight at him. Toad screamed somewhere near him. With no words, no grins, not even a look of victory, Beauty finished the job and pulled the trigger.

"Sammy!" Toad cried.

Sammy closed his eyes and heard the hand cannon erupt. A heavy weight slammed into him as his feet finally blasted, milliseconds too late to block the cannon's death shot. Something big hit the rear of the cruiser, away from him. Pieces of shrapnel grazed Sammy's trapped arm, stinging and burning him. He opened his eyes.

Toad's shrapnel-filled body was on top of him. Beauty looked dazed from her collision with the back of the cruiser. The side door to the cruiser jerked open. Sammy struggled to turn and face more enemies.

"Samuel?" Sammy couldn't see the face yet because his eyes hadn't adjusted to the light, but he knew the voice.

"Commander Byron?" Sammy said in response. It didn't seem possible. But when everything came into focus, he saw the commander. "Please. My friend—he's shot. And there's a Thirteen in here!"

"Get medical ready!" Byron spoke into his com. Then he spoke to two other Alphas. "Check out the cruiser."

Sammy looked to the back of the cruiser while the Alphas lifted Toad off him. Beauty was gone. Then he got his first good look at Toad, but what he saw was horrifying. Toad's chest and legs were like meaty pulp.

Blood was everywhere, leaking from every hole. His face was whiter than any normal person's face should ever be.

"Toad?" he whispered.

"Samuel, we have to go." Byron pulled the chair frame off of Sammy's arm and helped him to his feet.

Sammy allowed himself to be led out of the wrecked cruiser and down the hangar. Toad was already whisked out, but left a trail of blood. Sammy's mind was blank. Everything was right and wrong at the same moment. Byron was here, but Toad . . .

I promised to protect him. Sammy tried to breathe, but choked on the air. He thought he was going to vomit. Byron's support grew stronger.

"Did you know that boy?" the commander asked. Byron's voice was light and casual, probably trying to keep Sammy from going into shock.

He nodded weakly. The hangar was completely different now. The Thirteens and Aegis were gone. Most of the bodies were Aegis and security. The resistance had all left, too, the bodies of their dead carried off.

I promised to protect Toad. He meant to say it out loud, but didn't.

He repeated the words over and over in his head. Each time the resounding failure echoed deeper inside of him, mocking him along with the fresh images of Toad's body.

Byron gave up trying to talk to him, yet Sammy leaned on Byron more than ever. He was tired and beginning to feel sick. The pilot came out of the cruiser as they left the gaping hole that had been the hangar door. His gloved hands were stained with blood and bits of flesh. Sammy's stomach swirled again. The Elite's eyes said everything that needed saying.

"There wasn't anything I could do, Commander," the pilot said. "Even if Maad had been here . . ." His voice trailed off as he pulled off the dripping gloves.

This time the sensation in Sammy's stomach did not stop. He vomited onto the gray pavement, retching and retching until he felt he might vomit everything inside of him. In between retches he sobbed uncontrollably. He felt his mind unraveling again, fraying at the edges.

Why do things like this have to happen? How can things like this happen?

It was his fault. All his fault. If his gift had not been gone . . . *I would have beaten her. I should have beaten her!*

Beauty—whatever her name was. He ripped himself away from Byron and ran back into the hangar. Back to the cruiser to finish her off. He knew he could do it. Byron and several others caught up and grabbed him.

"No, Samuel," Byron said. "There is nothing there for you now. We have to leave, or there will be more trouble than we can handle."

"I have to kill her . . ." he cried out pathetically. "That woman . . ." His voice sounded weak and lame, even to him. What was the point in having these stupid abilities if all they brought was death? Martin. Cala. Kobe. Toad. His parents. Dr. Vogt. The Hernandes, too, probably.

When will it be Jeffie or Brickert or Natalia or Kawai?

"Whoever she was, she's gone now," he said. Then he steered Sammy to the back of the cruiser. The older Alphas avoided his eyes, but still stared at the boy they had come to rescue. Sammy strapped himself in, still sobbing.

I promised to protect him.

The cruiser took off very quickly. Toad's body was less than a meter away from Sammy, but he couldn't look at it. He knew if he saw it, the guilt of his failed responsibility would fall even harder on him. It might even crush him. But the presence of Toad's body behind him, ghostly, cold, and dripping red, stayed on his mind. He buried his head in his arms.

Not long after, one of the Alphas turned to face him and attempted some sympathetic conversation. She asked something about his being excited to get back home. Sammy stared at her with bleary eyes. He got up and went to the front, ignoring the Alphas who asked him to sit back down.

"Samuel, what—" Byron began.

"Wrobel is a traitor." Sammy stated this as if he'd said the sky was blue. "I saw him on camera in the factory. He betrayed us."

Commander Byron seemed to search Sammy's soul before he answered. "Thank you, Samuel." Then he turned to Tango Squadron and said, "You have all just heard classified information, understood?"

Byron muttered something into his com and began speaking. "Send a squadron for Commander Wrobel. He needs to be detained immediately and kept under guard. Check his office, personal quarters, everywhere. Confiscate his log reports and data systems, too. I will inform the general."

Sammy returned to his seat. Any Alpha who hadn't been staring at him before certainly was now. He didn't want their eyes on him. He wanted to be alone. It just wasn't fair. Going home was supposed to be wonderful. Toad was supposed to be an Ultra. He'd already helped Toad start his training, and for what?

Nothing.

The truth of that realization resonated like a gong in Sammy's soul.

Life isn't fair, Sammy. Life will never be fair.

That was it, plain and simple, laid out before his mind. At any moment it could be him, or anyone else he knew and loved, and there was no one above or below to guarantee promises of happiness or stability. He thought about his discussions with Al and Dr. Vogt about life after death and God.

Dr. Vogt is dead. And Al is wrong.

He, Samuel Harris Berhane Jr., was as alone in the world as he had ever been, dependent on his own strength and intelligence. A bolt of lightning could strike the stealth cruiser, shut down its power, and send them crashing into the sea. *And the sun will rise, the Thirteens will still exist, and people will still go on knowing nothing about what's really happening in the world.*

Bitterness crept into his heart, filling his stomach and chest with its poison. It was sour and it stank to high heaven, but at least things made sense to him now. He did not matter one iota in the grand scheme of things. And it sucked.

28 | Command

May 4, 2086

THE FLIGHT OVER THE ATLANTIC was uneventful, and the team arrived in Capitol Island in the late morning. Sammy hadn't slept a wink. Members of Tango Squadron, on the other hand, were sawing logs all around him.

How can they sleep with Toad's dead body in the back of the cruiser?

Byron left the co-pilot's chair and sat by Sammy. "We are stopping at Alpha Headquarters. I am not sure for how long. You need to meet with Psion Command for debriefing. Tango will be there, too. So will Albert."

"Can't you tell them that I just want to be left alone?"

"I know you would rather forget about all of this, but since you are not in immediate medical danger, I have no way to get you out of it."

Sammy nodded blankly and stared out the window, trying not to think of what would be done with the corpse of his friend.

When the cruiser touched down near the edge of a large airstrip, he was surprised to see several cars waiting to escort them. Byron led him to the closest car.

Sammy looked around him, trying to appreciate the fact that he was home, but unable to do so. The twilight air was cool with a fickle breeze that blew through his shaggy mane. It smelled clean and fresh, but did nothing to lift his spirits. Once seated in the car, he watched the rest of Tango Squadron through his window. They all looked tired and glad to be home.

"How long were they looking for me?" He watched the commander's reflection in the glass as he waited for an answer.

"Weeks," was the reply.

"They got my message?"

Byron nodded. Sammy hated the sympathy in the commander's eyes and focused his attention back on the Alphas.

"How did you do that?" Byron asked.

"It was your dad's idea. He wrote it."

"Where are we headed, sir?" asked the driver, another Elite officer.

Commander Byron's eyes stayed on Sammy for several seconds, and his face wore an expression of surprise. "Uh . . . War Offices. Then as an afterthought, he added, "If you please."

Byron raised a partition between them and the driver.

"You met my father, Samuel?" Byron's voice was very quiet, which wasn't like him. Sammy wondered if the commander really believed him.

"I met Thomas and Lara Byron. They helped me."

Byron swallowed twice and cleared his throat, turning away from Sammy as he did so for five or six seconds. "Does he still quote poetry all the time?"

Sammy nodded. "But I don't know who wrote any of it."

Commander Byron looked at his watch. "We have about ten minutes before we reach our destination. Will you tell me what you can?"

Sammy struggled to give the commander a true accounting of his time since Al's team went to Rio last November, so instead he spoke about how he walked to Wichita and found a resistance compound. Byron's face was as impassive as stone while Sammy explained how his parents were part of that resistance, and how they'd helped him get home.

The car pulled to a stop in front of a large metal door connected to a mound of concrete the size of a small shed. When they got out of the car, Byron thanked the driver very briskly and opened Sammy's door.

"Keep up with me, Samuel," he said.

Normally Sammy would have been interested to take a look around at Alpha headquarters, his future home. At this moment, however, he found himself detached from everything around him. The commander walked faster than his usual pace. The door was reinforced steel and had a palm and eye scanner along with voice recognition. Byron opened it, and they stepped into the small concrete bunker. Inside was a small flight of stairs with a second identical door at the back of a large landing. This time Byron stepped in front of a camera.

"State your name, rank, and identification number, please." The voice came from a small speaker on the wall.

"Psion Commander Walter Tennyson Byron." Then he listed off a long number that Sammy knew he should be able to memorize, but couldn't.

The door opened and a much longer flight of stairs appeared. Sammy didn't count them as they descended, but guessed they numbered far more than two hundred.

The third door at the bottom required even more identification and was about a foot thick. Blue light leaked through the widening crack. Before Sammy could get a good look at the War Offices, Byron tugged on his sleeve.

"In here."

He led Sammy to a men's restroom and checked to make sure no one else was inside the stalls.

He spoke in a low, rushed voice: "Samuel, I am terribly sorry for everything that has happened to you. I came to look for you in Rio the first moment I could, but you had already left."

Sammy met Byron's eyes. "You came to the—?"

"What Tango and I just did for you in Omaha was not known to Command. It was unauthorized. Not illegal, but I am still in a great deal of trouble. So I need you to be honest and tell them everything. I know it will be difficult. When you finish, Dr. Rosmir is going to want to see you."

Without another word, Byron led them out of the bathroom and down a hallway with blue carpet until they came to a room with a brass plaque that read Command Conference Room. The door was slightly ajar. Sammy heard at least a half dozen voices floating out of the small space. Byron pushed it open.

"Sammy!" Al exclaimed, grabbing Sammy's hand and pulling him into a tight hug. While Al tried to restrain himself, Sammy felt nothing more than a disjointed desire to feel gratitude. "I knew you were alive!" Al quietly told him in their embrace.

Order came to the meeting and everyone took their seats. Sammy sat between Commander Byron, who was at the head of the Command table, and a man Sammy vaguely recognized as the Alpha Doctor. He'd seen him once before, back when Jeffie broke her leg.

"General Wu cannot be here," Byron began. "Victor will not be here, either."

A short Asian man with a slightly bulging stomach and thinning hair spoke up. "Where are they? I was told this was of the utmost importance."

"The general is in a meeting with the congressional subcommittee on space travel and colonization. However, one of my pupils is here. Samuel Berhane."

Several people in the room turned to look at Sammy.

"This isn't—" another commander began. "You mean to tell me—?"

"Yes, Mabella, I do. Samuel, those here at the table are members of Psion Command. You would normally not meet them until your Panel, but allow me to introduce you." He gestured around the table. "Commanders Annaliese Havelbert, Chang Ling, Muhammad Zahn, and Mabella Iakoka."

Sammy received four gestures of acknowledgement. The smiles on the faces of the commanders were strained at best, as though they didn't know exactly what to make of his presence.

"How long have you known Samuel was alive, Walter?" Commander Havelbert asked. Like the others, she was middle-aged. Her blonde hair and brightly colored finger nails distinguished her from the pack. She sat with impeccable posture. Sammy guessed she was or had been a dancer.

Commander Byron stared at his hands for a moment and finally looked up at all the members of Command. "Samuel is sitting right here," he said, gesturing at Sammy, "and is available for questions. How about we allow him to talk first, and then I will share my story after—"

"But Walter—" Havelbert started to protest.

"Annaliese, please," Byron responded politely, but with a note of exasperation, "I think his account is more important."

No one seemed pleased about allowing Sammy to speak instead of making Byron answer their questions. Sammy didn't get it. All of these people had been trained by Byron, so why did he get the impression they were annoyed with him?

Reluctantly, he began telling them everything. He started with the Rio mission, how things had gone from bad to worse until he fell into a hole. Occasionally Byron interjected with his own comments. Each time he did, he got sour looks from his peers. When Sammy revealed that he'd seen Wrobel on the factory security tapes, the atmosphere in the room changed.

Commander Iakoka exchanged a look with Havelbert and Zahn. "You're absolutely positive you saw him?"

Before Sammy could respond, Byron interrupted. "I have verified everything Samuel has reported."

"And you're letting us find out from a kid?" Ling asked. His face and bald head had all turned bright red.

From the looks on the faces of the other commanders, Sammy could tell tempers were barely being kept in check.

"Do you know how insulting this is?" Iakoka asked.

Al shifted uncomfortably in his seat behind Sammy. Tango Squadron, who sat in chairs along the wall, exchanged glances.

Commander Byron employed his usual diplomatic tone. "I see your point, Mabella. Please see mine. I have had reason to suspect a mole in

Command for the last several weeks. Why would I have come forward with the information? That mole could have been you. I am telling you now because I now know who it is. I am assuming, of course, that the treason was limited to him. For all I know, it might not be. We have severe damage control to do. We need to start by figuring out exactly how much information Victor gave away, if he has sabotaged any of our systems and networks, and where he is right now. The moment I learned it was Victor, I requested his detainment. So far, no one has found any trace of him. Now, Samuel, please continue."

Sammy spoke quickly. He wanted to get out of this room. Keeping his eyes on the table, he told them about the Hernandes family, his capture and torture and escape. At this point, Byron interrupted him multiple times with questions, as did the Alpha doctor. When it became too difficult to speak about his journey with Toad, Al reached forward and put a hand on Sammy's shoulder. Then he got to the part about overhearing Thirteens discussing an attack on the Artemis launch, and commotion broke out again among Command.

"How can they know about that?" Ling asked his peers.

Commander Zahn dropped several curses.

Havelbert took off her glasses and rubbed her nose where they pinched.

Iakoka also made a noise but Sammy couldn't hear her over Zahn's swearing.

"You're forgetting what Samuel has already told you about Victor. General Wu is aware of everything. Why do you think he is meeting with the congressional subcommittee right now?"

The discussion then veered away from Sammy and onto whether Commander Byron had broken protocol by lying about Tango's whereabouts and then flying into Omaha without notice or proper procedure. Zahn and Iakoka were by far the angriest. Commander Havelbert listened to both sides, offering comments. But Byron didn't seem concerned about their opinions.

It bothered Sammy that these people, the leaders of the Psions, would sit and squabble while they had more important things to be discussing.

"Commander Byron," Dr. Rosmir said over the noise, "perhaps I might go ahead with my exam of Samuel. Is he still needed?"

Sammy put his hands up. "No," he told them, "I don't need to see anyone. I was examined by a doctor in Wichita."

Rosmir began to say more, but Byron cut him off. "I know, Samuel, but it is protocol, and given everything you told me—"

"But I'm fine!"

"Your back and arms have multiple lacerations," the doctor said. "You have bruising on your face and you're holding your shoulder funny."

"I want to go home, not to a hospital!" Sammy shouted. "Maybe you all could act like my opinion matters."

"Perhaps, given the circumstances," Byron offered, "you can make sure he is cleared to go back to headquarters for the night. Is that okay, Maad? I will come get him later."

Dr. Rosmir pursed his lips as he looked Sammy over. "I can't guarantee anything, but I'll try."

Sammy followed Dr. Rosmir out of the room. They left the War Offices and a driver took them to the Alpha infirmary. The doctor didn't speak much, which Sammy appreciated. He stared out the window during the drive, wondering how far he was from the Beta building, and wishing he could just be there now.

Dr. Rosmir let Sammy inside his office. He tapped on a closed door that read: Autopsy.

"Your friend is in here. Do you want to see him?"

Sammy almost said no, but realized he'd always regret missing one last chance to see Toad.

"Yes, please."

Dr. Rosmir opened the door and closed it behind Sammy.

It was a cold room full of steel cabinets and instruments. Three long tables were in the room on a clean white floor. Only one of the tables held an occupant. Toad's body was covered in a white cloth, leaving only his face exposed. Sammy's tears felt hot on his cheeks as they rolled down. He kept wiping them away only to have more fall.

Toad looked peaceful, his eyes closed and his mouth set in an expressionless way. Sammy sniffed, then laughed a little as he remembered all the times Toad had done the same thing.

"I'm sorry," he moaned as he placed his hand on Toad's forehead. "I should have died, not you. You must have moved incredibly fast to . . . It should've been me, Toad. Not you. Why did you have to be so fast?" The tears dripped off his nose, but he didn't stop them now. "The Alphas came right after you died. Seconds after. Why did you have to move so fast?" He struggled to breathe through his sobs, but he didn't want to leave Toad alone. "Thank you," he finally whispered to his friend.

When he couldn't take it anymore, he withdrew his hand and left the room. He tried composing himself as best he could, but ultimately failed. Rosmir watched him with a frown.

"It's been rough on you, Sammy," he said. "Hasn't it?"

Sammy wiped his eyes angrily. "What?"

"Life."

Sammy didn't answer. He didn't want to.

"I have this for you," Dr. Rosmir said. He opened his fist and revealed Sammy's Beta symbol. Sammy took it and examined it. "Commander Byron and I found it in Rio. I didn't know if you'd want it back or not, but it's yours to do with as you please."

Sammy slipped it into his pocket and muttered his thanks. He stripped down as Dr. Rosmir performed tests, exams, and scans. He removed the few pieces of glass and treated Sammy's wounds. They went on and on through what was left of the day. By the time the doctor was done, Sammy felt worse than when he'd come in. After they finished and Rosmir had typed up a summary of his findings, he took a seat across from Sammy.

"You're going to need more psych exams."

Sammy rolled his eyes. "I already spoke to a psychologist."

Rosmir shook his head. "You spoke to a medical doctor playing with psychology. I'm sure he tried and maybe he did help you, but I can't put you back in any type of training until we clear you here. I just can't."

Sammy didn't know this man very well, yet he knew he wasn't going to win an argument with him. "You said I could go home today."

Rosmir looked at his watch and sighed. "I guess so. I'll need to get you admitted first, anyway. But no Game. No sims. No instructions. I'll probably come by to get you on Monday morning, if not sooner."

Sammy cursed. "Why can't I just be left alone? Isn't it bad enough I've lost my Anomaly Eleven? I'm never going to be the same, I get that. I just want to try to be normal again."

"Your anomaly isn't gone. I don't think it can ever be gone. Think about it for a minute. When that Aegis was putting you through hell and back on a regular basis, your brain—your amazing brain—couldn't possibly cope. So what did it do? It shut itself down, or parts of it. That's what I'm guessing happened to you. I think it'll come back, and I think we can help you. And by we, I mean people who aren't me, because I really don't know much about psychology."

No answer came from Sammy. He just stared at the floor and sighed, wishing he could leave. He appreciated Rosmir's words, but doubted his brain would ever be the same.

"Anyway, Byron should be on his way to take you back as promised. When he gets here, I'll take you up to the roof."

Byron didn't arrive to take Sammy back until after midnight. Sammy didn't know where all the time had gone, but between traveling, the meetings, and Rosmir's tests and treatments, the day had flown by.

Byron asked Sammy to sit in the co-pilot's chair. It was not long before they were back in the air. Sammy knew he wouldn't have to wait before the commander broke the silence.

"You gave me quite a shock today."

"Your parents?"

"Yes." This was followed by a long pause. The only sound was the low hum of the cruiser's engines. "Are they okay?"

"You mean healthy?"

"Yes, but also are they—what are they like?"

"They're really great people, sir," Sammy said. "All the people there were great." He thought of Dr. Vogt again and closed his eyes. "They were so excited to meet someone who knew you. They—they said they were proud to be fighting on your side."

Byron didn't answer right away. He appeared to be lost in his own thoughts. "I wish you could have told them about Albert . . ."

"Why is that, sir?" Sammy asked, now looking at the commander.

Byron looked back at Sammy. "Albert is my son. Their grandson."

Sammy opened his mouth and then closed it. "That makes sense."

Byron chuckled lightly. "Easier to tell than with some families, maybe."

"Well, remember I saw that picture . . . in your office."

"I forgot about that. Yes, that helps, too."

Sammy remembered something. "Your dad gave me a letter—for you. Right before I left. Here it is." He pulled a small envelope out of his back pocket.

Byron reached across the cockpit and took it. "Thank you." He twirled the envelope a few times, considering it. Then he tucked it into a pocket on the side of his gray jumpsuit.

Sammy was mildly disappointed. He wanted to hear what it said.

"Samuel, I am sorry for all that you—"

"It's fine," Sammy said quickly, looking away.

"No," Byron said with force, "it is not fine. And I know I said it already, but now I have a better understanding of the horrors you had to face—" Byron paused for a moment to clear his throat. "You are a very strong young man."

"I did what anyone else would have done, sir."

"Perhaps," the commander responded, "but with what you have gone through, well, maybe you do not understand what I mean right now."

The commander was right, Sammy didn't know what Byron was talking about, nor did he care. He didn't even want to think. Not when he felt so bitter and empty.

Byron kept speaking. "You said that a doctor put you through some therapy for what you went through. Do you feel that those issues are resolved?"

"Sort of. I mean, I did," Sammy answered, turning away even further.

"Sort of?"

"I—I don't know if I'm cut out for this, Commander," Sammy said. "I don't know if this is the life I wanted—what I thought it'd be. I want to be at headquarters. It's my home. But I don't want to see any more people die."

Byron cleared his throat again. "You are going through something every Psion has to go through: the realization that our lifestyle is not glamorous like most think it is. I encourage you to think often about this."

Sammy nodded. Part of him wanted to tell Byron more. About how his anomaly was gone—possibly for good—and about his sudden dark feelings about his life, but he couldn't find the strength in himself to do it.

They touched down on the roof of headquarters. "I promise to continue this discussion with you another time, but unfortunately I must get back to Alpha. No one knows you are coming back today. So you can slip in quietly and sleep. Either use Brickert's room or an empty one. If you need anything, Major Tawhiri is here watching over the building and you can reach me on my com."

He laid an arm out on Sammy's shoulder, and Sammy noticed that Byron looked older than he remembered. Byron reached into a cubby under the controls of the cruiser and removed a brown box from inside. The box had Sammy's name etched onto the wooden cover. He knew that inside he would find his new com.

"You have done so much good, and you are not done yet. Welcome back."

Samuel choked out a word of gratitude, took the box, and left the cruiser.

29 | Confrontations

May 5, 2086

PHYSICALLY AND MENTALLY EXHAUSTED, Jeffie lay in bed knowing she wasn't going to get much sleep. She glanced over at the clock on her wall: 0105. With a sigh, she sat up in her bed. *Too tired to sleep.*

As a child, her mother would give her a glass of warm milk to help her fall asleep. Right now it sounded tempting, but the thought of getting out of bed depressed her.

Byron had arranged a tortuous night-Game for the Betas, and it'd lasted over three hours, not ending until after 2200. Most of the Betas had gone to bed right after it ended. A few had gone to the rec room to watch a movie. Jeffie went to the sims for more weapons training.

Ever since her conversation with Brickert in solitary, she'd lost her motivation for the Advanced Combat sim unit. She knew she'd have to go back to it eventually, but she wasn't ready yet. Nor was she ready to watch Sammy's recordings. Brickert invited her twice during the past week, and she'd declined both offers.

"I think I've learned everything I can from Sammy," had been her explanation.

If you can't sleep, she told herself, *you might as well do something productive. Hit the treadmill.*

She glanced at herself in the mirror before she left the room. Her hair was a mess from tossing and turning, and her face had pressure marks from her pillow.

"Looking good, girl," she whispered to herself.

Wearing only boxers and a tee shirt, she climbed the steps to the next floor. To her surprise, a light was on in the cafeteria. It threw a thin white line on the wall opposite the door. She heard the tinkling of metal on glass, which reminded her of when she and Sammy would eat ice cream in the middle of the night. A small pang hit her stomach, and she considered just going back to bed. Instead, she peeked around the corner and saw someone sitting at a table, his back to her. The long black hair and an ugly brown flannel shirt told her who it was.

Hefani.

She didn't want to see or talk to him, especially now. But since she was determined to get her milk, she'd have to put up with his company for two minutes. Her light footsteps betrayed her presence, and he turned to see who was invading his privacy.

"Hey Hef," she said in a friendly voice.

But it wasn't Hefani. This person didn't have Hefani's eyes, nor his chin and nose. Just his long hair and black skin. Now that she saw who it was, she wondered how she'd ever thought it was Hefani.

"Sammy?" she whispered as his eyes met hers. Her stomach turned cold and her feet felt like giant cinder blocks had been chained to them.

"Hi, Jeffie," he said kindly, but no smile came to his face.

The invisible weights on her feet were gone. She went instantly to him, throwing herself into him. He turned just in time to receive her embrace. She knew she was not dreaming. She smelled him deeply, reveling in his warmth and the feel of his heart beating in his chest against hers. The touch of his arms and the texture of his cheek witnessed to her how real it was.

They hugged each other for a long time, much longer than she'd ever held anyone. She feared that if she let go too soon, he might vanish. All the moments she'd spent mourning his absence seemed too small a price to pay for having him here now. Her thoughts were strangely clearer than they'd been in weeks. Her best friend, her hero, was back.

She laughed. "I hate you!" But her eyes betrayed her emotion as she covered her nose and sniffed. She playfully hit him on the chest.

"I know." He looked sad, but hints of happiness tugged at his mouth. "It's good to see you, too."

"What—how—when did you get here?" Her voice was shaky, but she didn't care. Giddiness had flooded her. "What's been—what happened to your hair?"

"Well . . . I got here about this much ice cream ago," he answered, putting his spoon near the top of the bowl. "And I haven't cut my hair in about eight months."

"So you haven't been here too long. That's good. Where'd you get the clothes?"

"Some bum on the street gave them to me. He said he liked my hair."

Jeffie laughed again. They both looked at each other for a moment, not saying anything.

"I missed you," they both said.

Jeffie laughed even louder. Sammy didn't laugh and his smile was gone quickly.

"What's wrong?" she asked, sitting down beside him.

Sammy turned back to his bowl. "I don't know. Maybe everything."

"Do you want to—?"

"No." He cut her off without looking at her. "I don't want to talk about it."

"Hey." She'd thought her smile might never disappear, but already it was wavering. She put her hand on his shoulder. "Aren't you glad to be back?"

Apparently this was the wrong thing to say. Sammy sat straight up, forcing her hand off his shoulder. "Well, I've been gone for six months," he said, still not looking at her. "And I'm leaving again."

"What?" She tried to scale back the frustration in her voice. "Sammy, please . . . tell me what's going on. I'm clueless."

"Stuff happened."

"What—"

"I don't want to talk about it!"

Jeffie involuntary leaned back from Sammy. What could she say that wouldn't make him mad?

"Please don't make me," Sammy asked. His gaze bored so intensely into her eyes that she almost wished he'd look away again. He'd never been this serious before. "I'm not the same person I was last November. I was so excited to see you and be back here. And now that I'm here I feel like there's nothing inside of me. And I'm different and I don't belong."

"What's changed?" she demanded. "You don't have to be like this."

Sammy put his head in his hands.

"Where do you have to go, Sammy?" She tried to speak gently, but she was losing patience with his unwillingness to tell her anything. "Will you at least tell me that?"

"What does it matter?" He dropped his spoon in his ice cream with a disgusted look on his face.

"It matters!" she said, almost swearing in anger at him. "I don't want you to go!"

"WHO CARES?" he shouted. His face was contorted into an expression of deep pain. "It's just a game!"

"What is a game?" As Jeffie asked this, she pulled on Sammy's shoulder until he was forced to look at her again.

"Everything. Life. And we're all going to lose it eventually."

"No, we're not!"

"Yeah? Tell that to my parents. Or Martin and Cala and Kobe . . . or Dr. Vogt . . . *or Toad!*"

"Who? Why? I don't understand."

"Because they're dead!"

A giggle escaped Jeffie before she could stifle it, but her hand flew to her mouth to try to stop it, anyway.

He doesn't know. Oh my gosh, he doesn't know.

"Sammy, you idiot, Kobe and Cala aren't dead. You saved Kobe's life!"

He stared at her, and she saw part of his anger melt away. His eyes softened a bit and the lines of hurt etched into his face lessened. "Really? He's alive? Is he okay?"

"Yes. He's completely fine. He thinks you're dead . . . everyone thinks you're dead."

He still wasn't happy. The hurt in his eyes went deeper than Jeffie could go.

"Who's Toad, Sammy?"

She wished she hadn't asked because Sammy began crying. "A kid—an Ultra that I met in Rio."

"And . . . he died?"

Sammy's shoulders shook and he covered his eyes with a hand. Jeffie put her hand on his back. "I'm—I'm—"

"Please don't tell me you're sorry," he said, breathing deeply. "I don't want to hear that anymore."

"Okay, that's fair," she hurried to say. "I mean . . . I can't—I don't even want to imagine what you've been through. But I'll be here whenever you want to talk about it."

To give Sammy time to calm down, Jeffie got up to make her warm milk. She couldn't help glancing at him every few seconds. He didn't do much but stir his ice cream and take small bites. Maybe the silence finally got to him, because it was Sammy who started talking next.

"So how have you been?" he asked. His pathetic attempt at sounding casual bothered her.

"What's to tell? Life's the same here—oh, but since you've been gone I've been honcho and beaten the two easiest three-Thirteen sims!"

"That's great. I knew you would." He smiled at her, but it was a really lame smile.

"Well, you helped." She gave him a wink and sipped her warm milk. It didn't taste as good as when her mother made it. She'd forgotten to add the sugar.

"Me? How did I help?"

"I watched the recordings of your sims. Brickert did, too. We even started copying your exercise routines."

He didn't say anything in response. His eyes were fixed on some spot on the white wall.

She couldn't help but think Sammy wanted to tell her something, but wasn't saying it. As she went back to the Robochef to add sugar, she debated whether or not to push him.

"When will you be back, Sammy?"

"Does it matter?" he answered.

Jeffie gave him a face that told him the answer should be obvious. "Yes. It does."

"Why?"

"I told you six months ago how I felt about you—that wasn't easy. My feelings haven't changed, and I don't want to go through that again."

He stood up with his unfinished ice cream and dumped the bowl in the cleaner. Jeffie thought she'd said the wrong thing again. The last time he'd been this bothered, he'd been telling her about his parents' death.

"You don't get it, Jeffie. I might die tomorrow. You might die tomorrow. What's the point in a relationship? This war is going to kill us."

Jeffie stared at him from her seat, trying to think of what she should say. She was not sure if Sammy was really back or not. Here he was, standing in the same room, but it was not him at all. *What am I supposed to do?*

"Commander Byron lost his wife to the war," Sammy continued. "What makes you think we'd be any different?"

"So am I just supposed to forget about you and all these crazy feelings inside me? Be a warrior-nun so I never have any tragedy?"

"I don't know what you're supposed to do. But Psions don't seem to have a great survival rate."

"You're being dramatic," she snapped.

"No, I'm not!"

"Yes, you are. How would you possibly die tomorrow? It's absurd!"

"Oh, I don't know, maybe the NWG is secretly launching a space shuttle to the moon! And maybe the CAG knows about it, and plan to attack the launch site! And maybe that means an all-out war will start, and we'll be right in the thick of it!"

Jeffie ran the words through her mind for a moment. "Are they going into open war with us?"

He jammed his hands into his pockets and shrugged. Jeffie wanted to smack him. And kiss him. And then kick him in the nuts.

"I'd rather be able to look back and say I did everything I could to be with you than live with the regret of never taking a chance."

"We can't be together," he said in a husky voice.

"Why? How can you say that?" Jeffie asked, spilling her milk on the table as she stood up. "We're not going to end up like them. We're not them. You're the smartest person I've ever met!"

"Not anymore. I've lost it. My anomaly is gone."

"It can't just be gone," Jeffie said, but something in the desperate edge to his voice scared her.

"There was this man, an Aegis . . ." He swallowed hard, as if the name was difficult for him to say. "I called him Stripe. I was caught and—and he tortured me . . ."

Jeffie gasped aloud and covered her mouth. Sickness reared up in her stomach and she wondered if he was concealing scars under his clothes.

". . . for two months." Again Sammy seemed on the verge of losing control over his emotions. Seeing him like that broke Jeffie's heart. "When I escaped, I noticed it almost immediately and ever since then . . ."

"Noticed what?" she asked.

"That I couldn't *see*—you know what I mean. No matter how hard I've tried, it hasn't come back. I've fought Thirteens, and—and some of them have been better than me. I relied on my anomaly too much. I never really developed the skills that I taught Al to do—real fighting skills. Even fighting them one-on-one. There was this one—a woman—I've never seen anyone move the way she did. So fast and agile. She was unlike any Thirteen I've met, and truthfully, Jeffie, I'm scared of her. Toad jumped in front of her gun. I should be dead." The hollowness in his eyes was more pronounced than before as he banged his fist on the table. "Toad shouldn't be dead! I should be dead!"

Jeffie was silent. There was no other sound in the room besides their breathing. The things Sammy said scared her, too, and it was magnified by his voice. It was far away and thin, like a child wandering in a desolate place. The light in his eyes had faded away completely.

"I'm just—I'm tired. I need to sleep." He yawned, and Jeffie suspected it might be fake, but she said nothing. When he made to leave, she went to him, cutting him off.

"Where are you supposed to sleep?"

"In Brickert's room. Apparently he's had it all to himself for the last six months."

"Lucky."

"Yeah."

Then what she wanted to say all along came out: "Please don't go, Sammy. *Please*. Stay here. I don't want you to leave yet, especially if you might not be here again tomorrow. We don't have to talk. We can just sit and I'll hold you if that's what you want. I'll do anything you want. Just stay with me for a little longer."

She knew he would give in. Every time she'd begged him to stay up later, he did. He just couldn't say no to her.

"I can't." And she saw in his eyes he meant it.

Crestfallen, Jeffie refused to be in a bad mood. Not with Sammy back. Maybe he just needed her to stay positive, to be his source of happiness until he found it inside himself again.

"Okay—okay. I hope you sleep well." Then she added, "Are you going to spend some time with the others later?"

"What do you mean?"

Jeffie rolled her eyes. "Duh, Sammy. Everyone's going to want to see you, touch you, make sure it's actually you. We thought you were dead for the last six months."

"Oh," he answered, nodding slightly to himself. "Was there a funeral, or something like that?"

"No, which all of us thought was funny for a while. Brickert made it out to be some sort of conspiracy theory, *I'll tell you.*" She chuckled lazily at her little joke.

Sammy looked straight at her. "And you? What'd you think?"

The mirth vanished from Jeffie's face. Her voice became quieter as she spoke. "I didn't believe it for a while . . . but I don't know—sometime—at some point—I did. Guess I'm not as stubborn as you always thought."

"There's nothing wrong with letting go," he responded in a tone she didn't like. He looked at her in a funny way, and for a second she thought he was going to stay after all. But then he gave her a wave and left the cafeteria.

Jeffie watched the doorway for a long time after he left, hoping he might come back. She could barely remember why she had even come up there in the first place. Then she saw the spilled milk on the table. It didn't matter. It wasn't needed now. There was no way she was going to sleep tonight.

She grabbed a few cloth napkins and cleaned the spill, then tossed them in the bin. After turning out the cafeteria light, she headed for the exercise room. Farther down the hall, she heard a door close. It sounded like the door to the fourth floor stairs.

"Hello?" she called out. "Sammy?"

The footsteps continued toward her, but she couldn't see anything in the darkness. She reached around the wall of the exercise room and fumbled for the light switch. When she turned it on, she screamed.

There was a loud sound followed by a sharp pain in her chest, but by the time she hit the floor, everything had gone dark.

Commander Wrobel surveyed the girl's body on the floor for only a moment, then stepped over it.

"Queen," he spoke to his com.

After a brief wait, the other line answered.

"What do you want?" the Queen asked. She sounded as if she had a cold and was speaking to a piece of dirt under her nails.

"I'm in the Beta facility. I have access to Samuel."

"You can't be serious. How did you get past the security?"

Wrobel crossed the floor to the stairs as he spoke. "Commander Byron trusts too much in his system. I put a nasty virus into a file I sent him a couple days ago. Your people have been working on it for months. It gives me access to everything. Do you still want to kill Samuel?"

"If you're there now, why don't you do it yourself?"

"I asked you if you want to kill Samuel." Wrobel reached the first floor and scanned himself into the boys' dormitory. "I want a yes or no." He didn't care about pushing her too hard. He knew enough now about her personality from dealing with her over the last weeks to guess what her answer would be.

After a pause of several seconds, she said, "It would bring me great pleasure to kill him."

"Then you'd better be willing to do it on my terms." He eye-scanned a second door, this one with the word PLACK above it in red lights. "Are we agreed?"

The room was silent except for the sounds of two boys sleeping soundly—one on a top bunk, the other beneath. Wrobel fired two shots. The first hit Samuel, the second hit the boy named Plack.

"Do I get to hear the terms first?" the Queen asked.

"No," Wrobel said. He dragged Samuel's body across the bed and slung him over his shoulder, grunting under the weight.

"You'd better have something good planned," the Queen said. Wrobel could practically hear her smiling. "I'm in. Give me the terms."

30 | Claire

May 5, 2086

A SMALL COUGH was the first thing Sammy heard. It reached him like static coming from a dying speaker, tinny and stale. He knew it was a cough, but he didn't care where it came from or who'd done it. Wherever he was felt so comfortable and warm, any type of concern was far from his mind. He smiled to himself, noticing distantly that a pillow was not beneath his head. *No big deal.* He adjusted his head slightly, but still found no pillow.

Undeterred that this rest would be a good one, he absentmindedly swung his arm up to feel for the pillow, his mind still hooked into the wonderful dream in which he was immersed. The arm did not move as well as he had hoped, in fact, it did not move at all. Sammy enjoyed the dream a bit more as footsteps went by his head. Sammy grinned vaguely.

Someone was humming in the background. That was nice. Sammy liked a good hum every now and then. But his dream began to melt away, and he did not want that. Not when everything felt so warm and good. He wanted it to stay that way. The humming and footsteps quickened the melting process.

Sammy reached for his pillow again, but once more found himself unable to move his arms.

"I've got the Beta," a voice said somewhere close by. It was a nice voice. "Everything is in place for you to pick up the Alpha. He'll be where I told you. Don't worry, I've arranged it."

In an instant, he was back to reality. The bindings around his arms and legs were very real. Gone was the comfortable warm sensation, and in its stead was the harsh carpet Sammy recognized as belonging to a cruiser. It was rough and punishing, the pebbles embedded in the fabric dug into Sammy's cheek. He lay very still and kept his eyes closed, waiting for the footsteps again so he could get a better bearing on his surroundings.

"Stop pretending you're asleep." The familiar voice had none of the charm Sammy had heard in it before.

He did not open his eyes.

"I know how long my doses of sedatives last. I'd give you more, but that'd be approaching the danger zone, which is not what I want."

Sammy refused to play along. He did everything he could to make it seem that he was still asleep. As he did so, he concentrated on the bindings, realizing strong metal cuffs bound his wrists and ankles together.

He heard two quick steps on the carpet, then a crushing weight hit his stomach. The air left Sammy's chest, accompanied by a fleeting sensation of panic as his lungs seemed to quiver from the force of the blow. After a couple of failed attempts, he managed to suck in oxygen, restoring calm to his brain. Reluctantly, he opened his eyes. Commander Wrobel stood over him.

"Thank you, Sammy. It's insulting to treat people like they're dumber than yourself, even if they are."

Sammy didn't respond. He was trying to figure out a way to remove himself from the situation. His eyes slowly moved around the cargo space to find something that could help him.

"I haven't underestimated you," Wrobel said, watching him. "There are no weapons here. Nothing you could use against me, either. Don't recognize where you are? Tsk. It's the same cruiser you took to Rio."

"Why don't you just kill me?" Sammy asked. "Why all this?"

Wrobel looked at Sammy with disappointment. "I'm not a killer, Sammy. Not like some in our ranks."

"What do you mean?"

"I mean just that." Wrobel squinted at the controls of the cruiser, probably checking the auto-pilot. "I have never taken a life, not even in battle."

"Then what do you call this?" Sammy asked him, struggling against his restraints. "Are you crazy?"

Wrobel's heavy boot came crashing into Sammy again, this time punishing his thighs and knees.

"You have no idea, you little bastard!" he screamed. "Just because someone acts sanctimonious, it doesn't mean anything! You don't have a clue what's going to happen to you!" He kicked Sammy twice more, scaring more than hurting him now that his legs had gone numb. "I am not going to kill you."

Wrobel stopped kicking and went back to the pilot's chair.

"Walter Byron is going to kill you."

Sammy looked at Wrobel as though he really were mad. "That's impossible."

"You wait and see . . . You just wait."

A beep from the cruiser console distracted Wrobel. Sammy kept searching for something to help him. *That might do it*, he decided when he saw a small fire extinguisher about a meter away mounted low on the wall.

"You've never been to Baikonur, have you?" Wrobel asked, his voice now quite pleasant.

"No." From his geography instructions, Sammy knew Baikonur was the NWG Space Organization's main launch site. No doubt the Artemis shuttle would be taking off from there.

Commander Wrobel smiled and steered the controls of the stealth craft.

"Hasn't the launch been postponed?" Sammy asked.

Wrobel snorted. "Do you have any idea how much it costs to launch a space mission with hundreds of people on board?" As he talked, Sammy slowly rocked his body in the direction of the fire extinguisher.

"No idea."

"Lots. They won't be rescheduling. They'll beef up security, monitor satellites and aerial stations, and consider themselves safe. Congress doesn't consider information from a fifteen-year-old kid to be worthy of changing the date of a moon launch."

"What time is the launch?" Sammy asked, moving centimeter by centimeter toward his target.

"1700," Wrobel answered.

"And when is Byron supposed to kill me?"

Wrobel glanced very seriously at Sammy and went back to his controls. "Shortly after."

"Going to be kind of hard, don't you think?" Sammy asked, nearly halfway to his goal. "Seeing as how he'll be busy if the Thirteens attack."

"You'll be surprised how things work out."

"And what's your role in this?"

"Let that be a surprise, too."

"I don't get it, though," Sammy said, willing to say anything to keep Wrobel's mind occupied while he got into position. "Byron saved my life, why would he kill me?"

Wrobel did not answer. Sammy wasn't sure if it was because he was concentrating on flying or because he had nothing to say.

He rocked his body a little more.

"Walter killed three people several years ago," Wrobel began. Again his voice was void of all charm or emotion. A dead man talking. "We were in the sewers in CAG territory trying to rescue refugees when the Thirteens attacked us. My fiancée was there with us. Her name was Claire. She wasn't the greatest warrior on our squad, but she had many talents. Walter had split us up into two teams, the eight of us. One team to escort groups of refugees to the cruisers, the other to keep watch on the rest. Claire was in the watch group with me, Emily, and Blake Weymouth. Have you heard of Blake Weymouth?"

Almost there, Sammy told himself. *Slow and steady*. "No, I don't know of him."

"Because he's dead," Wrobel stated. The deadness in his voice fell to a new level. "Blake Weymouth could beat the living tar out of any man on

- 434 -

this planet. He fought like a god among children. Watching him fight was like watching music being composed before your eyes. It was the most beautiful thing I've ever seen . . . except for Claire."

Wrobel's voice broke and he glanced back at Sammy, glaring. The hate on his face put a healthy measure of fear in Sammy's heart.

"The Thirteens came. We fought them in that little sewer. We called for help, for Byron's team to get back and save us, outnumbered three to one, trying to fight against the enemy and protect the refugees at the same time. I've never been anything but an average soldier—I admit that. My strengths lie in tactics and planning. Had it not been for Emily and Blake, I'd be dead, too. Instead, I watched as everyone else around me died."

Wrobel's empty eyes bored into Sammy's.

"You know what that's like, don't you?" he asked. "How many people that you care about have died?"

"Six," Sammy said. "Three of those were your fault."

Wrobel nodded slowly and turned back around. Sammy knew he should start heading toward the extinguisher again, but he wanted to hear Wrobel.

"Our job is death. Even if we don't die in battle like our loved ones, each loss kills a part of us until the only difference between us and those who die is the beating of our hearts. A Thirteen pulled the trigger on Claire. Her name's Katie Carpenter. You met her. She killed your friend, too. In that hangar."

Beauty.

"You're asking yourself why I'd work with her now, but it's easy. She can't help what she is. Walter . . . he should have known better. If he had put himself or Zahn on watch instead of Claire, we could have beaten them.

- 435 -

Claire and Blake and Emily would be alive. But even then, he still could have saved my Claire."

"You think he wanted his wife to die? Are you insane?"

The look in Wrobel's eyes answered Sammy's second question. "Don't ask me that again! I've been fighting to keep my sanity for the last several years. And believe me, it's been difficult when dealing with Walter's incompetence."

Sammy said nothing, but resumed his efforts to get the fire extinguisher.

"You insist on trusting him?" Wrobel asked. "I guess I can understand. I trusted him, too. Let me ask you one more question. Why didn't your mission team in Rio have any weapons?"

"I—I don't know."

"Walter insisted that Beta missions not have any. He believed they'd be a greater danger than good. 'A bunch of kids running around with weapons, ready to shoot at the first thing that moved.' That's what he said. You tell me, Sammy. Do you think Martin Trector would have survived if he'd had a weapon?"

"I don't know."

"You're wrong and you know it."

"I trust Commander Byron." Sammy got three fingers on the cylinder of the small fire extinguisher and pulled it from the mount, barely catching it before it hit the carpet.

"You're going to be very disappointed then."

"So what?" Sammy asked. "They came to you, offered you a job, and you signed up to get your revenge?"

"You think they came to me?" Wrobel replied. "I went to THEM! Three years ago. I'd had enough. If you stuck around long enough, you'd understand better."

Sammy's fingers found the pin in the firing mechanism, and slowly pushed it out. It was so quiet in the cruiser that Sammy heard the pin hit the carpet, but did Wrobel?

The cruiser began to descend. He tried to estimate when the appropriate time to act would be, but was afraid to trust his math without the aid of his Anomaly Eleven. He fumbled around with his cuffs, trying to find the keyhole. When his thumb brushed across it, Sammy fired a concentrated blast into it.

Nothing.

He fired again and again, focusing on making his small blast as powerful as possible. Still nothing. He gritted his teeth and pushed as hard as he could from his thumb. This time, something happened.

A burst of heat erupted from his thumb, something so hot, it burned him. He barely stopped himself from crying out in pain. An acrid smell reached his nose, the scent of burnt metal and flesh. But his hands were free. The scent, however, spread throughout the cabin.

"What is that?" Wrobel asked. He squinted back at Sammy, then kept looking around. It gave Sammy just enough time to pull the trigger of the extinguisher.

"What is that?" Wrobel asked again. Finally he spotted what Sammy was about to do. "Stop! Don't do that!"

Frigid white fog filled the cabin. Wrobel cursed in frustration, and Sammy rolled toward the door. Wrobel must have thrown his body at him, because a tremendous thump shook the floor. His large hands scrambled to pull at Sammy, who was only just able to get on his knees and reach the releasing mechanism of the cruiser door. He gripped the handle tenderly with his burned thumb. The door beeped red in warning.

"Don't open——!" Wrobel shouted as he clawed and grabbed at Sammy's bound feet.

Sammy threw himself into the door again. This time it opened. The fog spilled out, clearing the air in the cabin. The ground was far enough away that Sammy wasn't sure if he'd survive jumping. Wrobel got a firm grasp on his ankle, but Sammy made the choice. He leaned forward, tipping his weight over the edge of the door, and fell, ripping himself from Wrobel's clutch.

He knew there was no time to mess with his ankle restraints. Instead, he focused on projecting as much energy as he could into a landing blast. His ankles stretched against the restraints as he bent his mind on safely reaching the earth. Blast after blast fired from his palms and feet in rapid succession.

Fear gripped him as he imagined an ignominious death meters from the landing strip at Baikonur. Finally, he felt himself slow. He fired again and again, each time feeling the concentrated cushions of energy as they bounced off the ground and decelerated his fall.

The landing was still awkward, but not even painful. He immediately began fumbling with the metal cuffs on his feet, trying to find some way to get them off. Above him, the cruiser prepared to land less than a hundred meters away.

Placing his other thumb over the keyhole of the ankle cuffs, he fired another intensely concentrated blast, channeling every bit of energy he could into the tiny hole. He screamed in pain as he felt his flesh burn again.

He looked at his thumbs, both now severely red with spots where the top layer of flesh had been charred. But it did the job, enabling him to run.

So he ran.

13 | Artemis

May 5, 2086

SMALL CLUSTERS OF BUILDINGS stood along both sides of the landing strip that ran through Baikonur. Sammy had no idea what purpose they filled, but he knew he needed to find shelter and, if possible, come up with some way to get the attention of the Alphas in the area. The only idea that came to his mind was to set buildings on fire. Surely that would do the trick.

He jogged down the strip, staying close to the buildings on the right side. After passing the first bunch, he came to a stretch of land with no cover for about a kilometer. He stopped, afraid of making himself an easy target for Wrobel. The nearest structure was about the size of a modest house, flanked by two satellite dishes and a radio tower. He checked the double doors at the main entrance, but they were locked. Around the corner he found a smaller window partially covered by a tree. Blasts from his palms shattered the glass. Pain shot through his burned thumbs again when he blasted, bringing tears to his eyes.

The building was thoroughly modern and professionally decorated. Four rooms lined the main hall, each with large glass windows and doors and labeled with metallic plaques with the official NWG Space logo of the earth surrounded by a fiery ring. Quick glances through each glass door showed empty cubicles. Finally he came to an empty conference room.

Inside the room was a holo-screen. His curiosity got the better of him, and he turned it on. The channel was broadcasting live news coverage from the launch site. A crowd of thousands had gathered to watch the takeoff. Sammy saw no panicking, no fighting, only excited people anticipating the launch. A small countdown in the corner of the screen showed how much time remained: four and a half minutes.

As Sammy watched, his heart thumped madly. Any moment the CAG would attack all those people. He muted the sound and cranked the window open slightly so he could listen for sounds. Everything was quiet.

The excitement of the small crowd built into a fevered pitch as the few remaining minutes ticked away. Sammy, on the other hand, became more and more anxious. Would the CAG wait until the shuttle launched and shoot it down? Would they attack at the last possible second so it could not be aborted? Where was Byron and what was he doing now?

Only thirty seconds remained.

The reporters' enthusiasm visibly grew as the last seconds ticked. Sammy could read the lips of the audience members as they counted down in unison. Every few seconds the camera cut to shots of the technicians seated at their desks. Would all those people die?

His eyes hardly blinked as he stared, forgetting to breathe in the final moments. He was about to witness catastrophic destruction.

Five . . . four . . . three . . . two . . . one . . .

Through the open window, Sammy heard the rumbling of the space shuttle's gigantic engines and on the screen he saw the lift off. The shuttle launched into the sky, ascending on a perfect line. Billows of smoke and fire curled and blossomed around its base, following it past the clouds. He observed with fascination.

The attack didn't come. Why? What's going on?

CRASH!

Sammy jumped in his seat. An orange and red light streaked down the hall. Footsteps approached the conference room at a run. He snapped his body around, positioning himself with trained precision into a solid defensive stance. He hoped to see Byron, but he expected to see Wrobel. It was neither.

Katie Carpenter had arrived. And she toted the biggest gun Sammy had ever seen.

She wore the traditional uniform of a Thirteen, and its shiny metallic surface told Sammy she was more prepared than their last meeting. *A blast suit.* Her nose was slightly larger, still swollen. The thought of her broken nose put a sadistic smirk on his face, but he wanted to do more than that to her. Hatred boiled inside him as fresh memories of their last encounter flashed in his mind. Toad's raw meat-like body being carried away by medics, blood trailing from the cruiser in the hangar to the cruiser on the runway, his glazed eyes and his face as pale as the sheet that covered him.

Katie pulled the trigger and he heard a loud *FFSSS!* like the sound of dumping cold water on a hot pan. In all the training Byron had put him through at headquarters, Sammy had never heard a weapon that made such a sound. He crouched low, and used a broad shield to deflect whatever projectiles this machine could throw at him.

The next thing he knew, there was a blistering hot pain in his left leg—much worse than what he felt in his thumbs. A shrill scream exploded from his mouth. He wanted to glance down to see what happened, but Katie rushed him, using the weapon as a club. He tried to stand, but the pain in his leg was too intense. Instead, he did a half somersault and used his hands to blast himself to the ceiling. Katie swung at empty air, and Sammy kicked at her face with his good leg on the back end of his flip. He had to use his hand blasts to soften the landing, but with them he rolled to the back of the room, away from Katie. An office chair provided him some cover. The pain in his leg throbbed mercilessly, fetid smoke curled off his skin, but he saw no blood. Whatever it was, it had instantly cauterized the wound.

Why didn't my blasts work?

Katie whirled to face him and fired through the conference room's glass wall, this time using a handgun. The glass exploded, but Sammy threw himself to the side. Pain shot up the entire left side of his body starting at his injured thigh. He yelled out in agony, almost falling backward.

She's aiming low, he noted. *Why is she doing that?*

Katie stepped through the remains of the wall, crunching on the broken glass with her military boots. The angle gave Sammy a better chance to observe her weapon: an enormous black firearm with a dull red light on the top. Katie swung again, this time at his head, but he held the weapon at bay with a blast. The Thirteen almost lost her balance from the momentum shift, and the larger weapon knocked the smaller one out of her hand. He used that opportunity to straighten his legs, but found it nearly impossible to move his left leg laterally, even trying to do so made him want to scream again.

The red light on her gun turned green, and she took aim again.

FFSSS!

Sammy blast-jumped into the room across the hall and hit the floor next to her handgun. He jerked it around, flicking back the hammer, but Katie was not in his line of sight.

He remembered the red light turning green. *She's waiting for her next shot.*

The smell of burned plastic reached his nose. He looked around and saw that part of the chair had been melted away from her last shot.

Sammy cursed softly. He dared not move first . . . not without some clue as to where she lurked. That gave him an idea.

"Not trying to kill me, Katie?" he asked in his most juvenile voice. "Above such things now?"

She gave no reply.

"Who's calling the shots now, Katie? You answer to Commander Wrobel? Old Vicky? Is he your new girlfriend?"

The words came out easily enough but they did not take away the horrible ache in his leg, the burning in his thumbs (compounded by gripping Katie's fallen gun), or the piercing fear in his mind. Katie was the one Thirteen that Sammy wasn't sure he could defeat.

He heard a tiny sound like weight shifting on a few slivers of glass. He was pretty sure it came from the other side of the wall to his left. Was she in the room adjacent to him?

Using his hands as support, he scooted his body to his right to give himself a better angle. Katie must have heard the changes in his breathing, because at that moment she attacked. Again, Sammy noticed, she aimed away from any vital organs. His arm moved out of the way just in time, leaving him no chance to return fire. He felt the heat of the projectile graze his arm hair, and the next moment half of a palm-sized disk protruded from the carpet, smoking and singeing the fibers. From the combined effects of the pain and the overpowering scents of burning skin, hair, rubber, and carpet, Sammy felt nauseous and hazed.

It's a blitzer, he realized. Al had told him about it during their Rio mission briefing. *Super-heated discs that can cut through a blast shield.* If he wanted to block one of these, he'd have to use a strong, concentrated blast. The thought of doing so made his thumbs sting.

Katie hid behind the wall again. Sammy decided not to go on the offensive with so little distance between them. Instead he got his good leg underneath him, and maneuvered the bad one as best he could. If he needed to move quickly, he could use feet blasts. He held the gun in his hands with a steadiness that surprised him.

Katie whipped around for her next shot with breathtaking speed. Sammy fired three rounds right as she emerged. Reacting with perfect timing, Katie used the massive blitzer as a shield. Something inside the weapon ruptured and a billowing plume of steam erupted from the punctures. Katie aimed the jet of hot air at Sammy trying to cloud his vision. He used feet blasts to shoot over the growing fog, but Katie anticipated this and swung the blitzer hard.

Sammy realized his mistake, but could not change his course fast enough. He brought his hands up to block the blitzer, but felt a smacking thud against the side of his head.

"Ugh," was all he could say as he fell to the ground unconscious.

The blitzer was beyond repair. Not that the Queen was a weapons expert, but she knew enough. After all, the weapon was her own concept. The problem with prototypes like this was they were slow, fragile, and bulky.

Give it five years. The Fourteens won't know what hit them.

She looked down at the boy's unconscious form and moaned with desire to kill him.

He broke my nose!

The thought sent waves of rage rippling across her skin. She had already scheduled an appointment with the best plastic surgeons, but not until after this mission. She brought her foot down hard on Sammy's nose and heard a satisfying crunch.

"Now we're even." Then, over her com, she said, "I've got Sammy."

"What's his status?" came Wrobel's reply.

"Out cold."

"I've got your signal. There's a maintenance room in the back of your building. Take him there—it should do the job. On my way with the Alpha right now."

The Queen hauled Sammy by his hair to the back of the building, taking care to pull his body over as much glass as possible. Small lines of his blood trailed behind them.

At the end of the building's main hall and to the left was a steel door marked with electrical symbols that only an engineer would understand. Three savage kicks later, the door swung open, and the Queen pulled Sammy into the room over the cold bare floor.

The room was bigger than she'd expected. It probably serviced connections to the satellites and radio towers nearby.

She threw Sammy into a corner and sat cross-legged facing him, her third and last gun (a jigger, her favorite) was aimed at his chest. She could have picked up the pistol, but the filthy kid had touched it, even fired it. *No thanks.* All she needed now was an excuse—half an excuse—because she had very large doubts about the Fourteen's grand scheme to kill two birds with one stone.

The back door's handle emitted a hiss and small wisps of blue smoke drifted up from the keyhole. The Queen pulled a strand of hair out of her face and put it back behind her ear. The door opened and Wrobel came in. His right arm was wrapped around his own subdued hostage, his left carried several pieces of equipment.

"Take him," he told her. "Watch them both while I set up."

"Let's kill this one now," she said, pointing at Sammy, as she relieved Wrobel of a young Fourteen with brown hair.

"No!" Wrobel shouted.

"Kill him now!" the Queen yelled back. "This one is different. The longer he stays alive the more chance he has of—Byron will never even know!"

Wrobel ignored her, going about setting up two folding metal chairs less than half a meter apart as if she'd said nothing. Then he assembled a small camera on a tripod facing the chairs. She grabbed his arm.

"Wrobel! Kill that kid now!"

"No! We do this my way! You shoot him, I shoot you. Got it?"

The Queen pulled out her jigger again and this time aimed it at Wrobel. "The fox wants him dead."

"The fox wants me alive even more."

"You're useless to him now. They know about you."

"I'm the one that has access to everything!" he said, tapping his head and glancing at her with a look that instantly broke down her surety. "That virus I put in Byron's computer is going to be hard to shut down. In the meantime, I can do a lot of damage. If you don't believe that, kill me. Otherwise, shut up and put your kid on the right chair and the Alpha on the left. Make sure they're secure."

"Aren't you going to sedate him?" the Queen asked, gesturing to Sammy.

"No," Wrobel answered. "Any more could kill him."

"Why do we care?" She didn't bother hiding her dislike of him and his methods.

"I had him handcuffed," Wrobel said, "he figured out a way to use his blasts to break the cuff."

"Do you think I'd underestimate him?" she shot back.

"Of course not." He glanced at her broken and taped nose.

She shoved Sammy into his chair and taped each wrist and ankle separate, bending him over until his face was in his knees. His arms and legs were intertwined with the legs of the chair in such a way that his hands had no mobility.

"Ready to go," she informed him.

Wrobel had finished tweaking the camera, and after surveying her work, he cleared his throat and spoke: "Charlie. Six. Lima. Zero. Alpha. Seven. India. Four. Romeo. Three. Echo."

⑨ ⑨ ⑨ ⑨ ⑨

On the north end of Baikonur, Commander Byron, Commander Zahn, and Elite Commander Durrant oversaw the removal of over thirty Alphas and two hundred Elite from Baikonur. No attack had come. Not that

Byron wasn't grateful to avoid a conflict, but the whole situation was still a disaster.

For the last couple hours, every com worn by an Alpha had been dysfunctional.

"Oscar Squadron, move all the crates into the cargos!" Byron ordered.

Alphas and Elite soldiers moved like ants around the launch command center. Byron watched them with distant interest as so many unanswered questions wrestled for his attention. Why had there been no attack? What had gone wrong with the coms? Did Victor have something to do with it?

No sooner had the thought crossed his mind then his com screen flipped down.

Incoming call/video feed: Victor Wrobel

Byron's mouth went dry. He snapped his fingers loudly until an Elite intelligence officer looked up, then Byron waved the man over. "I need a tracer on the line calling my com."

The Elite officer got to work while Byron answered the call. "Hello, Victor."

"Walter. Are you tracing my line?"

The commander's com picked up Wrobel's video feed, and he saw two hostages in chairs. Cloth bags covered their heads. Byron knew of them was Sammy simply by the clothes he'd been wearing. The other was an Alpha.

"Why are you doing this, Victor?" As he asked, the notion that the Alpha might be his son struck him. "Are these your hostages?"

"No need for hostages anymore," Wrobel explained. "I'm already on my way out of here."

"Then what's the point of this?" Byron asked.

"Because today's your day of reckoning, Walter."

Katie Carpenter walked into the scene on the video. She held a jigger in one hand as she walked behind the two hostages and pulled the bags off their heads.

"Victor—Victor, what are you thinking?" Byron asked, trying to find his most calm voice, but failing.

"Think!" Wrobel shouted, looking more unhinged than Byron had ever seen him. Tears swam in his old friend's eyes. "Think about Claire!"

"Claire?" Byron repeated. "How does this have anything to do with her?"

"I said *think*!" Wrobel was still shouting while his face became streaked with his tears. His face got uncomfortably close to the camera and bits of his saliva landed on the lens, blurring the image. "You gave the orders on the mission. Do you remember what the order was?"

The memory came back to Byron as clear as if he was there again. Emily falling down the sewer ladder, bleeding, and he, Byron, diving after her, catching her and stopping them both from crashing to the ground with his blasts. Screams from a man and a woman. Blake lying in a pool of his own blood. Claire clinging to the same ladder, her neck bleeding. Victor pulling her the rest of the way up the ladder while she screamed his name. Chaos—chaos everywhere. The enemy retreating, but Emily still bleeding so much. Byron's hands trembling as he carried her. Trying to pull out the braxels that had drilled too deeply into her body.

"You blame me, Victor?" Byron pleaded. His hands now shook as badly as they had then. "I was trying to save my wife."

"Do you remember the order?" Victor's voice was an inhuman scream. High and shrill like a cat's.

Byron had to think for only a moment. "Yes, I remember. I was supposed to shield for Claire and myself up the ladder."

"You see? You see now you stupid son-of-a—"

"My wife was shot! You would have done the same for Claire."

"EMILY WAS ALREADY DEAD!" bellowed Wrobel. Tears streamed now from his red eyes. "And because of your incompetence Claire had to die, too! You murdered her in your stupidity."

"Murder—I—" but the words failed to come to him. How could Victor have kept this in for so long? Byron tried to explain, and as he did, his voice grew in power. "It was an accident. The Thirteens killed her. Look who is behind you, Victor. See reason, not madness! She killed them both!"

"Like I said," Wrobel continued, now with more composure, "this is your day of reckoning. I will not be guilty of murder as you already are. I will allow you to choose."

"Choose?"

"Which one dies—your son or your prize pupil? My assignment for the last fifteen months has been to kill Samuel. Fortunately, I can now hand that assignment to you."

"You call yourself innocent?" Byron responded. "Martin Trector? Is his blood not on your hands? What other lives have your actions—your treason—cost us?"

"His blood is not on my hands!" Wrobel said. "I told you—everyone on Psion Command told you they should have had weapons! You ignored us. You threw your weight around and ignored all of us! Now, I'm giving the choice to you. Samuel or Albert."

Byron's breathing was labored as he struggled to grasp the insanity facing him. Several people were gathered around him now, but he looked to the Elite intelligence officer who shook his head and pointed to his wrist.

"Give me time to think, Victor, please." His voice was desperate and solemn.

"One minute," Victor answered quietly. "And if indecision is your choice, she'll shoot them both."

On his small screen, Byron saw Katie standing behind Samuel. Her gun centimeters away from the crown of his head. Her face shone with pure joy. There was a ripple in one of the tiny flecks of spit on the camera, and Byron squinted to try to see better. He could not be sure what he saw. He wiped the sweat from his own eyes, and bowed his head in thought and prayer.

Just as suddenly he lifted it up again. "Have me instead," he announced. "I will give myself up, I swear it!" His voice was pleading, his tone urgent and humble. "You know I would, Victor. You know it!"

"Thirty two seconds."

"VICTOR!" Byron yelled, and many people around him jumped. "You are a better man than this!"

Wrobel said nothing, but continued to gaze at his watch.

Byron knew he had to choose.

"Twenty seconds."

The word coming out of Byron's mouth tasted obscene, but he said it with conviction. "Albert."

Wrobel looked at the camera as though he'd misheard. His face paled, and his lips went tight. "What?"

"Albert."

But Victor nodded to Katie, and she lifted her jigger away from Samuel's head. A single tear fell from Byron's eye, and he was grateful his com screen covered it. "I love you, son," he whispered so quietly that the words would never be heard by Wrobel.

⑤ ⑤ ⑤ ⑤ ⑤

Sammy's hands were useless, but his feet were in perfect position. When Byron chose his son, he heard the shock in Wrobel's voice. Katie had been standing above him, pressing the barrel of the jigger into his scalp in a very painful way. When the gun pulled away, he knew he had to act.

Using foot blasts, the entire chair shot straight up like a rocket. Sammy threw all his weight back and smashed the back of the chair into Katie's face. For the second time in two days, he was rewarded with the immense pleasure of hearing her nose crunch, this time, however, it was already broken. He wrenched and twisted his hands, blasting to help them rip through the tape. He succeeded in only loosening them. Then, balancing his weight just right, he landed back on the floor, only to repeat the jump.

Mid-jump, he whirled his body around, chair and all, and gripped her blast suit with his hands as she grabbed at her nose. He threw his weight backwards and jerked at her, flipping her over his head with his momentum. Katie flew into the camera, sending it crashing to the floor, and Sammy landed on the back of his chair, barely keeping his head from smacking the concrete floor. Lying on his back, he could see Wrobel staring at Katie in disbelief.

"Get up!" Wrobel yelled at her.

Sammy struggled with his feet, trying to free them, but Katie had done too good of a job on them. He was stuck. Raising his head as high as he could, he saw Wrobel pulling his own gun from his holster. Sammy did the only thing he could think of. He rocked his body forward with one great heave as he blasted himself bodily into Wrobel, catching the commander in the chest and landing in a heap on top of him.

The collision loosened up his right hand enough that he managed to wiggle it five or six centimeters back and forth. Before he could free himself, Katie got up with a grunt. She scrambled for her gun, moving too fast for Sammy to do anything but react.

He tipped himself off Wrobel and landed the chair on its feet, right side up. The broken tripod lay nearby. Sammy picked it up. Clutching it as best he could with his right hand, he leaned forward and blasted again, trying to stay low, knowing if he overshot his mark, she could easily kill him. Flying through the air, he extended the three metal feet of the tripod and jabbed at her just as she stood.

For Toad.

Two of the three feet caught her blast suit and dug two long bloody slashes in her skin. Then he shot a blast, catching her in the side and shoving her away.

Just before he smacked into a wall, he wrenched his right hand completely free and used a small blast to stop himself. It was not pretty, but he landed and rolled onto his back so he could see properly. Quickly, he released his other hand from the tape. Wrobel seemed down for the count, but Katie gingerly stood, bleeding now from her face, ribs, and arm.

"I can block whatever you've got." He was panting hard, working with one hand to free his feet, ready to shield with the other. "Your suit's worthless. And sooner or later, my friends will come."

He knew he was right. He looked ridiculous, and every part of his body hurt in a way he hadn't felt since being in Stripe's care, but she had lost.

Katie looked at him with an expression he could interpret only as curiosity. She had won the first and second rounds, but now he had beaten her. There was no fear in her eyes, only respect, intelligence, and ruthlessness so intense that Sammy knew he would never comprehend the depth. He didn't know how he could understand her so well. Even still, he hated her with such passion . . . because she scared him.

She crossed the room and stood at the entrance of a hallway. At her feet were several small streaks of what Sammy guessed was his own blood. She stopped, turned, and smiled at Sammy. He'd never seen anything so ugly as her perfect lips twisted in a smile. Then she lifted her gun and fired twice at Al. Sammy tried to blast at her, but she was too far.

Al's head jerked up as Katie left.

"Al!" Sammy fumbled again with the tape around his feet. In his panic, it took several extra moments to free himself. He crossed the room to Al, limping badly on his injured leg. A hole had formed in Al's clothes over his left breast, but worse, Sammy heard the soft whir of a jigger tunneling. Al's eyes were open as he gasped in shock.

"HELP!" Sammy screamed to no one as he ripped Al's flight suit. He tried to get his hands into position to reach the wound. "HELP!"

"Hey," Al whispered, his face twisted in a grimace of pain. "Hey."

Sammy stopped yelling.

"Can you stop screaming and pull the braxel out?" Al was trying to smile. "I can't die. I've got to get married soon."

"But how . . .?" Sammy sputtered.

"Reach in and get it."

Sammy held his breath as his index and middle fingers slid into the wound slick with blood and tissue, and pried away the muscle around it. Al moaned in pain and ground his teeth together.

"Don't do that," Sammy said through his own gritted teeth, trying to force his fingers deeper. Al cried out as Sammy did so. Finally the tip of his index finger felt the spinning metal object just below it. Taking a deep breath, he forced both fingers around it, and caught it between the tips of his fingernails. It spun hot between them, but he began teasing it out very carefully.

Al screamed longer and louder than Sammy thought was possible for anyone to scream. The braxel continued to spin against Sammy's flesh, bringing new sensations of pain to his burned thumb, almost causing him to lose his grip. Slowly he pulled it out and dropped it with a clank on the floor. Leaning back from the awkward position, he fell to the floor and breathed loudly. "Now what?"

Al panted and moaned. "Either I bleed to death or they find us . . . or Wrobel wakes up and kills us."

Sammy stripped off his shirt and compressed it against Al's wound as best he could. "Well, at least if I get left behind this time, I won't be in enemy territory."

Al snorted a tired chuckle. "Please don't make me laugh," he grunted. "It hurts just to breathe."

Sammy wanted to distract Al from the agony, but he didn't know how. He finally decided just to talk to him. "Can I ask you something?"

"Okay," came the response.

"It might seem obvious, but I really need to know what you think."

"Sammy, I'm bleeding badly, just ask . . ."

"Is it worth it? Getting married, having a family? Aren't you afraid of losing Marie?"

Al coughed a couple of times. The coughs were abnormally thick and heavy. Color drained from Al's face. "That's what we fight for, right? Families."

"Every family I've known has died. Stripe told me that pain is what makes us who we are. It molds us."

Al's face showed Sammy that he understood. "I'm not going to die. And I'm your brother. Jeffie and Brickert are your family, too. Pain teaches us . . . yes . . ."

His face went deathly white.

"But it's how we love . . ." Then Al's voice stopped. His eyes rolled back and then closed.

"HELP! HELP US!" Sammy shouted over and over again. Finally, the door burst open. Byron and Dr. Rosmir and an entire squadron of Alphas behind them stormed in. Byron saw Al first and ran toward him. Rosmir was right beside him ordering instructions to his medics. Another Alpha came and cut the remains of Wrobel's cuffs off of Sammy's limbs. Once they were off, the Alpha began to rub them to help the circulation and soreness.

"Wait here," the Alpha told him. "A medic will look at you."

"I'm fine," Sammy said, trying to get up, but his leg would not allow it.

"Kid, you're an awful mess. Sit there and wait."

Byron glanced at Sammy for just the briefest of moments, then he turned back to watch Dr. Rosmir and his team of medics remove Al as quickly as possible.

Sammy breathed a little easier when a medic announced Al still had a pulse. In fact, he felt lighter than he had in a very long time. It was hard to believe. It was over. He couldn't wait to see his loved ones. *Especially Jeffie,* he thought with the beginnings of a smile.

31 | Home

May 5, 2086

SAMMY RODE IN THE MEDIC CRUISER with Al, Byron, Dr. Rosmir, and Rosmir's team to the NWG hospital. Less than ten minutes into the flight, Al's condition had stabilized. Byron's careworn face still seemed troubled, but he thanked the doctor and the medics profusely. Then he returned to the pilot's seat where he remained for the rest of the flight.

Once the medical team's attention left Al, they strapped Sammy onto an exam table and got to work on him: First they removed all the large glass shards from his legs, hands, and backside.

"I can give you something for the pain," Dr. Rosmir told him, "but it won't do much. You've had so much sedative today, it's not safe to give any more."

He did, however, give Sammy a biting stick while they worked on him. With all his adrenaline gone, Sammy was left to feel most of the effects of the pain.

They reset his nose in place and injected a bone fastening solution. Then they examined his leg. Dr. Rosmir informed Sammy that his vastus lateralis had been almost completely severed from the blitzer. The skilled medical crew removed the damaged tissue and reattached the muscle. Dr. Rosmir apologized over and over while Sammy just kept biting down on the block in his mouth and tried not to scream. They squirted orange goo over the wound when they'd finished operating. "That'll speed up the healing and reduce scar tissue," one of the medics told Sammy. It burned almost as badly as his thumbs. Finished with the leg, they turned their attention back to the smaller pieces of glass embedded in Sammy. In the end, forty-seven pieces of glass were removed from his skin, the largest almost as long as his little finger. The last thing Dr. Rosmir looked at was Sammy's thumbs.

"How did you manage to do this?" he asked. "These are third degree burns."

They used a burn gun on his thumbs and a couple other areas where the blitzer had singed him.

When it was all over, Sammy rested for a good three hours. When he woke, his head was full of cobwebs. The cruiser was on top of the Alpha infirmary, where Al was being moved to another cruiser to fly to the main hospital on the island.

"Hey, bud," Dr. Rosmir said when their eyes met. "I got a call from the psych center. You're scheduled to check in tomorrow. I'm going to have to get a good look at that leg again while we're taking you there."

"Do I have to go?" Sammy asked. "I feel fine."

Dr. Rosmir's look reminded Sammy that the subject wasn't up for debate. Then Byron came over and helped Sammy into a wheelchair. The short ride to Byron's cruiser sent all kinds of awful sensations through Sammy's body, forcing him to close his eyes.

"How are you feeling?" the commander asked.

"Great . . ." Sammy responded slowly, his eyes still shut. "Am I going home now?"

"Yes."

"Right now?"

"Yes, just for the day. You deserve some time with your friends."

"I know."

Something else was in the back of Sammy's mind that he wanted to ask the commander, but his brain was too muddied to remember what it was. As Byron pushed him up the ramp into the cruiser, Sammy's head went light.

"Whoa," he mumbled, gripping the arms of the chair tight.

"Easy there," Byron said.

Sammy laughed at that, but he was not sure why. "The chair's kind of comfy," he commented.

"Try not to get used to it," Byron warned. "You will only need it for a week at the most."

Sammy laughed again lightly. Byron stopped the wheelchair for a moment and reached into his pocket. "Here, smell this." He held something small under Sammy's nose.

Sammy sniffed.

"Ugh!" he exclaimed, jumping in his seat at the intrusion. His head was clearer, but the smell was biting and rancid. "What is that?"

"Smelling salts," Byron answered. "Dr. Rosmir gave me it while you were asleep. I need to speak candidly to you while we still have time."

"About what?"

Byron locked Sammy's chair into place and got into the pilot seat. Within a minute, they were up in the air, flying to Beta headquarters.

The commander turned so he could look Sammy right in the eyes.

"Thank you," Byron said. His voice was very heavy.

Sammy realized he couldn't really imagine what the commander had gone through today, nearly losing the last member of his family. The commander continued to stare at Sammy until the seemingly impenetrable dam of his emotions broke. It embarrassed Sammy to see such a towering, solid person like Byron break down.

"I—I was just doing what we're supposed to do."

"No," Byron told him as he tried to collect himself. "You did more than anyone could have asked. When—when I was forced to make that choice, I was not sure if I had seen you move or not. I was going on something beyond hope—faith, really. I thought that was it. And then you came alive again, Samuel. What you did in there was unbelievable. I cannot—words cannot—" Byron gathered himself again before the dam crashed once more. "I am in your debt."

"There is something special about you, Samuel," Byron continued, but now not quite meeting Sammy's eyes. "You have got strong stuff inside you. I hope you know how much faith I have in you."

Sammy's face felt hot. He could barely stand to look at Byron, but he still nodded.

Byron turned back to the controls as Beta headquarters approached quickly on the midnight horizon. Sammy thought about how great it would be to go back home. He smiled even though it hurt his nose.

"Sir, what am I going to do when I finish everything here? I mean, I'm almost done with the sims and instructions."

Byron answered as though he had been thinking the same thing. "Some are suggesting that you graduate before you turn nineteen. Maybe even at sixteen. What do you think? Would you like to leave early?"

Sammy saw the rooftop door, the one he knew led to the stairs and then to home. He thought of who was behind the doors waiting for him. Then he thought of Al's words about the point of it all. "Not if you can help it, sir," he answered. "I'd rather stay."

"Noted," Byron said as he landed the cruiser. Then he wheeled Sammy down a ramp to the door of the rooftop. "Wait here," he said.

"I'm not going anywhere," Sammy joked.

The night air was cool and the wind was strong up on the rooftop. It whipped Sammy's hair, but felt wonderful on his wounds. Had he not been so anxious to get inside, he could have stayed up on the roof for a couple of hours to just enjoy being alive. A bowl of ice cream would be nice, too.

"Do you think my anomaly is back?" he asked the commander. "I mean, I fought well against Katie today. A lot better than last time, but it still wasn't the same as other times. Does that even make sense?"

"No idea. But keep me informed. You can speak to Dr. Rosmir about that, too. When you have your psych evaluation, there will be specialists who can help you. Some of them deal with the Tensais on a regular basis."

"Sure. I'll do that."

Byron went into the cruiser and came back with crutches. "If I help you, can you walk down the stairs?"

Sammy used his armrests to push himself into a standing position. Byron folded the wheelchair and carried it in one arm with the crutches. Sammy took Byron's free arm and limped carefully down the stairs. When they reached the third floor, Commander Byron set the chair on the ground and helped Sammy back in, setting the crutches on his lap.

"This is where I leave you," he said warmly.

"Thanks, sir."

"No, Sammy," Byron said. "Thank you."

"How am I going to get downstairs to my dorm?" Sammy asked.

"Don't worry about that," came the reply as the commander walked away.

"But, sir, my com . . ."

The lights were all off in the hallway as he wheeled himself to the cafeteria for a bite to eat. His com was downstairs in his room, so he couldn't call anyone to let them know he was here. He struggled to get his chair into a position that would allow him to swing open the door. As he did so, he wondered if this was Byron's way of urging him to get out of the chair as soon as possible. If so, it would certainly work.

Finally he got a handle on the door and pushed it open, forcing his chair through enough to stop it from closing again. A light came on in the cafeteria, blinding him.

Who would be up this late? Jeffie again? Does she know I'm coming?

His pulse quickened as he manipulated the wheels to push himself into the room. No sooner did he push himself through, than his ears were filled with the sounds of cheers. His own tears blurred the images of his friends clapping and rushing forward to greet him. Even people he didn't recognize.

Sammy grinned.

Home at last.

۩ ۩ ۩ ۩ ۩

After seeing Sammy safely to headquarters, Byron returned to his cruiser and left the building. He set his sights to the far northern edge of Capitol Island. The flight wasn't very long, and he had so many thoughts occupying his brain that it seemed even shorter. From far above he saw the blinking lights outlining a short landing strip. He called ahead to announce his arrival and request that a guard be there waiting for him.

When he touched down, a stern-looking woman stood at a safe distance from the landing strip holding an umbrella outside her car. She moved into position to help keep Byron dry in the pouring rain.

"Thank you," he told her, not expecting any response.

After she checked his clearance with a handheld print scanner, she drove him from the landing area through the gates surrounding the facility. Once in the building, they took an elevator deep into the earth. After three more clearance checks, Commander Byron came to the interrogation room where Victor Wrobel was being held. Byron watched his old friend for several minutes through the two-way mirror, remembering the words that had been shouted at him. Some of them were truer than he wanted to believe.

Victor's Alpha Command flight suit had been replaced with a bright orange jumpsuit. His head was shaved, and heavy shackles adorned his feet and hands. According to the record hanging on the wall, he'd been force-fed the anti-Anomaly Fourteen pill, too.

The surly female guard used three forms of ID to unlock the atrium of the cell: eye-scan, voice-matching, and fingerprint analysis. Once the atrium was secure, two more armed guards, each of whom held separate keys to the room, watched as she repeated the procedure again. After she successfully identified herself, the guards placed their own keys into separate locks more than a wingspan apart and simultaneously turned them. The door to the cell opened, bringing with it the smell of stale, filtered air.

"Ah, Father Abraham," Wrobel said with a smile. "I wondered when you'd be coming." Then he spat in Byron's face.

The guard reached for her electric stick, but Byron stopped her with a hand on her shoulder.

"I will be fine by myself."

The guard looked like she wanted to protest, but held her tongue. Commander Byron had plenty of rank in this situation. She had no choice. When she left, he removed a handkerchief from his pocket and wiped the saliva from his cheek and brow.

"We were friends for a long time," he said to Victor. "You have seen it all. You know how this will go. If you have enough information—"

"I don't care if they execute me. I've been dead for a long time. Might as well make it official."

"Are you going to—?"

"Did Sammy make it out alive?" Wrobel interjected briskly. He observed Commander Byron's face and eyes for a long moment. Then shook his head and laughed like Sammy's survival was the greatest joke ever told. "That lucky little kid! I can't believe it. I really can't believe it!"

Byron didn't know what to think. Victor truly seemed mentally unbalanced. "Will you please let me ask you some questions?"

- 466 -

"Absolutely. Go ahead."

Byron ignored the sarcasm in Victor's voice and pushed ahead.

"Why was the attack on Artemis called off?"

"How's Al doing?" Wrobel asked in response. "Does he harbor any animosity toward you?"

Byron calmly gazed back into Victor's green eyes, which held nothing but hate, despite the quick laughter he displayed.

Wrobel leaned forward. "You didn't tell him, did you?" He bounced his knee up and down as if it were some hilarious joke. "You're a cod, you know that? A sneaky, yellow-bellied cod."

"How did you get access to the Beta building after I terminated your codes from the system?"

"How could you choose your son?" Wrobel asked. "You could have made everything so much easier—I bet everything on you choosing Samuel. It never ever *ever* crossed my mind you'd pick your own kid. You really are a heartless prick. You know that, don't you?"

"Victor," a touch of impatience crept into Byron's tone, "you know what General Wu will do to get the information out of you. Why not talk? Give me some names of people you have had contact with."

But Wrobel seemed to have shut down, staring straight at the floor.

"Please. You have done so much good for us—"

"Go to hell, Walt!" Wrobel screamed violently, much like he had at Baikonur. Then he immediately calmed himself. "I made up my mind long ago. This is my path, and I got caught . . . so be it. I'm not giving you anything."

"You know they will get it out of you eventually."

"Let them try."

"Why do they want Samuel dead so badly?"

Victor said nothing.

"Is there something else about him I should know?"

Still nothing.

"Why did you bring Katie Carpenter into this?"

Victor sat as still as a corpse. Commander Byron brought his hand down on the table hard. The former commander jumped slightly.

"Please! I am sorry about Claire. And Emily. And Blake. I wish I could redo every decision that has led to deaths of Psions. You know I regret them, Victor. We were friends for years. Cooperate with me and undo some of this mess."

Wrobel turned his head slowly until his eyes rested on Byron. The deadness in them chilled the air in Byron's lungs. He saw nothing of his old friend left in his hollow pupils. Burying his hate for so long had taken Victor Wrobel to depths of insanity that Byron couldn't fathom. And he knew for certain that General Wu could not break Victor. He would try. Wu had to try. But this man would never break.

"You've got much bigger things to worry about now. So much more than before." He wore a smile that stretched from ear to ear, but his eyes were as void of life as ever. "You have no idea, Walter—how deep it all goes. You don't have a clue. And I sincerely pray that when you finally figure it out . . . it will be too late."

THE END

AFTERWORD

Thank you for reading *Psion Gamma*! I hope you appreciated a less-cliffhanger-ish ending. As you probably guessed, Sammy's adventures are not over. *Psion Gamma* will be followed by *Psion Delta*, *Psion Alpha*, and *Psion Omega*. My plan is to release one book a year over the next three years. I hope for your continued support and enthusiasm; it makes the writing and editing process more enjoyable to know that my Fellow Bookworms are excited to read more about our mutual friends.

The best way to continue to support the *Psion* series is to leave helpful Amazon and Barnes and Noble reviews, share your enthusiasm through social networking, and tell your friends and family about your favorite books. Word of mouth is the most powerful advertisement out there.

Another project currently in the works is an epic adventure series: *A Tale of Love and Adventure*. The first volume is already written, *The Flight from Blithmore*. It is not a science fiction novel, but an adventure story set in a pre-Victorian era in a fictional land called Blithmore.

As always, for more information on me, my writings, and for updates on my work, follow me on twitter @psionbeta or, even better, join the Psion Beta Facebook Fan Club.

Long live Sammy!

--Jacob Gowans

www.psionbeta.com

Made in the USA
Charleston, SC
19 November 2015